APPLEWOOD's
PICTORIAL AMERICA

# STAR-SPANGLED IMAGES

**APPLEWOOD BOOKS**
*Carlisle, Massachusetts*

## STAR-SPANGLED IMAGES

For prints of images in this book visit:
www.libraryimages.net/holidays/starspangled

Thank you for purchasing an Applewood book.
Applewood reprints America's lively classics —
books from the past that are still of interest to
modern readers. For a free copy of our current
catalog, please write to Applewood Books,
P. O. Box 27, Carlisle, MA 01741.
www.awb.com
www.pictorialamerica.com

ISBN 978-1-60889-010-1

# TABLE OF
# *Contents*

[ N⁰· 1 BIRTHPLACE OF BETSY ROSS.]

[ Nᵒˢ· 2–3 BETSY ROSS SCENES.]

BETSEY ROSS

[ *N⁰.* 4  YANKEE DOODLE.]

[ *N⁰.* 5  GREAT SEAL OF THE UNITED STATES.]

[ *N⁰.* 6  THE EAGLE AND THE FLAG.]

[ *Nᵒ·* 7  JULY 4ᵀᴴ POSTCARD.]

"The Day we celebrate"

1776

[ *No.* 8   JULY 4TH POSTCARD.]

"Then ring the bells
and fire the guns,
And fling the starry
banner out!"

[ *No.* 9   JULY 4TH POSTCARD.]

[ No. 10   FRANCIS SCOTT KEY AT FORT McHENRY, WAR OF 1812.]

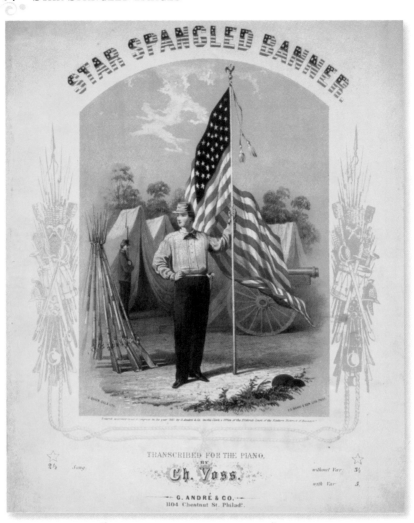

[ *N⁰·* 12   CIVIL WAR SCENE.]

[ *Nº.* 13   JULY 4ᵀᴴ POSTCARD.]

[ *No.* 14   CIVIL WAR SONG.]

[ *Nº.* 15  CIVIL WAR POSTER.]

[ *N⁰·* 16   JULY 4ᵀᴴ POSTCARD.]

[ *No.* 17   JULY 4ᵀᴴ POSTCARD.]

[ *No.* 18   JULY 4ᵀᴴ POSTCARD.]

[ *Nº.* 19 JULY 4ᵀᴴ POSTCARD. ]

[ *Nº.* 20 JULY 4ᵀᴴ POSTCARD. ]

[ *Nº.* 21 THE FLAG THAT WAVED FOR 100 YEARS, 1876. ]

[ *N⁰.* 22  JULY 4ᵀᴴ POSTCARD.]

[ *N⁰.* 23  JULY 4ᵀᴴ POSTCARD.]

[ *Nᵒˢ.* 24–25  BATTLE SCENES.]

[ Nº· 26   THE HUMAN FLAG, ALTOONA, PENNSYLVANIA.]

FLAG WOVEN AND MADE UP BY MILL-WORKERS AT MANCHESTER, NEW HAMPSHIRE

Unquestionably one of the genuine "war brides" of industrial America is flag manufacturing. Never before in the history of this country has there been such a phenomenal demand for flags—not only Star Spangled Banners, but the flags of all the European nations with which the United States has joined forces in order to banish autocracy from the world. The arrival in America of the various missions of the Entente Allies has further quickened the demand for flags of foreign countries. Formerly a star-maker employed the primitive tools of die and mallet, but, in the face of the recent enormous demands, the flag factories now use motor-driven machines to cut the 48 State emblems required for every national ensign. The flag in the above illustration weighs 200 pounds and is 50 by 95 feet in size. The stars are one yard in diameter and are placed 4 feet 9 inches apart. The field of the union is 28 by 38 feet. (For correct proportions of our flag see page 312.)

[ Nº· 27   FLAG WOVEN BY MILLWORKERS IN NEW HAMPSHIRE.]

[ N⁰· 28   HUMAN AMERICAN EAGLE, FORT GORDON, ATLANTA. ]

[ N⁰· 29   HUMAN U.S. SHIELD, CAMP CUSTER, BATTLE CREEK. ]

[ *Nᵒ·* 30  MAGAZINE COVER.]

FORWARD AMERICA !

[ *N°.* 31  WWI POSTER.]

For The SAFETY OF WOMANHOOD
For The PROTECTION OF CHILDHOOD
For The HONOR OF MANHOOD
And For LIBERTY THROUGHOUT THE WORLD

HELP 'TILL IT HURTS

LIBERTY LOAN COMMITTEE of WASHINGTON

[ *N⁰.* 33  WW I POSTER. ]

[ *N⁰.* 34  WWI POSTER.]

[ *Nᵒ·* 35  WWI POSTER.]

[ *Nᵒ.* 36  FLAG DAY DURING WWI. ]

[ *N⁰.* 37  FLAG DAY DURING WWI.]

[ No. 38  WWI POSTER.]

[ *No.* 39  WWI POSTER. ]

[ Nº 41  WWI POSTER.]

[ *No.* 42   WWI POSTER. ]

[ *N⁰·* 43  WWI POSTER. ]

# PATRIOTIC LEAGUE

⌈ NO. 45  **WWI POSTER.** ⌉

[ *N°.* 46  **WWII POSTER.**]

[ *No.* 47  WWII POSTER.]

[ *No.* 48   PATRIOTIC POSTER. ]

[ *N⁰. 49* PATRIOTIC POSTER. ]

[ *No.* 50   GOVERNMENT CENSUS POSTER DURING WWII.]

[ *Nº.* 51  PATRIOTIC POSTER.]

[ *Nº.* 52  WWII POSTER BASED ON IWO JIMA PHOTOGRAPH. ]

NOTES &
*Sources*

[Copyright Page] Page 2. Old postcard.

[Table of Contents] Page 3. c. 1898. *Don't Touch My Flag!* Henderson, W.D. (chromolithograph)

*Revolutionary War*

Page 4. No. 1. Old postcard.

Page 5. Image No. 2. c. 1932. *Betsy Ross, 1777.* Jean Leon Gerome Ferrus, artist. Foundation Press, Inc., Cleveland, Ohio. (photomechanical print, halftone, color)

Page 6. No. 3. c. 1908. *Betsey [sic] Ross.* From painting by G. Liebscher. Original copyright, F.A. Schneider. (lithograph, color)

Page 7. No. 4. c. 1876. *Yankee Doodle 1776.* Publisher, J.F. Ryder, Cleveland, Ohio. Archibald M. Willard, artist. (chromolithograph) SUMMARY: Willard's most famous work is *The Spirit of '76* (previously known as *Yankee Doodle*) which was exhibited at the Centennial Exposition. The original is believed displayed in Abbot Hall (Marblehead, Massachusetts), as Willard painted several variations of the now-famous scene. Another original variation of the work by Willard hangs in the United States Department of State.

Page 8. No. 5. c. 1850–1910. *Great Seal of the United States.* Andrew B. Graham, lithographer. (lithograph, color)

Page 8. No. 6. c. 1850–1869. *Eagle & Flag.* American Bank Note Co. (engraving)

Pages 9–11. No. 7-9. Old postcards.

*War of 1812*

Page 12. No. 10. c. 1913. *The Star Spangled Banner—Francis Scott Key.* Percy E. Moran. (photomechanical print, halftone, color)

Page 13. No. 11. c. 1861. *The Star Spangled Banner, National Song / Stackpole, sc.* Published by William Dressler, New York. (engraving, hand colored)

*Civil War*

Page 14. No. 12. c. 1861. *Star Spangled Banner, Transcribed for the Piano by Ch. Voss.* J. Queen del. & lith. P.S. Duval & Son Lith. G. Andreacute & Co. Philadelphia. Marian S. Carson Collection, Library of Congress. (print, chromolithograph)

Page 15. No. 13. Old postcard.

Page 16. No. 14. c. 1861. *All Hail to the Flag of Freedom.* Published by Skaats & Knaebel, Brooklyn. Ferd. Mayer & Co., lithographer. New York. (lithograph, color)

Page 17. No. 15. c. 1861. *Hail! Glorious Banner of Our Land, Spirit of the Union.* Gibson & Co. lith., Cincinnati. (lithograph, color)

*Scenes from the 1800s*

Pages 18–21. Nos. 16–20. Old postcards.

Page 22. No. 21. *The Flag That Has Waved One Hundred Years—A Scene on the Morning of the Fourth Day of July 1876.* Fabronius, E.P. & L. Restein's oilchromo. National Chromo Co., publisher, Philadelphia. Original copyright, J.M. Munyon. (chromolithograph)

Page 23. Nos. 22–23. Old postcards.

Page 24. No. 24. c. 1867. *The Uprising of the North.* Thomas Nast, 1840–1902, artist. Bequest and gift, Caroline and Erwin Swann, 1974, Library of Congress. (painting, tempera, 7 ft. 10.5 in. x 11 ft. 7 in.) SUMMARY: One of five surviving paintings from Thomas Nast's Grand Caricaturama—a humorous account of American history involving real persons and symbolic characters. Nast created 33 paintings, each approximately 8 x 12 feet, for display on a stage as a moving panorama accompanied by an explanatory talk and piano songs. The performances in New York City and Boston received a highly favorable popular response. Cartoon shows "a night scene. Columbia stands on a balcony draped with the United States flag, with the American Eagle beside her, wings outspread. She brandishes her sword, and below her, mounted knights salute her with drawn swords. In the distance is a wide landscape of mountains, valleys, rivers and lakes—a whole continent—with beacon fires everywhere. In the sky is a vision of the Capitol, with rays of light radiating from it like the aurora borealis....The painting reveals Nast's complete belief in the righteousness of the Northern cause. It also reveals the basic romanticism that governed his politics and art."

Page 25. No. 25. c. 1898. *U.S. Navy—First Hoisting of the Stars and Stripes by the Marines on Cuban Soil—June 11th, 1898.* Werner Company, Akron, Ohio. (photomechanical print, color)

*WWI*

Page 26. No. 26. c. 1912. *The Human Flag, Altoona, Pa.* Photo by A.R. Bardsley. (photographic print)

Page 26. No. 27. c. 1917. *Flag Woven and Made Up by Mill-Workers at Manchester, New Hampshire.* Photograph by Harlan A. Marshall. Illus. in *National Geographic,* 1917 Oct., p. 411. Published by the National Geographic Society, Washington, D.C. (photomechanical print, halftone)

Page 27. No. 28. c. 1918. *The Human American Eagle. 12,500 Officers, Nurses and Men. Camp Gordon, Atlanta, Ga.* Maj. Gen. George H. Cameron, Commanding. Photo by Mole & Thomas. (photographic print)

Page 27. No. 29. c. 1918. *The Human U.S. Shield. 30,000 Officers and Men, Camp Custer, Battle Creek, Mich.* Brig. Gen. Howard L. Lauback, Commanding. Photo by Mole & Thomas. (photographic print)

Page 28. No. 30. c. 1917. *I Want You.* James Montgomery Flagg. From Frank Leslie's illustrated newspaper, Feb. 15, 1917. (photomechanical print, halftone, color illustration)

Page 29. No. 31. c. 1917. *Forward America!* Carroll Kelly. Wright Henry Worth Inc. (poster, lithograph, color, 57 x 39 cm)

Page 30. No. 32. c. 1918. *It Protected You, Will You Defend It.* Wentworth Institute poster no. 1. (poster, lithograph, color, 88 x 64 cm)

Page 31. No. 33. c. 1918. *For The Safety Of Womanhood ... Help 'Till It Hurts.* Ker. from the *Delineator*, April 1918 issue. (print, poster, lithograph, color, 51 x 33 cm)

Page 32. No. 34. c. 1918. *Remember! The Flag Of Liberty—Support It!* Buy U.S. Government Bonds 3rd. Liberty Loan.  Heywood Strasser & Voigt Lithograph Co., New York. No. 6-A. (poster, lithograph, color, 76 x 51 cm)

Page 33. No. 35. c. 1917. *Women! Help America's Sons Win the War—Buy U.S. Government Bonds, 2nd Liberty Loan of 1917.* R.H. Porteus. Edwards and Deutsch Litho. Co., Chicago. No. 11. (poster, lithograph, color, 75 x 49 cm)

Page 34. No. 36. c. 1917. *140th Flag Day, 1777–1917. The Birthday of the Stars and Stripes, June 14th, 1917.* Forms part of Willard and Dorothy Straight Collection, Library of Congress. (poster, lithograph, color, 101 x 65 cm)

Page 35. No. 37. c. 1918. *Uncle Sam's Birthday, July 4th 1776–1918, 142 Years Young and Going Strong!* United Cigars. (poster, lithograph, color, 85 x 53 cm)

Page 36. No. 38. c. 1918. *Will You Have a Part in Victory?* James Montgomery Flagg. Caption: Every garden a munition plant. Charles Lathrop Pack, President, National War Garden Commission. (print, poster, lithograph, color, 84 x 56 cm)

Page 37. No. 39. c. 1918. *Be Patriotic—Sign Your Country's Pledge to Save the Food.* Paul Stahr. W.F. Powers Co., Lithographers. Promotional goal: U.S. J7. U.S. Food Administration poster. (poster,  color)

Page 38. No. 40. c. 1917. *Don't Wait for the Draft—Volunteer.* Guenther. Associated Motion Picture Advertisers, Inc. Poster No. 3. Compliments of Joseph H. Tooker. Forms part of Willard and Dorothy Straight Collection, Library of Congress. (poster, lithograph, color, 99 x 67 cm)

Page 39. No. 41. c. 1917. *Wake Up America! Civilization Calls Every Man, Woman and Child!* James Montgomery Flagg. Hegeman Print, New York. Promotional goal: U.S. J44. Mayor's Committee. (poster, color)

Page 40. No. 42. c. 1917. *The Call to Duty—Join the Army for Home and Country.* Published by Recruiting Committee of the Mayor's Committee on National Defence [sic]. American Lithographic Co., New York. Adapted from the sculpture by Edoardo Cammilli. (poster, lithograph, color)

Page 41. No. 43. c. 1917. *Follow the Flag—Enlist in the Navy.* Daugherty, composition, H.R. N.Y., Carey Print Lithography, New York. Promotional goal: U.S. J26. (poster, color)

Page 42. No. 44. c. 1917. *My Soldier—Buy United States Government Bonds—Third Liberty Loan.* H.H. Green, Matthews-Northrup Works, Buffalo, Cleveland, and New York. (poster, lithograph, color, 106 x 70 cm)

Page 43. No. 45. c. 1918. *Patriotic League.* Howard Chandler Christy. United States Prtg. & Lith. Co. SUMMARY: Includes open blue triangle, symbol of war relief work. (print, poster, lithograph, color, 70 x 51 cm)

## WWII

Page 44. No. 46. c. 1939. *Elmhurst Flag Day, June 18, 1939, Du Page County Centennial.* Beauparlant. WPA Federal Art Project, Chicago, Ill. Work Projects Administration Poster Collection, Library of Congress. (print on board, poster, silkscreen, color)

Page 45. No. 47. January 1943. *I Pledge Allegiance and Silence about the War.* WPA War Services of Louisiana. Byrne, Thomas A., artist. Federal Art Project, sponsor. (print on board, poster, silkscreen, color)

Page 46. No. 48. c. 1936–1938. *49th Annual Exhibition of American Paintings Sculpture.* M. Waltrip. Illinois. Federal Art Project. Works Progress Administration. (print, poster, silkscreen, color)

Page 47. No. 49. c. 1940. *51st Annual Exhibition—American Painting and Sculpture.* Chicago. Illinois WPA Art Project. Federal Art Project, sponsor. Works Progress Administration. (print on board, poster, silkscreen, color)

Page 48. No. 50. *It's Your America! Help the Ten-Year Roll Call—1940 Census, U.S.A.* U.S. Government Printing Office. Promotional goal. (poster, color)

Page 49. No. 51. c. 1941. *Defense! Long Island Women. Home Defense Day. Exhibits—Demonstrations—Lectures—Drills—Music.* JD. New York State WPA Art Project. (print on board, poster, silkscreen, color)

Page 50. No. 52. c. 1945. *7th War Loan: Now—All Together.* Cecil Calvert Beall, artist. From Associated Press photo. U.S. Government Printing Office, Washington, D.C. United States Dept. of the Treasury, funder/sponsor. Official U.S. Treasury poster. (photomechanical print, poster, halftone, color)

Page 55. No. 53. Old postcard.

[Back Cover] c. 1861. *Our Heaven Born Banner.* Painted by William Bauly. Lith. of Sarony, Major & Knapp. Published by W[illiam] Schaus. New York. (print on wove paper, lithograph printed in colors, image 25.2 x 32.3 cm) SUMMARY: A pro-Union patriotic print, evidently based on Frederic Edwin Church's small oil painting *Our Banner in the Sky* or on a chromolithograph reproducing that painting published in New York by Goupil & Co. in the summer of 1861. Church's painting was inspired by the highly publicized Confederate insult to the American flag at Fort Sumter in April 1861 and by a sermon by Henry Ward Beecher published shortly thereafter. The present print was deposited for copyright, with a companion piece, *Fate of the Rebel Flag* (no. 1861-21), on September 6. *Our Heaven Born Banner* shows a lone Zouave sentry watching from a promontory as the dawn breaks in the distance. His rifle and bayonet form the staff of an American flag whose design and colors are formed by the sky's light. Below, in the distance, is a fort—probably Sumter. The print is accompanied by eight lines of verse: "When Freedom from her mountain height / Unfurled her standard to the air, / She tore the azure robe of night / And set the stars of glory there. / She mingled with its gorgeous dyes / The milky baldrick of the skies, / And striped its pure celestial white / With streakings of the morning light." Unlike its companion piece, *Our Heaven Born Banner* is printed using brown instead of black ink for the primary tone.

UNITED
WE STAND

A GLORIOUS FOURTH.

[ NO. 53 JULY 4TH POSTCARD.]

LaVergne, TN USA
13 November 2009
164141LV00001B

# THE MUSLIM BROTHERS IN SOCIETY

Everyday Politics, Social
Action, and Islamism in
Mubarak's Egypt

Marie Vannetzel

Translated by David Tresilian

The American University in Cairo Press
Cairo • New York

First published in 2021 by
The American University in Cairo Press
113 Sharia Kasr el Aini, Cairo, Egypt
One Rockefeller Plaza, 10th Floor, New York, NY 10020
www.aucpress.com

First published in French in 2016 as *Les Frères musulmans égyptiens: Enquête sur un secret public*. Copyright © Éditions Karthala, Paris, 2016.

Dar el Kutub No. 10921/19
ISBN 978 977 416 962 5

Dar el Kutub Cataloging-in-Publication Data

Vannetzel, Marie
    The Muslim Brothers in Society: Everyday Politics, Social Action, and Islamism in
    Mubarak's Egypt / Marie Vannetzel.—Cairo: The American University in Cairo Press, 2021.
        p. cm.
        ISBN 978 977 416 962 5
        1. Islam — Egypt — History — 1981
        2. Egypt — Politics and Government — 1981
        297.8

1  2  3  4  5    25  24  23  22  21

Designed by Greg Jorss
Printed in the United States of America

# Contents

# Figures

# Tables

# Maps

# Acknowledgments

This book would not have existed without the help and patience of the men and women who have been my interlocutors during field research. Encountering them in the context of their daily lives, learning who they are as social actors and individuals, grasping their views of the world and coming to understand them, even if I did not share their opinions, enabled me to comprehend the multiple shades of being a Muslim Brother or Sister.

I owe special thanks to my academic mentors and supervisors, Professor Sarah Ben Néfissa from the Institut de Recherche pour le Développement, and Professor Jean-Louis Briquet from the Centre National de la Recherche Scientifique. The trust they placed in me from the very beginning of this work has always gone hand-in-hand with an intellectual rigor that pushed me to constantly deepen my thoughts and face the contradictions that arose in the course of the work. I want to pay tribute to them here. I also feel profoundly indebted to Professor Salwa Ismail from SOAS, University of London, Professor Jean-François Bayart from Graduate Institute-Geneva, and Professor Johanna Siméant from Université Paris Panthéon-Sorbonne, for their thoughtful and critical comments, as well as their influence and confidence. Each played a constructive role in this work.

In Egypt, France, and other parts of the world, there are many colleagues and friends who supported me through the rewriting of various drafts of this book. At the Centre d'Études et de Documentation Économiques, Juridiques et sociales (CEDEJ) in Cairo, I first wish to acknowledge the institutional help provided over time by its directors, the late Alain Roussillon, Karine Bennafla and Agnès Deboulet. I am grateful to Elisabeth Longuenesse and Nafissa Dessouki, who generously gave me access to their personal research archives. My dear late friend Gihan Basyuni was an amazing partner during fieldwork and I miss her very much. I am thankful to Hala Bayoumi, head of CEDEJ's Digital Humanities Department, for providing me with data, and to Neil Ketchley, associate professor at Oslo University, for his generous advice and for the maps he provided. At the Centre Universitaire de Recherche sur l'Action Publique et la Politique (CURAPP) in Amiens (France), I warmly thank Ana Perrin-Heredia, Patrick Lehingue, Romain Pudal, Pierre-Yves Baudot and Elodie Lemaire for their critical insights and friendly intellectual companionship.

I am also greatly indebted to Professor François Burgat, the principal investigator of the program, "When Authoritarianism Fails in the Arab World" (WAFAW), whose substantial support helped this project tremendously. I have benefited from vivid discussions with my colleagues of this wonderful team: Amin Allal, Robin Beaumont, Laurent Bonnefoy, Myriam Catusse, Vincent Geisser, Stéphane Lacroix, Monica Marks, Laura Ruiz de Elvira, and Dilek Yankaya.

In various contexts, Tewfik Aclimandos, Lydia Ali, Gabrielle Angey, Richard Banégas, Mounia Bennani-Chraïbi, Nathalie Bernard-Maugiron, Nicolas Bué, Michel Camau, Raphaëlle Chevrillon-Guibert, Hélène Combes, Youssef El Chazli, Florence Haegel, Amr Hashem Rabie, Béatrice Hibou, Malak Labib, Mailys Mangin, Igor Martinache, Elise Massicard, Thomas Pierret, Marine Poirier, Giedre Sabaseviciute, Amr ElShobaki, and the late Samer Soleiman, made useful and rich comments on earlier versions that improved the manuscript significantly.

This book owes much to Nadia Naqib and Laura Gribbon, from the American University in Cairo Press, for their endless efforts, patience, and kindness. I take this opportunity to express my sincere gratitude to Professor Sumita Pahwa, who graciously took the initiative to introduce my work to the AUC Press. I would also like to thank Editions Karthala in France for backing this project, and David Tresilian for the translation from French to English. This book was made possible thanks to the funding from the Centre National du Livre and from the WAFAW program.

*Ange* Farid Farid and *Dude* Victor made valuable contributions to this book by editing the text and helping me clarify my thoughts. Marine has helped shape my thinking and has given me unfailing support. *Mille mercis à vous trois*, as well as to my dearest Jean-Claude and Sélim for their supplementary revisions.

My family and my friends Abderrahman, Adrien, Ana, Arthur, Assia, Caroline, Carl, Celia, Charlotte, Dilek, Erica, Farah, Maaï, Mahmoud, Marie, Meeto, Merve, Mosaab, Naïké, Nathalie, Nicanor, Raffaella, Saker, Sarah, Sixtine and Taher also provided much help and support at different stages of this book. Ahmed Rady and Madiha Doss will be forever remembered. Their clever and tender gazes on Egypt and life have helped me see things differently. And, as always, Bob has been an indispensable companion.

# Introduction:
# Encountering the Brothers

Politics in Egypt relies on an unusual equation—which is that although the Muslim Brothers are banned, they are still very much present. Once you have understood that, you will be on the right path. (An official from the Muslim Brotherhood, speaking in August 2009.)

On 25 December 2013, the organization of the Egyptian Society of the Muslim Brothers, the Gama'at al-Ikhwan al-Muslimin, was officially declared a "terrorist organization." Six months after the removal of Mohamed Morsi, the president who was elected in 2012, the organization to which he belonged had become public enemy number one.

Yet the revolutionary uprising that took place on 25 January 2011 opened up an entirely new period in the history of the Society of the Muslim Brothers, or Muslim Brotherhood (MB). Founded in 1928 when Egypt was a monarchy under British control, the Brotherhood was first banned as early as 1948, after the assassination of the then-Prime Minister Nuqrashi Pasha, a crime for which it had been found guilty. It experienced a brief return to grace when the monarchy was overthrown in 1952, but it was then harshly repressed by the Nasser regime after 1954. In the 1970s, the movement slowly reemerged after Anwar al-Sadat came to power as president. From then on, the Brotherhood experienced changing fortunes as periods of repression came and went, and it eventually became an influential social and political actor[1] and an organization that, although banned, was tolerated. It was the fall of then-president Hosni Mubarak on 11 February 2011 that made this ban obsolete. At the same time that the former ruling party, the National Democratic Party (NDP), was dissolved, the Gama'a created its own first legal political party, the Freedom and Justice Party (FJP). In December 2011, a coalition led by the FJP won 47 percent of the seats in the People's Assembly, the lower house of the Egyptian parliament, and

1

then more than 58 percent of those in the Consultative Council, the parliament's upper house. In June 2012, MB candidate Mohamed Morsi won the first presidential elections in the country's history that were considered to be free and fair.

The 2011–12 period was crucial for the Muslim Brotherhood. For the first time in more than fifty years, not only did the Brothers have the historic opportunity to take control of the country's governing institutions, they also had the *duty* to reemerge from their underground status and reenter the legal fold. This reemergence was, however, an enormous challenge for the Gama'a. Rightly or wrongly, the overall impression of Brotherhood rule during Morsi's presidency was of opaque management of public affairs by an organization that was still largely hidden and that sought to monopolize control of state institutions in underhanded ways. It was this perception, a powerful force for the delegitimization of Brotherhood rule, that, when coupled with the continuing influence of networks from the ancien régime, the economic crisis, national and regional rivalries, and the influence of the media, led to the massive demonstrations that took place on 30 June 2013. These were used by General Abdel Fattah al-Sisi and his collaborators to carry out a coup d'état that overthrew Morsi and began a period of blanket repression of the Muslim Brothers.

In order to understand the importance of the challenges the Brotherhood faced in 2011–12 and the reasons it failed to meet them, this book examines the everyday lives of the Brothers over previous decades, a period when, before becoming a 'public enemy,' they had been a 'public secret.'

## A Public Secret
*Mosalsal*

An ordinary-looking student, his face somewhat tense, is making an urgent call from a public telephone booth. A few minutes later, a man in his fifties wearing a suit and tie, balding and with a carefully trimmed beard, appears on the sidewalk walking toward the student. As he passes him, he says, "You don't look happy," without looking at him. Following the man, his manner indicating a state of alert, the student asks to meet him in a quiet place. "With thousands of State Security agents watching us? Don't even think about it," the older man answers, adding, "Tell me what you have to report and be quick about it." The student says that all "their" candidates in the student union elections at Helwan, 'Ain Shams, Alexandria, and Mansoura Universities have been removed from the lists by the authorities. He holds out a piece of paper, which the man quickly tears up. If he is arrested, any documents found on him could be used against him. "We're not dealing drugs here," the student exclaims. "They let drug dealers go. But even an ordinary activist is important when it comes to the Brothers," the man replies, indicating that he will be turning into the next street and bidding the young man farewell.

In the next scene, the man, his grim manner echoed by the accompanying music, is shown walking around a western-style supermarket of which he is the manager. "This business of the caricatures of the Prophet is finished," he tells a worker at the dairy counter. "Get the Danish products out and hide the others so the Danish products will sell before their sell-by dates are reached." He is then seen in his office, closed-circuit TV screens on in the background, talking to an unknown person on the telephone whom he calls "my lord." With a nervous laugh, he arranges to meet the person for dinner in a local shawarma restaurant.

These were the first scenes of a television series broadcast on one of the Egyptian state TV channels in 2010 during the holy month of Ramadan, when Egyptian families habitually gather together in front of the television in the evening to watch that year's *mosalsal*.[2] Talk of this series, called *al-Gama'a* after the Brotherhood, was on everyone's lips during the summer before the parliamentary elections that took place in November of that year. Directed by Walid Hamid, said to be anti-Islamist, the series was mostly financed by public funds despite the usual ban on Muslim Brothers appearing in state TV programs as a way of denying them media coverage.

From the first episode onward, the series contained many striking elements that slowly came together to produce a full-scale portrait of the enigmatic Gama'a. First there was the emphasis on the organization's clandestine nature, expressed by secret meetings, high-handed commands for discretion bordering on paranoia, an insistence on confidentiality, and the sanctity of the Brotherhood's guarded nature. Then there was the emphasis on the organization's political power, shown to be targeting young people in universities, and on its financial power, like that held by the wealthy businessman presented in the first episode who was later discovered to be responsible for the management of Brotherhood funds. Finally there was the emphasis on fraud, shown through the hypocrisy of the MB businessman regarding Danish butter.

Later in the same episode, a dozen or so other mysterious figures appear during a secret meeting of the highest executive body of the Gama'a, the Guidance Bureau (Maktab al-Irshad). Gathering in opulent surroundings, it answers to the organization's supreme guide (al-murshid), whose hand these figures are shown kissing. Faced with the situation of *mihna*, or persecution, in which "we live and have always lived," the guide declares that "we have the necessary experience and determination, and most people sympathize with us . . . or at least, if they are not with us, they are not against us. The moment has come for us to show our strength and the extent of our influence among the students." The series then refers to events that took place in Cairo on 10 December 2006, though it does not explicitly refer to dates and presents the events significantly differently from the way they actually transpired. These events followed on from an affair called the "al-Azhar militias," in which some fifty students affiliated with the Brotherhood, all dressed in black, staged a demonstration on the premises of al-Azhar University in Cairo, the most prestigious Sunni Muslim educational institution in the world. Six of them had also carried out a demonstration of martial arts in protest against the arbitrary dismissal of some of their peers by the university administration.[3] Instead of six people, the TV series showed several dozen masked activists carrying out kung fu-type movements, brandishing copies of the Qur'an, and calling for a "jihad on the path of God." The security services were presented in a flattering light, with officers of the State Security (Amn al-Dawla) shown carrying out their work in a conscientious manner with the help of a model young prosecutor. The sequence that followed showed the satisfied face of the Brotherhood's guide, commenting that whatever criticisms might be made of the organization, its influence would continue to grow.

The series thus brought together two main aspects of the Brotherhood's supposedly all-powerful nature. On the one hand, there was its secrecy and violence, raising the specter of a conspiratorial force advancing under the cover of darkness. On the other hand, there was the idea that if it were able to advance, this would be because of its presence throughout society, the organization being presented as having tentacles everywhere and being particularly attractive to certain segments of the country's youth. Situations are depicted as if the Brotherhood is known to be everywhere, even if its presence is hidden. This representation of the organization, made explicit in the TV series, is telling of the manner in which the Muslim Brothers in fact appeared in public space during the Mubarak years in Egypt.

### Al-Mahzura

Even though the organization was illegal, its existence was well known and even partially recognized, as is clear from the daily articles about the Brotherhood in both the private- and the public-sector press at the time. However, many of these articles referred to the organization as *al-mahzura*, literally meaning 'the prohibited.'[4] This indicates not only that the Gama'a was a notorious secret: of all the clandestine groups existing in Egypt at the time, only one was unequivocally designated as *al-mahzura* because of its imagined size. However, unlike most secrets, it was also not the object of "a tacit arrangement . . . on the level of private communication between friends or acquaintances" (Thompson 2000: 21). On the contrary, it was as if this tacit arrangement were taking place at the level of Egyptian society as a whole, thus making the existence of the Brotherhood a public matter that was presented as a secret, or, in other words, simply a *public secret*. Everyone knew of the Brothers' existence, but no one knew exactly *who* they were. They were credited with having a presence throughout society, but no one knew exactly where this was located. They were imagined to have a network of social services, but in general very little was known about the charities, hospitals, and schools linked to the Brotherhood and how such connections worked. It is also a major characteristic of a public secret that it creates a scandal when it is publicly unveiled, and it was for this reason that the TV series mentioned earlier created such a stir. The secrecy of *al-mahzura* seemed to have been strikingly revealed.

The public denunciation of the hidden side of the Muslim Brothers came to a climax in the years between 2011 and 2013. But their secrecy had actually started to be questioned even before the fall of Mubarak. A heated debate had even taken place inside the Gama'a itself. The growing importance of the media in Egyptian life had led to the appearance of MB bloggers in 2006, whose criticisms of the organization's traditionally secretive culture had already provoked conflict and disagreement within it. Other activists had retorted that the clandestine character of the organization was a consequence of oppression, adding that the *mahzura* (banned) was also the *mazluma* ('wronged'). Others still had argued that the illegality of the organization had paradoxically endowed it with greater opportunities for action when compared to the conventional political parties whose activities were more strictly controlled. The Brotherhood's status as *mahzura* during the Mubarak years had by default given it a certain degree of freedom.

## Open Secrecy, Informality, and the State
The Gama'a has often been described in scholarly literature as a "banned but tolerated organization." However, even in repeating this assertion, its precise meaning is not clear. How is this banning and tolerance in fact manifested? What was the origin of this ambiguous status and what were its consequences for the activities of the Brotherhood?

Scholars underline either the permissive or the repressive consequences of this status. Some have emphasized the co-option of the Muslim Brothers by the Mubarak regime, while others have stressed their exclusion from the political system and retreat into the social sphere, whereby they were permitted to operate by the regime insofar as they helped compensate for the welfare-state crisis. However, rather than try to separate the repressive and permissive aspects of this situation, my intention here is instead to place this ambiguity at the center of my inquiry.

The notion of 'open secrecy' captures this ambivalence. The Brotherhood kept some of its activities secret and unofficial because of the limitations weighing on it as a result of its illegality and state repression. At the same time, however, because there was still a fluctuating margin of tolerance, it benefited from the de facto recognition of its existence in society. It could also take part, though in a limited fashion and only under certain conditions, in the official political sphere through the electoral process. 'Open secrecy' also led to informality: I use this concept to indicate both the undefined status of the Gama'a and the modes of its political, social, and organizational existence in the Egyptian authoritarian context. While the Brotherhood was not legally recognized, Muslim Brothers nevertheless took part in official political and social spheres in Egypt. They were thus *politically informal* as they were characterized by an ambiguous political positioning, being neither in the opposition nor co-opted by the regime, and neither completely outside the system nor completely inside it. They were also *socially informal* as they were present throughout society, though this was tacit or hidden. And the Gama'a itself displayed some informal aspects: it was a strongly hierarchical and closed organization, whose boundaries were nevertheless both vague and porous. The Brotherhood's informality was the result of three factors. Firstly its ideology, which viewed political action as being inseparable from religious, moral, and social action; secondly, the organization's strategies to ensure its survival; and thirdly, it was also the byproduct of the ways in which the Egyptian state controlled and regulated society. Indeed, as Julia Elyachar has noted, accounting for the 'informal' here "necessarily also means paying attention to the state" (Elyachar 2003: 580).

Rather than develop the hypothesis that the Brotherhood worked against the state or that it was entirely under its control, I use the approach of "politics from below" (Bayart, Mbembe, and Toulabor 1992) in an attempt to understand the Muslim Brothers as fully fledged actors in the "formation of the [Egyptian] state," here defined as "a largely unconscious and contradictory historical process composed of conflicts, negotiations, and compromises between different groups whose self-interested acts and mutual concessions made up the social spread of power" (Berman and Lonsdale 1992: 5). This conception echoes the definition of the state as a "structural effect" put forward by Timothy Mitchell (1991: 78), in which the state is not seen as a self-directing and autonomous structure differentiated from society by a clear and objective boundary. It is rather seen as the result of practices that bring this boundary into being and make it visible, with its production and maintenance being at the center of strategies used by many different actors. It is thus the local sites in which the 'state' is 'produced' that should be explored, which are also the sites in which the Muslim Brothers operated. In adopting the notion of the "everyday state" put forward by Salwa Ismail in light of Mitchell's ideas, the intention is to pay particular attention to "practices of government and power deployed at the micro-scale of everyday life" (Ismail 2006: xxxiii). This should enable a reexamination of the hypothesis of the Islamists as somehow compensating for the abandonment of various spaces by the state, and contribute to a description of how relations between state and non-state actors, the latter including the Muslim Brothers, functioned in them. These spaces were susceptible to being filled in all sorts of ways, and the limits of the everyday state were defined and redefined within them.

However, this book also intends to suggest an alternative way of thinking about the relationship between the Muslim Brothers and Egyptian society. This question has been the subject of much attention in recent years, and it has given rise to much lively debate, rendered more intense by the polarization that has taken place in the Egyptian political arena.

## The Gama'a and Society
### The Debate

Few scholarly works before the 2011 revolution examined the question of the social roots of the Gama'a. While another Islamist group, al-Gama'a al-Islamiyya, has been the object of careful studies into the everyday political practices and modes of inserting of Islamist activists into the social fabric of society (Ismail 2000; Haenni 2005a)[5], only one study, by Mohamed Fahmy Menza, has applied the same kind of analysis to the Muslim Brotherhood in Egypt, concentrating on the Cairo district of Misr al-Qadima (Menza 2012). The focus of Menza's study, however, was as much on the ruling NDP as it was on the MB, and while it did analyze the everyday relationships between the Muslim Brothers and local notables in the district, the Brothers' social activities were not systematically examined.

Generally speaking, the Brotherhood has been looked at in terms of a much larger Islamic social movement (Wiktorowicz 2001 and 2004; Bayat 2005, 2007; Singerman 2003). As a result of this theoretical framework, the connections between the different "institutions of the Islamic social movement" (Clark 2004) have been simply presupposed and not empirically explored. Carrie R. Wickham (2002), for example, argues that the private mosques, clinics, schools, companies, publishing houses, and Islamic banks that existed in Egypt in the 1980s and 1990s formed a "parallel Islamic sector" to the state and functioned to support the propaganda activities of the different Islamist groups. However, she does not explain exactly how they did so.

Much of this can be attributed to the absence of empirical data, since, as Steven Brooke justly remarks, "data on [the Brotherhood's social-services network] are frustratingly hard to come by. One cannot identify whom the Brotherhood's networks serve, how large they are, how they function, where they exist, or how they relate to the state" (2019: 3). Some studies have provided more information about aspects of the Islamist presence in Egypt's professional associations (Qandil 1994; Hasan 2000), as well as in various charities (Abed-Kotob and Sullivan 1999; Siyam 2006), yet the fact remains that here too the exact nature of the links between those structures and the Gama'a have not been examined. With the exception of the pioneering work by Sarah Ben Néfissa (2003) on the relations between the Brotherhood and the prominent charity al-Gam'iyya al-Shar'iyya, it was only after the 2011 revolution that new studies started to appear dealing with this question.

Among them is the excellent book by Brooke (2019), which scrutinizes the Islamic Medical Association (IMA), another important Brotherhood-linked charity. Many of the empirical difficulties stem from the fact that such connections are not visible from a distance, so to speak, since, as this book will demonstrate, they very rarely take an organizational form. Al-Gam'iyya al-Shar'iyya and the IMA are the two major exceptions to this rule (though in the case of the former, the organizational links between it and the Brotherhood were theoretically severed at the beginning of this century).[6] This does not mean that the Gama'a has no links with other associations, charities, or schools. It simply means that because these links are informal, they can only be observed by using ethnographic methods.

The question of the nature of the social services provided by the MB was closely examined in the post-2011 context for two main reasons: first, to understand the reasons behind the Brotherhood's electoral success before and after 2011, and second, to understand why it experienced such a sudden collapse in 2013. Regarding the first question, Tareq Masoud has argued that, before 2011, the provision of social services did not explain the MB's electoral performance. With the ruling NDP exercising a monopoly over the votes of the poor through its clientelist structures, the Muslim Brothers were only able to mobilize the then small number of middle-class voters, who were not captured by NDP patronage (Masoud 2014). But this was enough to win seats, given the low turnout and the lack of competition. After 2011, and with the NDP absent from the elections, larger numbers of poor electors redirected their votes toward parties that they perceived as being more inclined to distribute welfare resources, such as the MB and the Salafists, he says. It was these voters' disappointment at the absence of such social policies under Morsi's rule that later led to the drop in popularity of the Muslim Brothers (Masoud 2014). Brooke similarly argues that the Brothers' main priority was to mobilize the middle classes, but he also shows in a more systematic and empirical fashion the mechanisms for politicization that were at work in their provision of social services. His conclusions are consistent with mine, namely, that paradoxically the key to the political success of the Brotherhood's social activities lay in their depoliticization (Brooke 2019). The apparent depoliticized character of welfare provision had positive reputational effects for the MB, and in chapters three, four, and six we will examine in more detail how these reputational effects were brought about, as well as the subtle forms of politicization that resulted from them. The ethnographic approach adopted here also allows the idea of a break between the poor and middle classes in Egypt to be more nuanced, since in my view the authors cited above are too rigid in their descriptions of it. In fact, so extensive is poverty in the country that much of the middle classes would be better described as "subaltern groups with room to maneuver" (Schwartz 2011) than as genuinely middle-class.

Lastly, Brooke's explanation of the overthrow of Morsi in 2013 does not appear convincing. According to him, in the first half of 2013, the Brotherhood undertook a change in strategy and carried out a massive medical campaign in rural areas in order to win over poorer voters. So great was the impact of this campaign that it led the other political parties to appeal to the army to intervene, since, according to Brooke, they knew that they would not be able to compete with the MB in the subsequent parliamentary elections. My problem with this explanation is twofold. First, such medical campaigns were not new, even if it is true that on this occasion it was particularly broad and politicized (the importance of this is returned to in chapter six). Second, and more importantly, it should not be forgotten that this campaign took place after the clashes outside the Ittihadeyya Palace in December 2012 and at a time when the Brotherhood was already losing much of its popularity. There is no reason to think that the medical campaign would have allowed the Brotherhood to win the elections, since it had already ruined its reputational effects.

Other studies appearing after 2011 have looked at the question of the relations between the Brotherhood and wider society, as well as at the organization's sudden drop in popularity, by taking a very different approach. Here, the argument is that it was the internal structure of the Gama'a, the fact that it was cut off from the rest of society and that it notoriously indoctrinated its members, which best explains the Brotherhood's failure to establish a solid social base outside the narrow circle of its own activists. This, according to these studies, was revealed in the events that took place in 2012–13 (Kandil 2015; al-Anani 2016; Trager 2016; Ben Néfissa and Abo El-Kasem 2015). The issue of indoctrination will be discussed more fully in chapter five. For the time being, it is sufficient to point out that while these studies do manage to reopen the 'black box' of the Brotherhood, which had mostly been closed since the classic work by Richard Mitchell in 1969 (with the exception of the works by Tammam in 2006 and al-Anani in 2007), they nevertheless focus on the sectarian aspect of the organization, while almost completely ignoring its social dimension.

## The Purpose of This Book
This book is intended to make two distinct contributions to the debate on the Brotherhood. First, it aims to consider the public and the hidden faces of the Gama'a as the two sides of a single coin; the public face being turned outward, toward social embedding, and the hidden one being turned inward, toward the inner world of the organization. I aim to show that despite the tensions and contradictions that existed between these two facets of the Brotherhood's activities, the Gama'a as a whole cannot be understood without examining the relationship between them. In fact, neither facet can be fully understood without the other. Second, this book

offers an ethnographic analysis of the Brotherhood's everyday politics and social activities in three districts of Greater Cairo. How, concretely, did the Brothers relate to the local populations? What social services did they provide and how did they do so? How did they adopt different forms of mobilization according to local contexts, and what were the political impacts of these on a micro and macro scale? How did they deal with the distinction between the 'inside' and the 'outside' of the Brotherhood when organizing their activities? What forms of relationship did they have with the Gama'a and how did they juggle their membership in the Brotherhood with other social identities?

The chapters that follow examine the links between the social services that the MB provided and the group's everyday politics, through an ethnographic account of the activities of three Brotherhood MPs elected between 2005 and 2010. I investigate the various local networks in which these MPs and their staff of activists and volunteers operated, how they related to the state institutions and authorities, and how they mobilized during election campaigns. I aim to show how they maneuvered within the framework of what I call the "politics of goodness." This term is used to characterize the conflictual consensus that existed between the Brothers and local agents of the Mubarak regime such as NDP members and state functionaries. This consensus saw political activities in terms of practices that were non-specialized and, as paradoxical as it might seem, also mostly non-politicized. Such practices, having to do with the provision of *khidma* (pl. *khadamat*, social services) and *khayr* (goodness, charity), were implemented through tightly linked networks in which political divisions like those between the MB and the NDP were not largely apparent.

The politics of goodness, as a conceptual framework, allows me to demonstrate that there was no such thing as a parallel Islamist sector on the ground. It was much more fluid and intercutting. I also provide further evidence and explanation for the counterintuitive conclusions drawn by Brooke regarding the weak *direct* politicization of Brotherhood social activities. However, even though the politics of goodness demanded consensus, there was also conflict at play. Indeed, as I will show below, the Brothers strove to distinguish themselves from their competitors by means of a *symbolic economy of disinterestedness*. The main mechanism of this economy was the promotion of individual and collective forms of behavior that I summarize under the heading of 'ethical conduct.' This behavior was the vehicle for the informal social embedding of the Brotherhood. The Brothers acted as *virtuous neighbors* without making their identity obvious, but at the same time behaving in such a way that that they could also potentially be identified as members of the organization. It was this behavior, subtle and implicit, that led to judgments being made about the overall 'virtue' of the Brotherhood, and explains how affective and ethical bonds with constituencies were built. This ethical conduct made the MB attractive to several groups of people that have received little attention until now in the literature: the sympathizers, whom here I call "associated personalities." By definition, these individuals were non-Brothers (some even belonged to the former ruling party, the NDP), or half-Brothers of some sort. I argue that while they were not members of the organization, they nevertheless constituted a stratum of the Gama'a, very active in the provision of its social services and contributing to its daily existence on a local level.

It is here that the question of the hidden face of the Gama'a arises—that is, its internal rule and religious ideology. The involvement of 'non-Brothers' and 'half-Brothers' in the Brotherhood can only be properly understood if we are aware of the organization's porous boundaries even as it remained highly hierarchical in its internal structure. Understanding the hidden face is also important in understanding how 'ethical conduct' was not a spontaneously adopted code of behavior. Instead, it was the result of specific training that aimed to produce activists who understood that their mission was to bring about a moral transformation of society according to their vision of Islam. Members were trained to serve as exemplary models for other Muslims and were made to feel their own moral superiority to others. As a consequence, their relationships with people outside the organization were complex. They were caught up in a contradiction between their everyday activities as virtuous neighbors within local communities, and the need, flowing from their conviction of moral and religious superiority, to keep themselves to themselves as Brothers. The criteria of 'ethical conduct' also brought about a certain hierarchy and discipline within the organization, acting against other organizational patterns based on the specialization of skills and competences. This led to significant internal tensions, seen most notably in the opposition of young MB bloggers toward the leadership of the organization at the end of the 2000s.

The bloggers also contested the ambiguous political impacts of the 'politics of goodness,' which swung between maintaining the authoritarian order and nurturing latent conflicts that were only sometimes expressed in terms of clear divisions. The 2011 Revolution helped to bring these tensions out into the open, and the conflictual consensus that had been built around the 'politics of goodness' then collapsed into disarray. These dynamics were among the powerful factors causing the Brotherhood's historic downfall in 2013.

The results presented in this book were made possible by the use of close ethnographic investigation, a method not previously used in the case of the Egyptian Muslim Brothers.

## Investigating Open Secrecy
### The Local Offices of Brotherhood MPs

In carrying out the fieldwork for this study, I took the local offices of Brotherhood MPs as my base, an approach that had considerable theoretical and methodological advantages. The 2005 parliamentary elections had been exceptional for their relative transparency and had sent eighty-eight Brotherhood MPs to the People's Assembly, the lower house of Egypt's parliament, winning some 20 percent of the seats. These MPs then opened several offices in their constituencies to which local residents could bring their problems. It was the first time since the 1950s that the Brotherhood had been able to open offices in its name or under its umbrella in any district or village in Egypt. Indeed, except for the headquarters of its top institution, the Guidance Bureau, located in Manial (Cairo), the organization had no premises—at least no known or public ones. Each MP had between four and seven offices, making a total of more than 450. The fieldwork on which this book is based was carried out in three constituencies in Greater Cairo between 2007 and 2010, namely Helwan, Tibbin/15 Mayo, and Madinat Nasr. It allowed me to observe firsthand how the activities of the MPs, the social embedding of the Muslim Brotherhood, and its 'open secrecy' varied according to local circumstances.

During the Mubarak years, the role of an MP was essentially that of an elected local representative. For many ordinary citizens, parliament only existed as a kind of agency to which they could address requests for services (*khadamat*). It was the responsibility of the local MP to find the means to provide these by identifying the necessary resources and developing the necessary relationships with ministers, governors, and various state agencies. His local constituency offices thus constituted an 'ideal-type' space that straddled institutional and informal politics and mixed political activities with the provision of social services. Moreover, in his role as an interface between the state and the local society, the new Brotherhood MPs found themselves positioned precisely at the meeting point between the public and the hidden face of the Gama'a. The new MPs and their staff were responsible for relations with the residents of their constituencies. However, at the same time they were members of the *tanzim*, the organizational apparatus of the Gama'a.

Various activities took place in and around these offices, and activists with different social profiles rubbed shoulders in them, using them as a kind of local headquarters. They included MPs, staff members, candidates in local elections, local leaders of the *tanzim*, and young activists (with some of the latter later becoming opposition bloggers). I also met 'associated personalities' in these offices, along with local residents, some of whom were Brotherhood voters and some of whom were not. I have changed the names of my interlocutors to preserve their anonymity, although this was not possible for public personalities, such as members of parliament.

The fieldwork was rounded off by a smaller study of the Brotherhood MPs and their staff in two Alexandrian constituencies. I also conducted interviews with five distinct classes of actors: (1) various well-known figures or leaders of the organization, (2) political actors in competition with the Brotherhood, including other MPs, election candidates, members of the NDP, and members of opposition parties, (3) NGO activists, journalists, lawyers, and judges, and (4) young members of the Brotherhood who stood up against the leadership of the organization during the period of the study, some of them eventually leaving it. The relationships of trust that I built up during my fieldwork for this study later allowed me to meet a fifth group, MB activists in exile in Istanbul after 2013.

Lastly, various documents provided a third form of primary source. They included publications produced by the MPs' offices, election leaflets, internal memoranda, the texts of parliamentary speeches, candidate CVs, material from websites linked to the Muslim Brotherhood, articles from the local and national press, reports on elections, and so on. I explain below the ways in which the ethnographic method helps us to see what up to now has not been seen about the Brotherhood, while at the same time pointing to its limitations. It is only by becoming aware of the latter that they attain their full explanatory value.

## Ethnography and the Evidential Paradigm

In any piece of ethnographic fieldwork the researcher aims to understand the meanings that the actors give to what they do and say, paying particular attention to the social taxonomy categories that they use, the context of which they are a part and to which they refer to, and the paradoxes, ambiguities, and contradictions that are part of any human activity. By relating several specific cases, the ethnographer can have access to different points of view, amplified by the fact that the fieldwork is carried out in a milieu in which the different actors know each other and over a substantial time period. The aim is to produce a "thick description" of that milieu (Geertz 1973).

Details are treated by the ethnographer as 'traces,' a term referring to the 'evidential paradigm' developed by Carlo Ginzburg and Howard Becker. While Ginzburg talks of "clues" (Ginzburg 1989) and Becker of "what doesn't fit" (Becker 1998: 175), their modes of analysis are similar, depending on "traces that may be infinitesimal [but] make it possible to understand a deeper reality than would otherwise be attainable" (Ginzburg 1989: 93).

The 'evidential paradigm' is also particularly well suited to investigating a public secret. Not only are the observations difficult to repeat, something which is common to all sociological inquiry, but in addition a whole range of activities that one might wish to investigate are not directly observable. In the case of the investigation reported on here, the fact that there were whole areas set aside as secret was particularly limiting. Observations made as part of the inquiry must be treated as clues, particularly since they cannot be made systematically and cannot be exhaustive. From the study of what might seem to be unconnected details, it is possible to grasp what might be called the 'quality' of a given phenomenon and to capture something of its qualitative complexity. This complexity cannot be flattened out in order to allow for statistical generalization.

For example, the idea that the Brotherhood's popularity can be traced back to its provision of social services to populations that had been abandoned by the state has been advanced many times, but the value of this hypothesis decreases with the number of times it is reiterated. In the social sciences, unlike the natural sciences, the fact that a given observation can be reproduced does not necessarily increase its value, even if it helps to support its validity. On the contrary, it tends to reduce its explanatory power. Yet the very fact that various researchers have felt the need to reformulate this idea over and over again indicates that it has some hidden value or that the 'quality' of the phenomenon being described has not been exhausted. Investigating a phenomenon necessarily means examining a particular instance of it carefully in the same way in which a geologist might take a soil sample in order to test its 'quality.' Generalization should not take place by bringing a particular piece of data closer to the norm, something which would empty it of its content. Rather, the method that Becker, tongue in cheek, calls "not-so-rigorous analytic induction" (Becker 1998: 421) allows one to move from an individual observation to the theoretical generalization that explains it by setting out the premises that underlie such observations in logical terms. It is for this reason that Becker recommends that we pay attention precisely to "the detail that doesn't fit."

What was this detail in my case? I began the present study by carrying out an investigation into the mobilization of the Brotherhood for the 2005 parliamentary elections. My research question, at the time, was to ask how members of an illegal organization had nevertheless been able to stand as eligible candidates. I explained that the Brothers owed their success to their notably successful use of the patron–client relationships that govern the electoral system in Egypt. As a result, they were able to redeploy their grassroots support—in other words, the resources and competences they had gained in areas not directly seen as political, such as universities, charities, unions, and so on—for electoral purposes. I was particularly struck by the insistence of the MPs and activists I interviewed that this mobilization needed to take place over the long term and on a daily basis. This provided fertile ground for understanding how the Brothers had managed to emerge as local counter-elites and how they had managed to engage in forms of oppositional mobilization despite their illegal status.

However, at the same time I was also confronted by a detail in the field that did not correspond with my expectations. This detail was that this mobilization was not as regular, visible, intense, or politicized as I had expected. In particular, I ran up against an oddity or incoherence that emerged in most of the interviews I carried out with grassroots activists. They told me that though they worked their best to serve the people, they could not do this through institutions since as Brothers they did not have the legal right or the practical ability to set up charities, take control of mosques, or take part in union elections. They also said they would not brand the services they provided as strictly 'services delivered by the Brotherhood' for reasons that had to do as much with security as with morality. Not only did these assertions strike me as contradicting the widespread notion that the Brothers were somehow infiltrating the Egyptian state and society, but they also seemed to complicate the idea that the Brotherhood's grassroots base was being redeployed for political purposes. How could the Brothers be providing the very extensive social services that they claimed they were doing in the absence of institutional structures? And how could they be gaining people's loyalty by delivering these services if no one knew that it was the Brothers who were delivering them?

The statements could have been part of a dissimulation strategy on the part of the Brothers to disguise their real proximity to the structures of power and to cover up their instrumentalizing of poverty or their own lack of action. However, the fact that such statements were made to me over and over again, apparently in tones of genuine frustration, made me take them more seriously and ask myself what they could be leading toward as clues. What were the premises on which they were based? This type of questioning led me to the hypothesis of 'open secrecy.' Rather than assume that there was some kind of automatic conversion mechanism at work here by which a grassroots base was being transformed into political loyalty, I decided instead to look closely at how this transformation actually operated, with all its ambiguities and limitations. Drawing on Becker's work once more, I turned the question around, and instead of asking, "Why did this conversion mechanism work so well?" I asked, "How was it possible for it to work at all?" I thus paid attention to periods when nothing much seemed to be occurring other than banal everyday events, as well as to apparently insignificant and depoliticized practices. I discovered that the study of everyday experience did not discard mobilization and politicization, but on the contrary, these things reemerged in the form of a mass of minute details that came together to create larger patterns. Such details, rather than sustaining a fantasized vision of the Brotherhood's forms of mobilization and politicization, helped me to grasp them more fully, that is, by describing and making sense of their evasiveness.

During the course of the research, I became interested in the variations of opacity and transparency that characterized both the object of my study and the conditions in which I was studying it. Certain facts that were 'well known,' such as the Brotherhood's being an organization that was 'illegal but tolerated,' and one that was 'secret' but that nevertheless had MPs sitting in parliament, appeared to me in a new light as a result and reengaged my attention. One of the major principles of ethnographic fieldwork, self-reflection on the part of the observer, became an essential guide for me on the path to knowledge.

## The Role of the Researcher

I noted changes in the boundaries between secret practices and public ones depending on the different periods, places, and individuals concerned. While the offices of the Brotherhood MPs represented the 'known face' of the Gama'a, the boundary between this and the organization's 'secret face' was not so clear. The same activities could be made public to greater or lesser extents in different constituencies. In one office, activists happily provided me with information that their counterparts in another held back on the grounds that it was secret. Depending on the constituencies, the same activities set up by MPs' offices were more or less publicized. In the Madinat Nasr constituency, the local MP refused to let me meet the people in charge of his office's 'committees' (working groups on different issues such as education, infrastructure, and so on) on the grounds that no one apart from him knew who they were for security reasons. In the Helwan constituency, on the other hand, this information was publicly available, and a leaflet distributed during the local elections gave details of the biographies of the candidates along with their roles on various committees.

This example shows that decisions made by the MPs' staffs regarding what was and what was not secret largely depended on the local relationships the Brotherhood had with the regime, and on how members perceived these relationships. In Helwan, the social clout of the MP, a man respected and influential within the local community, meant that information could be given out. In Madinat Nasr, a more upmarket suburb in eastern Cairo, information could not be made public because social bonds were weaker in the area and the local MP held less sway for residents there. However, such differences in the management of MB secrets were also a matter of how far different groups and individuals had been shaped by the organization's culture of secrecy. Thus, after the interview with the Madinat Nasr MP in which he told me that it would be impossible for him to tell me the names of those responsible for the committees in his office, I was accompanied down into the street by a young activist. Not only had he written down all the questions that had been sidestepped by the MP and offered to answer them for me, but he also told me that he knew all the names of those responsible for the committees even if the MP himself thought otherwise. This anecdote not only shows that there were very different understandings of activist culture at work in this office, but it also reveals another important characteristic of the way in which the Brotherhood managed the question of secrecy—which was that not everyone had access to the same information within the organization even when that information directly concerned them. The most obvious case of this was the fact that some activists considered themselves to be fully-fledged Muslim Brothers, in other words members of the *tanzim*, whereas in reality they were only considered to be *muhibbin* (sympathizers, sing. *muhibb*) or *mu'ayyidin qawiyyin* (strong supporters, sing. *mu'ayyid qawi*) by the 'real' activists. Those who found themselves in these categories, well defined even if not exactly formalized, did not know of their existence.

It will thus be clear that the question of access had to be continually renegotiated. It was not simply a matter of making an agreement at the beginning of the fieldwork about the extent and limits of access, since in reality one had to be always feeling one's way forward, always testing the limits set by each new interlocutor, and always trying to push them a little further, according to changes in the boundaries between what was secret and what was public. During fieldwork, the interlocutor can try to maintain confidentiality, but in order to be sympathetic to me and to honor his initial acceptance of the interview, he tries to present himself as revealing secret information even if in reality he does not say anything confidential. At the end of one long and difficult interview with the man in charge of an office in Helwan, for example, during which my questions regarding the *tanzim* had been met with stony silence or evasion, my interlocutor said with an amused expression on his face, "Okay, in the end, I'll tell you everything, even about the *tanzim*, and then you can make what you want of it." We laughed and I said that this would suit me perfectly, though in fact I knew that he would tell me nothing about the *tanzim*. His main aim was to act 'as if' he had confided in me.

Another example took place during the Eid in 2008 when I asked a female activist in one of the constituency offices whether I could attend the celebrations, as she and other women were supposed to be distributing gifts of meat to poorer families in the area. She said no, telling me that it was "too dangerous," but invited me to dinner at her house the next day. To my surprise, this turned out to be a family dinner organized for the Eid. Obviously, it was not possible to pursue my inquiries on this occasion. Instead, I was encouraged to play with the children and give the baby its bottle. For this activist, bringing me into her private sphere allowed her to develop the relationship at a low risk: it did not require her to break secrets, while at the same time she was meeting my expectations, at least temporarily.

The game of inclusion and exclusion that inevitably takes place between the ethnographer and her interviewees is a complicated one. Access to the

Gama'a and penetrating its hidden recesses means taking part in interpersonal relationships that involve the mutual acceptance of each other's way of looking at the world. As this book shows, entering and belonging to the Gama'a means adopting a certain ethical code and using this as the basis for behavior. In carrying out the fieldwork for this book, it was as if my relationship with my interviewees was also subject to this mechanism of embodiment, and as a result, it seemed as if I had to display evidence of my morality. My interviewees brought judgmental elements into our relationship that, in my own view, should remain external to it. I wanted to be judged on the seriousness of my academic inquiry, something objective and essential to any researcher, whereas they wanted to judge me on my morality, something that I considered subjective and in any case a private matter. I wanted to present myself as first and foremost a researcher, leaving my other roles, whether as woman, foreigner, young person, or other sociological categories, to one side, even as my interviewees insisted on seeing me in these ways. Could I, or should I, impose my view on them, however? If my interviewees insisted on seeing me in these ways, was it not because these were the sole means they had of situating me and of reassuring themselves about some basic level of security?

The different ways my interlocutors and I saw the relationship led to a particular form of negotiation that had less to do with my insisting on my definition of the role of researcher and more to do with our 'producing' this role together. In other words, I had to understand and to accept that the situation between us was one that was being mutually defined, even if this meant bringing into it elements (my morality, as they looked at it) that I initially considered external to it. Gaining access to the hidden side of the Brotherhood meant undergoing a form of apprenticeship in which I would have to learn to accept, and then to get around, the obstacles that were being put in my way rather than simply being irritated by them, since in addition to my need to advance in my work there were also the rights of my interviewees that had to be taken into account. They, on the other hand, turned out to be ready to accept some of my requests, since if I had not made any at all I would have fallen into the trap of self-censorship. The Helwan MP, for example, eventually allowed me to come and go as I wished without insisting that he be informed of my visits to the offices. On the other hand, I learned to do without systematic documents (lists of activists, statistics), and to reconstruct this data from what could actually be obtained (my assertive approach was useful) and the informal traces that I was given.

It was a question of knowing how to play the game. Since in many cases the strategies used by the Brothers were informal ones, it was only to be expected that they were not described in precise terms or set out in supporting documents. My informants prevaricated, and so did I. One young activist, thrilled with my presence and hurrying through his explanation of the connections between the Brothers and various charities, let slip a piece of information that surprised the other activists in the room. "Now I have just returned from association A., which belongs to us," he said. No one is supposed to deliver this kind of information, that a charity belongs to the MB, in such a direct way. I did not dwell on what he said at the time, but I did try to get an additional clue later, in an interview with the wife of an activist working in the same office who was active in the charity A. but was not herself a member of the Brotherhood. "Is the association A. a Brotherhood charity?" I asked. She firmly said it wasn't. Her husband remained quiet. In fact, many charities were directed by Brothers who were unknown to the public as members of the Brotherhood. This kind of vagueness was emblematic of the ways in which the organization worked, and it was in line with the idea that it was 'illegal but tolerated.' It obliged the fieldworker to use the same type of indirect procedures in her own work, suggesting but not affirming, introducing elements of doubt, and gleaning information slowly and in multiple ways.

The methods used in carrying out the fieldwork thus took on the characteristics of the ways of working used by the informants themselves. The need for reflexivity in gaining access to the object of study itself became a tool of reflection. In sum, the question became not so much "What are the difficulties I am likely to encounter and how am I to get around them?" as "How can I use these difficulties as a way of revealing the characteristics of the organization being studied and the various ways in which it operates?" It was this experience that allowed me to understand the varying relationship between the public and the secret in the world of the Brotherhood. Using this experience as a path to understanding was also not only appropriate but was the only way of understanding what was meant by the Brotherhood's 'open secrecy.'

## The Structure of the Study

Chapter one analyzes the ways in which the Gama'a has participated in Egypt's electoral system in relation to the informal rules set out by the regime hampering the specialization of political activities. Because electoral politics in Egypt are closely linked to welfare provision, the Brotherhood used this to build a strong grassroots presence, as will be confirmed by analyzing the profiles of the MB candidates in the 2005 parliamentary elections.

Chapter two examines the careers of the Brotherhood MPs in the three Greater Cairo constituencies mentioned above, looking in particular at questions of eligibility. In each case, it explores the ensemble of practical and discursive arrangements by which the Brothers produced a 'symbolic economy of disinterestedness.'

Chapter three looks at the ways in which Brotherhood MPs took on their roles in the light of limitations associated with the condition of 'open secrecy.' It analyzes the ways in which these 'banned MPs' were nevertheless able to exercise their roles thanks to their organizational resources, their access to the state apparatus, and their social embedding at a local level.

Chapter four investigates the mechanisms of the 'politics of goodness' in detail, including the ways in which the Brothers related to their local communities and used 'ethical conduct' as a way of differentiating themselves from other political actors. These mechanisms allowed the Brotherhood to engage in subtle forms of politicization that appealed to people's moral sensibilities and emotions.

Chapter five explains how this social embedding and ethical conduct were the outcomes of the Gama'a's internal pattern of regulation and training. It explores the ways in which this pattern led to significant tensions within the organization that increased in the post-2011 period, leading to the opposition and disengagement of some members and the increasing discontent of others.

Lastly, chapter six describes the ambiguous impacts of the MB's everyday mobilization, seen as both subtle and unsystematic, which did not so much oppose the regime as *inhabit*[7] its structures, its norms, and its weaknesses in different ways. It shows how the politics of goodness collapsed in the crucial period between 2011 and 2013, giving way to increasing polarization, the redefinition of the Brotherhood's open secrecy, and the fragmentation of its internal organization.

# 1

# (In)formal Politics

The condition of 'open secrecy' in which the Muslim Brotherhood operated was the result of a historical process that saw developments within the regime, changes in the relationship between the regime and the Brotherhood and in the latter's internal dynamics, and changes to the political, economic, and social systems in Egypt from the early 1970s onward. This chapter does not aim to give a history of these changes or to present a history of the MB. Instead, it aims to describe the ambiguous position the Brotherhood enjoyed under Mubarak's rule, being neither legal nor entirely banned and neither part of the opposition nor a collaborator with the regime. It was neither completely integrated within nor completely outside the system, and it was positioned at the intersection of the political, social, and religious spheres.

As a result of this ambiguous positioning, the Brotherhood participated in the institutional political sphere in an informal way, though this informality, the consequence of the organization's ideology and specific relationship with the regime, was also a result of the tensions between formality and informality that shape the institutional political sphere in Egypt. The latter is characterized by a strong element of "institutionalized informality"[1] since many widespread political practices, though 'informal' in the sense that they are not covered by any particular legal provisions, are in fact 'institutionalized,' which transforms the activities and the roles played by actors in the political sphere into constraining norms even if these are not legally defined.

Yet, instead of its being the result of cultural factors or of hangovers from the past, the informal dimension of the institutional political sphere in Egypt comes from the way in which successive regimes have sought to depoliticize electoral politics. Their desire to establish their hegemony has meant that the 'non-specialization of politics' has been the rule governing the activities of MPs. This concept, referring to Bourdieu's theory of social differentiation, holds that politics in Egypt is a lesser-differentiated field in which activities are deeply entrenched in other social activities such as providing services and doing charitable works. Moreover, most political actors, including MPs, are not 'political professionals' since they do not live from politics alone, and many of them do not have specific political skills but instead are characterized by their ability to connect with local communities. To sum up, the non-specialization of politics means both the non-differentiation of political activities and the non-professionalism of political actors.

This chapter analyzes the ways in which the MB participated in Egypt's electoral system in relation to this rule of non-specialization. Its electoral successes were based both on following this rule and on using it to build a strong grassroots presence. As this chapter explains, the particular characteristics of Brotherhood MPs from 2005 to 2010 can be understood by examining the relationship between the organization's electoral politics and its strategy for social embedding. This also allows us to understand the reasons behind the Brotherhood's successes at the polls during the Mubarak period.

## The Brotherhood and the Local Road to Parliament

The reemergence of the Brotherhood in Egypt began in the 1970s when leading figures from the organization began to be released from jail after the repression of the Nasser era. The ways in which Sadat's policies contributed to this reemergence, whether directly or indirectly, have been well documented. As part of its policy of countering policies associated with the Nasser regime, the Sadat regime encouraged the "reorganization of the field of political struggle and domination in religious terms" (Ismail 2003: 56), with the political system as a whole being turned into a "liberalized autocracy" (Brumberg 2002) by the introduction of "limited political pluralism" (Linz 1975) from 1976 onward. Leading figures in the regime used Islamic references as a way of managing this still very limited political liberalization, ridding it of openly expressed social conflicts and imposing a kind of 'solidarity without consensus' around the use of Islam in politics. This means that forms of common understanding developed between actors not sharing the same political convictions but nevertheless drawing on "a common vocabulary that meant the . . . same system of references could be used even if they were interpreted in different ways" (Ferrié 2003). The regime's leaders imagined that the Brotherhood could be drawn into this 'solidarity without consensus,' even if necessarily in a limited way, since they would never grant the organization its legal status. However, it was precisely the limited margins for maneuvering that gave the Brotherhood the opportunity to rebuild itself from the 1970s to the 1990s. At first this meant operating outside of the institutional political sphere because of the constraints imposed by the regime, as well as because of the necessity to regain widespread grassroots support. Later the MB began to work within the institutional political sphere, precisely in order to consolidate its support at the grassroots level.

## Rebuilding an Undefined Organization
### Dynamics and networks of reemergence

The rebuilding of the Brotherhood took place at first through work in the two major areas of the charitable sector and on university campuses. The Sadat regime had supported the expansion of Islamic charities so that they could take responsibility for the social services that the state was abandoning in the wake of its adoption of economic liberalization policies. Egyptian entrepreneurs, some of them Muslim Brothers,[2] who had left for the Gulf, where they had made considerable fortunes, were urged to reinvest their money in Egypt, particularly in real estate. Tax privileges were granted provided that parts of the new buildings being built would be set aside for private mosques run by charitable associations often hosting social, healthcare, and educational services. These large "Islamic complexes" multiplied exponentially during the period (Ben Néfissa 1995), and MB businessmen coming back from the Gulf were able to rely on the support of influential "brokers"[3] within the ruling economic circles.[4] Such brokers were also to be found within the prestigious institution of al-Azhar, which consisted of the most important mosque in Egypt, a major university, and several bodies with authority over religious affairs. While al-Azhar represented, and still represents, the Islam of the state, influential ulama within it were able to use Sadat's new emphasis on religion to push for the social and legal re-Islamization of Egypt (Zeghal 1996). Al-Azhar also operated a network of primary and secondary schools across the country, and these now welcomed many Brotherhood teachers.

At the same time, in the context of the exponential growth of higher education[5] that was taking place in these years, the regime also encouraged the development of 'Islamic groups' (gama'at islamiyya) in the country's universities in order to counter leftwing student movements. These 'Islamic groups' enjoyed considerable success in student union elections until they opposed Sadat's peace treaty with Israel and were closed down as a result in 1979. However, it was through such developments that a new generation of young activists putting references to Islam at the core of their discourse and the center of their practices emerged and began to build connections with MB leaders who had also now been released from prison (Kepel 1985; Mubarak 1995; Tammam 2011; Al-Arian 2014). These young activists played a crucial role in rebuilding a broad, cross-class social basis for the movement. After

Sadat's assassination by Islamist militants in October 1981, his successor, Hosni Mubarak, adopted an accommodating attitude toward what was described as "moderate Islamism" (Abed-Kotob 1995). The Brotherhood resumed its activities in the country's universities[6] and charities, as well as in the professional syndicates (doctors, engineers, pharmacists, and so on), gathering momentum throughout the 1980s (Bianchi 1989; Fahmy 1998). Young, well-educated, middle-class activists rose to leading positions in the syndicates, and they were able to use these positions to reach out to new constituencies (Qandil 1994; Wickham 1997; Hasan 2000).

Mobilization of this sort continued until the regime cracked down on the syndicates in the 1990s after they had become more critical of the government and the Brotherhood's influence within them had become all too obvious (al-Awadi 2004). This repression was part of a broader reversal of political liberalization in the context of an economic structural adjustment program that was also introduced in Egypt during these years (Kienle 1998). The syndicates were 'frozen.' This official term meant that they were not dissolved, but rather that internal elections and various activities within them were now forbidden. The regime arrested several prominent MB syndicate figures who were subsequently tried before military tribunals.[7] It also strengthened its control over the country's charitable NGOs, reinforcing their supervision by the Ministry of Social Affairs and dismantling some of those that appeared to be too obviously affiliated with the Brotherhood (Siyam 2006). However, as will be described in more detail below, the Brotherhood was able to maintain significant influence in the charitable sector as well in the now 'frozen' professional syndicates,[8] even if this became less obvious. While the regime did not want to eliminate the MB's activities in the social sphere, it also did not want to draw too much attention to its own redistributive failures at a time of economic austerity. As a result, repression was mostly aimed at making the Brotherhood less visible.

### *Tanzim*, ideology, and undefined identity

For the Brotherhood, the incorporation of a new generation of activists in the 1970s and 1980s meant extensive reorganization, and this turned out to be a complex task because of the existence of three distinct groups of activists who did not share the same relationship to political action, legality, and clandestine activity.

## Three Generations of Leaders

At the beginning of the 1980s, the Brotherhood no longer possessed more than a few of its 'historic leaders,' the former associates of al-Banna who had been effectively neutralized as a result of long periods spent in prison. Many more were from the generation that came up during the 1940s and 1960s, and who did not constitute a homogeneous group. In addition to the sons of the Brotherhood's founders, or those who had been imprisoned in 1954 only to be released twenty years later, such as Mahdi 'Akif (future supreme guide of the organization from 2004 to 2009), there were also others who had been members of the 'Secret Apparatus.' The 'Apparatus' was the supposed 'armed wing' of the Muslim Brotherhood during the 1940s and 1950s.[9] Others, who had been members of the '1965 Organization' that had been created by young militants inspired by Sayyid Qutb's ideas to take action against the state, also rounded off this faction. Former members of these groups, who included Mustafa Mashhur, Gom'a Amin, Mahmud 'Ezzat, and Mohammed Badi' returned in force to the Brotherhood in the 1970s and took up positions of influence within it in a more and more visible fashion.

The third generation, sometimes called the 'intermediate generation' (*gil al-wasat*), is made up of activists that came from the vibrant Islamic student groups of the 1970s. One trend, advocating for public outreach, provided some of the MB's most prominent public figures, including men such as 'Isam al-'Iryan, 'Abd al-Mun'im Abu al-Futuh, Helmi al-Gazzar, and Gamal Heshmat. These were able to take up positions in the country's professional syndicates and later be elected as Brotherhood MPs. However, they were still often kept out of important positions in the tanzim hierarchy itself. Another trend gathered young activists, most notably Mohamed Morsi and Khayrat al-Shater, who were close to the former members of the 'Secret Apparatus.' Al-Shater, who eventually became a businessman and gained the reputation of being a martyr to the cause as a result of his many years spent in prison, played an important role working in tandem with Mahmud 'Ezzat, and he headed the so-called 'organizationist' current of the Brotherhood that gave absolute priority to the preservation of the *tanzim* (the *tanzimiyyin*).

The latter current was particularly important in the 1990s, a decade characterized by the repression of the MB, and then even more so between 2005 and 2010 when al-Shater was again in prison. The influence of the 'organizationists' over the rest of the organization culminated in the resignation of 'Akif from the post of supreme guide in 2009 and the election of Badi' against a background of intense internal conflict.

Building a firm hierarchy for the Brotherhood, called the *tanzim* and inspired by the hierarchical framework of al-Banna's original association, was a priority for former members of the organization's 'Secret Apparatus' (Tammam 2006). These men now holding positions of power within the organization considered that "the path of tanzim was preferable to any legal accommodation with the regime. They were not only convinced that the refusal [to accord the Brotherhood legal status by the regime] was final, but they also thought that the movement's illegal status was more favorable to it as it meant avoiding the costs of legality, which would be much greater than its advantages" (Tammam 2006: 7–8).[10] As an illegal organization, the Brotherhood could avoid legal restrictions that weighed on political parties that had appeared after 1977. These had turned the parties into co-opted organizations and had prevented them from developing any real grassroots support. On the contrary, it was precisely the MB's strategy to regain extensive support at the grassroots level that allowed the reborn organization of these years to reestablish itself. This strategy consisted of consolidating the Brotherhood's existence in a de facto fashion even while being denied the possibility of obtaining de jure legalization.

The strategy of building grassroots support also helped to bring the organization's ideological repertoire up to date, which had been inherited from the first period of the Brotherhood (1928–48). During this period, when Egypt, then a monarchy, was under British occupation, the Brotherhood existed as a legal association but it had been able to turn rapidly into a mass movement by multiplying its reach into different sectors of society. It had recruited supporters from the popular classes, the lower-middle classes, and the middle classes, and it had used sophisticated methods to attract young people from the country's growing number of students (Lia 1998).[11] Members of the association had been instructed to "spread the principles [of the MB] throughout their social spheres,"[12] meaning particularly their personal social circles and neighborhoods, as well as to develop local forms of solidarity. As a result, the development of the early Brotherhood's networks had relied upon actively engaging popular forms of sociability as well as on establishing educational, healthcare, and charitable programs in almost all its local branches.

It had thus constructed an alternative model of political action that was extraparliamentary and had not used the same methods as the political parties (Lia 1998). By bypassing the institutional political sphere, Hassan al-Banna's movement had extended its influence and attracted the support of the many young Egyptians who felt marginalized by the elite political classes. Moreover, this alternative model of political action, anchored in religious and social activism, led al-Banna to gradually outline the Brotherhood's ideology, as well as the way this ideology would be put into practice. Inspired by the ideas of the Islamic Renaissance,[13] this ideology held that political, proselytizing, educational, or charitable activities should be seen as one and oriented toward the same aim: bringing about the moral reconstitution of the individual and the moral refoundation of society on the basis of the doctrinal precepts and principles of Islam. In a formula that was to become celebrated and that is still used today in the organization's publications, including election manifestos and material on the Internet, al-Banna said that "reform" *(islah)* must concentrate on the "reform of the self" *(islah nafsi)*, the "formation of the Muslim individual and of the Muslim family" (or "household") *(takwin al-fard al-muslim wa-l-bayt al-muslim)*. This would then allow for achieving the virtuous guidance of society, the liberation of the nation, the Islamic reform of the government, and the rebuilding of a "state entity for the Islamic community" *(i'adat al-kayan al-dawli li-l-umma al-islamiyya)*—all of this to finally reach the "mastership of Islamic preaching over the world" *(ustadhiyyat al-'alam bi-nashr al-da'wa al-islamiyya).*[14]

Such ideas constituted a broad ideological repertoire that was readopted by the Brotherhood at the time of its reemergence in the 1970s. Even though most young members of the 'new' Brotherhood had not had firsthand experience of the period associated with al-Banna, leaders were able to claim continuity with the older organization by reviving this repertoire. The latter was well adapted to the circumstances of the 1970s and 1980s, as access to the institutional political sphere at the time was very limited, necessitating a strategy of moving into other social spaces. This ideological repertoire, making the movement protean and unclassifiable, gave the Gama'a its unique character. The organization therefore claimed the right to be recognized in terms of its sui generis status on the grounds that it was neither a political party, nor a charitable association, nor simply a religious brotherhood. For these reasons the Gama'a had also never sought recognition within the terms of any particular legal framework, since this would have necessitated its being classified within a preexisting legal category, whether as a political party, an NGO, or an association. Instead, its attempts at legalization consisted of demands that its illegality be canceled—in other words, the cancellation of the 1954 banning order directed at the organization.[15]

It was only from the 1990s onward that the first tentative steps were made toward the creation of a political party. Some members of the 'intermediate' generational group, used to the ways things were done in the professional syndicates, gradually began to come around to the idea that the movement should set up an associated political party (al-Anani 2007: 127). A small faction made up of these activists, led by engineer Abu al-'Ila Madi (who had been a student activist in Minya and a syndicate leader), ended up leaving the organization in 1996 in order to try to set up an independent political party in the form of the Wasat Party, illegal until the fall of Mubarak (al-Ghobashy 2005). However, the idea of setting up a political party associated with the organization itself never achieved unanimity within the MB, including among the members of the 'intermediate' generation. Neither did it call into question the existence of the Brotherhood itself, which in any case would have continued to exist as a parallel entity (Vannetzel 2017).

This debate reveals an important aspect, namely the non-defined identity of the new Gama'a. The old association set up by al-Banna already had a legally ill-defined status as an association that had operated outside of a strictly defined charitable framework and had been characterized by its multifarious nature. The founder of the Brotherhood himself had defined it as "a collective idea including in it all categories of reform," being at once "a Salafiyya message, a Sunni way, a Sufi truth, a political organization, a sports group, a cultural–educational union, an economic company and a social idea,"[16] for example. Decades later, and even as the Brotherhood reestablished itself without gaining any recognized status, the organization's 'undefined identity' became central to its own sense of itself and its identity.

However, from the 1980s onward, the debate around the party was distinct from the question of the MB's participation in the institutional political sphere, that is, in the electoral process (Pahwa 2013). The political liberalization of Mubarak's earlier years in power led the Brotherhood to take part in the electoral system from 1984 onward in order to position itself effectively in what was becoming a competitive system of politics. Yet this was not seen as a complete change of strategy, for the Brotherhood's inclusion in the institutional political sphere also constituted a continuation by other means of its strategy of building grassroots support. In order to understand how this was pursued through the MB's participation in the electoral system, it is first necessary to examine in more detail how the electoral system itself was also characterized by a kind of 'institutionalized informality.'

## Electoral Politics and Social Embedding

In what follows it will be shown that the imbrication of social action and electoral politics was not simply the result of the ideology of the Brotherhood, but that it was in fact more generally caused by the non-specialized character of the institutional political sphere in Egypt. Far from being a simple vestige of the premodern past, or of some local cultural tradition, the non-specialized character of politics in the country was, and is, a characteristic effect of the hegemony of the modern state. It is related to the developmentalist ideology of the state and to the state's emphasis on authoritarian control. Parliamentary politics in Egypt were not built as a space for expressing politicized conflicts, but instead as a channel for redistributing state resources. The role of an MP has historically consisted in assisting in the state's social management and delivering services to local constituencies.

## The non-specialization of politics: developmentalism and authoritarianism

From the Nasser period onward, the Egyptian state has been seen as the "architect of structural transformation" (Richards and Waterbury 1996: 234), whose purpose has been to reshape society and to fight against various aspects of "backwardness" (sic), thereby closely binding economic, social, cultural, and political issues together as facets of the same fundamental problem. In 1956, the newly independent regime began a program of ambitious socioeconomic reforms, including the redistribution of agricultural land, import-substituting industrialization, the expansion of the public sector, and widening access to education. This model of the state as the architect of development redefined the theory and practice of politics in Egypt, with the dissolution of all the country's political parties and voluntary associations in 1952 not only aiming at containing opposition, but also being related to a vision of politics as a potentially divisive threat to the nation. In Nasser's vision, politics was to be reshaped by the direct and fusional relationship between the leader and the nation, the corporatist and functionalist organization of society, and the active role for the army in protecting the nation and underwriting social modernization (Waterbury 1983; Fahmy 2002).

Political institutions such as the People's Assembly (the Egyptian parliament) were subsumed under the developmentalist mission of the state. The country's former political elites, most of whom were notables and large landowners, were in large part deprived of their access to elected authorities, and new representatives of the state bourgeoisie were promoted as *nuwwab* (MPs) and affiliated to the single party, the Arab Socialist Union (ASU). Rather than being seen as the political representatives of the nation, a role now claimed by the leader, these *nuwwab* were henceforward seen more as middlemen acting in the space between the state and society, their role being to redistribute public resources among the population. In consequence, the idea of politics was both broadened—the state and political institutions would now belong to the whole nation—and reduced to providing 'services' (*khadamat*) to the population.

Neither Sadat's infitah policies of economic liberalization carried out between 1970 and 1981, nor the neoliberal turn seen during Mubarak's rule from 1981 to 2011, greatly contradicted this representation of the state. It was still seen as being responsible for the development of society despite the economic shift from the public to the private sector from the 1990s onward, cutbacks in public expenditure, and declining state welfare provision (Harrigan and El-Said 2009). Although the *nuwwab* of the Mubarak era were increasingly faced with the problem of the continuing reduction in state resources, and were increasingly urged to resort to private ones instead, they still had to comply with their role as 'state agents,' which, as Patrick Haenni has rightly said, meant agents acting with the "spirit of service" (Haenni 2005a).

The Brotherhood and the Local Road to Parliament    29

Their failure to be seen as political representatives was also due to the absence of genuine municipal authorities in Egypt, a feature of the larger political and administrative system (Ben Néfissa 2009). The Nasser regime had set up non-elected local councils at the district and neighborhood levels, designed as simple administrative structures whose role was to "provide basic services to the poorest people in order to improve their economic conditions" (Ibrahim 2007: 13). In 1971, this system of local government was divided into a non-elected branch made up of local executive councils (LECs) under the authority of the provincial governors, and an elected branch consisting of Local Popular Councils (LPCs) that was entirely subordinate to the non-elected one. From 1975 to 1979, the elected councils had the power to oppose executive control, but this proved to be only a temporary arrangement. Indeed, it had led to MPs being stripped for a time of their local functions, which had had the indirect effect of encouraging the parliament elected in 1976 to play more of a legislative role and to criticize the actions of the executive. Therefore, this parliament was dissolved by Sadat in 1979, and from then on MPs were once again 'downgraded' to the rank of simply local constituency representatives, removing their national legislative role (Ben Néfissa and Arafat 2005: 69).

As a result, the typical Egyptian MP of these years was a local notable, a member of the "state bourgeoisie" (Waterbury 1983), and someone who held positions in local political and administrative structures linked to the party of the regime (by this stage the NDP). He was someone who fully mastered his role as a mediator between state and society and in redistributing state benefits at a local level. This typical profile did not fundamentally change until the 2000s despite the socioeconomic transformations. Even though elites associated with traditional forms of social hegemony (the rural notables) or more modern ones (associated with the infitah) started to return to the People's Assembly in the 1970s and 1980s, the state bourgeoisie remained dominant within it (Springborg 1982). Even when businessmen started to enter politics in large numbers from the middle of the 1990s onward, they also remained constrained by the demands of this role.

In fact, an unofficial rule was institutionalized at this time that required each MP to have access to the state apparatus (the rationale of power), an important position in local solidarity networks (the rationale of proximity), and the capacity to redistribute public resources on a discretionary basis (the rationale of service) (Ben Néfissa and Arafat 2005). As a result, the capacity to engage in political activities was defined more in terms of the ability to master practices that were little different from other everyday operations—knowing how to build relationships with the state apparatus as well as with society— than of having distinct competences in efficient management, ideological coherence, or public discourse. As Menza has brilliantly shown, candidates for election as MPs had to be able to connect with "lesser notables" who were "mostly illiterate or poorly educated local notables."

> [Lesser notables] were the ones "getting the job done" on the local/popular levels in terms of garnering the sort of infiltration and connectedness that the state party needed to have with the lower strata of society. This was usually attributed to their entrenchment within the community and their subsequent ability to utilise these social networks for the political and/or social purposes they desire. . . . [Such figures] played an essential role as intermediaries between other categories of notables in the higher echelons of the polity and at the grassroots basis at the popular level. . . . The mere existence of such an interlinked network facilitated the dissemination of resources from the higher echelon notables onto the lower strata within the popular community (Menza 2019: 102).

The idea that political activity was by its very nature non-differentiated and based on the central notion of *khidma* was thus established by the modernizing and authoritarian state. This had been a rule that had persisted despite the introduction of a multiparty political system and contested elections in the 1980s. It could even be said that the changes in the electoral system introduced under Mubarak's rule simply reinforced this norm and consolidated the idea that MPs played a purely local role.

### Electoral engineering, political co-option, and low turnouts
As is widely known, Egypt's 1971 Constitution did not grant effective powers to the People's Assembly and subordinated it to the executive. However, the presence of a large majority of NDP members in the Assembly still mattered to the regime, as until 2005 the president was chosen by a two-thirds majority of the People's Assembly and then approved by referendum. Controlling access to the Assembly was also a way for the Mubarak regime to secure legitimacy by co-opting local elites (Blaydes: 2010).

The complicated electoral engineering that took place during the Sadat and Mubarak years also shows that those in power saw elections as being potential test periods that required frequent readjustments (Kassem 1999). The electoral laws were forever being changed as a result, and in 1984 and 1987 the party-list system of proportional representation[17] was introduced to replace the first-past-the-post system that had been in effect since 1923. This change was to ensure that only members of the legal parties could stand for election. However, these parties, in any case only legal since 1977, had to meet drastic conditions of eligibility. In order to be recognized by the state, they had to seek authorization from the Political Parties Commission, whose members were appointed by the president, and after the assassination of Sadat their activities were significantly impeded by the 1981 Emergency Law that banned all public meetings without the prior authorization of the Ministry of the Interior. The parties also had few members, and they lacked significant grassroots support, making it impossible for them to field candidates in all constituencies. All these factors tended to give a free hand to the NDP candidates.

Nevertheless, the party-based electoral system encouraged alliances between the country's political forces and thus tended to "politicize" the role of MPs ('Awad and Tawfiq 1996). This caused the regime to take a step backward in 1990,[18] with a return to the first-past-the-post system and a reduction in size of constituencies to encourage local notables to stand in elections. While this had the result of reinforcing the idea that MPs were purely local or apolitical figures (Kassem 1999: 75–92), the system of competition between members of small local elites that it fostered led to the multiplication of independent candidates. These were presented as having no particular political affiliations, but in fact they were often NDP members whose candidacies had not been approved by party's management, or genuine independents who mostly joined the NDP after they had been elected.[19]

The growth in the number of such independent candidates had not been planned by the regime, and it was not able to control it. However, the NDP adapted its internal system to this increase in order to maintain its hegemonic stranglehold over the elections. Through the system of (re)integrating independent candidates into the NDP after their election, the party apparatus found a way of selecting for those elites who were most powerful on a local basis. It could choose not to field an official candidate in a given constituency in order to allow two local notables to fight things out naturally between themselves, or it could use the defeat of an official candidate in a battle against an independent as an opportunity to integrate the latter into its own ranks.[20] Such competition also gave the official NDP MPs additional incentives to foster their own local networks once they had been elected in order to ensure their reelection, distracting them yet further from their legislative role (Kassem 2004; Ben Néfissa and Arafat 2005). Moreover, the system of reintegrating MPs into the ruling party could also be used to target candidates from the legal opposition parties, though the majority of these were in any case more and more open to forms of co-optation from the 1990s onward, since their seats were mostly earmarked for them by those managing the process during the electoral negotiations. The NDP would agree not to field a candidate in a constituency 'set aside' for an approved opposition party candidate, for example, or it would field a deliberately weak candidate in order to facilitate the election of this opposition candidate (Albrecht 2005).

Finally, this electoral engineering was reinforced by the low participation of voters, with turnout rates declining between 1984 and 2005 (Table 1). Unlike the case today, such low turnouts were in fact in some ways desired by the regime, as they were one of the ways in which it sought to control the electorate. Only a small proportion of the latter was automatically registered on the electoral roll,[21] and only in rare cases was registration the result of individual effort. Instead, voters were registered by others. It was quite common for representatives of the candidates (*mandubin*) to collect up voting cards and use them to vote in the place of the voters concerned, for example. Even if they did not go that far, the lesser notables would manage the voting of the groups of voters over which they exercised most influence, gathering them together in order to take them physically to the polling stations on election day. It was thus more often a case of making vote rather than simply of voting, and in order to ensure that this happened it was necessary for the candidates concerned to have widespread grassroots support.

Table 1. Participation in Egyptian Legislative Elections, 1984–2005

| | 1984 | 1987 | 1990 | 1995 | 2000 | 2005 |
|---|---|---|---|---|---|---|
| Total population (millions) | 47.4 | 50.2 | 53.3 | 58.7 | 64.7 | 71.3 |
| Potential electorate (millions) | 27.5 | 29.1 | 30.9 | 34.1 | 37.5 | 41.4 |
| Number of registered voters (millions) | 12.6 | 14.3 | 16.3 | 21.0 | 26.9 | 32.1 |
| Percentage of those registered to vote from the total potential electorate | 46% | 49% | 53% | 62% | 72% | 78% |
| Number of voters (millions) | 5.4 | 7.8 | 7.5 | 10.5 | 7.4 | 8.1 |
| Percentage of voters from those registered to vote | 43% | 55% | 46% | 50% | 28% | 25% |
| Percentage of voters from total potential electorate | 20% | 27% | 24% | 31% | 20% | 20% |
| Percentage of voters from total population | 11% | 16% | 14% | 18% | 11% | 11% |

Source: Calculations from data in Soleiman, 2006.

The alliances (*tarbitat*) between the candidates and those they made vote for them were strengthened during election campaigns by other *tarbitat* between the candidates themselves. Each constituency had two seats in parliament until 2010, one reserved for workers and peasants (flexible categories, as we shall see) and the other reserved for all social categories (*fi'at*). This system encouraged candidates not competing for the same seat to come to a strategic agreement, mobilizing their supporters toward a common goal. One candidate might enlarge his base by benefiting from the support of the lesser notables ranged behind his electoral ally, for example. It was also not unusual for electoral alliances of this sort to be made between candidates representing different political tendencies, and lesser notables might thus simultaneously support candidates from the NDP as well as independents and members of the co-opted legal opposition (table 2). They might also support Muslim Brothers, as we shall see (Menza 2012).

Table 2. Results of Egyptian Legislative Elections, 1976–2010

| Date and voting system | NDP MPs | Legal opposition MPs | Muslim Brother-hood MPs | 'Genuine' indepen-dent MPs | Total (Elected not appointed MPs) |
|---|---|---|---|---|---|
| 1976 Individual | NDP: 280<br><br>Total: 280 | Right Platform:[22] 17<br>Left Platform: 2<br>Total: 19 | 1 | 50 | 350 |
| 1979 Individual | NDP: 330<br>Defectors from other parties: 16 to 24<br>Total: 346 to 354 | Ahrar Party: 3<br>Labor Party:[23] 34, then 10<br>Total: 37, then 13 | 2 or 3 | 2 to 10 | 382 |
| 1984 List | NDP: 390<br>Total: 390 | New Wafd: 50<br>Total: 50 | 8 | 0 | 448 |
| 1987 List + Individual (quota = 48) | NDP: 308<br>Independent NDP: 40<br><br>Total: 348 | New Wafd: 36<br>Ahrar Party: 6<br>Labor Party: 16[24]<br>Total: 58 | 38 | 4 | 448 |
| 1990[25] Individual | NDP: 225 to 348<br>Independent NDP: 60 to 125<br><br>Total: 350 to 408 | New Wafd: Boy-cott - 14<br>Ahrar Party: Boy-cott – 1<br>Tagammu': 6<br>Labor Party: Boy-cott - 8<br>Total: 29 | Boycott | 0 to 56 | 444 |
| 1995 Individual | NDP: 319<br>Independent NDP: 91<br><br>Total: 410 | New Wafd: 6<br>Liberals: 1<br>Tagammu': 5<br>NADP:[26] 1<br>Total: 13 | 1 | 20 | 444 |
| 2000 Individual | NDP: 172<br>Independent NDP: 218<br><br>Total: 390 | New Wafd: 7<br>Liberals: 1<br>Tagammu': 6<br>NADP: 2<br>Total: 16 | 17 | 21 | 444 |
| 2005 Individual | NDP: 152<br>Independent NDP: 172<br><br>Total: 324 | New Wafd: 6<br>Tagammu': 2<br>Ghad: 2<br>(Karama:[27] 2)<br>Total: 12 | 88 | 8 | 444 [28] |

| Date and voting system | NDP MPs | Legal opposition MPs | Muslim Brother-hood MPs | 'Genuine' indepen-dent MPs | Total (Elected not appointed MPs) |
|---|---|---|---|---|---|
| 2010 Individual | NDP: 424 Independent NDP: 53 to 56<br><br><br>Total: 477 | New Wafd: Boy-cott of second round - 6 Tagammu': 5 Ghad (Boycott):1 (defector) Others: 4 Total: 15 | Boycott of second round: 1 (defector) | 12 to 15 | 508[29] |

Sources: Ben Néfissa and Arafat, 2005; 'Awad and Tawfiq, 1996; Kassem, 2004; DRI, 2007; press sources, 2010; IPU Archive, diverse years.

The latter were able to take advantage of what for them was a paradoxically beneficial situation. Since the most important factor in electoral politics was grassroots support and the ability to redistribute services, the MB had obvious comparative advantages over the legal opposition parties in running for election. On the one hand, the Brotherhood's informal status meant that it could escape the legal restrictions weighing on the political parties. On the other hand, its grassroots support meant that it could conform to the spirit of service while at the same time increasing its public outreach by virtue of its informal involvement in the electoral system.

## The Brotherhood as an Informal Player

In a statement published on the organization's official website, the then supreme guide, Mahdi 'Akif, justified the Brotherhood's participation in the 2005 parliamentary elections in the same way as he explained its presence in civil-society organizations

> The goal of the Muslim Brothers, whether in getting elected to parliament or to other elected councils or winning positions in the professional syndicates or in any civil-society organization, is the establishment of a Muslim society leading to the establishment of an Islamic state that will act for the good of all the people, whether or not they are Muslims. . . . Our way is known, our goals precise, and our intentions realistic and not imaginary. Our practices, those which belong to us as Muslim Brothers, in the various domains of civil, social, popular, political, and parliamentary work are known to everyone, and all those who are able to see clearly and perceptively are well aware of them and do not deny them. [They are to work in] institutions from student unions to professional

syndicates, including teaching associations, youth clubs, charitable associations, local councils, and parliament. People have already reaped the fruits of these practices, so why not give them the opportunity to be set to work once again in order to bring goodness, mercy, and justice to the people as a whole?

However, taking part in elections had by no means always been seen as legitimate by the Brotherhood, which in fact had always been divided on this issue and had been harshly criticized for it by other groups claiming to represent political Islam. Accusations of compromise directed against those participating in a system founded on institutions judged as not being in conformity with the divine law had long been common among part of the group. Without going into details, it is enough to emphasize here that the MB's decision to take part in elections during the Mubarak period should be seen not so much as an ideological turn, but instead as the effect of a particular political opportunity (Schwedler 2006). This explanation takes into account the dynamic relationships between the political structure, behavioral changes, and partial modifications in the organization's ideological repertoire. Though the latter had been inherited from the past, it was never simply frozen, and its components were continually rearranged according to the circumstances in which the political actors found themselves and the debates they were engaged in as a result (Schwedler 2011; Pahwa 2013).

### From 'free-riders' to 'independents'
The problem of the lack of an Islamic character to Egypt's political institutions was toned down for the MB by a constitutional amendment making the shari'a the main source of legislation in Egypt in the early 1980s. However, what really led the Brotherhood to take part in the competitive electoral system was its desire to present itself as a de facto political actor despite its illegal status ('Awad and Tawfiq 1996). Now was the time when the Brotherhood could position itself in an electoral landscape marked by the policy of dialogue introduced by Mubarak after the assassination of his predecessor, the emphasis being put on democratic reform. There had also been the reestablishment of the New Wafd Party in 1983, which in a previous form had been the main rival of the MB in the struggle for independence under the monarchy and during the colonial period. The new opportunity for the Brotherhood to position itself collectively and publicly as a player in the electoral system was also linked to the 1984 law on the party-list voting system, which had turned out to be a boon for the Gama'a and had given it unprecedented access to the institutional political sphere.

Under the 1984 law, the lists of candidates standing in elections could not include candidates from different political parties. But electoral alliances were made practically indispensable because the eligibility threshold for representation in the People's Assembly was set at 8 percent of the vote and the weakness of the legal political parties made it impossible for any one of them alone to produce a list of candidates that could meet this figure in the country as a whole. Paradoxically, only the Brotherhood was in a position to be a partner in electoral alliances, since its members, not being members of a political party, could appear on the lists of other parties by registering fake memberships and concluding informal alliances with them. This it did with the New Wafd Party in 1984, as well as with the Labor Party (Hizb al-'Amal)[30] and the Liberal Party (Hizb al-Ahrar), two parties that had emerged from the left and right wings of the former ASU, in forming a coalition favoring the application of the shari'a in Egypt and called the 'Islamic Alliance' (al-Tahaluf al-Islami). This 'free-rider' (or perhaps 'hidden-rider') strategy brought immediate gains in terms of the number of Brotherhood MPs elected, with eight seats going to the MB in the 1984 elections and up to 39 in 1987.

However, the later return to the first-past-the-post voting system put an end to this strategy. The unexpected success of the electoral alliances entered into by the Brotherhood had shown that the party-list voting system encouraged the opposition to join forces and called into question the "system of divided contestation" (Lust-Okar 2005) that the regime had been promoting by maintaining the Brotherhood's illegal status. Even so, the return to the first-past-the-post system in fact only reinforced the position of the MB vis-à-vis the legal opposition parties. It placed the emphasis more than ever on the resources available to local notables in fighting elections by making it possible for them to stand as individual (independent) candidates without party affiliations. This result was probably not anticipated by the regime. Not only did Brotherhood candidates have the advantage, when compared to their competitors, of strong grassroots support, but their particular conception and practice of politics as a non-differentiated activity was also bolstered by the structure of the institutional political sphere as a sphere of non-differentiated activity anchored in social action.

The Brotherhood began to take part in a systematic way in Egypt's legislative elections after the boycott of the 1990 elections by all the country's opposition forces with the exception of the Tagammu' Party. In the 1995 elections, it fielded around one hundred and fifty candidates as independents, but because of widespread electoral fraud and repression (a thousand MB members were arrested) only one of them was elected.[31] It was only when public debates took place in the 2000s on the rules of the electoral system that the Brotherhood finally imposed itself as the most important organized political force in parliament, even if still an informal one. It won seventeen seats in the 2000 elections, and, remarkably, eighty-eight in 2005, winning 20 percent of the parliament's 434 seats as against 3 percent for all the legal opposition parties. At the same time, the weaknesses of the NDP were becoming more and more evident, and it was only able to maintain its two-thirds majority in parliament by co-opting more than one hundred and sixty independent MPs.

### New rules, new games: The politicization of elections

Significant debates began to take place in 2000 regarding the supervision of Egypt's elections. The Supreme Constitutional Court issued a decision giving responsibility for these to the country's judges, making it obligatory for them to be present in all polling stations in accordance with Article 88 of the Constitution instead of functionaries appointed by the Ministry of the Interior. The first effects of this reform were felt in 2000 in the shape of a reduction in obvious fraud, but it was only in 2005 that the new system of judicial control became more effective and the counting of votes more transparent (Bernard-Maugiron 2010).[32] The 2005 elections[33] also took place in a context that politicized the "electoral moment" (Kohstall and Vairel 2010). Domestically, there was growing political mobilization against the succession of Gamal Mubarak, the son of Hosni Mubarak, under the slogan of "Kefaya," which gave the movement its name (Enough!). Protest movements were developing in various sectors for social demands such as better labor conditions and higher salaries, and in the wider world the Bush administration in the United States was demanding that its Egyptian ally take steps toward opening up politically as part of its project to bring democracy to the greater Middle East (Arafat 2009).

The Brotherhood took part in the Kefaya movement to a limited extent, while at the same time prioritizing its preparations for the fall 2005 parliamentary elections. These were a turning point for the MB in that the campaign gave unprecedented publicity to its candidates. Though these were still officially labeled as independents, they nevertheless openly used the name, logo, and slogans of the Gama'a, abandoning the evasive formulas that had previously been used, such as al-Tayyar al-Islami (the Islamic Current) and al-Tahaluf al-Islami (the Islamic Alliance) (see images 1 and 2). Brotherhood activists whom I later interviewed about the 2005 campaign often emphasized that it represented a new development both for the collective history of the organization and for them personally. For some of them it marked the first time they had officially admitted to the residents of the areas in which they lived that they were members of the Muslim Brotherhood. The elections were the first time they had been seen marching under banners bearing the symbols of the Brotherhood. This moment underlined the importance of the electoral campaigns as a way of increasing the organization's grassroots support by greatly boosting its visibility.

Figure 1. (top) Leaflets of the MB candidates in Helwan, 1995, identifying them as candidates of the 'Islamic Alliance.' Figure 2. (bottom) Leaflet of 'Ali Fath al-Bab, MB candidate in Tibbin/15 Mayo, 2015, showing logo, name and leaders of the Brotherhood.

The Brotherhood and the Local Road to Parliament    39

This feature of the 2005 elections also explains why the Brotherhood also took part and attempted actively to campaign in the 2008 local council elections and the 2010 parliamentary elections that followed them,[34] even though these, unlike the 2005 elections, were strictly controlled by the regime. Internal documents for the 2010 parliamentary elections[35] were prepared to help train MB activists in explaining the "importance" (*ahamiyyat*) and "goals" (*ahdaf*) of the campaign (*al-hamla*):

1. To spread our message and our election manifesto to all segments of society and to persuade them that it is right;

2. To seize the opportunity of mobilizing (*taharruk*) society in an almost official fashion (*bi-sifat shibh rasmiyya*);

3. To train our members to work with the surrounding community and to convince them of this work's importance;

4. To make our political and social figures known to every citizen and to the community in every constituency;

5. To help our members acquire skills such as negotiation (*al-tafawud*), openness (*al-infitah*), and attractiveness (*al-isti'ab*);

6. To communicate with the media and to promote our activities and campaign events [*idarat al-hamla al-intikhabiyya*, 2010].

The campaign thus aimed less at making electoral gains as such and more at various forms of mobilization, including spreading MB ideas, communicating with the media, and above all establishing greater links with the local community in "an almost official fashion" through the mechanism of the elections. The campaign was not only an opportunity for the Brotherhood to make itself better known to the "surrounding community" and to "mobilize" its support; it was also a way of pushing its activists to work with this community and to provide them with the training needed to do so. Electoral mobilization was thus seen as valuable in itself and not only in relation to the results of the elections. It helped both to mobilize external support for the Gama'a and mobilize the latter from the inside.

Such claims can be illustrated by looking at the sociological backgrounds of the MB candidates in the 2005 elections. These were well adapted to the rule of political non-specialization, and they also contributed to the Brotherhood's strategy of social embedding. Analyzing their profiles also offers a valuable opportunity to gain a more precise picture of the activist base of the Gama'a and its local networks.

## 'Making Do': Methodological Questions

In the study, I have chosen to include both candidates who were elected as MPs in the 2005 elections and those who were not elected, with no distinction being drawn between them. This lumping together of the two categories not only allows for a larger sample to be used, but it is also in line methodologically with the way in which the elections themselves were carried out. It will be argued that whether or not they were elected, the Brotherhood representatives were chosen according to the same criteria. Moreover, those who eventually failed to be elected had generally gathered significant support, as is shown by the fact that a third of these were selected for the second round. Their failure to win is best explained by the way in which the elections were conducted, which differed from one governorate to the next. Indeed, the elections were organized in three geographical phases (because there were not enough judges to supervise all the polling stations at the same time), and the level of repression dramatically increased during the second and third phases.

The sample studied thus includes the 170 MB candidates who ran in the 2005 elections and whose personal details were for the most part published on an Internet site set up for the election campaign.[36] However, while these documents constitute an invaluable source of information on the candidates, they also suffer from certain gaps. Some candidates gave more details than others, partly depending on where they came from. In fact, the candidate CVs seem to have been produced according to instructions given out on the local level in the Brotherhood governorate section concerned, which interpreted the national organization's instructions differently. Each candidate also seems to have been given significant freedom regarding what information to include. In short, the documents are the result of a process of negotiation between the candidates and the Brotherhood hierarchy, with the former being allowed some control over the way in which they chose to present themselves to the electorate and election observers.

The lack of uniformity in the documents has methodological implications, in that the number of respondents for each indicator (N) chosen for the study vary according to whether or not information was included in the CVs. In the sociological analysis presented here, the following indicators have been chosen: date of birth (N = 152); educational achievements and highest qualification obtained (N = 158); subject studied at university (N = 124); professional membership according to last known profession (N = 164); participation in various public activities such as memberships in student unions, professional syndicates, and trade unions, and social, political, or charitable activities (N = 155 or 129).

## The 2005 Elections: Knowing the Brothers

An examination of the social backgrounds of the Brotherhood candidates in the 2005 parliamentary elections reveals that they conformed to the pattern of the local MP as a 'distributor of services.' It also shows that the election period was an occasion for the Gama'a to select individuals who could then be held responsible for matters essential for its survivalist ability to mobilize grassroots support on an everyday basis.

### Brotherhood Candidates: Non-professional Participants

The MB candidates in the 2005 parliamentary elections had many of the characteristics of other parliamentary elites in Egypt, who for the most part came from the NDP or independents, while also having specificities of their own. However, the latter were not necessarily those commonly associated with the ideal type of Brotherhood MPs. Concentrating on the careers of MB figures well known in the media, such as senior figure 'Isam al-'Iryan, has conveyed the misleading idea that all those put up by the Brotherhood for parliament followed the same linear path of politicization that started in the student unions and continued into the professional syndicates. This conception has also tended to suggest that the Brotherhood MPs were all part of the organization's "reformist current" *(tayyar al-tagdid)* that wanted to see greater political professionalization and rejected the old guard that was reluctant to get involved in the political system (ElShobaki 2009). However, the empirical material presented here indicates that most of the Brotherhood's parliamentary election candidates had not in fact followed a political trajectory of this sort and that they were not necessarily members of the "reformist current."

### Beyond the intermediate generation

At first glance the Brotherhood candidates in the 2005 elections mostly corresponded to the ideal type incarnated by al-'Iryan, for the vast majority of them belonged to the demographic cohort typical of the intermediate generation and had completed some higher education (Table 3). There are, however, three features that tend to contradict any monolithic conception of this intermediate generation and that draw attention to the various sociopolitical trajectories followed by these figures.

Table 3. The Educational Backgrounds of MB Candidates in the 2005 Elections

| Date of Birth (N = 152) | Level of Education (N = 158) | Subjects (N = 124) |
|---|---|---|
| Before 1950: 15%<br>1950–54: 14%<br>1955–64: 62%<br>1965 and later: 9% | University graduates: 79%<br>with graduate-level education:<br>22%<br>Technical institutes: 4%<br>High school graduates: 14%<br>Basic qualification or no qualifica-<br>tions: 2% | Medical: 27%<br>Engineering and agriculture:<br>20%<br>Basic sciences: 6%<br>Business: 16%<br>Literature and education: 16%<br>Law:10%<br>Religious studies (major): 6%<br>Religious studies (additional):<br>30% |

Source: Vannetzel, 2012. *2005 Parliamentary Elections Brotherhood Candidates Database.*

## 'Isam al-'Iryan: A Misleading 'Ideal-type' Career

Born in 1954 and a doctor by profession, 'Isam al-'Iryan is a typical figure from the MB leadership's 'intermediate generation.'
He began his political career in 1972 as an amir in the *gama'at
al-islamiyya*, the Islamic groups engaging in social, religious, and
political activities that had begun to appear on university campuses
in Egypt at the beginning of the 1970s. Building on his position
as an amir, al-'Iryan was elected president of the Cairo University Faculty of Medicine student union in 1975, and in the same
year he joined the Brotherhood, which was looking to recruit
members of the *gama'at* as part of its strategy of reconstruction.
Al-'Iryan was made responsible for the MB's student section, and
some years later, in the 1980s, he became secretary-general of the
Doctors' Syndicate after the victory of the Islamic current in the
professional elections. At the same time, he headed the list of the
Brotherhood/New Wafd Party coalition candidates for the Giza
constituency in the 1984 parliamentary elections. In 1987, aged
thirty-three, he was elected a member of the People's Assembly.

In 1995, al-'Iryan was sentenced to five years of hard labor,
officially for "belonging to a clandestine group seeking to overthrow the state," but in fact as a result of his syndicate activities.
On his release from prison he became a symbol of the reformist
current of the Brotherhood by helping to draw up a document
calling for the drastic reform of the regime, called "An Initiative
for Reform," in March 2004. He continued to climb the ranks,
eventually joining the Guidance Bureau, the organization's highest executive body, in 2009. He was reelected an MP in the first

parliament of the post-Revolution period that sat from January to June 2012, while also becoming vice-president of the Freedom and Justice Party.

In the first place, the vast majority of the MB candidates in the 2005 elections were born some years after al-'Iryan (in other words, after 1954). Trivial though this might seem, it becomes important if this generation is viewed as a group sharing a common historical experience (Mannheim 1952). Most of the candidates who were university graduates had gone to university after the end of the period when the *gama'at* dominated the student unions, between 1974 and 1979, and three-quarters of them did not mention in their CVs that they had taken part in student unions. Secondly, they graduated in a range of subject areas: while more than half of them (53 percent) studied scientific subjects, in particular medicine and engineering, a large number studied business, literature, or law. Only seven studied religion as their major. Finally, almost a quarter of those making up the cohort of individuals born between 1955 and 1964 did not attend university at all. Some only completed secondary school, often in vocational programs, or graduated from technical institutes. The latter offer two-year training programs to high school graduates and train technicians to work in industry.

### Beyond the professionals

This variety of educational experiences among the Brotherhood candidates is also reflected in their occupational careers (Table 4). While 19 percent of the MB candidates in the 2005 elections declared themselves to be members of medical professions requiring advanced qualifications, such as doctors, dentists, pharmacists, or veterinary surgeons, this was true for only 3 percent of non-Brotherhood MPs.[37] Engineers occupying positions in the public sector or private enterprise made up 10 percent of the Brotherhood candidates in the elections, whereas they accounted for only 3 percent of non-Brotherhood MPs. When lawyers and the single journalist in the sample are added to these figures, it emerges that 37 percent of the MB candidates were professionals (miheniyyin), which tends to confirm the pertinence of the ideal type represented by al-'Iryan. However, there are still two further observations that need to be made.

**Table 4. Professionals and Others: The Occupations of the MB Candidates in 2005**

| | |
|---|---|
| Professionals: 37% | Medical professions: 19%<br>Lawyers and journalist: 8%<br>Engineers: 10% |
| Teaching professions: 22% | University teachers: 10%<br>Teachers in primary and secondary schools: 9%<br>School inspectors, supervisors, etc: 3% |
| White-collar state employees: 24% | Senior civil servants: 9% (3% engineers)<br>Middle management: 12%<br>Employees: 3% |
| Public- and private-sector employees: 14% | Employees: 6%<br>Technicians and skilled workers: 6%<br>Unskilled workers: 2% |
| Company bosses: 6% | — |
| Religious professions: 3% | — |

Source: Vannetzel, 2012. *2005 Parliamentary Elections Brotherhood Candidates Database.*

The strong presence of professionals in the sample reflects the Brotherhood's overall membership. However, it should not be allowed to obscure the fact that other categories were also represented among the MB candidates in the elections. Thus, there were also significant numbers from the educational professions, in the broad sense of the term: 22 percent of the Brotherhood candidates. Ten percent of these were academics, and 12 percent were teachers or schools inspectors.[38] While the former might be added to the professionals category, the latter two groups belong more to another sociological group just as prominent among MB candidates—state employees. These individuals, usually occupying senior or middle-management positions—or more rarely being ordinary employees in the local or national state administration—made up a quarter of the Brotherhood candidates (the same proportion as in parliament, where they made up 23 percent of MPs).

In addition, teachers and administrative personnel were overrepresented among Brotherhood candidates from the Upper Egyptian governorates—in other words, from the historically and sociologically marginalized rural areas. Whether or not the authorities had intended to recruit Islamists to the educational system and the local administration, the fact remains that a significant number of Muslim Brothers seemed to have succeeded in occupying such positions as mediators between the state apparatus and local communities. The large number of teachers and state white-collar workers among MB candidates in the 2005 elections—36 percent of the total—gives some indication of the extent of the influence of the Brotherhood in these socioprofessional categories. It also shows how readily a large proportion of

MB candidates met the typical profile of mediator as described above. One final feature of the data, equally remarkable if less obvious, is that 14 percent of the Brotherhood candidates were regular employees, unskilled or skilled factory workers,[39] when members of these categories made up around 13 percent of MPs as a whole (Soleiman 2006).

On another note, the strikingly strong presence of professionals among the MB candidates does not in itself indicate a greater degree of political professionalism among them. From the point of view of the Brotherhood's overall techniques of mobilization, doctors, pharmacists, state white-collar workers, and teachers all share the essential characteristic that they come into contact with a broad range of people in their work. Such people were recruited as election candidates by the Brotherhood because they corresponded to a particular functional type: individuals who had extensive relationship networks, were involved in providing services, and were able to contribute to integrating the Gama'a into both local communities and the state apparatus.[40] Such grassroots influence in local communities and local services was sought after when the Brotherhood was recruiting professionals to stand as its candidates, and it was far more important than any supposed advantage in terms of political professionalism that their professional profiles might have given them because of their management or other skills.

Moreover, experience in the professional syndicates—which, as we have seen, has sometimes been considered an important step in the Brotherhood's political professionalization—was only a factor in 43 percent of the careers of the professionals selected as MB candidates in the 2005 elections. This experience would also have meant very different things to different people, since some of the candidates had never been elected to leading positions in the syndicates concerned, merely declaring themselves to have been active members of such and such a committee within them. Others had carried out elective functions in syndicates that had been frozen by the regime from the mid-1990s onward. Since these syndicates neither held elections nor engaged in overt political activities, the main task of elected board members was to provide social services. Finally, combining this percentage with that of candidates who had taken part in the student unions,[41] it becomes apparent that the ideal-type trajectory of 'student union–professional syndicate–political election' does not hold true. It is only really observable in at most eight cases out of all the Brotherhood candidates in the 2005 elections.

As a result, the Brotherhood's professional MPs were characterized less by their politically professionalized profiles than by their capacity to act as services candidates with significant local support. It was exactly this point that was emphasized by Mohamed Habib, the Brotherhood's former deputy guide, who was responsible for recruiting candidates for the 2005 elections. He said in an interview, "We choose leading figures who have strong positions in local communities, such as the presidents of charitable associations or doctors who have good relations with people. That is to say, individuals who are active in [providing] services for the local population."[42]

The importance of the spirit of service in selecting the MB candidates also clearly appears in their engagement in various kinds of public work *(al-'amal al-'amm)*, an expression which in Egypt covers activities in charitable and religious associations as much as in syndicates, unions, and political parties. It says a lot about the ways in which political and social activities are interrelated. The areas of public work in which the MB candidates worked were at the meeting point of state, social, and Brotherhood networks, and it was there that they departed most from the ideal type represented by al-'Iryan.

## A Local Public–Work Elite

Involvement in local charitable activities was a characteristic of practically all the Brotherhood candidates in the 2005 elections, including most of those who were also activists in professional syndicates. Fifty-nine percent of the candidates declared that they worked in legally registered charitable associations, often linked to a mosque and usually having a dispensary and/or child-care center, and 56 percent said they took part in more informal charitable activities (Table 5). For the most part, the latter consisted of organizing mobile medical clinics (called 'medical caravans') for outlying areas, holding charity sales, helping with marriage costs, managing food distribution, or providing medical supplies or school books. They could also consist of fostering programs for orphans and poor families, or programs to help build medical or social facilities such as hospitals, child-care centers, educational and literacy centers, schools, mosques, religious institutes, and even housing.

Table 5. Public Work Activities of the MB Candidates in 2005

| Type of Activity | | Percentage of candidates participating |
|---|---|---|
| Formal charitable associations* | | 59% |
| Including: | Local development associations | 9% |
| | Official *zakat* committees | 8% |

| Type of Activity | | Percentage of candidates participating |
|---|---|---|
| Informal charitable activities* | | 56% |
| Popular justice associations* | | 23% |
| Pro bono preaching activities* | | 17% |
| Youth centers, clubs, parents' associations* | | 25% |
| Workers' mutuals and cooperatives* | | 11% |
| Workers' unions** | | 15% |
| Including: | Teachers syndicate | 8% |
| | Professional syndicates** | 32% |

Source: Vannetzel, 2012. *2005 Parliamentary Elections Brotherhood Candidates Database.*
*N = 129, ** N = 155

Such informal initiatives were a response to the growing control by the state over the NGO sector from the beginning of the 1990s onward. Associations that were 'satellites' of the Brotherhood—in other words, that were well known to have been set up and run by the organization—were almost all closed down during this period. There were, however, two major exceptions: the Islamic Medical Association (al-Gam'iyya al-Tibbiyya al-Islamiyya), a prototype of the 'satellite' Brotherhood associations tolerated by the regime, and al-Gam'iyya al-Shar'iyya, an association which had not been set up by the Brotherhood but which had long had significant MB membership. This meant that al-Gam'iyya al-Shar'iyya could be seen as a 'Brotherhood-ized' association, at least until the Brothers were formally ejected from it in the 1990s.

### 'Brotherhood' or 'Brotherhood-ized' Associations

#### The Islamic Medical Association
The Islamic Medical Association (IMA) was established in 1977 by senior Brotherhood figures, among them Ahmad al-Malt, a former member of the Secret Apparatus, and young recruits who had recently graduated from medical school, such as Abu al-Futuh and al-'Iryan in Cairo and Gamal Heshmat in Alexandria. The IMA controlled twenty-three hospitals across the country, along with

many smaller clinics or dispensaries associated with them, and it was undoubtedly the most important of all the medical associations. While the IMA is only mentioned three times on the CVs of the MB candidates in the 2005 elections, it was nevertheless probably responsible for setting up the medical facilities that are mentioned more frequently. As will be seen in the following chapters, IMA facilities played an important role in helping to mobilize voters and supporting the activities of Brotherhood MPs. Its seizure by the state was ordered in the wake of a decree classifying the Brotherhood as a "terrorist organization" in December 2013. The board of the IMA was then swiftly purged by the intelligence agencies, and after a year in which its fate was unclear, its assets were seized by the authorities (some LE300 million) at the beginning of 2015, and its managerial staff replaced by individuals supporting the regime (Brooke 2015).

### Al-Gam'iyya al-Shar'iyya

Set up in 1913, al-Gam'iyya al-Shar'iyya (GS) is one of the most important Islamic charities in Egypt. At the beginning of the 2000s, it had 457 subsidiaries across the country and nearly 6,000 associated mosques providing medical and social services. It was able to reach out to between two and a half million and five million people (Ben Néfissa 2003).

Ben Néfissa has drawn attention to the relationship between the GS, the Brotherhood, and the regime, writing that throughout the 1970s and 1980s the GS "was used by the Egyptian authorities as much as by the Muslim Brothers" (Ben Néfissa 2003: 216). After Sadat came to power in the early 1970s, the GS, originally a proselytizing association, became a para-public organization aiming to take under its control the private mosques that were growing exponentially in number at the time. It did this by setting up educational, medical, and social services within the mosques, thereby contributing to "the new social policy [of] charity 'in the name' of Islam" (Ben Néfissa 2003: 222) and establishing itself as "a rampart against extremist Islamism by encouraging the membership of representatives of moderate Islamism in the shape of the Muslim Brothers" (Ben Néfissa 2003: 246).

The integration of the Brothers into the GS hierarchy thus came about as a result of the role assigned to them by the authorities at the time, and one they continued to play almost without incident until 1990. In this year, the Brotherhood's victory in the elections to the GS board led to a change of attitude on the part of the regime and the board's sudden dissolution. According to Ben Néfissa, the Brotherhood's victory in the GS board elections indicated the latter's growing "autonomy" from the regime as a result of the influence of its MB members, leading to efforts by the authorities to eject them (Ben Néfissa 2003: 215).

Thirteen percent of the Brotherhood candidates in the 2005 elections indicated that they were or had been members of a local branch of the GS, and in eight cases out of a total of 17 they also indicated that they had been either the founders of the branch in question or were presently its managers. Such figures give some indication of the importance of the involvement of the Brothers in the GS, the charity most often mentioned in the candidate CVs, as well as of the significance of attempts to eject them from it from the early 1990s onward. The details of individual involvement in the GS, with dates and functions, are mostly sketchy, however. Some candidates put their involvement in the past, even if it was in fact continuing, though informally, as will be seen in the case of an MP from Helwan. It seems likely that the relationship between the MB candidates and the GS was played down in many cases, perhaps on the orders of senior figures in the organization.

However, despite these two exceptions at the national level, most MB candidates in the 2005 elections declared that they took part in activities run by mostly local associations not specifically linked to the Brotherhood. A significant proportion said that they took part, usually more or less anonymously, in local parastate associations, including local development associations,[43] official zakat committees,[44] youth centers, sports clubs, or parents' associations. These are all examples of the characteristic social spaces in which local notables are formed in Egypt, and therefore they are essential to non-differentiated political activities.

The involvement of Brotherhood candidates in parastate networks also took place through the workers' unions (different from the professional syndicates) attached to the government-controlled Egyptian Trade Union Federation (ETUF). There were also MB activists in the Teachers' Syndicate, also under the control of the state. Others worked in cooperatives, mutual societies, and solidarity funds attached to their workplaces.

The participation of MB candidates in preaching activities and in customary justice (sulh) shows more acutely the intertwining of state, social, and Brotherhood networks that took place at the time. Seventeen percent of MB candidates gave freely of their time as imams or preachers in mosques (there were only five cases of candidates who worked professionally in the religious field). Some said they were imams appointed by the Ministry of

Awqaf. One said he worked as an imam in prisons under the direction of the Ministry of the Interior, and three were *ulama* recognized by al-Azhar.[45] Nearly a quarter of the candidates engaged in dispute resolution activities or customary justice, meaning settling quarrels between neighbors. At the end of the 1990s, the regime tried to exercise greater control over the sulh system by introducing reconciliation committees linked to the Local Popular Councils (LPCs) (Ben Néfissa 2000). Nearly a third of the Brotherhood candidates involved in sulh practices explicitly said in their CVs that they had done so as members of these official LPC committees.

Moreover, despite the control exercised by the NDP over the LPCs, 15 percent of the MB candidates for the 2005 parliament had previously served as elective representatives in such LPCs. Thirteen percent of them had also already been MPs, for the most part elected in the 2000 elections.

## Conclusion

The MB candidates in the 2005 parliamentary elections were members of a local elite that was politically unprofessional but that was well known for its social and charitable activities taking place at the intersection of state, social, and Brotherhood networks. This allows us to make two observations. The first is that the Brotherhood was able to meet the regular political eligibility criteria in Egypt when selecting its election candidates. This means that we should not necessarily consider votes for the Brotherhood as purely ideological ones, which would obey very specific logics. On the contrary, the MB vote, analyzed here in terms of the mobilization—the making vote—that produced it, needs to be seen within the overall framework of electoral politics in Egypt. The second observation is that the results of the 2005 elections called into question the widespread idea that there was a parallel Islamist countersociety at work in the country. Instead, it appears that the public-work networks in which the Brotherhood candidates were involved, whether in an informal, hidden, or negotiated manner, penetrated both inside and outside the state, revealing the latter's "elusive" boundaries (Mitchell 1991).

However, such hypotheses need to be supported by exploring the dynamics of the local political arena in greater depth. How did the Gama'a manage to develop its networks in the face of regime limitations on its activities? How, moreover, did its candidates manage to pull off the successes they did in the face of NDP candidates who had much greater resources? Whether they were local figures well placed in the political and administrative structures of the regime, and therefore had easy access to state resources, or businessmen *(rigal a'mal)* able to call upon their own private wealth, the NDP candidates would seem to have been much better placed to demonstrate the spirit of service necessary to succeed in the electoral system. Finally, while the Brotherhood's support in the elections was not purely ideologically motivated, it was not only the result of client-based mobilization either. The question remains of how the Brotherhood's overall aim of moral rebirth and the need to comply with the spirit of service necessary to win in the elections were connected.

# 2

# Mobilizing Disinterestedness

The electoral successes of the Muslim Brotherhood in the Mubarak era have often been explained by two arguments that might seem to be contradictory. On the one hand, they have been put down to the influence of the organization's social base with its vast, and, as we have seen, sometimes mythical 'parallel' redistribution system. On the other hand, they have been described as the result of ideological voting practices that are in principle incompatible with clientelist ones.

Both these arguments have been refuted in a recent work by Masoud (2014), who shows that the "ideological" argument does not stand up when the "socio-structural" factors of elections held under the Mubarak regime are analyzed. Clientelism largely determined votes, Masoud says, and in any case voters constituted a limited, mainly poor, fraction of the population, due to the weak participation in elections. Yet, in his view, the "redistribution" argument that held that voters voted for Brotherhood candidates because of the social services provided by the organization was not a convincing one either. This was because the Gama'a, banned under Mubarak, was not in a position to provide enough social services to guarantee the loyalty of poor voters, who in fact had no other choice but to cast their votes for the ruling NDP that controlled state resources. According to Masoud, the Brotherhood thus only won votes by mobilizing a small number of voters from the middle classes who were not susceptible to being controlled by patronage. While such middle-class voters were a minority, given the very low turnouts, they were enough for the MB candidates to win a limited number of seats in the elections, as was the case in 1984, 1987, 2000, and 2005.

The analysis presented here agrees with that of Masoud on the socio-structural factors at work in the elections and the small size of the active electorate, but it also differs with it on two important points. The first regards the nature of the middle classes, since a large part of these is so impoverished in Egypt that it would be better to call them "subaltern groups who are not poorly off" (Schwartz 2011). They were not immune to clientelist relationships. Not only can these groups benefit from the types of redistribution considered here, but they may also play the role of intermediaries in their implementation, or be witnesses of them in a way that is far from simply anodyne. The second point is, precisely, that in clientelist relationships symbolic resources typically count for as much as, and often more than, the amounts distributed. This chapter will aim to show that the clientelist distribution of resources practiced by the Brotherhood was characterized above all by a symbolic economy—in other words, by its supposed disinterestedness. It was not only the poor categories of the population that could be attracted by this symbolic dimension despite the limited material resources at the disposal of the MB when compared to those available to the NDP or various businessmen. The middle classes were also able to play a role in such symbolic exchanges, as will be shown.

I use the concept of 'eligibility' in an anthropological sense in order to capture the sociological and historical conditions that enable an individual to obtain electoral support, such as being entrenched in community networks and in local memory (Abélès 1991). In analyzing eligibility at the local level, the intention is to go beyond the normative opposition between the ideological and the clientelist patterns of voting, in order to investigate their interpenetration on the ground through an in-depth exploration of the three Cairo constituencies of Helwan, Tibbin/15 Mayo, and Madinat Nasr. The overall aim is to contribute to an understanding of the practical and discursive ways in which Brotherhood candidates constructed their 'symbolic economy of disinterestedness.'

## Statesmen, Businessmen, and Men of God?

There were very few businessmen or business leaders among the MB candidates in the 2005 elections—only 6 percent of the total. However, this occupational group nevertheless became one of the most represented in parliament[1] and became more and more powerful within the NDP (El-Tarouty 2015). Why did the Brotherhood not field more candidates from the business community? How should one understand this specificity? The argument that will be presented here is that the Brotherhood aimed to maintain a division of labor between local leaders known for their public service and businessmen. While the first group was selected in line with the rules of clientelist relationships in Egypt that emphasize the non-monetary dimensions of the spirit of service, the second group was responsible for financing their campaigns. This division of labor was central to the economy of disinterestedness that the Gama'a relied upon in its electoral mobilization. This symbolic economy also contrasted with the disenchanted clientelist practices that had become more and more widespread because of the greater involvement of businessmen in elections.

## Patterns of Eligibility
### Economic privatization and electoral politics

The entrance into politics of the business elites was a result of the crony capitalism that characterized Mubarak's regime. The business bourgeoisie used its links with the state apparatus to obtain permits, favors, and positions from which it could then extract rents (Sadowski 1991; Sfakianakis 2004). In the 1990s, few businessmen stood as candidates in elections, their involvement mostly being restricted to financing the campaigns of others by giving money to local charities or putting votes at their disposal by mobilizing the employees of companies they owned on election day (Longuenesse and Youssef 1999). However, in the 2000s, businessmen got more directly involved. This was enabled by the mode of recruitment that the NDP developed at the time, by using independent candidates (see chapter one).

However, this new and significant presence of businessmen among election candidates did not lead to major changes in the legitimate criteria of eligibility. While the businessmen used their own money to finance their campaigns, the image of MPs as distributors of state benefits limited the ways in which they could use private resources in their clientelist practices. They often sought to combine their personal fortunes with traditional political careers in the local political and administrative apparatus. However, even so, their very presence made the direct use of money (either by handing it out or in the shape of gifts and so on) both more visible and more widespread. While the exchange of votes for money was not new in the history of Egyptian politics, such financial arrangements had usually taken place between a candidate and lesser notables, such as popular local leaders, the heads of leading families, the presidents of associations, and the like (Menza 2012). These exchanges were also accompanied by favors that had some collective benefits, such as the building of new schools, bridges, or clinics, which allowed appearances to be saved and monetary transfers hidden (Ben Néfissa and Arafat: 2005; Kassem 2004). In contrast to this traditional system, by 2005 the Egyptian press was denouncing the new and visible payment of electoral bribes (*rashawi intikhabiyya*) to voters at polling stations, along with an increase in the number of election brokers (*samasir*). The businessmen were considered much more likely to use the services of these agents than the traditional candidates fielded by the NDP. Unlike lesser notables, brokers did not have any long-term links with the candidates concerned, but instead simply bought votes with money from the candidate making the highest offer, seeing their services as simply something that could be bought and sold.[2]

The increase in the number of businessmen in parliament was also a symptom of the socioeconomic changes taking place in the 1990s and 2000s, when many large companies were being privatized and there were moves to deregulate the labor market. These changes impacted both the nature of the services that were demanded by the voters and those that the candidates might offer them. Such demands were more and more likely to be for jobs, and while the businessmen enjoyed obvious advantages over the traditional NDP candidates in this regard, since they could simply hand out jobs in their companies at least on a temporary basis, neither they nor the traditional candidates were able to meet the demand for public-sector jobs, which had become more and more difficult to come by but were the only ones many voters considered to be sufficiently secure (Aclimandos 2010; Dessouki 2010). Such considerations could in part explain the number of MPs who at the end of their terms in office had difficulty being reelected, something which particularly affected the NDP. In 2005, 73 percent of MPs were elected to the People's Assembly for the first time, while in 2000 this figure had stood at 70 percent, and it was only 42 percent in 1995 (Rabi' 2002, 2006a). The high turnover rate of MPs could thus have been the result of the chronic instability of the networks on which they depended.

However, such developments were felt differently in different contexts. Constituencies with highly stable relationship networks, such as Helwan and Tibbin, need to be distinguished from others where social bonds were weaker and electoral volatility was more marked, such as Madinat Nasr. The three constituencies examined here had one point in common, however. All three were ministerial fiefs whose MPs, statesmen or stateswomen, were ministers who were able to call upon the state apparatus—police, state security, governors, Local Popular Councils, executive councils, and so on—in their campaigns to control the local voters or to lavish services on them (for example, by providing residential areas with electricity, opening dispensaries, or rehousing the inhabitants of informal areas).

### Helwan and Tibbin/15 Mayo—Constituencies 24 and 25

Constituency 24 comprised most units (shiyakhat) of the Helwan administrative district (qism), including the highly populated area of Ma'sara. The constituency had more than 133,000 voters on the electoral roll in 2005 (Rabi' 2006b). A former spa town (sulfurous water) for aristocrats and European residents, surrounded by agricultural villages, the area became a suburb for the educated middle classes at the beginning of the twentieth century (Prestel 2017). In 1959 Helwan became the site of a major industrial city, as part of Nasser's attempts to industrialize Egypt. Housing developments and then areas of informal housing sprang up to house industrial workers, who came from all over Egypt. These workers were attracted by the area's large public-sector factories making material for the military (al-masani' al-harbiyya), its car factories (Al-Nasr), and its cement works. The latter began to be privatized at the end of the 1990s.

Constituency 25 (around 84,000 registered voters in 2005) included three shiyakhat of the Helwan qism and the Tibbin qism as a whole, as well as the City of 15 Mayo. The area contains the major national steelworks EISCO (the Egyptian Iron and Steel Company, in Arabic al-Hadid wa-l-Sulb) that still employed more than 13,000 workers in 2009, down from the 25,000 employed in 1990 shortly before the employment cutback in Egypt's public-sector industries imposed by the period's structural-adjustment programs (Makram-Ebeid 2012). The constituency also contains factories belonging to the country's largest textile company (Misr Helwan li-l-Ghazl wa-l-Nasig). Workers' housing was built there in the 1960s near the old rural villages of Helwan al-Balad and Kafr al-'Ilu (Fakhoury1972). Today this housing is occupied by former agricultural workers who have retrained to work in factories, craftsmen, and workers in the informal sector. The City of 15 Mayo is the only one of the new cities built in the desert periphery of Cairo that has been able to attract a significant population of workers from Cairo and from other governorates (Jossifort 1995; Depaule and El Kadi 1990). Mainly residential, it was lived in at first by skilled workers employed in the nearby industries, and then by middle-ranking public-sector managerial staff and employees.

The Helwan/Tibbin area is characterized by strong ties of family and regional solidarity, due to the tightly knit character of the large families originating from the former rural villages of the area and the way in which immigrants from various regions of Egypt settled together in the different districts (Longuenesse 1997). In the older neighborhoods and in informal areas, the leading families, both original and immigrant, often have a *mandara* (reception room) that is used for family reunions. It is also used to host receptions for election candidates, in which the services the candidates intend to offer to the leading figures in the district are negotiated. The original familial and regional loyalties have been rewritten as neighborhood ones based on direct interpersonal knowledge (Haenni 2005a). Similar feelings of solidarity based on common residence can be found in workers' housing projects in Helwan and Tibbin ('The Old Steel City,' 'The Housing,' and so on) (Makram-Ebeid 2012). In 15 Mayo City, residential links develop along separate housing blocks called *mugawarat*, each of which has its own shops, school, and mosque, and where feelings of neighborliness can be intense.

Factory identities carry weight in electoral politics, too. In Helwan (24), the military factories are said to determine the results of elections, and the same thing is true for Tibbin (25) regarding the EISCO steel plants. It should be added that very often workers vote in the constituencies in which they work rather than in those in which they live, a possibility permitted by law and widely exploited by employers. The Helwan and Tibbin workers also played a leading role in the episodes of popular revolt that took place in 1968, 1971–75 (on this occasion, the president of the ETUF was held prisoner at EISCO), 1977 (in protests against reductions in consumer subsidies), and finally in the summer of 1989 when massive strikes took place at EISCO. The intensity of the repression used against the latter has stayed in the collective memory, but the later granting of certain privileges, such as promises to employ the sons of workers at the steelworks, weakened collective action while maintaining ties of solidarity between workers (Makram-Ebeid 2012).

The effects of this highly structured social fabric are also seen in local politics. The Tibbin constituency (25) was for many years under the control of Mohamed Mahgub, a former minister of *awqaf*, who was the perennial MP for the *fi'at* seat from 1979 to 2005. Presenting himself as an *ibn al-balad* (a son of the country), Mahgub was related through his wife to the largest of the original resident families in Tibbin. However, from 1995 onward, he was obliged to compete for the seat with Mustafa Bakri, an independent candidate who combined national fame with local popularity (see Table 6).

Table 6. Main Candidates in Tibbin/15 Mayo (25)

| Seat | Result | 1995 | 2000 | 2005 | 2010 |
|------|--------|------|------|------|------|
| *Fi'at* | Elected | Mohamed Mahgub, NDP, minister of *awqaf* | Mohamed Mahgub, NDP, minister of *awqaf* | Mustafa Bakri, independent, media figure | Constituency suppressed |
| | Main challenger | Mustafa Bakri, independent, media figure | Mustafa Bakri, independent, media figure | Nasir al-Gabari, NDP, head of the National Cement Company | Constituency suppressed |
| Worker | Elected | 'Ali Fath al-Bab, MB, worker EISCO | 'Ali Fath al-Bab, MB, worker EISCO | 'Ali Fath al-Bab, MB, worker EISCO | Constituency suppressed |
| | Main challenger | Mohamed Mustafa, NDP, worker EISCO | Mohamed Mustafa, NDP, worker EISCO | Mohamed Mustafa, NDP, worker EISCO | Constituency suppressed |

In the case of the Tibbin workers' seat, the NDP found itself in competition with local leftists who had emerged from the earlier workers' uprisings. In the 1990 legislative elections, Mohamed Mustafa, the leader of the 1989 uprising at the EISCO steelworks, won the seat running against the NDP, though he joined the party a few months later. In the 1995 elections, he faced two other candidates. One was a member of the Tagammu' Party who had been a leader of the 1977 uprising at the textile factories and the founder of a center for workers' rights that presented itself as a sort of independent syndicate.[3]

## Mustafa Bakri—Scandal Specialist and 'Godfather' of the Sa'idis

While it would not be correct to call Mustafa Bakri a business-man, he nevertheless possessed financial assets that, while opaque in character, allowed him to be active in the media for several decades. After having been editor of the newspaper of the al-Ahrar Party, during which time he caused a crisis by criticizing the party's president for supporting the privatizations that were taking place at the time as well as the party's alliance with the Brotherhood, Bakri later founded and largely funded the weekly paper *al-Usbu'*. This was one of the first private-sector media entities to receive a license in the 1990s.

This favor, rare at the time, says much about the good relations Bakri enjoyed with the Mubarak regime, but it can also be explained by the necessity incumbent on the latter to promote journalism that looked 'anti-governmental' in order to compete with the discourse of contestation being promoted by another newspaper, *al-Dustur*, that was enjoying growing success at the time. Bakri's style of journalism was based on the reporting of scandals, and it depended on the close links he enjoyed with the security apparatus. This meant he could carry out multiple media campaigns aimed at intimidating opponents of the regime while at the same time not signaling any obvious loyalty to it.

Bakri combined acerbic criticism of the government with support for President Mubarak personally, and while some voters saw him as an opponent of the regime, others saw him as an independent, and still others as a supporter of the NDP. On the constituency level, Bakri possessed an influential newspaper, Sawt Helwan, established in 1995 and run by his brother Mahmud Bakri, who was seen locally as the strongman of the two. He emphasized his origins in the Sa'id (Upper Egypt) and therefore his closeness to migrant workers who had originally come from there. After Mahgub's death, Bakri managed to have himself elected to the fi'at seat in 2005 instead of the new NDP candidate.

The other was a Brotherhood member, 'Ali Fath al-Bab (one of the three MPs whose careers are examined here), who was standing at the time as a Labor Party candidate and had himself been a worker in EISCO. Mustafa (NDP) and Fath al-Bab (Brotherhood/Labor Party) went through to the second round. The defeat of the Tagammu' candidate in the first round was seen as the result of an error of judgment in not choosing a candidate from EISCO (Longuenesse 1997). Despite the support of the local NDP apparatus for Mustafa, it was Fath al-Bab who in fact was elected, and he held the workers' seat without interruption from 1995 to 2010. His victory—unique in the 1995 elections, when he was the only Muslim Brother to be elected to the People's Assembly at a time when hundreds of the organization's activists were being imprisoned—was the result of the *tarbitat* strategy pursued by the candidates for the *fi'at* and workers' seats. Fath al-Bab benefited from an alliance with Mahgub during the second round when the latter was trying to pick up votes from outside NDP circles to counter competition from Bakri.

The Helwan constituency (24) was the traditional fief of the minister of military production Sayyid Mish'al, who held its *fi'at* seat from 1999 to 2011. The workers' seat was held by Mohamed Mungi, vice-president of the ETUF since 1979, president of the Military Production Workers' Syndicate since 1978, and president of a syndicate committee in a military factory in the area since 1964. Mungi had been an MP from 1984 to 2000, and he was again a candidate in the 2005 elections.[4] The fact that all the workers in the military production factories were registered on the Helwan constituency electoral roll meant that these two candidates, both representing the authorities, could comfortably expect to be reelected. The tight control exercised over the military factories explains in part why the left and various protest movements had never been able to make inroads in them. However, the Brotherhood, identified as the Islamic current at the time, fielded heavyweight challengers in the 1995 elections in the shape of Abu al-'Ila Madi, representing the Engineers' Syndicate,[5] and Mohamed 'Abd al-Ghani, a worker in the military factories. In the 2005 elections, Sheikh al-Muhammadi 'Abd al-Maqsud, whose career is analyzed in detail below, won the workers' seat in competition with Mungi in the first round. Mish'al, standing for the fi'at seat, also had to compete with an 'NDP independent,' businessman Isma'il Nasr al-Din, in the second round, the latter having made a *tarbit* agreement with Sheikh al-Muhammadi (see Table 7).

**Table 7. Main Candidates in Helwan (24)**

| Seat | Result | 1995 | 2000 | 2005 | 2010 |
|------|--------|------|------|------|------|
| *Fi'at* | Elected | Mohamed al-Ghamrawi, NDP, minister of military production | Sayyid Mish'al, NDP, minister of Military Production | Sayyid Mish'al, NDP, minister of military production | Sayyid Mish'al, NDP, minister of military production |
| | Main challenger | Abu al-'Ila Madi, MB, engineer | ? | Isma'il Nasr al-Din, independent, NDP, businessman | Mustafa Bakri, independent, media figure |
| Worker | Elected | Mustafa Mungi, NDP, ETUF military production | Ibrahim Lutfi, NDP, ETUF military production | al-Muhammadi 'Abd al-Maqsud, MB, worker military factory | 'Ali al-Guhari, NDP |
| | Main challenger | Mohamed 'Abd al-Ghani, MB, worker military factory | Mohamed 'Abd al-Ghani, MB, worker military factory | Mustafa Mungi, NDP, ETUF military production | 'Salah,'* MB, worker cement plant |

* Name changed for interviewee protection.

### Isma'il Nasr al-Din, *Ibn al-Balad* and Independent Patron

Born in Helwan al-Bahariyya in 1953 to a family that he has described as "modest"[6] and that had lived in the area for several generations, Isma'il Nasr al-Din was a real estate developer responsible for several major urban projects in Saudi Arabia in the 1980s, a career he continued in Qatar even after his return to Egypt in 2003. He was also the president of a charity in Helwan al-Bahariyya that he founded in 1993 and that he had been able to finance as a result of his success in business. The many trophies—plaques bearing expressions of gratitude of various kinds—that decorated his office in Helwan bore witness to his patronage. This office had nothing to do with his business activities but was devoted to public relations and looked like an office in which an MP receives his constituents.

During the 2005 election campaign, Nasr al-Din did his best to promote an image of a rich *ibn al-balad* (al-Messiri 1978) who was using his wealth to serve his local community and the place of his birth. He received significant support from the local newspaper *Helwan al-youm*, which publicized his charitable activities by showing him, for example, at the inauguration of a welfare association one day and at the opening of a training school for young soccer players the next. It also gave him regular opportunities to appeal directly to readers: an article with the evocative title of "The Love of People Protects against Power and Money" (*Hubb al-nas abqa min al-gah wal-mal*) is a typical example.

However, such patronage was not enough to beat Sayyid Mish'al and get elected in the 2005 elections, despite a remarkable result in the first round, in which Nasr al-Din received 1,576 more votes than the minister.[7] When interviewed, he was silent about his past as an NDP representative on the Local Popular Council (I learned about this elsewhere), and instead emphasized his independent credentials. Eventually he rejoined the ranks of the NDP. He was not selected as the NDP candidate in the fall 2010 People's Assembly elections, a slot reserved for the minister (Mish'al), but he was selected as the Party's candidate in the June 2010 elections to the Consultative Assembly, to which he was duly elected.[8]

The example of Nasr al-Din shows that in order to get elected it was necessary to mobilize many other forms of solidarity besides simply relying on money. The failure of his career as an independent also shows that while private resources were on their way to becoming necessary, they were still not sufficient to counter the greater influence available to candidates who had the resources of the state behind them.

### Madinat Nasr—Constituency 6

Built in the 1960s on desert land used for army barracks, Madinat Nasr was originally designed to house administrative agencies and those who worked in them. Over the decades that followed, the area attracted senior civil servants, company managers, engineers, technicians, and teachers (El Kadi 1990; Denis 1995). Madinat Nasr is a very large area crossed by freeways, hosting major facilities such as hospitals, shopping malls, the Cairo Stadium and the al-Ahli Soccer Club, as well as the al-Azhar University student dormitories. Its different districts are independent of each other and are divided into wealthy neighborhoods, areas for employees, shopkeepers, small businessmen and professionals, and informal areas. The most important of the latter, 'Izbat al-Haggana, housed between 200,000 and 400,000 people in 2006 (Sabry 2009: 31). At the other end of the spectrum, 'Izbat al-Muslimin is a tiny informal 'island' crammed into the much wealthier area of Misr al-Gedida. Constituency 6 also includes Qattamiyya, which takes in both the golf courses and luxury villas of Qattamiyya Heights and the housing projects and informal areas that house some of those who escaped the 1992 Cairo earthquake.

The fact that turnout in this constituency was lower in the 2005 elections (at 15.3 percent of a total of 150,000 registered voters) than in Helwan (19.8 percent) and Tibbin (22.3 percent) can be interpreted as a result of the more fragmented nature of the electorate.[9] The desert grid, the type of urban planning used, and the socio-professional composition of the constituency are all factors that do not encourage the kind of complex group loyalties described earlier. The concept of the *ibn al-balad* has little relevance to a constituency of this sort, whereas it had been taken up and reinvented in Helwan and Tibbin.

However, the informal areas were an exception to this rule, since their specific histories, the types of development, and the forms of buildings in them were all factors encouraging the formation of local loyalties around the earliest families settling in the area, the establishment of migrant communities on a neighborhood level, and the emergence of natural leaders (*al-qiyada al-tabi'iyya*) who controlled local support networks. Sayyid 'Abd al-Ghani, twice elected the constituency's MP in 1990 and 2000, enjoyed this status, having stood as an independent who later joined the NDP. He had left school at the end of the primary level and then worked as an employee at EgyptAir, the national carrier, and owed his rise (and victory in the elections against the official candidate of the NDP) to his popularity in the 'Izbat al-Muslimin neighborhood where he lived and where he was president of the Charitable Association of the Residents of Misr al-Gedida (Zahran 1996). Now deceased, he still lives on in local memory, reminding local political actors of the strategic importance of the informal neighborhoods and the kinds of exchanges that can take place within them.

The major oil companies were another important factor in the battles for election in this constituency. In the 1995, 2000, and 2005 parliamentary elections, the NDP candidate for the workers' seat, Thurayya Labana, was an assistant to the minister of petroleum. In 2010, the minister in person, Sameh Fahmi, successfully stood for election to the *fi'at* seat. The oil companies were important because whether they wished to vote or not, workers in them were physically transported to the polling stations on the day of the elections. And similar procedures could be used on the employees of various state agencies, al-Azhar University, and even the members of sports or social clubs.[10] In 1995, the NDP MP for the fi'at seat was none other than the former president of the Higher Council for Youth and Sports and president of the Cairo Stadium.

However, despite the influence wielded by these individuals, often parachuted in from another area, Constituency 6 saw particularly intense struggles for power within the NDP, perhaps because the members of different and competing elites lived there. The independent candidate Sayyid 'Abd al-Ghani, a lesser notable from the 'Izbat al-Muslimin neighborhood, twice won the workers' seat at the expense of the NDP's ministerial candidate Thurayya Labna before himself entering the ranks of the party. He had benefited from the support of the local section of the NDP against the official candidate (Zahran 1996). For the *fi'at* seat, two leading businessmen, one in construction and the other in ceramics (Mustafa al-Sallab, described below), fought over the candidature after 2000. After the death of al-Sallab in 2010, the seat was taken over by the minister of petroleum. The other businessman, who then sought the workers' seat (due to his relationship to the building industry), was headed off by the NDP, which selected another candidate whose profile underlined the nature of the competition between the different political and economic elites. This candidate, Tawfiq 'Abd al-Salam, an MP since 2010, was neither a local NDP figure nor a local notable with his own networks from previous elections. While he had played a role in the 2005 election campaign, this had only been as an electoral broker providing votes in exchange for money to benefit Mustafa al-Sallab (Table 8).[11]

**Table 8. Main Candidates in Madinat Nasr (6)**

| Seat | Result | 1995 | 2000 | 2005 | 2010 |
|------|--------|------|------|------|------|
| *Fi'at* | Elected | 'Abd al-Mun'im 'Imara, NDP, minister of sports | Fawzi al-Sayyid, then Mustafa al-Sallab, both NDP, businessmen | Mustafa al-Sallab, NDP, businessman | Sameh Fahmi, NDP, minister of petroleum |
| | Main challenger | 'Adil Husayn, Labor Party, journalist | ? | Makarim al-Diri, MB, academic of al-Azhar | Manal Abu al-Hasan, MB, academic |
| Worker | Elected | Thurayya Labna, NDP, ETUF oil sector | Sayyid 'Abd al-Ghani, indepen-dent, NDP, employee | 'Isam Mukhtar, MB, employee oil company | Tawfiq 'Abd al-Salam, NDP, former electoral broker |
| | Main challenger | Sayyid 'Abd al-Ghani, indepen-dent, NDP, employee | Thurayya Labna, NDP, ETUF oil sector | Thurayya Labna, NDP, ETUF oil sector | Fawzi al-Sayyid, indepen-dent, NDP, businessman |

### Mustafa al-Sallab: Ceramics Magnate and New NDP Elite

Businessman Mustafa al-Sallab was a member of an Egyptian private-sector dynasty.[12] Head of one of the country's largest ceramics groups that he had inherited from his father and grandfather, and in which he later also placed his son, al-Sallab also possessed shares in a major Egyptian satellite TV channel (al-Mehwar) and in real estate. Said to be close to Gamal Mubarak, the president's younger son, he became a symbol of the generation of businessmen who had entered politics in order to promote their businesses. He joined the NDP in 1991 after a period in which he had kept a distance from politics on the advice of his father, and rapidly became a member of the party's Economic Bureau, the youngest at the time. He was elected to the Cairo Governorate's LPC in 1996 and joined the party's leadership at the governorate level.

In 2002, al-Sallab continued his ascent by being elected to the *fi'at* seat in parliament for the Madinat Nasr constituency after another construction magnate, Fawzi al-Sayyid, elected in 2000, had been removed as a result of corruption. The two men then competed for the seat in the 2005 elections, and al-Sallab found himself competing against MB candidate Makarim al-Diri in the second round. He only managed to win the seat after negotiations with the Brotherhood, since al-Diri had won more votes.

The Madinat Nasr constituency was identified in the independent press at the time as a classic case of a constituency in which money had obviously been used during the election campaign and where workers from the oil companies and public-sector office workers had been bused in to the polling stations in order to vote. However, at the same time al-Sallab had used more traditional ways of winning votes in some neighborhoods in the constituency. In 'Izbat al-Muslimin, for example, residents said that he had been introduced to them by former MP Sayyid 'Abd al-Ghani, a native of the area, and that this had helped al-Sallab to win more votes. He was also careful to attend to his image as a good man, notably by astutely mixing his appeal. In one avenue in Madinat Nasr, for example, there was a veritable 'al-Sallab complex' in a building hosting his company headquarters, one of his constituency offices, and a charity bearing his name. Al-Sallab also ordered the construction of a charitable hospital, also bearing his name, that opened its doors in 2010. However, he did not have the time to reap the rewards of this activity, as he died of a stroke just before the 2010 elections.

The Brotherhood's first success in an election in Madinat Nasr took place in 1984 with the election of Muhammad al-Matrawi (on the MB–Wafd list). The organization's future guide Mahdi 'Akif, a senior civil servant at the Ministry of Reconstruction, was then elected in 1987 together with syndicate activist and lawyer Mukhtar Nuh, and al-Azhar sheikh 'Abd al-Hayy al-Farmawi. In 1995, the main opponent to the holder of the NDP *fi'at* seat (the president of the Higher Council of Youth and Sports) was president of the Labor Party and editor of the national opposition paper *al-Sha'b*, 'Adil Husayn. The Labor Party had many MB members at this time in the wake of its agreement with the Brotherhood as part of the Islamic Alliance. In 2005, two MB candidates, 'Isam Mukhtar (employee in a petrol company) and Makarim al-Diri (a professor at al-Azhar University), won both seats. The subsequent forced withdrawal of al-Diri from the *fi'at* seat to the benefit of the NDP prefigured the situation in the 2010 elections, when the Brotherhood candidates, along with other opposition candidates, were prevented from running.

Despite the sociological differences between the Madinat Nasr constituency and the constituencies of Helwan and Tibbin, together with their differences in urban layout, Brotherhood candidates scored victories in all three constituencies in the elections. In the 2005 elections, they did better than the official NDP candidates in each constituency, despite the fact that the latter benefited from the support of the state apparatus. In Helwan, Sheikh al-Muhammadi, elected in the first round, even scored by far the most votes, with 15,871 as against 6,082 for his opponent, the NDP candidate Mustafa Mungi, and 9,321 for Mish'al standing for the *fi'at* seat. The question arises of how the electoral success of these candidates can be explained despite their lack of *nufudh*, or access to state resources. In order to answer it, we need to examine the profiles of the three MPs.

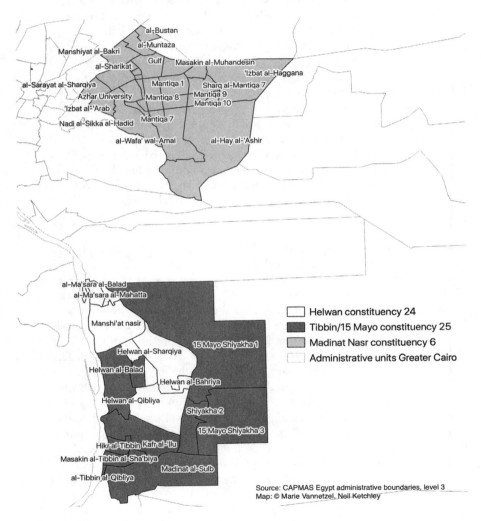

Map 1. Electoral constituencies of Helwan, Tibbin/15 Mayo and Madinat Nasr, 2005-2010.

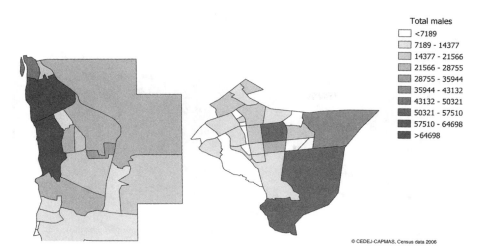

Map 2. Demographic disparities between subdistricts (total male population, headcount).

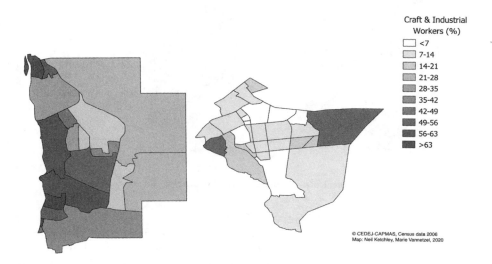

Map 3. Craft and industrial workers by subdistrict (% of total employed people).

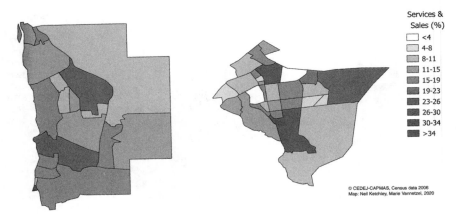

Map 4. Services and sales workers by subdistrict (% of total employed people).

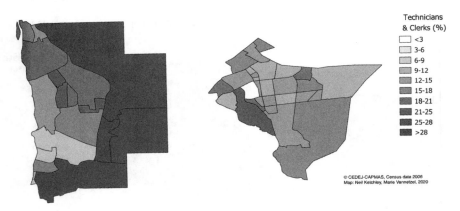

Map 5. Technicians and clerks by subdistrict (% of total employed people).

## Serving Society and Serving God

Contrary to what is often claimed, the MB candidates were not entirely deprived of *nufudh*, owing to their cooperation with the local authorities and involvement in organizations providing social services linked to the state. Even beyond the limited volume of material resources at their command, when compared with those enjoyed by their rivals in the NDP, the MB candidates drew heavily on a symbolic economy in order to distribute these resources. This symbolic economy could compensate for their relative lack of *nufudh* and turn it into a positive factor. While their ability to provide social services was certainly quantitatively reduced, at the same time it was qualitatively enhanced by the existence of an entire panoply of symbolic and practical arrangements that rendered it 'disinterested.'

Map 6. Professionals in technical and scientific occupations by subdistrict
(% of total employed people).

Map 7. Employees in the public sector by subdistrict, all occupations
(% of total employed people)

## 'Ali Fath al-Bab, workers' MP for Tibbin/15 Mayo (1995–2010)

'Ali Fath al-Bab was born in 1957 in Fayoum, a governorate of Upper
Egypt, and came to Tibbin when he was twenty-three years old to take a
job as a skilled worker at EISCO, following his graduation from a technical
high school. When I met him twenty-seven years later, he had become head
of a department. He started his career in public work (*al-'amal al-'amm*)

Statesmen, Businessmen, and Men of God?    69

by founding a *zakat* committee and preaching as imam of the company mosque. From 1990 to 1996, he served as union representative in the same steelworks, and in 1995, he ran as a candidate in the legislative elections. He won thanks to the *tarbit* agreement he made with Mahgub, the minister of *awqaf*, and he was therefore elected with the partial support of the NDP. This agreement was facilitated by an ambiguity about his true identity as a Muslim Brother, as he was also a member of the Labor Party at the time.[13] After his election to parliament, he was ousted from the union in 1996. However, far from abandoning his activities at EISCO in favor of his new responsibilities as an MP, he sought to keep them going for as long as possible, becoming the workers' representative on the factory board from 2001 to 2006. When he unsuccessfully stood for a second term on the board in the 2006 elections,[14] he based his campaign on what he had been able to achieve for the workers through serving as an MP.[15] Conversely, in the 2005 parliamentary elections, his manifesto, entitled "The Voice of the Workers," contained entire sections explicitly targeting the steelworkers and indicating the interdependence of his different roles and the ways in which they could be used to accumulate influence (see images 3 and 4).

Fath al-Bab saw his role as an MP as being naturally connected to his role in the plant, saying that "there is a common thing in being an MP and a workers' representative, which is the Service to People" *(al-khidma li-l-gamahir)*.[16] The two roles gave him a capacity for such service, whose electoral possibilities he fully recognized. While he did not seek to deny the possibilities for patronage that the two roles gave him, he nevertheless tried to turn the idea of service into a moral principle through discursive means.

> The other parties and the government accuse us of seeking to extend our influence through charitable activities, but this is not the case. It is a general rule for every human being to be interested in others regardless of their religion. And the establishment of the Brotherhood took place long before there were any elections. . . . For the Brothers, gaining power is only useful as a way of reforming society *(islah al-mugtama')*. Power is not an end in itself but is a way of working for the good of society. Moreover, through this work I am coming closer to God. When I help people, I am pleasing God, and I am coming closer to Paradise. . . . I don't expect anything in return from the person I help or his thanks. Even if he then ignores me entirely, I have to accept it, since all this is part of obeying God's will.[17]

In this extract from an interview, Fath al-Bab does not present the provision of social services as a *way* of gaining power, but instead as the *aim* of having power.

الإسلام صوت
هو الحل من العمال

انه لشرف عظيم لي أن أفوز بثقة اخواني العاملين لعدة سنوات ..بذلت خلالها
كل ما في وسعي حتي أكون نائباً يليق بهم .. نائب ثابت علي العهد والمبدأ ..
نائب يحضر كل جلسات المجلس .. لا يبزوغ ولا ينام .. نائب يناقش بكل قوة
وشجاعة ومنطق سليم مدافعاً عن حقوق العمال .. وراعياً للمصالح العليا
للوطن .. نائب ليس له مصالح شخصية من أي لون أو نوع عند جهة أو وزارة
معينة

## نائب لكل الناس

الكبير والصغير .. الغني والفقير .. القوي والضعيف .. من نعرفه ومن لا
نعرفه .. قبلي وبحري .. من انتخبنا ومن أعطي صوته لغيرنا .. يعني نائب لكل
الناس بكل ما تعنيه الكلمة .

**واليوم** .. أقدم لكم نفسي مرة ثانية آملاً أن تستمر هذه الثقة الغالية إن
شاء الله تعالي .

**لقد** شاهد الجميع وشهد علي ما قدمته في البرلمان من كلمات ومواقف
شجاعة -استجوابات وبيانات عاجلة وطلبات إحاطة- استمرنا كل الأدوات الرقابية ..
ولم نخشي في الله لومة لائم ..فلا مصالح شخصية نخاف عليها ..ولا بزنس
خاص نسعي للتوسيع فيه وهذا ما تشهد به أيضا مضابط مجلس الشعب
والصحافة وشاشة التليفزيون .

**والحمد لله** فقد تم توثيق هذه الأعمال والمواقف وتسجيلها بالصوت والصورة،
وسوف يتم عرضها علي الجماهير بكل الوسائل الممكنة ، كما يمكنك الحصول
عليها من خلال الاتصال بمكاتبنا المنتشرة في الدائرة .

**ومع ذلك** فإني أقدم لك أيها القارئ الكريم بعض من هذه المواقف لأن
المقام لا يتسع لها كلها بل لأنها وحسب طبيعة البشر منا من ينسي أحياناً ..ومنا
من لم تصله المعلومة علي الرغم من انتشارها في نطاق واسع .. ومنا من
يشكك .. وهناك من يزايد .. وهناك من يفعل كذا وكذا مما لا يعف اللسان عن
ذكره .

صحيح أنها مرحلة انتخابات .. وفيها كل شيء .. ولكننا لن نقول إلا ما يرضي

---

Figure 3. (top) Fath al-Bab's electoral leaflet "The Voice of the Workers," Tibbin/15 Mayo, 2005.

Figure 4. (below) Parts of the leaflet focusing on the Steel Workers.

---

ربنا وحده .. قلوبنا جميعاً ... كل قلوب البشر بيده سبحانه وتعالى وحده
يقلبها كيف يشاء .

**من هنا** أقول لبعض زملائي من المرشحين : أن الطريق إلى قلوب الناس
وإلى كرسي البرلمان لن يكون من خلال تشويه صورة الآخرين بالباطل ...ولن
يكون بتمزيق الدعاية واللافتات عن عمد .. ولن يكون بالوقوف في طريق من
يعمل ..ومحاولات الضرب تحت كل الوسائل الرخيصة وغير المشروعة ..إن
الوصول إلى قلوب الناس يكون من خلال مرضاة رب الناس ..وحسن الصلة
بالله والسعي بين الناس ..والنائب من خلال تعريف المرشح لنفسه أمام الجماهير
ومحاولة إقناعهم بأهليته لتمثيلهم من خلال سرد تاريخه ومواقفه وعمله
ونشاطه وخبراته في العمل العام ، أما من ليس عنده ما يقدمه للجماهير
فليجأ إلى الأساليب الأخرى فأقول له :

[نص داخل إطار أسود غير واضح]

**والآن** .. تعالوا معاً لنتذكر بعض المواقف والإنجازات .. أقول بعضها لأن
المقام لا يتسع لكثير منها :

● ضم العلاوات الاجتماعية إلى معاشات أصحاب المعاش المبكر فالكل يشهد
علي ما قدمته في هذا المجال ( مضابط مجلس الشعب - الخطابات المتبادلة
بيني وبين وزارة التأمينات الاجتماعية - شهود العيان من أهل الدائرة والذين
حضروا معي بعض المناقشات في مجلس الشعب ) .

● التصدي بكل قوة وشجاعة لمحاولة إضفاء الصناعة الوطنية :

## أولاً : الحديد والصلب :

● لن ينسى مجلس الشعب استجوابي الشهير .. الذي تحركت
بعده الحكومة وفرضت العديد من الرسوم على الواردات من الخارج .

● التصدي لمؤامرة شركة حديد أسوان حتى تم كشف أبعادها وحسمت
المحاكم أمرها .

● أعتقد أن عمال الحديد والصلب لن تنسى العديد من البيانات العاجلة
والاستجوابات الأخرى بشأن مشاكل شركة الحديد والصلب المالية وغيرها
حيث تم إعلان ذلك في التليفزيون كما تم نشره في الصحف المختلفة وفي
نشرات خاصة داخل الشركة .

---

● كما أن العمال يتذكرون جيداً يوم أن تدهور إنتاج الأفران العالية بسبب أزمة
فحم الكوك الشهيرة ...مما دفعني إلى طرح هذه القضية على مجلس الشعب
وتوالت الاجتماعات حتى تم حل هذه المشكلة بالشكل الذي يحقق مصالح
شركة الحديد والصلب وشركة الكوك .

**➤ تمليك المساكن :**

أقول بكل صدق وأمانة ... هذه القضية غير مطروحة لتكون ورقة إنتخابية أو
مجال للمزايدة من أحد .. وذلك للأسباب الآتية :

1- إن الأمر شأن داخلي يخص شركة الحديد والصلب .

2- هناك قرار من الجمعية العمومية بالموافقة على تمليك المساكن ( وهذا لا
يعلمه كثير من المزايدين على هذه القضية ... والقرار عندي مرة ..

3- تم تأجيل العمل بهذا القرار لأسباب ترجع إلى تعليب مصلحة الشركة
والعاملين بشكل عام .. قبل مصلحة الأفراد بشكل خاص وخاصة عند: إعادة
تقييم الأراضي والمدينة السكنية عند إعداد الميزانيات للتأكد على المستويات
في الدولة ( وهذا الإجراء كان يتم تحت علم وبصر وموافقة أعلى المستويات
في الدولة ، وليس في غفلة من الزمن كما يوحي للبعض أن يتوهم ) وإلا ..
لكان البديل المطروح :

تصفية الشركة طبقاً للقانون ...وهذا ما لا يمكن قبوله بأي شكل من الأشكال
ومهما كلفنا ذلك .. فبقاء الشركة واستمرارها ... وهذا ما أراه على العاملين ولصالح
الوطن أهم من تمليك بعض المساكن .

أما اليوم فالوضع أصبح مختلفاً .. خاصة بعد تحقيق الشركة لأرباح حقيقية
لأول مرة في تاريخها ... ومحاولة تكثيف الجهود لحل مشكلة المديونية
التاريخية ....لذلك فطرح الأمر سيصبح مناسباً .. ولكن من خلال القنوات
المشروعة وفي الوقت وبالشكل المناسب الذي يضمن مصلحة الشركة
ويحقق آمال العاملين .

## ثانياً : عمال النصر للسيارات

هل ننسى يوم أن أوشكت الشركة على التوقف التام بسبب عدم وجود مستلزمات
الإنتاج المستوردة ( 60 % من مكونات السيارة ) فكان التحرك السريع والجهود
الجبارة في مجلس الشعب مع كبار المسئولين لدرجة أنه تم تدبير مبلغ 30 مليون دولار
لإنقاذ الشركة .. وهذه المناسبة وإنني أتقدم بخالص الشكر
لنقابة الشركة وجميع العاملين على تقديرهم لجهودي في هذه القضية .

---

Statesmen, Businessmen, and Men of God?     71

For the members of the Brotherhood, he claims, such services would have a value that is independent of, or superior to, winning elections, since they would be undertaken with a view to carrying out God's will. Serving people and serving God are seen as two facets of the same action, which is why the idea of service is seen as taking place on a different timescale from that of an election campaign ("the Muslim Brothers have provided services for a very long time and long before they started to take part in election campaigns"). Rather than simply allowing elections to be won, service would help carry out the moral reform of society. On a personal basis, it would enable the one who serves to secure his own position in the afterlife. This discourse was not only to be found in the interviews I conducted with Fath al-Bab; it was also broadcast throughout his election campaigns. The following text appeared in a campaign leaflet produced for the 2005 elections, for example.

> People's hearts can only be reached by pleasing their Lord . . . and by ensuring that there is a good relationship to God as well as by doing good among people . . . and by the way in which the candidate presents himself to the people. He can convince them of his capacity to represent them through his past history, his convictions, his actions, and his activities and experience in public work.

The discursive repertoire of religion is used here to justify public services and to mitigate their utilitarian and strategic character. As a result, this ideological discourse does not so much rule out patronage relationships as serve to legitimate them. However, the language of religion cannot work unless it is linked to practical action. The case of Sheikh al-Muhammadi 'Abd al-Maqsud is even more significant in this regard.

### Sheikh al-Muhammadi, workers' MP for Helwan (2005–10)

> "If the slogan 'Islam Is the Solution' is employed by people who cannot be trusted, what is the value of the slogan? If the slogan and those who employ it contradict each other, it will rebound on them, and the slogan itself will be discredited."[18]

It was in these terms that Sheikh al-Muhammadi, in an interview for this study, described the supposed importance of religious discourse in mobilizing the electorate. In his view, such discourse could only work if it was supported by the candidate's continuous investment in providing social services. Sheikh al-Muhammadi perfectly embodied the local leader engaged in public work described in the previous chapter. His 2005 campaign literature gives an account of his career, illustrating it with religious quotations ("We are working to guide people on the way of God far more than we are working for ourselves" and "Indeed, my prayer, my rites of sacrifice, my living and my dying are for Allah, Lord of the worlds (Qur'an, al-An'am, 162)") (see images 5, 6 and 7).

Figure 5. Sheikh al-Muhammadi's electoral leaflet, Helwan, 2005. The last line indicates: "We are working for God far more than we are working for ourselves."
Figure 6. Verso of the leaflet titled, "Letter to the People of Helwan," reminding them of the Local Popular Council experience (1992-1997).

Born in 1945 in the Minufiyya governorate in the Delta and a graduate of a technical high school, Sheikh al-Muhammadi was later a skilled worker in the Helwan aeronautical industry at the military production plants. He began his career as an activist in the 1960s when he was in charge of the factory-based section of the Nasserist Socialist Youth Organization, before experiencing a "reorientation toward Islamic activism," according to his 2005 campaign leaflet, in the 1970s. Being the head of a local-development association (*tanmiyyat al-mugtama'*), he was also the founder of the local mosque in Madinat al-Huba in 1971. This served as the anchor of a local branch of the Gam'iyya al-Shar'iyya, which by 2002 had more than four hundred members and possessed a hospital, several schools, and an extensive care program for orphans. It had thiry offices, and more than thirty thousand people benefited from its services. However, Sheikh al-Muhammadi was ousted from his position as director of the branch by State Security in 1990 on the grounds that he had stood in the 1987 parliamentary elections on the Islamic Alliance list in the former South Cairo constituency.[19] However, despite his 'official' departure from the Gam'iyya al-Shar'iyya in 1990, fifteen years later he was still strongly connected to the association in the memory of local people.

Figure 7. Sheikh al-Muhammadi's electoral leaflet, Helwan, 2005. The first line is a Quranic verse: "Indeed, my prayers, my rites of sacrifice, my living and my dying, are for God, Lord of the Worlds."

The powerful influence of the Gam'iyya al-Shar'iyya probably explains why the Islamic Alliance list, led by Sheikh al-Muhammadi, won all the seats in the Helwan LPC in the 1992 elections. This remarkable victory, unparalleled elsewhere, was explained by Sheikh al-Muhammadi as a sign of the "popular reaction" to his being ousted by force from the Gam'iyya. He also emphasized the paramount importance of the role he had played in the LPC in paving his way to parliament not only because of the services that he had been able to provide through it, but also because of the relations he had been able to foster with local state officials. "We changed the face of Helwan between 1992 and 1997 thanks to the services we were able to provide in terms of piped water and sewerage," he said. Sheikh al-Muhammadi also made no attempt to hide his *nufudh* with some of the local authorities. Finally, also during the 1990s he became a leading figure in the Labor Party, setting up various party bureaus in Helwan through which he continued his social work and climbed up the party ladder until he reached the national level.[20]

In his electoral leaflets, Sheikh al-Muhammadi laid claim to "forty-two years immersed in local society," seeing this as a source of strength and describing himself as a "natural leader." In our interviews, he explained how his legitimacy relied on his sharing in the everyday lives of the local people. He stood ready, he added, to come to their aid at any moment.

> For the Brothers, a leader is not someone who is born in a day, but instead is someone who has always been present in a society and cannot be separated from it because of his deep roots within it. People knew me before I was elected to any position. For example, I played a role in the popular justice committees to find solutions to marriage problems, as well as problems with neighbors, in the family, with local businessmen or at work. . . . If someone had experienced a bereavement in the family, I was always there to present my condolences. I used to help people if there had been a fire in an apartment, helping them to repaint it and refurnish it. If someone was marrying off a daughter, I would go along to congratulate him, and if he needed anything, I would help him. . . . The intellectual class *(tabaqat al-muthaqqafin)* always want a program, but normal people *(al-nas al-'adiyya)* feel that the program is the candidate himself. If they trust a person, they will vote for him, because they know that he will always be at their side just as he always has been.

The idea of "roots" came up often in interviews with Sheikh al-Muhammadi, as it did in the way he described his own career, in his leaflets, and in his articles in local newspapers. Whatever the voters might make of it, it was an essential part of his strategies of self-presentation, the performative dimensions of which could not be ignored. An article that appeared in the newspaper *Nuhud Helwan* after Sheikh al-Muhammadi's 2005 election victory was entitled "Honesty, Historic Authenticity, Deep Roots, Forceful Gifts—Such Are the Qualities That Have Made This a Well-deserved Victory,"[21] for example. "Rootedness" here, depending on daily public service rather than on an idea of origins, was seen by the sheikh as a kind of moral guarantee of good conduct.

> The Brothers possess credibility *(misdaqiya)* among the people because they are men of principle *(ashab mabda')* who don't change their views. . . . They are rooted in society *(nebt al-mugtama')*. They are the bearers not of tradition, but of conviction and of the conscious awareness that the country must experience freedom and well-being

*(nuhud)*. Not a single Brother has ever forgotten the people or neglected them after being elected. Not one has lived in palaces while the people live in tombs *('a'ish fi-l-qusur wa huma fi-l-qubur)*.

What distinguished the Brotherhood candidate from others here was the fact that not only was he already (and had been for many years) in the service of the community, but also that he would remain in that community's service, since public service for him was a matter of principle. From this came the idea that if the sheikh did not hesitate to assert a direct link between the vote of the electorate and his service to the community, this was in order to underline the durability of that service, his own disinterestedness, and the fact that he personally did not benefit from it.

> People voted for me because they wanted to be closer to the man who had helped them and wanted to say that they understood what he was going through, as one day that man had been there for them. On polling day, one old woman came limping into the polling station as she had got so tired walking all the way through the streets. People said, "Why are you tiring yourself out like that? You should stay at home instead." But she said, "No, this man has helped me such a lot over the years that I wanted to make sure I came to give him my vote today." She wanted to pay me back *(al-muqabil)* for what I had done.

While the sheikh spoke of *al-muqabil* (payback) here, it was not to emphasize the strategic character of the services rendered. On the contrary, what he was trying to do was to transform the system of rendering services in return for a vote (the service/vote system) into one of gift and counter-gift, the 'gift' here being a gift of the self. As a result, the *muqabil* was not so much a matter of recognizing the existence of a debt as of engaging in an act of pure recognition. As Pierre Bourdieu put it, this manner of transforming clientelist practices into disinterested ones "represses the objective truth of practices" brought to light through the analysis by hiding it behind a subjective feeling. Yet this subjective feeling of disinterestedness, which Bourdieu calls the "lived truth of practices," should not be seen as a "cynical lie," but instead as "part of the truth of practices in their complete definition" (Bourdieu 1998: 114). In other words, it is not a matter of trying to decide on the sincerity of the intentions of the sheikh in this example, but rather of seeking to analyze how such repeated discursive acts can produce a symbolic economy of disinterestedness. Two main components of this economy are the *religious motivation of service* and the *long-term temporal framework* within which it is carried out, which make such service appear to be independent of electoral considerations (see Table 9).

**Table 9. Six Aspects of the Symbolic Economy of Disinterestedness**

| Religious motivation of service | Transformation of social service into a moral and religious principle<br>Activities of candidates in religious organizations plus the 'giving of the self' on an everyday basis |
|---|---|
| Timeframe of services | Local embedding of the candidates over the long term<br>Services provided long before and after elections |
| Dissimulation of Brotherhood identity | Services provided through semi-state structures<br>Never explicitly admitting membership in the Brotherhood |
| Effacement of the individual self | Principle of 'talib al-wilaya la yuwwala' (the one who asks to govern does not do so)<br>Mobilization of the entire activist group and collective organization |
| Collective mediation | Co-engagement of personal activist networks<br>Involvement of local notables and popular leaders (notable mediation) |
| Symbolic staging | Theatralization (doctors seen by the side of the poor and *masirat* as expressions of collective action)<br>Consideration given to voters (good manners, individual attention, provision of information, emphasis on awareness-raising and positivity) |

An examination of the case of 'Isam Mukhtar in Madinat Nasr, much less well known on a local level and having a correspondingly lesser capacity to arrange social services, draws attention to two other aspects of the symbolic economy. The first is the way in which his identity as a Muslim Brother was concealed and the second the self-effacement of the individual when compared to the collective.

## 'Isam Mukhtar, workers' MP for Madinat Nasr (2005–10)

Born in Cairo in 1961 and also a graduate of a technical high school, 'Isam Mukhtar started working as an employee for one of the major public-sector oil companies in Egypt in 1982. In 1993, he ran in the LPC elections for the neighboring *qism* (district) without revealing his identity as a member of the Brotherhood. This disguise allowed him to play a social role in his workplace, where he was a member of the board of the company's Pilgrimage Association, and it was this charitable activity that provided the springboard for his candidature in the company union elections in 1995. It was also the role that he played in the workplace that led to his being selected as a low-profile candidate in the 1995 parliamentary elections.[22]

However, Mukhtar had been engaged in few activities outside his professional milieu. It was not until 2004 that he set up a *zakat* committee at the Gam'iyya al-Shar'iyya mosque in the popular district of Qattamiyya, his place of residence. Nevertheless, when he announced he would be standing in the legislative elections on the eve of the final deadline for submitting candidatures, the committee was shut down by the authorities: as treasurer, Mukhtar was accused of using *zakat* funds to finance his campaign, and a court case was filed against him. Up until that day, Makarim al-Diri, the MB's sole female candidate in the 2005 elections, was the only candidate standing for the *fi'at* seat in the constituency. The announcement of Mukhtar's candidacy at the last minute as the Brotherhood candidate for the workers' seat thus created some surprise. He was not particularly well known to the security services, and he said that his candidacy in this election was the first real occasion on which he had publicly announced his identity as a Brother.

While it said something about how little known Mukhtar was in the local community, his earlier disguise of his identity as a member of the Brotherhood was also not without its positive aspects. For one thing, Mukhtar used it as 'proof' that he had been providing services to members of the local community over the years without at any time explicitly seeking to link these to the Brotherhood and *as if* these services had been entirely disinterested.

> During the elections, people found out that the person [he was speaking about himself] who had stood up for them had been a member of the Brotherhood. They therefore looked back at the experience they had had of this person. People know that I serve as their voice because I live among them and I provide services for them independently of elections because doing so is part of my religion. People will always find me to be the first person they can turn to, because when I am helping them, I am also satisfying God. Therefore, it doesn't much matter if the media attempts to blacken the reputation of the Brothers, saying that they are extremists or terrorists . . . when you deal with me you will no longer believe any of that, since you have already been able to test me out even before the elections when you did not know that I was a member of the Brotherhood.[23]

The selection of a little-known candidate like Mukhtar was also presented during the election campaign as proof of his lack of any egotistical motivation. He was not seeking personal gain, since he had not chosen to run as a candidate, something which Mukhtar himself explained in an interview published during his 2005 campaign.

> We Muslim Brothers do not put ourselves forward as candidates ourselves, and we do not seek any kind of worldly position. Instead, we joyfully align ourselves with the wishes of the Brothers and

their decisions, and we agree to bear the burdens that are put upon us. Perhaps my consistent presence in the constituency over the past few years and the services that God has allowed me to deliver in it through charitable activities and the *zakat* committee have made the organization look favorably on my candidacy.[24]

All the MPs and Brotherhood leaders that I interviewed referred to a principle of Islamic law in this regard that says that "the one who asks to govern does not do so"*(talib al-wilaya la yuwwala)* precisely in order to deflect any suspicion of acting out of self-interest.[25] In this way, religious discourse was once again mobilized in order to emphasize the personal humility of the candidates concerned.

However, such strategies of self-presentation, or rather of self-effacement, would probably not have been enough in themselves to make up for Mukhtar's lack of a public profile and his limited capacity to provide services in a constituency as large and as fragmented as Madinat Nasr. It was here that the Gama'a's organization and networks—the *tanzim*—took on their full importance. As one of the activists working for Mukhtar's election campaign said, "'Isam Mukhtar's activities on the *zakat* committee have only made him popular in his own neighborhood. I myself didn't know him at all. However, the Brothers put out information supporting his candidacy."[26] As a result, Mukhtar was introduced into a larger local network, in which each member had been expressly instructed to work to ensure the victory of the MB candidate in the constituency. This form of collective mediation, seen in all three of the constituencies studied, is the fifth aspect of the symbolic economics of disinterestedness identified above, all the more so as it extended beyond the Brotherhood networks and included intermediaries outside the tanzim.

## "A House Does Not Only Have Foundations"

Mukhtar himself emphasized the importance of collective mediation by saying:

> In the street marches *(masirat)* organized by the Brothers the Sisters come with their children, holding them with one arm while holding up a flag with the other. They pay with their own money to come in order to make sure that the Brotherhood candidate wins, because this is what they want, whereas the other parties are all obliged to pay people to come to their meetings. Everyone taking part is sure that the candidate's success will be a success for the group as a whole. Everyone plays his part to make sure that the outcome is a success; it is a complementary work *('amal mutakamil)*.[27]

In fact, the modus operandi employed by MB activists in the election campaigns contrasted strongly with that used by political parties. Not only were the Brotherhood's resources more extensive, but they were also used in a more rational fashion thanks to the hierarchical structure of the *tanzim* in which local units, or *shu'ab*,[28] in the same constituency operated in a coordinated way. In the 2005 elections, systematic use was also made of individually tailored methods to canvas voters and to 'produce voters.'

However, while he recognized the important role played by the large team of highly engaged MB activists that worked with him during his election campaign, Sheikh al-Muhammadi of the Helwan constituency also made mischievous mention of a second aspect of this collective mediation.

> A house does not only have foundations . . . the Brothers constitute the foundations, and the edifice as a whole would not be possible without them. . . . But then people see this edifice and it is their actions which complete it.[29]

While it made up the foundations of the electoral edifice, the team of activists working to make sure the MB candidate was elected did not hesitate to approach individuals and groups outside *tanzim* networks and to solicit their support.

### Producing Voters

A flyer circulated in Helwan during the 2005 election campaign bore a picture of the sheikh next to a copy of the Qur'an illuminated by a ray of light on one side. On the other side, a hand was shown pointing to the sky and clutching an Egyptian flag in such a way that the hand and the flag were inextricably intertwined (see image 8).

The aim of this iconography was not only to present the sheikh as a candidate who was morally accountable to God, since he was presented as having sworn 'on the Qur'an,' but it was also intended to link his religious credentials to his civic ones in that the hand pointing to the sky, signifying that God was watching, was intertwined with the national flag. The flyer carried two slogans: the traditional "Islam the Solution" and another one that became a leitmotif of the 2005 election campaign, "Together, we are working for the good of Egypt" *(ma'an nuhaqiqu al-khayr li-Misr)*. The latter played on the multiple meanings of the word *khayr*, signifying at the same time 'welfare,' 'fulfillment,' and the idea of good as opposed to evil. The text of the flyer read, "Brother Voter, Sister Voter: *sawtak amana* [meaning both your vote is your conscience and it morally binds us], and we expect your vote. Don't waste your vote, as it is a hope of change. Work with us to bring about reform." The MB candidates were not the only ones who used the expression "*sawtak amana*." But they put particular emphasis on the double meaning, civic and religious, of the word "conscious," as is illustrated in this extract from a tract produced by 'Ali Fath al-Bab aimed at steelworkers:

> The people [al-gamahir] are conscious to the highest point ['ala daraga 'aliya giddan min al-wa'i]. . . . and are fully awakened [sahiya giddan] . . . and they refuse to allow defamation or attacks on the sanctity of the lives of others . . . in the same way that they refuse to allow clannishness or sectarianism if not for the sake of law and reform. . . . One thing is certain: only their conscientiousness (damiraha) can tell the people how to conduct themselves in the polling booth. . . . Consciousness is one . . . and we all know that God is forgiving, but not careless, and that he will not set at naught the reward of the one who has worked the best.[30]

Figure 8. Sheikh al-Muhammadi's electoral leaflet, Helwan, 2005: "Sawtak amana"

In contrast to the accusations of apathy frequently made by the Egyptian media and political elite against the country's voters, the emphasis here is on the idea of an electorate that is fully aware of what is going on around it. The voters are conscious in the sense of being informed (wa'i), awake, and attentive (sahi), and thus capable of discernment, but also in the ethical sense of being morally conscious or conscientious (al-damir) and subject to God's judgment. While the voters are seen as being part of the collective (al-gamahir), their identity as individuals is shaped by their intellectual and above all their moral capacities. Understood in this way, the individual voter is seen as being partly responsible for the social and political order.

He is presented as being alone, in possession of his consciousness/conscientiousness, before God in the polling booth, and he is presented as choosing "the one who has worked the best"—in other words, the candidate who has made the best efforts to serve the people and to satisfy God.

Rhetoric of this sort was accompanied by intense efforts to mobilize the voters behind MB candidates in the 2005 campaigns, with these voters being seen as conscious individuals and not as passive members of a group controlled by local notables. While it is difficult to measure the effects of such efforts, two hypotheses can be advanced.

Firstly, they may have had an effect on turnout in the elections, which increased between 2000 and 2005 and particularly in the Madinat Nasr constituency, where the turnout nearly doubled. While this was not due solely to the activities of the Brothers, their efforts intended to reshape an electorate that had previously been 'left to rot.' One of the most successful methods used in areas lived in by white-collar workers and executives in Madinat Nasr was door-to-door canvassing (*tarq al-abwab*), in which young activists, in groups of two and elegantly attired, would go from door to door throughout the district to raise the awareness of elite residents of the need to take part in the elections and to help them to do so. This was because, while the voters in these districts had a greater amount of social and cultural capital than those living in the popular areas, they often had more problems when it came to actually going out to vote. Fewer of them had voting cards (necessary to vote in the 2005 elections), and fewer of them were aware of the procedures that needed to be followed, since the regime had deliberately sought to limit turnouts in previous elections. In particular, many such voters simply did not know where they were supposed to vote or at which polling station they were registered. This information was kept by the local authorities and the ruling NDP, allowing regime agents and their *mandubin* to control groups of voters. While all the candidates could ask for copies of the electoral roll, a technical issue made this useless for the purposes of canvassing voters, since before the 2005 elections the electoral roll was only available to non-NDP candidates in paper format and the names of voters were not given in alphabetical order. However, in 2005 Brotherhood activists managed to type up the electoral roll and produce digital versions of it, allowing them not only to search for the names of the voters more easily, but also to tell them which polling station they were supposed to go to in order to vote. By creating these digital versions of the electoral roll, MB activists were able to use the lists effectively in preparation for the polls, during doorstep meetings, and on polling day itself, when they would appear outside the polling stations armed with laptop computers. All this represented an extension of the idea of service, one that reached out to social categories that did not exactly require material assistance, but that could benefit from help navigating the state bureaucracy. According to Singerman, the latter kind of help should be considered no less important, as it supplied a need that was a fundamental feature of political exclusion in Egypt (Singerman 1995).

Secondly, canvassing voters as individuals had cognitive effects since it was a sign of distinctiveness in Egyptian electoral politics. Well-off individuals were usually not the focus of such politics, and they used to show the highest record of abstention in elections. For them, the fact of being solicited for a vote by young people "who are educated and make a good impression"[31] was in itself a non-negligible factor. This effort to "make a good impression" aimed to counteract the terrifying image of the Gama'a served up by media loyal to the regime. The flyers handed out during the door-to-door canvassing aimed to present a reassuring image of the Muslim Brothers, with photographs of Hassan al-Banna and later guides of the organization appearing next to the question "Who are we, and what do we want?" An answer consisting of fifteen points was given. Emphasizing their vision of Islam as a whole system, the text of this flyer underlined the moderation of the Brothers' conceptions of religion and of their methods ("We do not claim to be above criticism," it read), and it informed readers of the organization's long history and the extent of its influence worldwide. At the same time, it hammered home the idea that the Muslim Brothers were attached to their country, while explaining the importance of the Islamic umma and emphasizing their engagement in support of the Palestinian cause. Two paragraphs were also devoted to the idea that "you [the voters] should not despair, since despair is not part of the Muslim ethics, and the rights of today were the dreams of yesterday, and the dreams of today will be the rights of tomorrow," along with the role of the Brothers in "spreading the spirit of hope in the hearts of Muslims."

Combining civic and religious morality together once again, such efforts to produce voters went hand in hand with an appeal to the positivity that each citizen had within himself. This was explained by Mustafa, a young activist working for the Mukhtar team in Madinat Nasr who was also responsible for the organization of the campaign.

> Our main message is to say, "Be positive and take part in the elections." The young activists use two methods of doing this, one religious and the other intellectual *('aqliya)*. The intellectual method means convincing people that their votes can change the situation, like what happened in Ukraine and Latin America, the idea being to spread hope in people's hearts. The religious method means saying "Your voice is your conscience." "God will hold you accountable on this, since our religion rejects being retiring or passive and encourages participation and a positive attitude."[32]

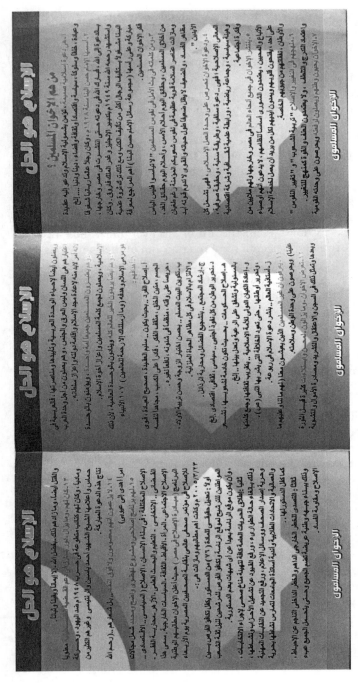

Figure 9. 'Isam Mukhtar's electoral leaflet, titled "Who are the Brothers?" Madinat Nasr, 2005.

The intensity with which the work was carried out and the efforts made to adapt the Brotherhood's discourse to different groups in the constituency also impressed an independent journalist who covered the elections, someone who was by no means a sympathizer of the Gama'a.

> What made the difference was above all the fact that the Brothers showed themselves to be educated and cultivated, while the people working for the NDP and those assisting their candidates unfortunately were absolutely not. Individuals posted to stand in front of the polling stations did not know how to speak to people, whereas the Brothers were very well organized. When a voter arrived at the polling station who was not registered on that station's list, they would look on their laptop computers to find out which station he was registered at and then direct him to it. If you had asked the same thing of someone working for the NDP, he would not have been able to help you. In addition, the NDP did not know how to rationally plan a campaign, and it carried it out in a chaotic manner. People working for the NDP would ask people living in certain districts to talk to others about their candidate, but this would not cover the whole constituency. The Brothers, on the other hand, would take part in marches every day, each time in a different district, and use them to talk to people in the streets and in neighborhood cafés. . . . People could see how well-organized and "civilized" they were because they were educated. For example, the Brothers set up a mini puppet theater about elections near the exit of a cinema in a local shopping mall. People coming out of the cinema saw it and reacted very positively to it. So, in my view the two reasons for their success are the level of education of their members (muthaqqafin) and their good organization (takhtit).[33]

This account emphasizes the new techniques of information, communication, and public education that the Brothers used in reaching out to voters in the constituency, breaking with the conventional methods used in ordinary campaigns. The introduction of a mini puppet theater also indicates the importance they gave to the way in which such mobilization was presented, even theatricalized. This was also the aim of the campaign marches (masirat) that they held. The idea of the marches was to take over public space in a disciplined way and without disorder, aiming to be more reassuring than frightening to those around them and making sure that women and children were placed in prominent positions.[34]

Women were also at the forefront of the Brothers' election campaign in 15 Mayo City. In the mugawarat (residential blocs), women had tightly knit social networks thanks to the welfare associations and Qur'an recital classes at the local mosques of which they were members, as well as through daily neighborhood visits. According to Salma, in charge of the women's section of Fath al-Bab's campaign team since 1995, door-to-door canvassing in the constituency was undertaken by women because "they can enter houses more easily" than men. She also said that on polling day groups of women had "secured" the transportation of the ballot boxes from the polling stations to the places where the votes were counted by closely following the vehicles carrying them.[35] Like the young and educated Brothers who had made such a good impression in Madinat Nasr, the mobilization of female MB supporters in 15 Mayo acted as a sign of distinctiveness, setting the Brotherhood off from its competitors, who had very little of this sort of thing to fall back upon. Voters were encouraged to take part in the elections by the Brotherhood's strategy of mobilizing its weakest supporters, including women, old people, and even children, who according to Salma "handed out fruit juice in the street," in sharp contrast to the violence and repression that usually characterize Egyptian elections. The use of women in the election campaigns turned out to be a powerful advantage for the Brothers, and the scenes of women (not only Muslim Sisters) climbing ladders to get over the walls of polling stations blocked by the security forces on polling day were among the most memorable images of the 2005 elections (Blaydes 2009).

The importance of neighborhood networks, emphasized by Salma, also indicates that despite the urban character of the 15 Mayo constituency, people's direct knowledge of each other was a major resource, even if, unlike in the informal districts where the limits of people's direct knowledge of each other would be defined by the *hara* (alley) in which they lived, the relevant unit was the apartment building. Women members of the Gama'a, but also male doctors, pharmacists, teachers, lawyers, and shopkeepers, could be expected to invest a lot of their time building relationships with their neighbors, and this meant that the Brotherhood's *tanzim* networks could be extended by the social networks of its individual activists in what might be called the sharing of personal networks for electoral purposes. According to Mustafa, in Madinat Nasr a "committee of personalities for mobilization" was formed, consisting of Muslim Brothers who were also "well-known personalities."

> People did not know anything about 'Isam Mukhtar, but the Brotherhood personalities persuaded them to vote for him because people trust them and can turn to them for help if they have a problem.

In the Helwan constituency, the sheikh also relied upon the personal social networks of members of his campaign team and particularly on those who "had their own *'asabiyya*."[36] A good example of this was Ayman, the son of a leading Helwan family and a leading figure on the sheikh's staff, who was also selected as the substitute candidate for the sheikh and succeeded in winning a significant number of votes in a sign of his own personal popularity. (A substitute candidate stands for election to the same seat as the main candidate and replaces him in cases where the latter is unable to stand at the last minute because of action by the security services.)

However, besides the networks provided by the activists, there were also other non-Brotherhood individuals, notables of different sorts, making up additional and more open networks with deep roots in the local community. These intermediaries, not part of the MB *tanzim*, proved indispensable in reaching into districts where the Brotherhood had little local presence.

### External Networks: The *'Izba* Politics

The individuals making up these external networks were described as the "keys" to the districts in question or as popular "ambassadors" by former deputy guide of the Gama'a Mohamed Habib.

> A personality is the key *(muftah)* to a district and someone whom it is absolutely necessary to approach before being able to address people directly. In Cairo, there are such personalities in the apartment blocks in the different districts who are distinguished by their presence among other people and by the respect and esteem with which they are treated. As a result, if we can manage to persuade people of this type to be our ambassadors *(sufara' lana)* to the wider population, we have won. We speak to such people and tell them what we would be able to do for them were we to be in parliament, and eventually they are persuaded so that they put us in contact with those close to them as well as members of their entourage and family.[37]

The deputy guide was vague about the precise content of such exchanges, but he saw it as being very much related to the idea of service ("what we would be able to do for them were we to be in parliament"). The example of the election campaign in 'Izbat al-Haggana, a large informal area of Madinat Nasr, makes the content of such exchanges clearer.

According to Mustafa, responsible for Mukhtar's campaign, while "the Brothers do not win the most votes in the informal areas," the group of activists to which he belonged made particular efforts to reach them. Aged only twenty-five at the time of the elections and recently qualified as a dentist, Mustafa described with some emotion how he and his colleagues, often students of medicine or engineering, had gone to "see people in their homes and cafés, stay with them, sit down with them on the ground, and talk with them, as these people feel forgotten." He added that "we are not the state, and our capacities and resources are limited," but that "people's dreams in these districts are very straightforward, and they are only asking for small things." As a result, the Brothers were able to provide services that were inexpensive but had a strong symbolic charge.

> For example, there was an area full of rubbish in 'Izbat al-Haggana that the local people asked us to clean up. So, we rented the necessary equipment, put on old clothing, and planted trees in the area to replace the rubbish. Even today, people remember this episode, and what touched them the most was that we had done it with our own hands. After the elections, we went back every two months to sit with people in cafés and in the street, and as a result they were able to see that we were on their side and not like the NDP, which people only see during elections.

This story shows the way in which MB activists sought to make up for their lack of material resources (compared to the NDP) by staging a reversal of roles in which doctors and engineers gave up their time, sat on the ground, and put on old clothes in order to clear up the rubbish of the poor. However, this type of activity was only possible when local personalities who were not part of the activist network assisted in mediating between the Brotherhood activists and the local population, particularly since the Brothers themselves very rarely lived in 'Izbat al-Haggana. Such personalities could include anything from the local *baltagi* (strongman) to the local imam and could include popular leaders such as Hagg Nabil, who was a perfect example.

> Mustafa al-Sallab will buy you by giving you money. He is all about *gineh*.[38] (Silence). *Gineh gineh*. No doubt about it! He is a millionaire. Money—with money he does everything, meaning that he buys people. He supplies food in Ramadan and blankets in winter. But he doesn't give any of these things to the people directly. He gives them to the *samasir* (brokers) so that they will work for him in the elections. . . . But giving money like that is *haram* (immoral). Isn't your voice your conscience *(mish sawtak amana)*? The Brothers can't behave like that. So they provide services instead, like solving water problems, or engaging in charitable activities . . . things that are in the general interest. So, helping them is an honor *(sharaf)* for me.

### Hagg Nabil, popular leader of 'Izbat al-Haggana

Hagg Nabil, a baker by trade, was born in another Cairo district and moved to 'Izbat al-Haggana in the 1970s when he was twenty-two years old.[39] His father, also a baker, gave him a taste for charity work; Hagg Nabil commented that "he always gave some bread to those who were hungry, and he used to tell me to give my clothes to children in need even though we ourselves did not have much money." When he arrived in the 'Izba, together with a group of friends he began "to organize in order to collect money and help those in need." Over time, and as a result of his informal charity work, Hagg Nabil established a reputation in the district. A charismatic figure, he was also good-humored while having a certain authority.

"How does one become a popular leader?" he asked. "It is one's love for people that makes them listen to what one has to say. If you love them, they will listen to you, like children listen to their father. You also need to have clean hands *(nazif al-yid)*. This means that I have no personal interests invested in what I do; my interest is in *khayr* (welfare, goodness) and nothing else. I was once invited to join the NDP and to be a member of the local council. I said no. I am independent, and I am not looking for a position. I am not with the Brothers either. I am someone who keeps himself apart, someone who is himself alone *(haga li-wahdaha)*. I am not like anyone else. There are many people who are better than me, but people like me as I am: independent. However, if I had to be something, it would be with the Brothers, as their approach and their principles are the right ones *(al-nahg sahh, al-mabda' sahh)* from the beginning and at the roots *(min al-asl, al-guzur)*. Hagg Nabil's apartment was on the first floor of one of the red brick buildings that fill Egypt's informal areas, and it had no pretensions. He continues: "I met Dr. Mustafa through the charity work. As I know the people here well, I was able to tell him who really needed help."

During the election campaign, it was Hagg Nabil who helped the Brothers to organize a popular *masira* in the 'Izba, and it was he who led the march with the MB candidates, presenting them to the local people and persuading the latter to take part in the *masira* as well. "That *masira*—you have never seen anything like it. Normally when a new candidate makes himself known, nothing like that happens. It was huge. Everybody was in the streets, from the entrance to the 'Izba, and with their cars, horns, flags, and children with them. We have never been able to organize anything like it up to now . . . even though usually when it is an NDP candidate he comes to see me very readily." Hagg Nabil paused for effect, as he was very often solicited by the candidates during elections. "It was a wonderful *masira*, and people were happy. I presented Mr. 'Isam Mukhtar to them, and I said, 'Hey, guys, this one has very clean hands, and he wants to do good. Tell people around you about him.' So, when people love me, and when I love them, when they see me with him at the *masira* or at the polling station, that encourages them to vote for him. Their love for me makes them understand that what I say is true. In the end, Dr. 'Isam won."[40]

Hagg Nabil drew a clear distinction between his own role and that of the *samasir*, or election agents, who only worked during each election season. He said:

> The *samasir* are often members of the local councils. They take people's voting cards, including from very poor people who don't know what an election is. They then keep their cards, giving them some money in exchange, and go and vote in their place. Either that or they hand out money, food bags, or sandwiches in front of the polling stations and tell people who to vote for. But I never take people's voting cards. I tell them that they should vote for Dr. 'Isam, or someone else, why? Because I know that he will do the work, and he won't put anything into his own pockets. People listen to me because of my morality. I have never said I would do something and then not done it. . . . One day, a *simsar* asked me how many votes I had. I said, 'Forget about it—you don't have enough to pay me.'

According to Hagg Nabil, 'Abd al-Mun'im 'Imara, the NDP MP in the 1995–2000 parliament, also "did something" for the residents of the 'Izba. He had brought in piped water, but that "was to win the next elections." "How do I know that the Brothers are not doing what they are doing just to win? It's simple. The NDP will come to see you and give you LE10,000. They say, 'take that and get us as many votes as possible.' Does the NDP want to use me? I won't serve them. The Brothers don't do that. That's all. And it is from this that they get their credibility (*khadu al-misdaqiyya min hina*)."

In a system where the NDP candidate made greater use of electoral brokers and monetary transactions than of negotiations with lesser notables, people like Hagg Nabil risked losing their positions of authority. Their desire to keep their social prestige intact could thus lead them to work with candidates, such as the MB ones, who were looking for their help because they either did not want to rely or could not rely on financial resources. 'Isam Mukhtar's victory in the elections came as a source of comfort to Hagg Nabil in his role as an intermediary between the district's residents and its MP. He was happy to produce documents showing the actions undertaken by 'Isam Mukhtar since the election, including the construction of a new access road to the 'Izba at his request, and thus to satisfy demands made by the area's residents over more than a decade. In opposing honor (*sharaf*) to money, he was also signaling his desire to preserve his image as a man of integrity ("Isn't your voice your conscience?"). He linked his social authority tightly to his morality and considered himself to be bound by a moral contract to the groups that he controlled, from which came his "duty" to support the candidate whose hands were perceived to be as "clean" as his own. In Hagg Nabil's view, by rejecting the use of money but emphasizing the provision of services in the "general interest," the Muslim Brothers were keeping their "hands clean." The *masira* of historic size that he described manifested this care for the general interest, since "everyone was outside." His description of it placed the candidate, his intermediary, and the local voters in a configuration dedicated to collective action that would demonstrate the moral motivation of the participants. It was this motivation that constituted the comparative advantage of the Brotherhood candidate when faced by competitors better provided with material resources.

A similar way of thinking could be found in statements made by another lesser notable, the head of a leading family in a popular area of Alexandria, the aptly named Hagg Muftah (which translates literally as 'key').

> I didn't support the Brothers in 2005, as I was supporting a relative of mine who was the NDP candidate. However, today I regret that choice. While he was a relative, he has done nothing for "us," and he has not given us any of the things he promised. So, another time I won't support the NDP. In any case, they don't do anything. I prefer to support the Brothers, even if they can't arrange major services, like having the streets resurfaced. But *at least they try*.[41]

The moral motivation of the Brothers was seen here as indicating a *willingness* to do something, which was seen as more valuable than the supposed *capacity* to do something enjoyed by the NDP. While the "morality" of the MB candidate benefited the popular leaders who did not 'dirty their hands' in supporting him, the opposite was also true, since in giving him their support the popular leaders guaranteed the "morality" of the MB candidate. This phenomenon might be termed 'notable mediation,' and was a significant part of the symbolic economy of disinterestedness promoted by the Gama'a.

In Helwan, Sheikh al-Muhammadi signaled the importance of this 'notable mediation,' in this case by capturing intermediaries usually used by the NDP. He said:

> There are four sorts of popular leaders who deal with the NDP: those looking for personal prestige (al-wagaha); those looking for money (al-ghana'im); those who have something preying on their minds and are looking for protection; and finally those who want to serve their country out of conviction. It is the latter who come to us. They do not always have the means to resist (yuqawimu) the blandishments of the NDP candidate, and they feel ill at ease and do not know what to do. But in 2005, they didn't want the NDP candidate who was not from here, and they wanted to have someone that they would see more often, someone to whom they could speak, and someone who would be present in the constituency. All this came about quite naturally.

The interrelationship between the NDP and MB networks at the local level could be seen clearly here. The Brothers were able to use the NDP client system, borrowing certain elements from it[42] and drawing distinctions between good and bad agents of the NDP and between self-interested intermediaries and popular leaders serving out of genuine conviction (and not out of a desire for personal prestige, wealth, or impunity) who might join the Brothers in an act of resistance (muqawama). This showed the ways in which client relationships could be subtly politicized.

## Conclusion

This chapter has explored the local operation of the six aspects of the symbolic economy of disinterestedness used by the Muslim Brothers as part of their election strategies (see Table 9). References to Islam were an integral part of this symbolic economy. Articulated around a discourse of giving and the giving of the self, religion was emphasized as a morally disinterested source of motivation and as a guarantee of moral probity far more than as part of an ideological program. This religious discourse was also often hybridized, being mixed with other discursive elements such as worker solidarity, rootedness, or civic morality (sawtak amana). But as the statements made by the sheikh indicated, "If the slogan 'Islam Is the solution' and the person pronouncing it contradict each other, this can have significant repercussions and reduce its credibility." It was thus not enough to invoke the name of Islam in order to profit from it. During Mubarak's rule, religion was used by many candidates (Haenni 2005a) and not just by those from the Brotherhood. For example, in Tibbin, Mustafa Bakri and the NDP candidates reproduced the same verses from the Qur'an in their electoral tracts as those found in material produced by Sheikh al-Muhammadi in Helwan.[43] In fact, references to Islam in politics at this time functioned as a kind of "discursive policy" (in the sense used by Foucault). From the 1970s onward, power struggles taking place in the political realm had used Islamic references as a way of closing down competition and displacing political debates onto religious and moral terrain, where they became debates about religious orthodoxy without calling into question social relationships and domination (Ismail 2003).

As a result, the Brotherhood election candidates did not seek to mark their differences from others only by the use of Islamic references. It was the way in which they used these that was more important. They tried to make their religious discourse credible by deploying continuous practices of service; by establishing themselves in religious charitable structures (Islamic associations, mosques, and *zakat* committees) that allowed them to gain access to spaces that were otherwise tightly controlled (such as the Tibbin steelworks and the oil company in Madinat Nasr); by staging themselves as being on the side of local residents and having genuine consideration for them; and by making use of the networks of activists and intermediaries that carried out more systematic electoral work, gave a collective character to popular mobilization, and camouflaged the personal interests of a given candidate. In sum, the use of religion, with its discursive, organizational, and behavioral components, was part of a larger and more complex symbolic economy.

This symbolic economy functioned as a way of compensating for the MB's limited access to public resources when compared to the NDP candidates. However, it was also a reflection of the social and political existence of the Brotherhood under the conditions of open secrecy. The intertwining of different networks, the importance of local friendships, the greater or lesser dissimulation of Brotherhood identity, and the presentation of the self as a model of morality were all fundamental aspects of the social anchoring of the Gama'a on an everyday basis and not only during election periods. The following chapters investigate these things more fully.

# 3

# Banned MPs

The Muslim Brotherhood MPs in the 2005–10 Parliament embodied a flagrant paradox: how was it possible to have been legally elected to parliament and yet at the same time be members of a banned organization? The election of these men significantly altered the terms of the 'public secret' of the Brotherhood. We have already seen that their election campaigns had been a kind of 'public emergence' for MB candidates. Following their election, the presence of these 'forbidden MPs' in parliament, now too many and too obviously members of the Brotherhood to be ignored, continued to disturb the public/secret equilibrium that had underpinned the modus vivendi between the Gama'a and the Mubarak regime.

Such disturbances should also be seen in a larger sociopolitical context that contained its own paradoxes. Immediately after the 2005 elections, the relative opening that had previously been the policy of the regime was brutally ended. The repression of the Brothers intensified, seen in particular in the wave of arrests that followed the martial arts demonstration at al-Azhar University in Cairo in 2006 (see the introduction). Forty leaders of the Brotherhood were arrested afterward, most of them businessmen, and they were later hauled up before military tribunals on charges of belonging to an illegal organization, money laundering, arms smuggling, and providing training in the use of arms. Twenty-five of them, among them MB deputy guide Khayrat al-Shater, were sentenced to long prison sentences in 2008.

However, the tightening up of the regime did not affect only the Brotherhood. In the spring of 2007, new constitutional amendments were introduced aiming to clamp down on election procedures, including the removal of the requirement for judicial supervision, and legalization of police procedures that up to that point had only been possible under the Emergency Law in the name of antiterrorism. The latter law, passed after the assassination of former president Sadat in 1981, was extended for the umpteenth time for two more years in 2008.

Major changes were also afoot in the Egyptian public sphere as a result of the development of the private-sector press, satellite TV channels, and the Internet. These outlets had covered the political demonstrations that had taken place in 2004–2005 as part of the Kefaya movement, and they had also covered the parliamentary elections in a more independent fashion. They were now giving greater visibility to the social protests that had been taking place across Egypt since 2006.

This paradoxical context of institutional clampdown and social opening had repercussions on the internal equilibrium of the Gama'a. The liberalization of politics and the media that had taken place in 2004 and 2005 had encouraged the promotion of certain figures called reformers *(islahiyyin)* inside the Brotherhood and the development of a new communication strategy for the organization that was particularly apparent in media appearances made by MB guide Mahdi 'Akif. However, after 2006 the new atmosphere of repression in Egypt saw a change of direction with the reemergence of leading figures in the Brotherhood called organizationists *(tanzimiyyin)*, who prioritized the preservation of the organization and argued for a policy of strategic withdrawal. It was in this double context, external and internal, that the Brotherhood's young bloggers also emerged, who will be examined further in chapter five. It is also against the background of this dual context that the activities of the Brotherhood MPs elected to the 2005–10 parliament should be understood.

The evident contradiction between the presence of the MB in parliament, pointed out by the private-sector press, and the official policy of repression led the regime to deal with the situation in a haphazard manner. In summer 2007, two Brotherhood MPs[1] had their parliamentary immunity lifted and were arrested and then charged with having attempted to "reconstitute the banned Muslim Brotherhood group." In fact, however, their arrest was linked to debates that had been taking place in parliament since 2006, when then prime minister Ahmed Nazif had been questioned in a plenary session by Brotherhood MPs after he had declared at a session of the World Economic Forum in Davos that Egypt was a secular state and there was no group called the Muslim Brothers in the country. Fathi Surur, speaker of the People's Assembly during the Mubarak years and a major political figure of the time, then declared in parliament that there was no Muslim Brotherhood organization in Egypt, and that if such an organization were uncovered, those found to be part of it could have their parliamentary immunity lifted. At the same time, however, he congratulated members of the Brotherhood bloc *(al-kutla)* in parliament for their work.

الكتلة البرلمانية للإخوان المسلمين ٢٠٠٥

Figure 10. The Parliamentary Bloc of the MB (Brochure, 2010).

A battle over the labeling of this bloc was taking place at the time. Surur had refused to allow it to use the term 'parliamentary group' *(hay'a barlamaniyya)*, which was the term used by the legal parties in parliament and which the Brotherhood MPs in the 2005–10 parliament had demanded to use. The latter referred to themselves as "Muslim Brothers" in their speeches. A rumor started that Surur, irritated by the polemical statements made by the Brothers in parliament, had stopped talking about the Brotherhood 'bloc' *(al-kutla)* and now talked about the Brotherhood "killers" *(al-qatala)* instead, in a play on the resemblance of the two words in Arabic (Rabi' 2009a: 31–34).

These developments indicated the strength of the paradox that the forbidden MPs represented. How would they be able to carry out their duties in parliament and fulfill the roles of mediator and distributor of services usually played by members of parliament? And how would the Brotherhood MPs, the public face of the Gama'a, be able to sustain a role that saw them as—at the same time open to the outside and turned inward toward the organizational apparatus—the *tanzim*?

In playing their role as MPs under such conditions they encouraged the emergence of new forms of interaction between the Gama'a and wider society. The establishment of parliamentary offices and staff by the Brotherhood MPs created a new and legal interface between the organization and society that was managed in different ways by the *tanzim* according to the local context. Moreover, this interface gave the Gama'a the new and incongruous function of mediating between the government and the governed—since Brotherhood MPs were approached on a daily basis to play a mediating role of this sort—while also using this function to deepen the Gama'a's reach in the wider society.

## Dealing with the *Tanzim*

The presence of a Brotherhood MP in a constituency led to the emergence of a specific structure—the MP's team and its offices—which is only partially integrated into the *tanzim*. This organizational division corresponded to a division of labor between the *tanzim* itself, responsible for Brotherhood affairs, and the MP's team, responsible for relations with the wider society.

### Internal Positioning of the MPs

At first glance, the way in which the *tanzim* was organized might seem to be clear, as this had been set out in a text developed out of the internal regulations governing the original association set up by al-Banna in the 1930s. These regulations had been modified in 1951, taken over as they stood in the 1970s, amended in 1982 and 1990, and then amended again in a more limited fashion in 2009 and 2010. However, when asked to describe exactly how the *tanzim* worked, MB activists typically came up with contradictory or confused accounts. They frequently described it as being "decentralized," while at the same time representing it as also having a pyramid-shaped and centralized organizational structure. The *tanzim* was thus both rigid and loose in its organizational structure, and it is important to try to sketch out how it worked in order to understand the nature of the relationships between the Brotherhood MPs and the *tanzim*.

### The *tanzim* between hierarchy and confusion

Looked at more carefully, the *tanzim* was less like a pyramid and more like a juxtaposition of three different dimensions—administrative, educational, and corporate—whose interconnections were not always well defined and whose functioning presupposed a certain amount of vagueness.

The administrative dimension of the *tanzim* followed the Brotherhood's internal regulations quite closely. The organization's supreme guide headed the MB Guidance Bureau (Maktab al-Irshad), its executive body—which was theoretically made up of fifteen other members elected from the ninety members of the organization's General Consultative Council (Maglis al-Shura al-'Amm)—and its legislative body. The latter were mostly drawn from the Governorate Consultative Councils (Magalis Shura al-Muhafazat), each of which elected a Governorate Administrative Bureau (Maktab Idari al-Muhafaza). The governorates were also divided into regions (*mantiqa*, pl. *manatiq*), each of which also had an Administrative Bureau. These were composed of representatives of local sections (*shu'ba,* pl. *shu'ab*) consisting of fifty or so Brothers and varying in number between three and ten depending on the size of the region. The lowest level of the organization below the *shu'ba* were basic units called families (*usra*, pl. *usar*).

Unlike meetings at the regional or governorate level, those taking place at the level of the *shu'ba* brought together all the members of the *usar* present in the area, making the *shu'ba* the only structure in the organization's administrative units that did not consist of delegates only. This is because the *shu'ba* was both an administrative and an educational unit. Together with the *usra*, it constituted the educational branch of the *tanzim*. The *usra* also had a delegate (*naqib*) who had greater contacts with the representatives of the *shu'ba* to which he belonged. This individual was usually called a trainer (*mudarrib*) rather than a delegate, however, to emphasize the educational function of the *usra* in providing training and producing socialization. The educational branch was connected to the administrative decision-making apparatus not only through the representatives of the *shu'ab*, but also through the Education Committee (*lagnat al-tarbiya*), which will be examined in chapter five.

The Education Committee also related to the third and final dimension of the *tanzim* structure, the corporate one, consisting of committees (*lagna*, pl. *ligan*) at the national, governorate, regional, and section levels that were responsible for activities similar to those outlined during the time of al-Banna. There were committees for welfare (*lagnat al-birr*), financial and legal matters, fatwas, preaching, workers, professionals, women, and students, among others. There was also a political committee, though this was only set up in 2005 (al-Anani 2007: 109). Committee members were not necessarily drawn from the Administrative Bureau, and the committees themselves functioned like working groups, sending proposals up to the national committees directly connected to the Guidance Bureau. If the proposals were considered to be good, they were looked at by the Guidance Bureau, and then sent back down again to lower administrative levels if they were adopted as decisions or directives. It can thus be seen that the administrative branch and its centralizing tendency predominated over the corporate and the educational branches.

At the same time, the *tanzim* worked in practice in a highly decentralized and informal manner, owing to the government's repression of the Brotherhood. Public meetings of more than five people not authorized in advance, and *a fortiori* meetings of the Muslim Brotherhood, were illegal under the Emergency Law at the time, and this made plenary meetings of the General Consultative Council, the Governorate Councils, and the section General Assemblies a mostly theoretical proposition. In a best-case scenario, such meetings could still be held in a disguised fashion camouflaged as social occasions, with the wedding of a Muslim Brother being an opportunity for a *shu'ba* meeting, for example, hidden behind the façade of a family celebration.[2] Another solution was to employ the then new communication technologies and hold meetings by videoconference. However, meetings held under such conditions had a direct impact on the way power was divided up between the different organizational levels of the *tanzim*. While instructions could easily be sent from top to bottom (for example, by text messages), the fact that it was impossible for members of the different organizational units physically to meet meant that the people with managerial positions in the *shu'ba* and the regional and governorate bodies had significant autonomy in making decisions. The *usra*, the only bodies that, because of their size, could meet easily, also acquired considerable influence in the lives of MB activists as a result of the provisions of the Emergency Law, even if in theory they were on the lowest level of the administrative ladder.

Lastly, the fact that the Emergency Law made it impossible physically to meet restricted the possibility of internal elections. Despite the provisions made for elections in the internal regulations of the Brotherhood, they were only actually held in the late 2000s under pressure from internal dissidents. The composition of the Guidance Council and the General Consultative Assembly had not been renewed since 1995, and a series of changes took place after May 2008, leading to various crises of leadership. In order to make up for the absence of the leading figures imprisoned after the 'al-Azhar militias' incident, four new members were elected to the Guidance Bureau, bringing the total up to nineteen (in addition to the Supreme Guide) instead of the fifteen specified in the regulations. When confronted with internal opposition from the reformer wing and the young bloggers, the Brotherhood's deputy guide, Mohamed Habib, said that the regulations could not be changed, as it was impossible to hold a full meeting of the General Consultative Council. However, exactly such changes did take place in May 2009 with the amendment of articles that had earlier caused the problems. After the resignation of Supreme Guide Mahdi 'Akif and the marginalization of the internal opposition, new elections to the Guidance Bureau took place in December 2009 that sealed the victory of organizationists such as the new supreme guide, Mohamed Badi'. The composition of the General Consultative Council also changed for the first time in years in July 2010.

### The MPs between autonomy and subordination
The Brotherhood MPs enjoyed a particular status within the *tanzim*, as they were not directly under the authority of the administrative branch and they had more autonomy than members of the corporate branch committees. There was a parliamentary committee[3] attached to the Guidance Bureau, but this only served as an interface between the bureau and the parliamentary bloc of Brotherhood MPs, which drew up its policies relatively independently of the organization and had its own means of doing so, among other things by maintaining premises separate from the Guidance

Bureau headquarters and its own staff of specialized assistants (Shehata and Stacher 2006). According to the head of the bloc, Saad al-Katatni, the MPs enjoyed "total freedom *[hurriyya tamma]* as far as their activities in the constituencies are concerned," and they did not receive instructions from the organization's leaders on these matters.[4]

However, the idea that the MPs were autonomous with regard to the *tanzim* needs to be qualified, for at least four reasons. First, the vast majority of MPs did not have a significant position in the *tanzim* hierarchy. According to the sociological study based on the CVs that I presented in chapter one, only six percent of the MB candidates in the 2005 elections held leadership positions in the organization at either the regional or national levels. All the rest were at best post-holders in either a *shu'ba* or an *usra*. This was due to the way in which the candidates were selected by the *tanzim*, since as a result of the principle of '*talib al-wilaya la yuwwala*,'[5] managerial figures at the governorate level preselected the names of potential parliamentary candidates and then submitted these to the Guidance Bureau, which had the final say. The choice of Saad al-Katatni as head of the parliamentary bloc and Mohamed Morsi (head of the bloc in 2000) as chair of the parliamentary committee was therefore not accidental. Because they were close to the *tanzimiyyin* leaders, both Morsi and al-Katatni were among the small minority of Brotherhood MPs that had held previous positions in the *tanzim* before being elected. They then began their upward climb to the Guidance Bureau, arriving there in 2004 (Morsi) and in 2008 (al-Katatni) after controversial internal elections. The two men's special links to the *tanzimiyyin* also enabled the latter to keep the Brotherhood's parliamentary bloc under their tight control.

Second, in the eyes of the *tanzim*, an MP was simply a member of the Brotherhood like any other, and despite his parliamentary position he also remained (in his guise as MB activist) under the direction of his administrative superior. Therefore, an MP did not have any organizational authority over the activists among his staff, who might hold the same administrative position that he did in the *tanzim*. In fact, the principal assistants of the Brotherhood MPs were in practice mostly the heads of an *usra* or *shu'ba*.

Third, the regulations stated that the staff of a Brotherhood MP should be drawn from his campaign team and be selected by the *tanzim*'s regional administrative managers (who would decide where each activist should go), and not by the MP himself. Asked to describe the "complete freedom" of Brotherhood MPs in more detail, Saad al-Katatni admitted that there were indeed certain limits.

> There is no separation *(infisal)* from the *tanzim*, and instead there is coordination *(tansiq)* . . . the head of the Administrative Bureau holds his power from the organization . . . and so he exercises his authority over the MP. . . . The latter enjoys complete freedom of

action within the area of his activities and with his own staff, but in cases where his actions touch on the activities of the Brotherhood, or involve other members beside his own staff, then such actions have to go through the administrative manager.

The problem was that in reality there was often no clear-cut distinction between the activities of the Brothers and the activities of the MP. The former did not refer only to the activities of activists within the organization, but could also include activities designed to provide services to the wider population, among them the activities of the welfare committee (*lagnat al-birr*), for example. Akram, the staff coordinator for Sheikh al-Muhammadi in Helwan, drew a distinction between non-charitable social activities, such as the provision of private lessons for schoolchildren and mobile medical clinics, which are part of the MP's duties, and activities that were purely charitable in nature (*'amal khayri*).

> The MP's office does not engage in charitable activities . . . since it cannot be the recipient of gifts as this would be illegal. . . . However, if someone goes out and buys things to distribute through the office, or provides the money to do so, then yes, I can buy things and distribute them.[6]

Thus, charitable activities could take place through the office of the MP, but they could not be carried out as part of his staff's own activities. However, the distinction was not as hard and fast as it seemed, since activists who were members of the MP's staff also played other roles, such as an organizational role as members of the administrative branch of the *tanzim*, and a corporate role as members of various committees. They might also play social roles as a result of being members of an association, for example, or of a *zakat* committee, or of a welfare fund for colleagues. They might also engage as individuals in various informal charitable activities. When Akram distributed the goods that had been sent to the MP's office, in theory he was doing more than he should have been doing as a staff member. However, he was also taking advantage of the possibilities that his various roles offered him in order to engage in charitable activities, acting as a mere individual or as a member of the Brotherhood.

Moreover, the distinction between charitable and non-charitable activities could change from one period to another, as can be seen from the example of food distributions in Ramadan or on the day of the Eid. In 2008 in Madinat Nasr, for example, Ramadan food parcels were distributed to local residents bearing the name of 'Isam Mukhtar and with the Brotherhood's signature slogan emblazoned across them ("Islam Is the Solution"). In contrast, in Helwan Akram said that "the Brothers take care of this," though this did not mean that Sheikh al-Muhammadi could not be involved, at least symbolically, by being present at some of the food distributions.

Akram's reference to the regulations governing the financing of MPs' activities draws attention to another, fourth dimension of the control exercised by the *tanzim*. This is because the MPs did not have their own budgets and were only allowed to claim a personal allowance. Fixed by law at LE5,000 in 2005 and increased to LE7,000 in 2008,[7] though this was a non-negligible sum when compared to the average salary in Egypt at the time it was still not enough to pay for charitable activities. The Brother-hood probably also helped to finance the budgets of the offices of its MPs, although this was, of course, not communicated since it fell in the secret domain of 'open secrecy.'

There was thus a tension between autonomy and subordination in the relationships between the Brotherhood MPs and the *tanzim*. However, there were also important differences in the way this was experienced for the three constituencies studied, and this was seen particularly in the composition and operation of their respective staffs.

## Local Variations in MP Staff
### Helwan: A network of networks around Sheikh al-Muhammadi
The six offices of Sheikh al-Muhammadi in Helwan were easily identifiable from the streets outside by illuminated signs bearing his name and often also his portrait. His main office was on the floor below his private apartment.[8] Neither the words 'Muslim Brothers' nor the organization's logo appeared on the signs, though this did not mean that the sheikh was trying to disguise his identity as a member of the Brotherhood. On the contrary, this was always quite obvious, given the fame of the sheikh and that of members of his staff. The autonomy that the sheikh and his team enjoyed in Helwan highlighted the wide reach of the Gama'a in the local community.

Table 10 gives details of the fifteen main activists making up the core of the MP's staff in Helwan.[9] Aged between forty-five and fifty years old, nearly all of them had been born in Helwan, and most of them came from the popular classes, with fathers who had been farmers, factory workers, office workers, or shopkeepers. They themselves had attained higher social positions, included three professionals, two entrepreneurs, two civil ser-vants working for the Ministry of Education, and a shopkeeper who owned several small groceries. However, the majority of them were factory work-ers, with the one major exception being General S, a former army officer and now a senior executive at Military Production Factory 99, a particular case. Six of the activists described themselves as skilled workers, and it was they who managed the sheikh's offices near the area's factories and workers' housing developments.

The workers among them engaged in at least one form of community work within their respective factories. Ayman had served from 2001 to 2006 as a workers' representative on the board of the Military Factory 45 where he worked, before being transferred by the authorities to another factory in a remote area north of Cairo at the end of his term in office. Gabir and Ashraf, workers in two other military factories in the constituency, had run in workers' elections several times but had been removed from the lists each time as a result of interventions by State Security. Salah, the successor to the sheikh in the 2010 parliamentary elections, was an exceptional case. He was a technician in a private-sector cement factory and had been an elected member of the union committee of his company (ETUF local branch) from 1996 to 2011, in other words continuously over a fifteen-year period. However, most of the activists worked in other spaces of services (*magalat li-l-khadamat*) in their respective factories, including *zakat* committees, cooperative associations, solidarity funds, and pilgrimage associations, along with the prayer rooms attached to their workplaces. Security constraints, particularly in the military factories, had also led them to look for other ways of carrying out their activities, sometimes in wholly informal ways.

All the core members of the staff were actively engaged in social work outside of the plants, in their neighborhoods. They were members of charitable associations, local-development associations, *zakat* committees, or administrative boards of mosques. In some cases, they were unofficially preaching as imams in mosques, or acted as members of popular justice committees (*sulh*). Most of them also engaged in informal mediation efforts between the poor and the rich. These activities varied according to the social position of the individuals concerned. Hamdi, for example, one of the two entrepreneurs on the staff, who described himself as a "businessman who had returned from the Gulf," paid for the construction of sanitation and educational facilities in his area. Gamal, a shopkeeper and the son of a shopkeeper, had not only inherited his father's grocery stores, but had also acquired his status as a natural leader of the area.

> My father was someone who was well known in the area, and even today people know that he was a good man. He has been involved for a long time in social work in various associations. I used to work with him, and in the same way that he was well known, I have also become well known in turn.[10]

Table 10. Profiles of Brotherhood MP Staff in Helwan, 2005-2010.

| Name | Function | Social Origin | Profession | Associations | Union / Company Workers Representative | Preaching as imam | Labor Party | Experience on Local Popular Councils (LPCs) in 1992 |
|---|---|---|---|---|---|---|---|---|
| Akram | Coordinator of the offices | Born in Helwan in 1960, parents farmers originally from Qalyubiyya | Accountant | Yes | - | - | Yes | Yes |
| Ayman | Manager of the main office | Born in 1962, son of a leading local family in Helwan | Foreman, military factory | Yes | Yes | Yes | Yes | Yes (elected to the LPC) |
| 'Abd al-Rahman | Manager of the Helwan Center office | Born in Minufiyya in 1965, parents farmers coming to Helwan in 1991 | French teacher in a public secondary school | Yes | - | - | Yes | Yes |
| Gamal | Member of the Helwan Center office | Born in Helwan in 1972, father a grocery store owner originally from Fayoum | Shopkeeper | Yes | - | Yes | - | Yes |
| Muhsin (non-Brotherhood) | Member of the Helwan Center office | Born in Helwan in 1960, father a butcher and employee originally from Qalyubiyya | Businessman | Yes | - | - | Yes | Yes (elected to the LPC) |

| Name | Function | Social Origin | Profession | Associations | Union / Company Workers Representative | Preaching as imam | Labor Party | Experience on Local Popular Councils (LPCs) in 1992 |
|---|---|---|---|---|---|---|---|---|
| Hamdi | Member of the Helwan Center office | Born in Helwan in 1968, father a worker in the military factories originally from Upper Egypt | Businessman | Yes | - | - | - | - |
| Gabir | Manager of the Mashru' Amriki office | Born in Shubra (Cairo) in 1966, came to Helwan as a child, father a worker in the military factories | Skilled worker in a military factory | Yes | Yes | - | - | Yes |
| Salah | Member of the Mashru' Amriki office | Born in Helwan in 1963, father an electrician | Technician in a cement works (private sector) | Yes | Yes | Yes | - | Yes |
| Ziyad | Member of the Mashru' Amriki office | Born in Helwan in 1963, family from Mashru' Amriki | Skilled worker in a private-sector factory making construction materials | Yes | - | - | - | - |
| Ashraf | Manager of the Madinat al-Huda office | Born in Helwan in 1971 | Skilled worker in a military factory | Yes | Yes | Yes | Yes | Yes |

| Name | Function | Social Origin | Profession | Associations | Union / Company Workers Representative | Preaching as imam | Labor Party | Experience on Local Popular Councils (LPCs) in 1992 |
|---|---|---|---|---|---|---|---|---|
| Ibrahim | Manager of the Hadayek Helwan office | Born in Helwan, parents originally from Cairo | Educational adviser | Yes | - | Yes | - | Yes |
| General S. (non-Brotherhood) | Member of the Hadayek Helwan office | Born in 1945, originally from Minufiyya | Former general, senior executive of a military factory | Yes | - | - | - | - |
| M.* | Team member | Born in Helwan in 1955 | Skilled worker in a military factory | Yes | Yes | - | Yes | - |
| A.* | Team member | Born in Helwan in 1964 | Lawyer | Yes | Yes | - | Yes | Yes (elected to the LPC) |
| T.* | Team member | Born in 1960 | Architect | - | - | - | - | Yes (elected to the LPC) |

Source: Interviews and/or short CVs included in 2008 local election leaflets (those not interviewed are indicated by an asterisk). Names have been changed.

Apart from this strong participation in local public work, the second main characteristic of the Helwan staff lay in the long-standing relationships that its members had both among themselves and with Sheikh al-Muhammadi. Akram, the coordinator of the sheikh's office and an accountant by training, explained:

> It was the sheikh who asked me to work with him, and I said "*hader*" [at your service]. That was in 2004. We had known each other for twenty-five years through the Gam'iyya al-Shar'iyya Mosque even before we became Brothers. He was president of the local association and sheikh of the mosque, and I was a young man, a friend, who used to come to it. Later I joined the Gama'a.[11]

Most of the members of the sheikh's staff had first come into contact with him through al-Gam'iyya al-Shar'iyya (GS hereafter)[12] at a time when they were often still quite young. Hamdi said that he had made his first investment by contributing to the construction costs of one of the GS schools, even though he had still been a student at the time and had only been able to contribute in a very modest way because of his limited income (he gave LE100 that he had inherited from his father, about $150 at the time). While Hamdi had already joined the Brotherhood at that time, this was not the case for Gamal, who remembered that his father had sung the praises of the sheikh for his charitable activities even though he himself had been a member of the NDP.

> My father always used to tell me, "Don't join the Brothers," as he was frightened of State Security. He was always terrified of the Brothers. But he liked Sheikh al-Muhammadi a lot, as he knew that he had the reputation of being a good man *(ragil tayyib)* who used to come to the 'Izba whenever there was a problem and used to do many things for it. We didn't know he was a Brother, however. We knew he was an Islamic figure, but we didn't know he was a Brother.

While General S. was quite reticent about his own personal activities, he did say that he had been a "neighbor of the sheikh for thirty years" and that they had founded the GS schools together and were both members of the parents' associations of these schools. It was this that had led the general to become one of the managers of the sheikh's Hadayek Helwan office even though he was not himself a Brother. It was thus clear that the GS had forged the sheikh's local reputation and that it had also served as a place where long-term relationships and loyalties could be established.

The two other places where long-lasting loyalties were built were the Local Popular Council (LPC) and the Labor Party. The sheikh headed the LPC from 1992 to 1997 after an exceptional victory in the local elections as a member of the Islamic Alliance list, which united the Labor Party and the Brotherhood. The sheikh had headed the party's branch in the south of Cairo in the 1990s, and Ayman (the worker in a military factory), T. (the architect), and A. (the lawyer), all members of the party, had been elected to the LPC along with the sheikh. Muhsin, the other member of the sheikh's staff who was not a member of the Brotherhood, was a member of the Labor Party and had met him through this connection. He was also elected to the LPC. Akram, the staff coordinator, had not been elected to membership of the LPC, but he acted as "director of the sheikh's office at the LPC," in his words, and managed the party's premises in the center of Helwan. Ashraf (the worker in a military factory) was the manager of a party office in 15 Mayo City that in fact served as the constituency office of 'Ali Fath al-Bab, then recently elected to his first term as an MP (1995–2000). He was thus also brought into the sheikh's orbit through a Labor Party network and during the period of the sheikh's tenure on the LPC, and it was at this time too that he had started to work with him. Salah (the technician in cement works), who was living in the adjacent *qism* of Maadi north of Helwan at the time, was not a member of the Labor Party, though he had stood as a candidate "under the party label" in the 1992 local elections in his district. While he knew of the sheikh's reputation as the founder of the GS, of which he was also a member, Salah had only begun to work with the sheikh directly in 1992 during the election campaign.

'Abd al-Rahman (the teacher) had moved to Helwan in 1991 when he was twenty-seven years old and a new recruit to the Gama'a. He joined the Labor Party and worked on the sheikh's election campaign while also getting to know him personally. The stories of Gabir (the worker in a military factory), Gamal (the shopkeeper), and Ibrahim (a school adviser), aged twenty-six, twenty, and twenty, respectively, at the time, were similar, since it was by working on the LPC election campaign in 1992 and then on the parliamentary election campaign in 1995 that they had moved toward joining the Gama'a, although it is difficult to be sure of the exact dates on which they joined.[13] Their campaign work had consisted of distributing flyers, putting up posters, and canvassing voters, having been trained to do so by friends or neighbors in the area. They had thus gotten to know the sheikh by working on his election campaigns and then as volunteers on activities organized by the LPC. Ibrahim, for example, described how he had helped to clean up the district of Ma'sara. His first steps in public work are closely linked to the experience of the LPC.

The LPC experience continued even after the end of the sheikh's term of office in 1997. Victims of the fraud that characterized the subsequent elections and swept them off the LPC, the sheikh's staff managed to stay together by regrouping at the local Labor Party offices, where they formed what Muhsin did not hesitate to call a *"maglis mahali al-zil,"* or shadow LPC, that continued to provide certain services to the local population. Muhsin was in charge of the party's office in his home area of 'Izbat al-Qibliyya, a popular and semi-informal district.

> The office was closed two years after the party's activities were frozen, but we used it from around 1997 to 2003. We used to deal with people's problems even though we were not elected representatives. The Labor Party "held onto" the 'Izba, and we were an extensive team consisting of twenty-seven people in total and three leaders, H.S., A.H., and me. We knew the 'Izba well, and three of us were not members of the Muslim Brotherhood, even if Brothers worked with us. Sheikh al-Muhammadi always used to come to planning meetings.[14]

The staff working with the sheikh in the 2005 election campaign thus came together as a result of long-standing personal relationships that were in part outside of strictly Brotherhood circles. Because of this, they were also to an extent brought together apart from the *tanzim*. This was due to the close neighborhood relations in the area, the institutional role played by the Gam'iyya al-Shar'iyya, the important resources that could be mobilized by the Labor Party in Helwan, and the central figure of Sheikh al-Muhammadi himself. However, Akram, the coordinator of the sheikh's election offices, seemed to also be the regional administrative officer of the *tanzim*.

> When we [the *tanzim*] were selecting the MP's staff, I brought together all the administrative figures from each *shu'ba* and asked them to look into who might have the ability and the means to join the staff.

However, the central role that Akram played on the MP's staff did not indicate that the *tanzim* controlled the MP. On the contrary, Sheikh al-Muhammadi had the final say, though this was also based on his personal relationship with Akram. In sum, in the Helwan constituency the *tanzim* adapted itself to the local situation by capturing the network of networks that had long been built around the sheikh.

### Madinat Nasr: The influence of the *tanzim*
In contrast, in Madinat Nasr, things indicated that the balance of power was to the advantage of the *tanzim*. Only three constituency offices were opened, one in the popular and peripheral district of Qatamiyya (Mukhtar's

home area), a second near the informal area of 'Izbat al-Muslimin, and the last, the main office, on the ground floor of a building in the socially intermediate area of al-Hay al-'Ashir. The staff included a dozen or so activists who had earlier played a role in the campaign's organizational committees, but most of them had not known Mukhtar before the elections took place. They included two young IT engineers,[15] two professionals in their thirties (Mustafa the dentist and Bassim the accountant), and a small shopkeeper in his fifties (Husayn, the manager of the 'Izbat al-Muslimin office). According to the MP, there were also a lawyer, some public-sector workers, and a few doctors, engineers, and university professors, although I did not have the chance to meet them. Hadi, the MP's secretary and manager of the main office in al-Hay al-'Ashir, was a paid employee and not a member of the Brotherhood. He had also not taken part in the earlier campaign. While at least Bassim and Mustafa had some activities in associations, these were nothing compared to those of the activists in the Helwan constituency. Husayn, the small shopkeeper, even claimed that he had "no social activities outside the MP's office."[16] It therefore seemed that the local social resources that could be drawn upon by the Madinat Nasr staff were far fewer than those available in Helwan.

However, not much could be discovered about the backgrounds of the individuals in Madinat Nasr, since the conditions under which the fieldwork took place meant that only half of them could be interviewed. This, according to Mukhtar, was for security reasons, since only he was allowed to know who was in charge of the committees making up the campaign team.[17] In other words, the other staff members did not know who chaired which committee, whereas in Helwan this information had been made public. However, Bassim, the accountant in his thirties who had been present during an interview for the study with the MP, later said that in fact he did know many of those chairing the committees, not because he had been told who they were by the MP, but because he had been able to guess from what had gone on in working meetings.

> I am a member of the political committee of the MP 'Isam Mukhtar, and I am a member of the student committee in the *tanzim*. The members of the political committee accompany the MP when he is traveling around, but as there are not many of us in the committee, the Brothers who live in each district, and who know it well, help us in our activities [when we visit them]. There are around five committees in Mukhtar's team, like the welfare committee and the services committee, for example . . . but we do not hold meetings together. The heads of the committees can always meet in an informal and friendly [widdiyyan] way as they go in and out of Mukhtar's office. The relevant committees were there when the

office opened, but the welfare committee, for example, had nothing do with it.[18]

Oddly enough, Bassim mentioned the existence of a welfare committee in the MP's team, going against the idea that there was a division of labor, charitable and non-charitable, between activities carried out by the MP's staff and those carried out by the *tanzim*. Even so, he said, the welfare committee had "nothing to do with" the MP's office. The confusion here had nothing to do with Bassim's misunderstanding of the question, but instead revealed the relationship between the MP's staff and the *tanzim*. The welfare committee was actually not staffed by the MP's team, but by the *tanzim*. Many of the activities of the Madinat Nasr offices were organized by Muslim Brothers who were "not members of the team" but who used the premises for their own purposes. This was especially the case for events held there from time to time, such as the cheap clothing sales and mobile medical clinics (medical caravans) described in the following chapter. According to Hadi, the MP's non-Brotherhood secretary,

> If the Brothers want someone to represent the MP's office, someone from the staff will go, or Mr 'Isam himself, with the proviso that it is always he who decides who will represent the office. He might tell me that they are having a health clinic come next week and give me instructions on what to do. If someone calls, I will tell them where they should go, etc.[19]

Hadi's position was particular since he was, on the one hand, the centerpiece of the MP's team, managing both relations with the administrations and the demands of the inhabitants. On the other hand, however, since he was not himself a member of the Brotherhood, he had only a subsidiary role to play in events organized by the Brothers, with his words suggesting that the latter acted from outside the regular staff. Moreover, when I visited these events, I noticed that none of the activists who met in the MP's offices took part in them. Therefore, strangely enough, the separation between the areas for which the MP was responsible and those which were the responsibility of the *tanzim* was at the same time more distinct and less significant than it was in Helwan. More distinct because, as suggested by Hadi's comment, everything that did not come under his management was the responsibility of the Brothers who were not members of the MP's staff. And less significant, since the staff in Madinat Nasr was less well-structured and less self-directing. The *tanzim* intruded into it on a daily basis. It was also more secretive and more rigid in the way it was organized than the Helwan staff.

A good example of this rigid way of working and of the control of the *tanzim* was during the distribution of food in Ramadan. When the MP described this to me, I mentioned that one of the three informal areas on the outskirts of the constituency ('Izbat al-'Arab) had not received any food. Mukhtar explained that this was because the Madinat Nasr constituency was between two Brotherhood regions and 'Izbat al-'Arab was in the region that he did not belong to as a member of the *tanzim*. As only the leader of an *usra*, he could not mobilize activists in the other region to take care of the food distribution. In order to do so, he would have needed to get permission from the head of the welfare committee in the region concerned, whom he had not had the opportunity to meet as part of his activities in the *tanzim* and whose identity he said he did not even know. As a result, he had had to ask his own regional superior to contact his counterpart in the other region so that the latter could give instructions to his subordinates that they should get in touch with the MP's staff in order to carry out the food distribution. All of this Mukhtar justified on the grounds of the risk of repression from State Security, whose headquarters were also in Madinat Nasr. However, it was also the result of the particular layout of the constituency, which was large and fragmented, and the few resources owned by Mukhtar and his staff.

### Tibbin/15 Mayo: Guest *na'ib* and self-managing offices

In the constituency of MP 'Ali Fath al-Bab a different situation reigned. I only met the women activists in the 15 Mayo constituency office. They were the ones who were running the office. While there were other offices in the constituency,[20] I was systematically steered toward the one in 15 Mayo, presented as being the most important, and attempts to get in touch with the manager of the other offices all met with no response. As a result, what is described here cannot be used to draw final conclusions about the way the MP's staff was organized across the constituency. However, remarks made on several occasions by my main interlocutor, Salma, in charge of the women's committee in the MP's staff, led me to believe that there was a clear division of roles between the MP on the one hand and the different offices on the other.

> Salma: All the activities taking place in the office are managed by the staff, and they are responsible for everything. The MP comes as a guest *(deif)*, except when he is holding regular meetings with constituents.

> Fath al-Bab: We decide on the main lines together, but after that the staff act in an autonomous fashion. I am only present on the days events take place, as a way of signaling my role as a representative, but I don't organize them. That is the role of civil society and voluntary workers. The MP is there to put his contacts at their

disposal. Each office carries out different activities depending on the needs of the local population in the areas in which it is situated and on its own human and financial resources. Women are much less active in Kafr al-'Ilu than they are in Mayo, for example.

Salma: The coordinator of the offices might tell us about the activities taking place in other districts so that we can learn from them. But there is no permanent cooperation between the different offices, even if we do meet each other from time to time.[21]

The 15 Mayo office thus operated "autonomously" not only with regard to the *tanzim*[22] but also with regard to the other offices and the MP himself. The cohesion of the 15 Mayo group of activists was noticeable, and all those I met said they had been members of the staff for at least five years, with some, such as Salma, having been already there in 1995. They had known each other before through their activities in welfare associations in 15 Mayo and as members of the local women's section of the Gama'a. When it was created in 1995, the MP's team was originally an ad hoc construction, unique in the whole country. It was both not really detached from the *tanzim*, and linked to the Labor Party, as the local premises of the latter in 15 Mayo served as Fath al-Bab's constituency office. Later, other offices were opened, which were apparently accustomed to working separately from each other over the course of Fath al-Bab's three terms in parliament. Over time, they became routinized and their activities slowed down. According to Salma, the amount of time people spent working in the office depended on the events going on at the time.

I am in charge of the women's committee, but I don't go to the office every day. In fact, we only really start working when there is a particular project on, once every two months approximately.

'Ali Fath al-Bab held regular meetings with residents in his constituency offices every other week, but he maintained a distance from the other activities. He spoke of "decentralization" (al-la markaziyya) as a way of describing how they worked and confirmed that he only attended as a "guest."

It can thus be seen that there were major differences between the staff of the Brotherhood MPs. In Helwan, there was a network of networks centered on Sheikh al-Muhammadi, while in Madinat Nasr there was a weak staff dependent on the *tanzim*, and in Tibbin/15 Mayo there was a configuration of many separate groups. These contrasting models were connected to the different ways of playing the role of MP in each constituency, since each MP had different resources at his disposal when it came to dealing with the state.

## Dealing with the 'Everyday State'

MPs in Egypt have to have good relations with individuals occupying senior positions in the state apparatus, such as ministers, governors, senior civil servants, and highly placed figures in state agencies, in order to be able to honor the spirit of service and expectations of the electorate. Being a member of the opposition can represent an obstacle to playing this role, which is why independent MPs so often join the NDP after winning elections. However, the prerogatives belonging to MPs, even if mostly formal and having limited margins for maneuver, should not be considered as being entirely without value: the Brotherhood MPs were used to deploying various strategies to access state resources, whether material or more abstract in the form of 'visas' or *ta'shirat*, the authorizations and recommendations issued by ministers or governors necessary before services could be provided to a given constituency.

## Three Models of Negotiating Access to Resources

Three ideal-type models can be identified for negotiating access to resources: parliamentary pressure (much used by 'Isam Mukhtar), local legitimacy (demonstrated by Sheikh al-Muhammadi), and elite complicity (characteristic of 'Ali Fath al-Bab).

### 'Isam Mukhtar: Parliamentary pressure

In an unpublished study, 'Amr Hashim Rabi' analyzed the interventions made by Brotherhood MPs in parliament between December 2005 and January 2007 and came to the following conclusions

> On many occasions, MPs in the Brotherhood bloc used parliament like MPs wanting to secure services for their constituencies, not only because they used it to gain access to ministers in order to obtain the authorizations needed to meet requests made by residents of their constituencies, but also because they used various parliamentary procedures to provide local services, even if the latter should probably have been dealt with by Local Popular Councils at the governorate level (Rabi' 2009a: 43–44).

Rabi' emphasizes the use of parliamentary procedures such as requests for information (*talabat ihata*) and questions (*istigwabat*) by Brotherhood MPs as a way of making demands on behalf of their own constituencies, even if these procedures were supposed by law to be used to deal with regional issues (for the former) and national issues (for the latter). I observed the same thing when examining the parliamentary interventions made by the three MPs studied here,[23] in particular those by 'Isam

Mukhtar. For an MP possessing little by way of *nufudh*, these procedures were his only resource. Most of the requests for information and questions found in Mukhtar's record for the 2005–2006 session of parliament concerned purely local requests: lighting and paving of streets in one area, lack of local shops in another, problems related to the construction of housing units in a given district, the opening of a post office, or public transport congestion. Some of Mukhtar's interventions sought to frame local requests and observations by relating them to more general problems, such as hospital failures or the high cost of telephone calls. However, this was less frequent in Mukhtar's case than it was in the case of interventions by the two other MPs.

This diversion of parliamentary procedures for constituency ends could also be used to get around obstacles thrown up by figures in the administration. Mukhtar's struggle with the governor of Cairo might be mentioned here, as the latter refused to accept a decision by the Ministry of Local Administration ordering the end of the demolition of housing in 'Izbat al-Haggana after a request to this effect from Mukhtar. Mukhtar made a complaint to the speaker, Fathi Surur, during a parliamentary session, who instructed the governor to respect the decision. Such pressure exercised in parliament by Mukhtar was not in itself decisive, and his success in forcing the governor to carry out the order owed much to the balance of power between NDP figures at the time. Indeed, it should be mentioned that the governor was also involved in a conflict over the same housing with the other MP from Madinat Nasr, the NDP businessman Mustafa al-Sallab, and the issue of the housing became a way for the two men to get back at one another. On this occasion, Mukhtar found an ally in his dispute with the governor in the person of al-Sallab, indicating that a Brotherhood MP could benefit from divisions in the ruling party that were sometimes even more divisive than differences of party label.

On another occasion, a decision by the governor overruled an authorization delivered by parliament. Mukhtar described how he finally obtained authorization to develop an area of green space in the 'Izbat al-Haggana district, only to have it blocked by employees of the local executive council on the orders of the governor. "They didn't want to hear it said that 'it was the Brotherhood MP who did that' . . . and after a bit they were going to dig up the idea of the garden again and say it was their idea," he said.

In Helwan, fewer requests of this kind were being made through parliamentary interventions. The MP, Sheikh al-Muhammadi, exercised such a significant influence in the area that he was able to directly address local authorities to make similar requests.

Figure 11. Examples of Mukhtar's parliamentary interventions (Leaflet 'Lamahat,' 2010).

## Sheikh al-Muhammadi: Local legitimacy

Sheikh al-Muhammadi enjoyed frequent contacts with the local authorities *(mahaliyyat)* in Helwan, including the elected members of the LPCs, the chairs and staff of the government-appointed local executive councils (LECs) at the district and governorate level, and the local managers of decentralized government services and independent state agencies, such as the electricity, water, and gas companies. This local structure was headed by the governor, who was directly appointed by the head of state and had the rank of minister (Ibrahim 2007; Sa'id 2005). The governor acted both as the incarnation of the centralization of state power, being responsible for implementing government policy at the local level, and as the main actor in the "informal, irrational decentralization [which] has a principal characteristic: it is not financed by the state budget. It is financed directly by citizens, NGOs or other private entities" (Ben Néfissa 2009: 189). While the regime refused to carry out any genuine reform of the state administration, in practice "the governors have been asked to develop their own resources; that is, fundraise from the private sector, without a fixed, precisely defined financing plan" (Ben Néfissa 2009: 193). As a result, the system at the local level was characterized by a multiplication of petty fiefs and an opaque and informal system of management. In addition to the possibilities for corruption to which this gave rise, it also led to multiple conflicts between the different actors.

It is not easy to find one's way through the maze of Egyptian local administration, but those who have tried will know that the existence of such internal conflicts can be a considerable resource. The record of the sheikh's activities for 2008 indicates that he knew quite well how to play the system. Not only did he often meet with the individuals concerned, who willingly accorded him their cooperation—supporting a longstanding request for the creation of an independent *qism* in Ma'sara in the north of the constituency, for example—but he also intervened with the chair of the governorate council to put an end to the conflict between the latter and the staff of the local executive council (LEC) and encourage "good relations that will allow everyone to work together to help solve Helwan's problems."[24] This role of mediator played by the Brotherhood MP may at first glance appear to be surprising, but it is readily explained by the extent of his local influence. When he chaired the Helwan LPC between 1992 and 1997, the sheikh had already established close relations with members of the executive council, with the chair of the latter having attended all the meetings of the LPC, when ordinarily, in Egypt, LPC elected representatives and LEC civil servants were in conflict and ignored one another. As a result, one-third of the recommendations made by the LPC were carried out by the executive council (Ben Néfissa 1999).[25] This was a considerable amount, when one remembers that according to figures from the Local Administration Committee of the People's Assembly, of the 66,979 recommendations made by LPCs across Egypt in 2000–2001, only 6,344 were carried out by the relevant executive councils, for example (Ben Néfissa 2009: 186).

In his role as MP, the sheikh thus continued his cooperation with local civil servants, as was seen in the creation of the new, but temporary, governorate of Helwan in 2008, for example. The decision to create the new governorate had been made without any thought being given to the budget required or the means needed to set it up, however, and as a result several decentralized state services found themselves without offices. Local staff working for the Ministry of Health appealed to the MP for help, as 'Abd al-Rahman, the teacher on the sheikh's staff, explained.

They wrote a letter to the sheikh asking him to intervene with the ministry in order to find the necessary funds. This is what happened, and the sheikh managed to arrange for the provision of LE4 million. The staff could not have asked for this directly, as they would not have received an answer. Being employed by the same ministry doesn't necessarily make things easier.[26]

In this case, a Brotherhood MP was thus asked by state employees to intervene with their own superiors so that the latter would implement a government decision (creation of a new governorate). The sheikh's role may appear to have been surprising here, but it can be perfectly well understood if one remembers, on the one hand, the relationships he had with the local authorities, and on the other hand, the kind of informal decentralization that had led to reduced funds being made available at the local level and made local civil servants the subalterns of the administrative order (Ben Néfissa 2009). The second case mentioned by 'Abd al-Rahman that concerned the local offices of the Ministry of Education was even more indicative of this type of informal decentralization.

> The civil servants in the local offices of the Ministry of Education came to see us to ask if we would finance the furnishing of the new offices they had been given. As a teacher, I knew them a little, so I was put in charge of the case. I suggested that the MP could make an official request to the governor, but they refused. They didn't want our involvement to be so visible. Instead, they wanted hidden cooperation. They wanted us to find them private donors, using our network as members of the Brotherhood. I helped them because I couldn't let them sit on the floor: they didn't even have chairs! We went to see furniture merchants we knew, asking for chairs from one and shelves from another . . . They gave me what they could, as they knew I wasn't doing it for myself. It was voluntary work, and they may have wanted to participate and make a donation. But normally there should be a budget for such things, as it is not always possible to count on *al-maghud al-dhati*.

*Al-maghud al-dhati* literally means 'self-effort,' that is to say, the idea of doing things by oneself, of counting on one's own effort. It became popular from the 1980s onward when the state began cutting its provision of social services. It is a form of self-financing comparable to "neoliberal techniques of government" that depend on transferring state responsibilities onto individuals (Foucault 2004). However, while it "apparently signifies the effort to rely on the self without calling on the state," it was actually endorsed by the state itself (Ben Néfissa 2009: 190). In 1988 this *maghud al-dhati* was introduced into law through a reform of the local administration (Law 145 of 1988). As the local authorities in Egypt do not have control over their own budgets and do not raise money through their own taxes, the law encourages them to resort to appeals to the spontaneous efforts of the local population in order to fund public projects. For example, a youth club might be built thanks to the contributions of local shopkeepers who are asked to provide building materials (such as cement and bricks) in lieu of paying fines for various minor offenses, something which is more advantageous for them in terms of time, money, and the avoidance of administrative problems (Ben Néfissa 2009: 191). In fact, the local population often has no choice but to participate in such endeavors, and as a result *al-maghud al-dhati* is more like a constraint than a matter of spontaneous effort. In a certain way, therefore, the MP's staff was obliged to respond to the civil servants' request ("I couldn't let them sit on the floor"), and since the latter were not able to organize the appropriate *maghud al-dhati* themselves they turned to an intermediary in the shape of the sheikh, who was also able to show off his ability to play a local role.

However, making up for the failures of the state was not in itself a source of political gains for the Brotherhood MP in this case, since, as 'Abd al-Rahman explained, the civil servants involved did not want to see their cooperation with the Brotherhood revealed. The sheikh's staff accepted their demand, but depended instead on a more discreet but more uncertain way of building political loyalty.

> The civil servants were afraid that it would get out that that they had cooperated with us. But in their heart of hearts they were completely with the opposition, even if they would not admit it. Most of our activities would conclude with mutual understanding based on the relations of trust that we are able to establish. But they didn't want to see anything written down or anything to be made official. The civil servants in the Education Ministry were worse in this respect than those working for the Ministry of Health, as they were worried about their salaries. They didn't want to see anything happen that might threaten them professionally.

Such observations illustrate the close links between Sheikh al-Muhammadi's staff and local state employees and the importance of these links for carrying out his staff's activities. However, even so, Akram, the coordinator of the constituency offices, cautioned against what he called the risks of "complacency."

> Relations with the governor of Helwan are very good, as they are with the head of the district *(ra'is al-hayy)*. We present our plans for street-cleaning, resurfacing the roads, the provision of water, etc., and together we manage to get the funds from the state to

carry them out. We go to see them, we talk together, and contrary to what people say about the Muslim Brothers, here in Helwan we have never had any sort of problem. But good personal relations do not mean complacency *(mubaha)*. If the governor does something good, we say that he has done something good. If he does something bad, we say that as well.[27]

Such limits seemed to be more easily crossed by 'Ali Fath al-Bab in the Tibbin/15 Mayo constituency.

Figure 12. Sheikh al-Muhammadi's publication announcing his success in opening a Youth center; editorial pieces written by Akram and Dr. Ehab insisting on their strong ties with Helwan and on the need for "citizens' positivity" (Ma'a al-nas, 2008).

### 'Ali Fath al-Bab: Elitist connivance

'Ali Fath al-Bab was a past master at using his local relations to get what he wanted from various authorities. An article that appeared in a leaflet produced by his office in May 2006 explained the long and tortuous procedure that had been followed after the request Fath al-Bab had made to the governor of Cairo concerning a vacant plot of land that had formerly belonged to the Misr Helwan public-sector textile company. Fath al-Bab wanted to see this plot used for a school. In the article, he presented himself as an expert negotiator of complex bureaucratic processes, including with the public property administration, the planning authorities, and the school buildings authority. In the same way, the example of a project to set up a technical college within the framework of the German–Egyptian "Mubarak-Kohl" Cooperation Program that was supposed to promote public–private partnerships indicated how the MP's network of relations could be used in addition to the parliamentary means at his disposal. Three days after he made the request in parliament to fund the project, in May 2007, a meeting was held with investors in the offices of the chair of the 15 Mayo executive council, during which the MP assured those present that he would personally take charge of the procedures necessary with the ministers concerned.

As Fath al-Bab explained to me one day when we were driving back from 15 Mayo to Cairo, a Brotherhood MP possessed two forms of power. On the one hand, there was "parliamentary pressure" *(al-daght al-barlamani)*, and on the other there was the "personal dimension" *(al-ganib al-shakhsi)*. The extract from the interview below explains what was meant by the second form of power.

> Something that is very important for us in Egypt is the personal dimension *(al-ganib al-shakhsi)* in the relations between individuals. The same thing is true of relations with the authorities. The fact that an MP is a member of the Brotherhood does not mean that he cannot have good relations on the personal and human level with a minister or someone belonging to the NDP. For example, the road we are driving along used to be in a very bad condition. There were potholes everywhere, and there was no lighting. When I made a proposal to have it renovated, it was immediately accepted by the governor, even though it cost LE45 million. My relations have always been very good with the governor . . . and the one before him as well. Besides that . . . there is also the example of the former minister of the environment. We have major pollution problems in Helwan, but improvements have been made. Contacts with this minister in particular were very good. The minister was

a very good woman, very well educated, someone who had lived in the United States. We used to have lunch together quite a lot . . . Even the minister of the interior—I have always been very welcome when I have called on him, even when, you know, the arrests that we are seeing at the moment, it is the same minister that is behind them. . . . Anyway, I am convinced that direct dialogue between people can resolve a great many problems. It's like with a married couple. Relations are often made difficult by an absence of communication. But if a man is ready to try to understand what his wife wants, and vice versa if she makes the effort to understand him, and they discuss things together, then in general any problems will solve themselves.

The seniority of Fath al-Bab as an MP, and his manner of envisaging relations with the state-like relations between individuals in dialogue with each other, had allowed him to develop personal acquaintances with individuals in the regime, even when these people were openly engaged in the fight against the Brotherhood (such as the minister of the interior). The schizophrenic attitude of the regime toward the Brotherhood MPs was mirrored in a similar behavior among some of them. Fath al-Bab's connivance with leading figures in the regime probably explains the fact that he came very close to being elected as chair of the parliamentary Workers' Affairs Committee, when in general everything possible was done to block Brotherhood access to such positions (Rabi' 2009a). At the local level, his reputation was one of "not making waves with the authorities,"[28] and he himself admitted (laughing) that he had received an offer to join the NDP.[29]

In sum, these three types of strategy—parliamentary pressure, local legitimacy, and elite connivance—had a common feature in that all three aimed to exploit the "zones of uncertainty" (Crozier and Friedberg 1980) created by conflicts between different political and administrative actors, including internal rivalries in the NDP, struggles between diverse authorities on the local level, and personal disputes between individuals. The second common point was that these strategies produce variable results depending on the interlocutors and the moments, but also on the publicization of the actions. It was when the services provided by Brotherhood MPs could be visibly attributed to their own action that state coercion manifested itself. This was not only because the Gama'a was obliged to observe a policy of limited publicity, but also because the appropriation of public space was in general something that was reserved to the state in Cairo and was a way for it to manifest its power (Ismail 2006). As a result, the cooperation between the sheikh and the civil servants in Helwan had to be disguised if it was to have a chance of continuing. In Madinat Nasr, proposals to create a green area in 'Izbat al-Haggana that would have been identifiably the work of the Brother-hood MPs were turned down.

There were other, less visible practices that made up the lion's share of the MPs' daily activities. These were intended not so much to earmark resources that could be used to provide constituency collective services as to respond to the individual requests for aid that residents might make to local constituency offices.

Figure 13. Publication from Fath al-Bab's office announcing the approval of his request for the renovation of the highway, his participation in a parliamentary committee, and his celebration of "exemplary mothers" (Li-kull al-nas, 2006).

## Meeting Individual Requests: Mediation, Instruction, and Ascription

Individual requests could concern a whole range of services involving the state in one way or another and testifying to the ways in which the state was perceived on a daily basis by those it governed. Such requests could have to do with applications to change schools after moving house, or applications to be moved from one governorate to another, from one position to another, or from one grade to another for public-sector employees. Above all, they could relate to applications for jobs in the public sector. Public employment had historically been an entitlement for all university graduates but had been in abeyance since the 1990s.

An MP was seen as an intermediary in such requests, since he could directly meet the governors and ministers concerned and could obtain the necessary *ta'shirat*. These requests were not made only by the poorest categories of the population, either, since there were also many members of the middle classes who lacked *wasta* (connections) and needed help in accessing the administration.

### "At least they try": Interactional and symbolic resources

Most of the work carried out in constituency offices consisted of collecting such individual requests, producing written requests signed by the MP, and sending them to the 'MPs' affairs departments' of the agencies concerned, generally the governorate and the regional offices of the ministries. This work was done by Hadi (the non-MB salaried secretary) in Madinat Nasr and by the activists working for the sheikh in Helwan. Every two weeks, the MPs would be physically present and would receive residents themselves. Observations made during a face-to-face meeting with the residents of the constituency at the MP's office in Helwan Center are reproduced below, the sheikh himself attending but arriving a little late. 'Abd al-Rahman, the office manager (a teacher by profession) and Abu al-Qasim (the office's 'jack of all trades,' not a member of the Brotherhood, but salaried and responsible for maintenance and reception) had taken over in his absence.

In these cases, services were provided in the form of advice, hints about savoir-faire, and the guarantee of some degree of protection. The sheikh told the former microbus driver that he would follow up his case and gave him step-by-step advice on the correct procedures to follow. The father worried about his daughter's education was advised by an 'expert in education' who gave him proper advice and promised to help him. It was clear that advice and instruction were the first main resources offered by the sheikh and his staff, with a clear sense of pedagogy. While the cost of this is nothing, its benefits were also uncertain, especially when the beneficiary upped the ante of his or her demands.

## A Face-to-face Meeting with the MP in Helwan Center

Abu al-Qasim was receiving residents coming to the office in Helwan Center with cups of coffee, tea, or anise, his desk overflowing with files and papers and situated in the center of the office's main room.[30] There were three sofas, a number of chairs, and a television mounted on the wall and set to Al Jazeera. Also on the wall there was a photograph of the MP and a 2008 calendar with another picture of the sheikh making a speech in parliament. A woman in her fifties and an elderly man in a *gallabiyya* were waiting while watching television. The woman told me that she had "come to ask for Sheikh al-Muhammadi's help" in finding new premises for an association that helped disabled people that she was involved with. The previous premises had burned down, and though they had belonged to the NDP, when she had asked the party for help and then the head of the district, she had been told they could do nothing to help her. She had sent a letter to the governor, but this had not received a reply. Then she had come to see the sheikh. She had already come three weeks previously, and the MP had told her to come back again. She had come back today to see whether things had advanced since her last visit. Did she think that the sheikh would be able to help her? "I don't know. We'll see. If our Lord helps him, yes. Everything depends on the will of God." The elderly man, a former microbus driver, was hoping that the sheikh would be able to help him with procedures to increase his small pension. Gamal, an activist (the shopkeeper), was also present and was commenting on what was being shown on television.

'Abd al-Rahman arrived and went into the other room to receive the constituents. Abu al-Qasim invited people in turn to go to see 'Abd al-Rahman, but they didn't go in in the order in which they had arrived. A woman and her daughter in her twenties were received first, even though they had just arrived. It was a request for employment, as could be overheard from the other room. They came out looking disappointed. Then it was the turn of the woman from the association. She told me in parting that 'Abd al-Rahman was going to talk to the sheikh again about the matter and that he would keep her updated. A fashionably dressed young woman accompanied by an older man waited for twenty minutes or so, and then started to complain to Gamal about the waiting time. 'Abd al-Rahman saw her for a few minutes, but then they left (they came back later). Gamal kept telling everyone that the sheikh was on his way. A man whose shabby clothes spoke volumes about his situation took his turn in the main room. The older man in the *gallabiyya* was still waiting.

The sheikh entered, a broad smile on his face. Everyone got up to greet him, shaking hands or embracing him if they were activists. I was asked to sit on the sofa in the second room, it being agreed that the sheikh would see the people who had been waiting for him before speaking to me. 'Abd al-Rahman sat down beside me, and the sheikh sat behind his desk with Gamal on his right taking notes.

The elderly man came into the room, his body held stiffly and looking intimidated by what was going on around him. He started to speak in a very low voice without coming near the desk. The sheikh interrupted him, grasping his hand warmly. But the rather startled look of the man showed that they did not know each other. The elderly man was also short, which added to the oddity of the scene. The sheikh asked him to sit down. The man then explained that he had been to see the head of the district about his tiny pension, but he had been sent to see someone else in another institution.

The sheikh (speaking formally): What did they tell you?
The old man: (No reply)
The sheikh: Did you go or not?
Gamal, reacting to the old man's silence: Come on, tell the sheikh what you told me a little while ago.
The old man: They told me that they couldn't solve the problem.
The sheikh: So, ask them to produce a written response, and then go to see the head of the district with the letter. Then come back here if that doesn't solve the problem.

The old man nodded. The sheikh told him the same thing again, and then he checked that he had understood by getting him to repeat what he had said. "So, what are you going to do? Tell me." After a second warm shaking of hands, the old man left, to be replaced by the fashionable young woman wearing a fuchsia-colored veil.

She didn't seem to be in the least bit intimidated. She sat down and made her request in a very direct fashion. It turned out that she was a graduate of a technical institute in electrical engineering and wanted to find a job in the offices of the electricity company or something else that suited her level of education. The sheikh advised her to write an application to the South Cairo Electricity Company on a computer in the first room. She cut him off, saying, "You told me to do that several months ago. I followed the procedures, but it didn't work, as there are no jobs. I have to find something else." The way she put this and the tone she used were quite critical. The sheikh explained, without batting an eyelid and retaining his usual bonhomie, that there were three thousand students in Helwan, and he couldn't find a job for all of them. Then there was a discussion about the idea of *wasta* (connections). The young woman said that she refused to find a job by using *wasta* and that she wanted to find one on the basis of merit. The sheikh approved what she said and added that if he recommended her for a job it wouldn't be because of *wasta*, as he had every reason to believe in her skills and her merit. Then he suggested that she go to apply for a job at the textile factory in the production department as a supervisor. She got quite angry. "But I don't want to do that." He said in reply, still retaining his calm and collected manner, that it was the labor market that decided things and that she would have to adapt. She wasn't satisfied. He explained things to her again, and then told her to go and write her application. She showed him another piece of paper, probably relating to another application for a job, and asked him to stamp it. I noticed the huge stamp with pink-colored ink sitting on the middle of the desk. It had been there since the MP arrived. Apart from this stamp, apparently the MP's main working tool, there was also a notepad, Gamal's notebook, and some documents left by people coming to see the sheikh. Otherwise, the desk was empty.

The young woman left, and a man in his forties entered the room, seemingly as timid and intimidated as the old man in the *gallabiyya*. He started to talk while still standing up, and the sheikh asked him to sit down. The man wanted to have his daughter transferred to a school closer to where he lived, as the school she was going to at present was a long way away. The sheikh asked whether the problem was one of distance or of quality. The man said it was distance. However, the headmistress of the school in question had asked for an authorization signed by the minister of education before she would agree to a transfer. The sheikh turned to 'Abd al-Rahman, presenting him as an education specialist because of his profession as a teacher. 'Abd al-Rahman explained that it was possible to arrange transfers without authorization at the beginning of each academic year, as long as the necessary procedures had been carried out in advance. In his view, changing a child's school in the middle of the year could harm her. The sheikh and 'Abd al-Rahman then started to reason with the girl's father, saying that they would deal with his request for the beginning of the following academic year in June. The man seemed to be satisfied, thanked them, and left.

Lastly, it was the turn of a student. Like the man before him, he seemed to be intimidated, but he sat down in the chair next to the desk and explained his situation. He had failed his exams, and he wanted to ask the sheikh to intervene with the administration so that he could get his certificate anyway. The sheikh hesitated, looking at the young man with a smile on his face but without seeming to understand what was being asked of him. The young man raised the stakes a little by giving the example of Mustafa Bakri, the MP in the neighboring constituency of Tibbin, who had done this for other students. The sheikh started to laugh. "But the problem was that you didn't revise for the exams," he said. A bit taken aback, the student said that the result had seemed to him unjust. 'Abd al-Rahman said that there was no proof of injustice. Then the young man said that he didn't have the means to do the year again, as he had to find a job, and he knew that an electricity company was recruiting workers. He wanted to apply, and he wanted a recommendation from the sheikh. The latter mentioned to 'Abd al-Rahman that they should tell the young woman in the fuchsia-colored veil about the company, and he agreed to recommend the young man for a job there. But he didn't change his mind about the exams. "Go and write your application on the computer next door," he said. The young man hesitated for a moment in silence. Then he pulled an already written application out of his pocket. There was laughter in the room, the stamp appeared, and then there were thanks all around. The sheikh seemed amused by the audacity of the student's request and started to joke about it with 'Abd al-Rahman.

Each case took about ten minutes.

The discussion between the sheikh and the young woman was interesting in this regard, since the latter did not hesitate to remind the sheikh of his role (he was expected to find a solution to her problem of unemployment) even though she rejected the patronage relationship implied if he were to carry out this service (she refused to make use of *wasta*). Here, the patron–client relationship was paradoxically reaffirmed on a functional level, but contested on its symbolism, as the young woman dismissed the asymmetrical power relations it implied and demanded that her case be seen in terms of a norm that she had chosen (individual merit). The sheikh had no difficulty in dismissing any suspicion of *wasta* in the relationship, since he wanted to see the exchange above all in terms of disinterestedness (as described in the previous chapter). Moreover, when faced with the young student later, he used the same arguments as the young woman in order to condemn the practices of Mustafa Bakri and emphasize his distance from them (merit versus *wasta*). However, once the ideas of norms were introduced into the transaction, it was the young woman who scored off the sheikh in terms of power, since she was the one who made him submit to what she wanted. In fact, she gave him a piece of paper which he stamped without complaining.

This stamp was the second major resource used by the MP in these interactions, its pink ink signaling a service that once again cost nothing, but whose benefits were once again equally uncertain. However, the major limitation the sheikh mentioned—the lack of skilled work opportunities—was structural in character, and he could not be held responsible if his stamp failed to help in this regard. The idea that "the Brothers at least try to do something" was often heard from the beneficiaries interviewed. The reaction of the sheikh when he heard (from the young student) that the company the young woman was interested in was recruiting bore witness to a certain level of engagement on his part.

However, it was still necessary that the Brotherhood MP should appear credible in his attempts to do something. The pink stamp signified the existence of social capital, and it had no value unless it symbolized the real or imaginary connections enjoyed by the MP. Sheikh al-Muhammadi was richly endowed in this regard, since he was able to imply that he had influence over the head of the district and to mention his relations with the management of the public-sector textiles company. It is clear that he did not resort here to any parallel Islamic sector. On the contrary, he emphasized his capacities as a mediator with the local political and economic authorities. It was also evident that the label of 'Muslim Brotherhood' was not foregrounded in his activities as an MP. The term was not mentioned once throughout the session. In Helwan, the signs on the constituency offices bore the name of the local MP, sometimes accompanied by his photograph and the slogan "Islam Is the Solution"*(al-islam huwa al-hal)*. But they did not include any logo or the words "Muslim Brothers." Inside, the décor consisted of posters and photographs showing the MP, with only a few discreet mentions of the Brotherhood (for example, a quotation from Hassan al-Banna). The MP's public bulletins detailing his activities were called "Ma' al-nas"(With the People), or, in a highly significant fashion, simply "al-Muhammadi," using the sheikh's first name. As a result, in his interactions with the local population, the sheikh's identity as a local notable and a popular leader took precedence over his identity as a member of the Brotherhood and even over that of MP.

There was a surprise as the meetings with constituents continued.

### A Local Court of Justice in the MP's Office

Twenty or so people suddenly came into the room. The staff brought extra chairs, arranging them in lines facing the desk. Four men aged between thirty-five and forty-five, all dressed in suits and ties with carefully polished shoes and the latest mobile phones, sat down in the chairs facing the desk. The others, dressed far more modestly and mostly in their fifties, sat down in the chairs at the back. The two women present were seated next to me. Gamal stayed sitting by the sheikh, a little behind the desk. As the scene unfolded, I began to understand that those present were members of the housing cooperative of a cement works and that there was a conflict between the four men sitting at the front, two of whom were lawyers, and the group of employees and workers at the back. The sheikh was being asked to help resolve this conflict.

The sheikh introduced the discussion relatively calmly. "*Bismi-llah al-rahman al-rahim.* Thank you for your presence today, and I am happy to be at your service . . . at the service of all of you." He summarized what he knew of the situation, having been informed about it the night before, and asked Sayyid, sitting in the chair closest to the desk, to speak, reserving the respectful title of *ustadh* for him at first before changing to the much stronger one of *hagg.* Sayyid, who turned out to be the president of the housing cooperative, launched into a long monologue in standard Arabic. He was speaking quickly and was visibly nervous. The conflict turned on some new apartments that the members of the cooperative had invested in. Not only had these apartments not corresponded to what had been advertised (there were problems with the plumbing, the electricity, and elevators that didn't work), but also the amounts demanded from the members had increased over what had been initially asked for. Sayyid was held responsible for this situation by the workers. In response, he accused them of not wanting to pay the sums they owed and of not honoring their pledges. During his speech, 'Imad, the lawyer of the group of workers, sitting opposite him, tried to interrupt, but he was immediately stopped by his neighbors, who told him to hold his fire. At the end of twenty minutes of monologue from Sayyid, someone interrupted him again, and this acted like a signal for the knives to come out. Everyone started talking at once, raising their voices and interrupting each other. Some stood up in order to express their indignation more forcefully. In just a few seconds, the solemn calm that had previously reigned in the room was replaced by general chaos. The sheikh tried to restore order. "If you would allow me" *(law samahtuli)*, he called out, with a certain sang-froid, while still retaining the smile on his face. He struck the desk several times with the stamp. A new function was revealed for this object—it could also be used as a judge's gavel.

Ten minutes at least went by before the sheikh was able to speak without being interrupted from one side or the other in the dispute. He was much more successful in obtaining the silence of the workers, all the while expressing himself with great politeness, than obtaining it from Sayyid and his supporters. Sayyid also did not hesitate to use his telephone while he was in the room and sometimes even interrupted the sheikh. This did not mean that the sheikh was unable to command a certain degree of respect from him, however, and Sayyid would occasionally voice approbation or deference when the sheikh was talking. Moreover, as the discussion continued, those present started to address the sheikh not as "Sheikh" but as *al-Ra'is al-Shaykh* (president), meaning that the situation had now turned into a court of popular justice *(sulh)*.

One of the most vehement of the workers, Abu Hamid, who had been getting up frequently to protest, then obtained official leave to speak, but Sayyid interrupted him. Abu Hamid replied by saying, "Shame on you *('eib)* for interrupting me." Sayyid got very angry and violently shouted, "Make it quick!" *(ikhlas)* at Abu Hamid. Efforts were made to calm the two parties, but the sheikh did not react directly to Sayyid's aggressiveness. Abu Hamid, doing his best to stay calm, then started to speak. "I was not born in Helwan . . . " The sheikh interrupted. "Where do you come from?" "Minufiyya." The sheikh cried out in delight. Gamal said, "That's the home of the sheikh." There was a smile from Abu Hamid. The sheikh then asked him his family name, the village he came from, and so on. A relationship of complicity had been established, and Abu Hamid continued his speech.

It looked as if the sheikh was doing everything he could to keep Sayyid from losing face—an influential man whose status he recognized by using an honorific title—while at the same time appealing for calm and trying not to make it look as if he were criticizing

Sayyid directly. The sheikh said several times: "We are here to solve the problem, not to make it more complicated" (there was a play on words between *hal*—"solution'—and *hila*—"obstacle' or "complication'). On the other hand, the sheikh was also doing everything he could to make it look as if he were not on Sayyid's side in the eyes of the workers, notably by making sure that they had a chance to speak and establishing relationships with them that relied upon proximity. He said his role was to be "of service to all," for example, and used the terms "sister" and "brother" to address the workers. He also employed politeness, humor, and some degree of pedagogy in his appeals for calm. He made a number of jokes about the fact that Abu Hamid seemed to feel a constant need to get up out of his chair in order to speak, ordering that several chairs be "piled up, as he will be higher up," while telling him that if he wanted to speak he would have to remain seated. At the same time, he was careful to mention the close personal relationship he felt with Abu Hamid as a way of recognizing his distinction and counterbalancing the humiliation that Sayyid had attempted to inflict upon him.

At the end of nearly two hours of debate, the sheikh suggested a way of beginning to resolve the conflict that was deliberately neutral in form. He proposed the formation of a committee that would study the problem and find a solution to it, to be composed of members from both sides in the dispute as long as they were calm. Those present agreed on the choice of the five people who should be on the committee. They refused to appoint Abu Hamid, who himself said that he wasn't calm enough to sit on the committee, and a debate then ensued about whether or not to appoint 'Imad ("He interrupted several times"; "Yes, but he is our lawyer"). There was then a discussion about one of the women, an engineer, who was duly appointed to the committee. She then put forward the names of several members of the cooperative who had not been able to come to the meeting but were calmer than those who had, she said. These names were approved. One of the lawyers accompanying Sayyid was also selected. The sheikh noted down all the names and took the telephone numbers of those who were absent so that he could contact them. He said the committee would have a month to find a solution to the dispute and proposed that they should meet again once it had done so.

The meeting ended with the sound of the stamp hitting the desk. People left. 'Abd al-Rahman said to me, "You see? People come because they trust Sheikh al-Muhammadi. We can solve a problem among ourselves without needing to go to a court or a representative of the state."

The case of Sheikh al-Muhammadi gives an indication of the multiple possible identities that could be taken on by social actors, even when they were members of the Brotherhood. Indeed, it is this multiplicity that is too often forgotten when 'Islamists' are discussed. It was his capacity to draw on a whole range of different identities that allowed a Brotherhood MP like the sheikh to adapt so readily to various situations and interactions. The capacity to switch identities as the need arose was also in evidence in Madinat Nasr in the case of 'Isam Mukhtar, though in a very different manner. The latter was less well endowed with personal resources, and he tried to hide his identity as a Muslim Brother behind that of an MP.

### Glossing over identity and the mechanism of ascription

Mukhtar's choice of Hadi, not a member of the Brotherhood, as his secretary was part of a larger strategy designed to gloss over his identity as a Brother with regard to the authorities. Authorizations were needed in order to have access to the MPs' affairs departments of the various government ministries and state agencies, and not being a member of the Brotherhood, hence not having a file with State Security, could help to obtain them. Mukhtar also emphasized his identity as an MP, presenting this as neutral and defined by his function and not his political affiliation. Though he was a member of the Brotherhood, the MP was nevertheless a cog in the Egyptian political and administrative system, and he had the right to make use, within certain limits, of the prerogatives that came with his position. Therefore, ruling elites were partly constrained in their interactions with Brotherhood MPs when the latter were able to present themselves not as Brothers but as elected representatives of the people. State officials symmetrically used certain euphemisms to explain why they were refusing or acceding to Brotherhood MPs' requests, as Hadi explained in the case of Mukhtar.

> Me: Did the governor ever refuse any of Mukhtar's requests because he was a member of the Brotherhood?
>
> Hadi: No, no, no. They would meet face to face, so he couldn't refuse him just like that. What would happen is that he would agree, but not one hundred percent. When a request came from an NDP MP, the governor would write "agreed" (*muwafiq*). For us, he would write "no objection"(*la mani'*), or if he wanted to cause problems, "no objection depending on the situation."[31]

Having MPs also gave the Brotherhood access to a social protection scheme that had been growing over previous years, at no cost to the organization.

This system, called 'healthcare paid by the state' *(al-'ilag 'ala nafaqat al-dawla)*, was a system of healthcare coverage that was in addition to the medical insurance that, in any case, only benefits half the population and certain restricted categories, such as civil servants and the employees of major companies. The system of 'healthcare paid by the state' was made available out of grants made by the minister of health on a discretionary basis, and it paid for expensive treatment needed by poorer patients. In 2004, the total amount of these grants represented more than half the amount spent on the medical insurance system as a whole, with nearly 1.2 million patients benefiting from it (Clément 2007b).

A large part of these grants went through the hands of MPs, who would draw the attention of the minister to the cases of individuals in need of expensive treatment. In 2009, all the MPs, all parties taken together, had obtained LE3.9 billion in medical grants, while the program had cost the government around LE8.4 billion over three years (Leila 2010). The requests made by Brotherhood MPs under the program were generally accepted, meaning that they could use their positions in parliament to redistribute public resources on an individual basis. This was seen as proof of their effectiveness as MPs and maybe even of the effectiveness of the social services provided by the Brotherhood. This is what I call the "mechanism of ascription, ' by which the MP takes credit for (good) actions that are not entirely his responsibility, let alone that of the organization.

Another example of this mechanism of ascription related to the financing given to micro-projects by the Social Development Fund *(al-sunduq al-igtima'i li-l-tanmiyya)* managed by the prime minister's office. This fund, provided by various international donors, had been set up in 1991 in order to help protect social groups at risk of being negatively affected by the structural adjustment program that was then in place and to promote the development of small businesses by young graduates (the priority target) newly entering the labor market. Akram explained the role of the small enterprises committee set up by the sheikh's staff in Helwan.

> In the first year, one hundred young people benefited from it. Later, there were fewer, but even so there have been some three hundred up to now [2008]. We don't give them money. Instead, we help them with the paperwork they have to do with the government. We help the young person concerned to prepare a dossier, and then we tell him where to take it. We don't have any direct relationship with officials from the Social Fund, and they don't know that the young person in question is being sent by us.

Not only was the cost of the service provided minimal, as it was once again advice and pedagogical instruction, but the chances of being given a grant were not compromised by the Brotherhood origin of the request, which was carefully hidden. While the "officials from the Social Fund . . . don't know that the young person in question is being sent by us," that young person does know it. It was this asymmetry of information that the Brothers counted on to ensure the loyalty of the beneficiary.

## Conclusion

The Brotherhood's banned MPs thus maneuvered between the resources of their staff and the organizational weight of the *tanzim*, and between the prerogatives that came with their position in parliament and the limitations imposed on them by the state when exercising their local roles. Their choice of strategies just as clearly depended on the nature of the local situation. A longstanding MP like 'Ali Fath al-Bab in Tibbin/15 Mayo could use his contacts in the corridors of power, while leaving members of his staff to do their own thing on an everyday basis. The risk was that he could then appear to be less involved in his own constituency. An unknown MP like 'Isam Mukhtar in Madinat Nasr, on the other hand, having fewer resources of his own and lacking the connections that would get him access to state agencies, needed to emphasize his neutrality as an MP and remind others of the privileges that came with this role. His strategy involved glossing over his identity as a member of the Brotherhood and opting for a general pragmatism, as a member of his staff admitted: "We want to see the services provided, so we tend to avoid making it obvious what the governor gives us, since if we did, he might put a stop to it."[32] This set of activities was handled by the MP and his non-Brotherhood secretary, while another set, not involving access to the state, was organized by activists connected to the *tanzim*. Lastly, the popular MP, Sheikh al-Muhammadi in Helwan, drew upon the authority and legitimacy he enjoyed with his local and regional interlocutors when framing his strategy. He was also supported by a staff that was both active and well embedded in the social networks of the constituency.

Despite the limitations they suffered in accessing state resources and public space, the Brotherhood MPs did their best to comply with the requirements of their role. The examples of *al-maghud al-dhati*, the instruction provided during constituents' meetings, the session of popular justice, the ascription of healthcare paid by the state and the Social Development Fund, all show that they have invested this role with particular "arts of doing" (De Certeau 1980) and different forms of savoir-faire in order to symbolically compensate for their comparative material disadvantage when faced with NDP MPs. The MPs' offices were a new way of increasing the grassroots influence of the Gama'a, by reaching out to a wider public and providing new types of services, such as access to administrations.

It was also with this double aim of symbolic compensation and enhanced local anchoring in mind that the various MPs' staffs introduced practices that did not require any dependency on the state and that reshaped the role of an MP. These will be examined in the following chapter. Studying them will allow us to better understand the ways in which the Gama'a spread its influence through society and the ways in which social relationships were politicized.

# 4

# The Politics of Goodness

This chapter focuses on the social services delivered by the staff of the Brotherhood MPs that did not require dependency on state resources. Although these might be regarded as a transfer of resources that are negligible from a quantitative point of view, they were highly significant on the symbolic level since they allowed the Brotherhood MPs to differentiate themselves from their NDP rivals, not because they were the only ones to deliver such services, but because they were the only ones to deliver them in the way that they did. Analyzing such practices sheds light on the Brotherhood's distinctiveness in the framework of the politics of goodness.

By this notion, I mean that the state and the regime, as well as the Brotherhood and other social actors, were together involved in "relocating welfare" (Ismail 2006) through their charitable activities and in reducing politics to the micro-level of social services. Perceptions of who serves (*beyekhdem*) and who does not serve (*mabeyekhdemsh*) were determining criteria in popular judgments of the political elites, often expressed in the moral terms of *khayr*, or 'goodness.' During the 2005–10 parliament, the Brotherhood MPs used the slogan "Together, we are bringing goodness to Egypt"(*ma'an, nahmal al-khayr li-Masr*), encapsulating both the Brotherhood's commitment to spirit of service and the pivotal role played by religion in the politics of goodness. As has been seen in earlier chapters, the Brotherhood's service and charity networks were intertwined with the regime's own social-service networks. The latter tried to keep the myth of state-led development alive, burdening the NDP MPs with local roles of resource distribution and public work. However, the politics of goodness was also a competitive framework in which actors struggled in order to be perceived as  those who serve and to enjoy the symbolic benefits of social actions. As a result, the politics of goodness is defined here in terms of a conflictual consensus built on entrenched welfare networks and as an imaginary matrix mixing state-led development and religious charity. The aim of the chapter is to further the study of this entrenchment of networks, and to understand how the Brotherhood tried to secure a distinctive moral position on the common but competitive grounds of *khayr*.

The staff of the Brotherhood MPs typically engaged in four kinds of social services, the first being education and leisure activities. This included classes in literacy, English, IT, cooking, and sewing, as well as after-school tutoring. There were also Qur'an recital competitions, day trips in Cairo or further afield, marriage-preparation classes for girls, and in-service training for teachers, among other things. Such activities were intended to enlarge the audience for MB social services by reaching out to different sections of the population, from the poorest of the poor to the lower middle classes, who had also been negatively impacted by the shortcomings of the public education system and had little money to spend on leisure activities.

Figure 14. Mukhtar's assessment leaflet showing celebrations and services (Lamahat, 2010).

Figure 15. Some examples of services shown by Sheikh al-Muhammadi's publication (Ma'a al-nas, 2008).

Second, the MPs' offices organized various public events on an annual basis, including prize-giving ceremonies *(hafalat takrim)* for valedictorian students *(al-mutafawwiqin)*, and exemplary mothers *(al-umm al-mithaliyya)* or workers *(al-'amil al-mithali)*.[1] There were also charity events such as Orphans' Day *(youm al-yatim)*, school supplies and clothing sales *(ma'arid khayriyya li-l-takaful al-igtima'i)*, group marriages *(zifaf gama'i)*, and food distribution during Ramadan or on the Eid. The Brotherhood MPs organized annual draws for the pilgrimage places *(qur'at ta'shirat al-higg)* that each year were allocated to members of the People's Assembly. The Brotherhood MPs claimed they had been the first ones to share out these places to constituents on this basis.[2]

A third type of activity included public-service campaigns, ranging from mobile medical clinics or medical caravans (*qawafil tibbiyya*) to street-cleaning operations. A fourth type, less visible and less official, but nevertheless taking place on a daily basis in all the offices visited, was the handing out of financial, medical, or food aid to local residents, who would come to the offices with this in mind, either occasionally or at monthly intervals.

Questions about the everyday forms of MB politicization arise from the study of these activities. What was their political meaning? Or, more precisely, what was the political work that they were doing? These practices were not political per se: they were not provided with an explicit ideological discourse, nor were they accomplished by activists with a systematic political aim in mind. Instead, politicization was produced in the course of interactions between Brotherhood members, the beneficiaries of the social services concerned, and also the intermediaries and even the spectators of such social-assistance practices. Politicization is understood here in two complementary ways. On the one hand, it is seen as a process of requalification of what is or is not political: it then refers to "ways of designating" (Lagroye 2003). On the other hand, politicization is seen as a process of reappropriation and diversion of the norms to which the governed are subjected (Bayart 1985): it then resides in "ways of doing" things (De Certeau 1980). The Brothers took over the "framework" (Goffman 1974) of the interaction between the MP and the governed with "ways of doing" that opened new possibilities for reappropriation for some among the governed, those that I call "associated individuals." The latter then enunciate ways of designating these practices by comparison and, often, in opposition to those they consider characteristic of the dominant order—that is, the practices of NDP officials. Taken together, such "ways of doing and designating" did not, strictly speaking, lead to the subversion of that order, but they did produce a belief, shared by the actors involved, that they were acting differently within the framework of the dominant order. Politicization in this context meant a series of operations engaging the requalification and reappropriation of the existing norms, thereby producing an impression of distinctiveness from them.

In the course of such operations and in the broader context of the politics of goodness, religious morality, seen as a set of practical activities and relationships to the self and others—in other words, as ethics—was crucial. I build on Saba Mahmood's understanding of the Aristotelian tradition of ethics and on how she used it, in her work on the mosques movement in Egypt, to explore some of the infinite number of "dimensions of human action whose ethical and political status does not map onto the logic of repression and resistance"(Mahmood 2005: 14). Referring to this nonbinary logic, I argue that the Brotherhood politicization mainly took the form of building distinctiveness through a specific ethical conduct.

## The Social Spread of the Gama'a: The Networks of *Khayr*

The regular activities and public events organized by the MPs' offices depended on three different types of networks: the Brotherhood networks, made up of activists and the social spaces in which they were active; the semi-Brotherhood networks, made up of partner institutions; and the enlarged networks that also took in non-Brotherhood intermediaries and associated individuals. All these networks underlay the social spread of the Gama'a, with their extent and character making the boundary between the Gama'a and the rest of society notably porous.

### Brotherhood Networks: Activist Groups and Extensions
#### Core members, intermittent participants, and benefactors
A Brotherhood MP's main resource was his staff, though as we saw earlier the composition and strength of this varied according to context. Each staff had a core of active members around which other activists, whether staff members or working on behalf of the *tanzim*, also worked on an irregular basis to help carry out the activities of the office concerned. Some of these individuals might help organize educational workshops, while others might make financial contributions to help fund special events or regular activities. The question of finance was in general swiftly dealt with by my interlocutors; they mentioned only the subscriptions that activists needed to pay to the Brotherhood in line with its internal rules. However, these subscriptions would certainly not have been enough to pay for the activities carried out by all the Brotherhood MPs during the 2005–10 parliament, especially since the repression of the period meant that the organization also experienced additional costs relating, among other things, to legal aid for prisoners and care for their families.

The English classes given by Mukhtar's staff in the Misr al-Gedida office of the Madinat Nasr constituency, for example, were attended by a dozen female secondary-school students who paid a symbolic amount to attend them. The teacher giving the classes had been contacted through an advertisement he had put up in a private language center he worked in. He was not a member of the Brotherhood, and he taught classes in the MP's office simply as a way of making some extra money. The special events and ceremonies organized by the MPs' offices also entailed significant expenses, including the rental costs of the premises and audiovisual equipment used as well as prizes and publicity materials.[3] As a result, another category of actors would regularly appear, opaquely identified as "benefactors" *(ahl al-khayr)*, who in addition to their regular subscriptions would make donations to pay for particular activities.

For example, 'Isam Mukhtar explained that, regarding the special events organized by his staff,

> The benefactors do not like to see their names published. However, they could be MB businessmen whom we approach directly when we are organizing special events. But they are not businessmen like Ahmed Ezz,[4] who owns whole factories. They are men who work in the private sector and who own a shop or a small company or two and are not employees.[5]

It was no coincidence that all my attempts at contacting Brotherhood businessmen in the constituencies studied drew a blank, being met with silence or refusals justified by the need to respect anonymity and the modesty associated with acts of *zakat*. At the same time, the period of the fieldwork should be seen in the context of the years between 2006 and 2008 when forty members of the Brotherhood, mostly businessmen or company bosses, were put on trial in military courts on charges of money laundering for the Brotherhood's benefit and subsequently sentenced to long prison sentences.[6]

All the activists interviewed also emphasized the substitution for financial resources of "work that was freely given in the shape of time and popular efforts" *(al-guhud al-sha'biyya)*,[7] as Akram, the coordinator of the Helwan offices, put it. It was a question of capitalizing on the social roles connected to the professional positions of the Brothers living in the area in order to support the activities of the offices. When a patient arrived at an MP's office, for example, asking for help in getting treatment for his condition, he would be sent to an MB doctor working either independently or in a hospital, who would then treat him without payment. The free medical care provided by the doctor was part of his support for the MP's activities. Pharmacists (a source of medicines), teachers (who could give lessons), lawyers (useful for legal advice), businessmen (a source of jobs), shopkeepers (who could provide food or other items), or civil servants who were also members of the Brotherhood could also be solicited for help. During a face-to-face meeting with constituents in the Helwan Center office, for example, 'Abd al-Rahman told a resident who had come with a problem regarding his health insurance to go to see a certain civil servant who worked in the local health department. "He . . . he is one of us *[wahid mennena]*," 'Abd al-Rahman carefully said, indicating that the civil servant concerned, a member of the Brotherhood, would be happy to help out a resident who had been sent by the local Brotherhood office.

In addition to their professional positions, local members of the Brotherhood could also be solicited because of their social roles in various welfare activities. It is for this reason that it is important to consider the extensions of the activist groups, that is to say, the different social services and charitable institutions in which the MB members were active.

## Patterns and techniques of social entrenchment

The official ban on the existence of the Gama'a and its corollaries—the absence of physical premises until at least 2005, the surveillance of the boards of unions and charities, and the need to disguise any identification with the Brotherhood—meant that the involvement of the organization's activists in the charitable sector could only take place in two main ways.

The first was through social activities that took place outside any legal framework and had no physical location, such as through the welfare committee *(lagnat al-birr)* attached to the *tanzim.* Branches of this committee operated in each district thanks to funding from activist subscriptions and donations made as *zakat* by local MB benefactors. However, the activists interviewed also worked through other committees collecting *zakat* donations that were not related to the *tanzim* and that had no legal status. These non-official *zakat* committees, distinct from the official ones registered with the Nasser Bank, consisted of groups of local residents, friends, or work colleagues who had decided to group together their own resources as well as gifts made to them by various acquaintances with a view to distributing these to poor families and orphans in their neighborhood. One intermittent activist member of the Helwan staff told me that the non-official *zakat* committee of which he was a member managed to give financial support to two hundred and fifty families and nine hundred orphans a year by distributing a total of LE250,000 (in 2010). While such figures need to be viewed with caution, this form of local self-organization seemed to exist on a considerable scale and was reminiscent of the *gam'iyyat* that are widespread in Egypt (Singerman 1995). The phenomenon was thus not restricted to the MB, and the groups involved were formed on the basis of local friendships rather than on membership in the Brotherhood, even if MB members tended to stick together, according to the young activist providing the information. Similar social activities could be carried out on the individual level, with Ayman (the worker in a military factory), Ibrahim (the school adviser), Gamal (the shopkeeper), and 'Abd al-Rahman (the teacher) in the Helwan constituency all describing themselves as "intermediaries" *(wasit,* pl. *wusata')* known in the neighborhood or their workplace for putting people needing assistance into contact with others who had various kinds of resources. Sheikh al-Muhammadi also described himself as "a mobile charity institution" *(mu'assasat khayr mutanaqqila)* during the period "before the office existed."[8] According to Akram, the coordinator of the sheikh's offices, it was this capacity to mediate between different social groups that gave the Brotherhood much of its influence. "Other donors *(ahl al-khayr)* have money, but they are not organized, whereas we are organized, and people trust us to be able to raise funds. The Gamaʻa has popular recognition and legitimacy even if it is not recognized by the government," he said.[9]

The second major form of entrenchment of the Brotherhood in the charitable sector took the form of the symbolic appropriation of spaces not otherwise linked to the organization, including charities, official *zakat* committees, mosques, workers' unions or professional associations, workers' cooperatives, mutual societies, and solidarity funds. This form of involvement can be seen as part of a strategy aimed at the "control of positions," to use the term coined by Bourdieu in the context of the Roman Catholic Church (Bourdieu 1998: 124). Brothers would carry out social activities through organizations that were not connected to the *tanzim*, but whose involvement could be used to spread confusion about who was really responsible for the activities in question. MB members therefore occupied certain positions in such organizations, including in those linked to the state, from which they could deliver social services at the lowest possible cost for the Gamaʻa since they were not using the latter's own resources to do so.

The "control of positions" presupposed a whole set of techniques intended to get around the banning order hanging over the Brotherhood. One of these consisted of using Brothers 'in disguise,' in other words, individuals not known to the security forces. This was the case of Ayman and Gabir when they started to work for the official *zakat* committees in their respective companies. As they had only recently joined the Brotherhood, or were still in the process of doing so, they were not known to be members of it. The case of Bassim, who was a member of al-Gamʻiyya al-Sharʻiyya in the Madinat Nasr constituency, is an example of the tactics that could be used to remain 'in disguise' and thus to remain off the radar of State Security. As he explained,

> I joined the Brotherhood in 1998 but was only detected by the security forces in 2001 because of my university activities. When I stood for election to the administrative board of the local branch of al-Gamʻiyya al-Sharʻiyya in 2003, I didn't provide my photograph and only gave my name, because there are lots of people that have the same name as I do. I did not give in my ID, because if I had, the result would have been different. My friends who worked in the same association knew that I was a member of the Brotherhood, but the people at the top did not know. It is a large organization.[10]

If they were later unmasked as Brothers and therefore expelled from other organizations, MB activists could use another technique, which consisted of placing people who were close to them or sympathizers of the organization in such positions, rather than holding them themselves. This allowed them to still make use of these organizations through the intermediary figures. A third technique consisted of getting involved in the organizations as ordinary members (afrad) without seeking to play leadership roles within them or taking them over collectively. The case of Ayman, manager of the sheikh's main office in Helwan, shows how these techniques worked.

---

### Control of Positions and Informal Activities in a Factory Environment

The son of a leading family in the informal area of Helwan al-Balad, Ayman began his social activities even before joining the Brotherhood by assisting his father on the informal popular justice committee that the latter headed in the area.[11] Employed from 1978 in one of the military production factories in the area, at the end of the 1980s he joined the factory's official *zakat* committee, which had been set up by the Muslim Brothers. This brought him into close contact with the Gama'a.

In 1990, he became the secretary of the *zakat* committee, and at the same time he was elected to the factory's cooperative association. These two parastate organizations had advantages that the workers' union did not have, among them the possibility of providing the most basic services to those in need. He explained:

> The workers take part in the *zakat* committee by making donations, and at the end of each month we look at how much has been collected and who has problems and then we try to help them from *zakat* funds. The Nasser Social Bank supervises the committee's work . . . The cooperative association is also a government organization, and it helps workers to buy furniture and so on at reduced prices. Every month, twenty-five people or so are able to buy the appliances they need thanks to their contributions to the cooperative, things like a refrigerator, a washing machine, or canisters of gas in winter. The union doesn't do anything like this.

Later, the *zakat* committee was ordered to be closed; Ayman said that "the minister of military production [Helwan MP Sayyid Mish'al] thought that it was through the committee that people had been drawn to the Brothers." However, Ayman continued his work, this time outside of any legal framework. "We all work on the factory floor . . . We get to know the people we work with, and we try to help if they have problems . . . We try to put them in touch with someone who can help them, a resident of the district who knows of a charity or a mosque, for example." Ayman also kept his unofficial position as imam in the factory mosque.

In 1995, he was prevented from running for the election as the workers' representative on the factory's board and put in prison for fifteen days. He set up an official *zakat* committee outside the factory in his home area. In 2001, he managed to be elected as the workers' representative, thanks, he said, to "the workers being careful to check the supervision of the balloting." He was finally transferred against his will to another factory in north Cairo in 2006. The *zakat* committee he had set up in his neighborhood was closed at the same time, though Ayman managed to stay on as its informal manager thanks to the actions of friends. "State Security removed my name and gave instructions to this effect to the Nasser Bank. As a result, I couldn't be listed as one of the managers, even though the committee continued to exist. There weren't any Brothers who were not known as such working in it anymore, but there were people who would work with us and liked us. We brought them in, and they kept the committee going. But they were not members of the Gama'a."

These forms of local entrenchment thus depended on the blurring of the activists' identities as Muslim Brothers and on the embedding of the Gama'a in social networks that mixed together Brothers, half-Brothers, and non-Brothers. This kind of blurring and intertwining also characterized the organizations described here as "partners" of the Brotherhood; in other words, organizations that had been founded or were directed by members of the Brotherhood without its presence in them being made public or its members having exclusive or even majority membership in them.

## Semi-Brotherhood Networks: Local Partner Institutions
Many studies have assumed the existence of links between Islamic social organizations and the Brotherhood. However, these links have only rarely been the object of empirical investigation.[12] Yet, in my view the very fact that these links are often simply assumed to exist reveals an important feature of the way they operate. Two examples of organizations linked to the Brotherhood are examined below in order to add to an understanding of how such links worked in practice.

### Medical partner organizations
Three medical institutions regularly took part in activities organized by the staff of the Helwan and Tibbin/15 Mayo MPs. These were al-Hadi

al-Islami Hospital and two clinics, one specializing in ophthalmology (and occupying premises in the same building as the sheikh's Helwan Center office) and the other in infertility treatment and in-vitro fertilization. Doctors from all three institutions actively participated in the mobile medical clinics organized by the offices of the Brotherhood MPs, and they also treated patients sent by them on a non-paying basis.

Al-Hadi al-Islami Hospital, founded in 1985, was a *khayri* (welfare or charitable) institution as opposed to a private *(khass)* or public *('amm)* one. It was part of the Gam'iyya al-Tibbiyya al-Islamiyya network described earlier as a "satellite association" of the Gama'a.[13] The hospital had sixty-five beds and could treat 1,200 patients a day.[14] It had a maternity and a dialysis clinic and offered twenty-six other specialized services. It had four operating theaters where operations including open-heart surgery took place, and it employed some two hundred doctors and more than three hundred and fifty other employees. According to Ehab, a Brotherhood official and former medical director of the hospital, the *khayri* status of al-Hadi al-Islami Hospital meant that it was able to charge "prices that are below market rates, while at the same time maintaining a high level of quality."[15] In 2009, the price of a consultation was LE11, as compared to LE30 at a private doctor's office. Prices a third of market rates were charged for all the services it offered, and patients considered poor could expect to be treated for free.

This was possible thanks to three main sources of finance. The vast majority of costs were absorbed by the hospital directly, while another part was absorbed by the doctors themselves, as they were usually paid between 50 and 60 percent of the cost of the procedures they carried out, though some would work for free or accept a smaller percentage. A third source of income came from donations from the local community to an assistance fund *(sunduq ri'aya)*, amounting to some 10 percent of the total. When deciding how much to charge an individual patient, the hospital would examine the financial situation of the individual concerned and make a decision about what percentage to charge, or, if the situation warranted it, write off the charges entirely. Such decisions could also be made before the treatment was started by the charities with which the hospital worked, the MPs' staff, or some other intermediary. Ehab emphasized that the hospital worked with all the relevant organizations in the area without exception and that its Brotherhood label was largely ignored.

Ehab also said that when it came to the recruitment of staff ("5 percent of the staff at most are members of the Brotherhood, most of them in management"), acceptance of patients ("there is no particular religious orientation"), internal rules,[16] or workplace management ("there is nothing in the hospital to indicate that it belongs to the Muslim Brotherhood"). This was confirmed by a visit to the hospital, where no Brotherhood signage or "Islamic design," to employ the term used by Farag (1992), could be observed. Only the Gam'iyya al-Islamiyya al-Tibbiyya logo appeared here and there, though in order for this to be understood as pointing to the Brotherhood one would have to have known in advance that the charity was linked to the organization. Most patients would not have known this. The doctors at the hospital worked there in addition to their main employment elsewhere, something that was readily admitted by Ehab. "They make a calculation. They stay in their offices for five hours, and perhaps five patients, maybe ten, come to see them. If they work at al-Hadi, even though they will get a smaller fee they will see twenty-five patients in three hours, which is more advantageous," he commented. In addition to the usual professional standards, the only additional condition that those working at the hospital had to observe was the need to respect a certain "moral" framework, which was defined by Ehab.

> There is a basis, a moral framework *(akhlaqi)*, which involves quality of service, equality of treatment, and the social care of the patient. Those who come to work here do so to earn a living and to experience the social message of the Brotherhood, not for the sake of appearances, but for the way in which the Brothers move in society, how they work compassionately *(bi-rahma)* to deliver top-quality services that add to social well-being. *The hospital is the message.* Everyone here will treat a poor patient for nothing. There is a consensus on this, and anyway it's not only the Brotherhood's idea, as everyone agrees on *khayr* (goodness) that is so characteristic of Egypt. We begin from this idea, and then other people see that it's a good one and start to implement it themselves.

Ehab considered that this moral framework was the distinguishing mark of al-Hadi Hospital and that it was perceptible to all those who used it. It led them to suppose that the hospital belonged to the Brotherhood, he said. He also emphasized the inclusivity of this moral framework, which showed that "the Brothers don't want to stay among themselves and only work in their own corner. On the contrary, they want to work with all the components of society." The two other medical centers, both of which he had also helped to establish, were based on the same model of a handful of Muslim Brothers founding the institution and then a majority of non-Brotherhood personnel managing or working in it.

For local inhabitants, the identification of the links between the Gama'a and these institutions was thus largely a matter of guesswork or even rumor. Ehab confirmed this when, after emphasizing that the hospital's connection to the Brotherhood was glossed over, he said that "people do know that a given individual is a member of the Brotherhood and that another one is as well. They get to know it during the elections." Ehab himself had been the manager of the MB candidates' election campaigns in Helwan since 1987. While he had never stood as a candidate in the parliamentary or local elections himself, he considered his role to be a crucial one, not least because he enjoyed a personal popularity linked to his job that could be used for the benefit of the candidates.

> Egyptian people have an absolute trust in doctors. After God, there is the doctor—an honest one, of course. So our role is an important one as we have people's trust. But we would never campaign inside a hospital. That is a strictly professional environment, a place where we would not engage in politics.

While the 'no politics in hospital' rule was one that Ehab seemed determined not to break, the relationships that were either observed or attributed between the hospital staff and local Brotherhood figures involved in politics encouraged the supposition that the Brothers lay behind the hospital's services. This was despite another manager insisting during a visit to the hospital that "we are not looking to ensure that people know the hospital belongs to the Brotherhood." Ehab was also a member of another 'semi-Brotherhood' network in the area, since he had been the manager of two clinics owned by al-Gam'iyya al-Shar'iyya, and he was still a member of the general assembly of the charity (in 2009) despite efforts by State Security to have him expelled.[17]

### Al-Gam'iyya al-Shar'iyya

The importance of the Gam'iyya al-Shar'iyya (GS) network has been mentioned in previous chapters. Even though it was well known in Helwan that the local branch of the GS had been founded and directed for many years by Sheikh al-Muhammadi and that there were partnerships between the sheikh's staff and the GS,[18] there were also hesitations on the part of my interlocutors when I mentioned this subject, reflecting the ambiguous position of the Gama'a in relation to the organization.[19] Sheikh al-Muhammadi himself only ever talked about the GS as something belonging to the past, and very few activists would speak openly about it. In fact, the GS was a sort of taboo subject for the Brothers, something like another public secret within the larger public secret of the Brotherhood itself.

The ambiguous proximity between the Brotherhood and the GS led to confusion in identifying the two organizations' actors. A Brother who had been expelled from the GS could still continue to be perceived as a member of the charity and could still benefit from the legitimacy that this identification could bring for his own individual and informal charitable activities.

Akram commented,

> Let me tell you something: we are present in the streets in a real way and independently of the authorities or any official or legal regulation. The Brother who was here a little while ago used to be the president of a charity he has now left. However, he hasn't stopped his charitable activities. Most Brothers who leave charities continue with their social activities, continuing to make charitable contributions with or without the charity behind them. We don't need the charities. It is the trust that people have in us that allows us to do what we do. It is that trust that makes people come to see us, saying "I have LE500 or LE1,000. I want to give it to poor people or orphans and so on." We say, "Give it to us, and we will distribute it." People trust us to do that, and it is that trust that enables us to work. It is not an organized and official movement. It is a popular movement, and I think it is that which gives it its size.[20]

The "trust" referred to probably owed a lot to the activities of the person concerned in his previous charity, all the more so since this was the GS, with its unparalleled reputation. I was able to be present during a conversation between two residents of Helwan that clearly expressed the confusion between the Brothers and the GS and the movable boundaries between formal charitable activities and informal ones (see conversation on page 153).

In addition to the debate on the question of the elections,[21] this conversation also showed how a completely informal organization—in this case a group of Brothers linked in some way to the official GS—could take on a real existence in people's minds such that they even began to refer to it in the same way (as "the GS of the Brothers"). Rawda readily understood who Hisham was talking about when he referred to the group in this way, for example. This intriguing conversation corroborates the idea that there was some confusion between the Brotherhood and the GS, and it stresses the importance of identification mechanisms. A further example, this time of a mobile medical clinic, or medical caravan, in Madinat Nasr, underlined this confusion.

## A Non-official al-Gam'iyya al-Shar'iyya

The conversation in question took place on the premises of a small NGO working on raising awareness of human rights in an informal area of Helwan.[22] The manager, officially a member of the NDP, was also close to the Center for Trade Union and Workers Services run by Kamal 'Abbas (a leftist). I met a woman, Rawda, who used to come to the NGO's premises from time to time, and Hisham, its jack of all trades. Rawda told me that her role was to help widows (like herself) by teaching them how to sew so that they could sell the products they made. She then talked about another charity that made small loans so that the women could buy sewing machines. I asked her to tell me more about it.

Me: Are you talking about the GS?

R.: No, not everything is connected to the GS, only the mosques.

H.: There is also an independent GS not linked to the mosques.

R.: What are you talking about?

H.: The GS of the Brotherhood.

R.: OK.

Me: There is a GS that belongs to the Brotherhood?

H. & R.: Yes.

Me: Here in Helwan?

H.: But it's not official (heyya mesh mu'lana).

Me: What does that mean?

H.: It means that they get together among themselves and distribute things for the elections. It's well known . . .

Me: Can you explain?

H.: They distribute things. They collect them, as well as money, and they distribute them to people.

Me: They do this in the GS?

H.: No, the independent GS.

Me: Independent?

H.: They do things like that themselves, without using GS premises (min ghayr maqar).

Me: They do that all the time, or only during elections?

H.: All the time . . . but apparently for the elections as well . . .

R.: No, it's not for the elections!

H.: Yes, it's for the elections. I am not talking of the official GS here . . . they distribute . . .

R.: Yes, but it's not clear! It's not been proven . . .

## A Medical Caravan in 'Izbat al-Haggana (Madinat Nasr)

The idea of a medical caravan (qafila tibbiyya) was to hold 'medical days' during which doctors (both GPs and specialists) and dentists would come together in a particular place on a particular day to offer a range of free consultations and services.[23] In the example described here, the place chosen for the event was particularly interesting, since it took place on the premises of the GS mosque in 'Izbat al-Haggana after the Friday prayer. The mosque was run by a sheikh who, like Hagg Nabil (earlier studied in detail),[24] was a popular leadership figure who had supported 'Isam Mukhtar in the latter's election campaign. The decision to hold the medical caravan on the premises of this mosque thus symbolized the informal partnership arrangement between them.

On that day, the GS premises were awash with children and young mothers lining up in front of different rooms that had been taken over for temporary medical practices run by young doctors who were giving their services for free. Not all of the doctors were members of the Brotherhood by any means. They were most often the colleagues of MB doctors who had agreed to take part in order to donate their professional skills for welfare purposes. Their participation was thus the result of Brotherhood activists mobilizing their personal networks among their professional peers. The leaflet publicizing the event presented it as a "free medical caravan under the patronage of MP 'Isam Mukhtar, member of the People's Assembly," as did the banners hanging over the entrance of the mosque on the day itself. It was also Mukhtar who opened the event by leading the weekly prayer at the mosque and giving the khutba. However, despite appearances, in reality it was the tanzim that lay behind the event, which had been organized by the welfare committee of its local branch. None of the activists of the MP's staff were present at the mosque on the day of the caravan (Bassim only went there to accompany me). This situation illustrated the relative importance of the tanzim compared to the staff of the local MP. However, at the same time the prerogatives enjoyed by the MP had opened up possibilities for welfare activities that the tanzim alone did not have. As one young MB doctor put it on the day of the clinic, "It is easier to organize medical caravans now that we have the MP on our side, as before the name of the Brotherhood never appeared. We had to organize them using the names of charities even if in reality they had been put on by the Brotherhood."

The young doctor's comment showed how the Brotherhood had been able to publicize its social activities through the election of its MPs to the People's Assembly in 2005. When he said that "we had to organize them using the names of charities even if in reality they had been put on by the Brotherhood," he actually described the 'control of positions' strategy referred to above. The problem was that this strategy did not allow the Brotherhood's influence to be made public. However, thanks to his position, an MP was allowed to organize public events, and it also made it possible for the mark of the Brotherhood to appear, even if it had to remain discreet. Neither the Brotherhood's name nor its logo appeared on the banners publicizing the event, which was only identified with the organization through Mukhtar's name. Lastly, such events publicly showed how the Gama'a was in fact embedded into neighborhood social networks, thereby reducing any stigma that could have been felt regarding its influence. The part played by the associated personalities follows the same path.

## Neighborhood Social Networks and Associated Personalities

The support of individuals external to the group was not called upon only during election campaigns. These individuals, or associated personalities, also played a crucial role in the everyday activities of the MPs concerned. Some of them had had long relations to the Brotherhood, such as Muhsin in Helwan. Others had only recently been in touch with them, such as Wafa' in Madinat Nasr.

### Muhsin, a relational entrepreneur in Helwan

Muhsin had established his own office in 'Izbat al-Qibliyya, in the building in which he had grown up and in which his sisters still lived.[25] It was a working-class neighborhood that traditionally had been inhabited by craftsmen, and parts of it also consisted of informal areas. Although Muhsin did not live in the district anymore, he was not at any great distance and he would still spend most of his time there when he was not away on business. He was a forty-eight-year-old entrepreneur, the owner of a small business making spare parts and of a company importing cosmetics, and the son of a government employee who had later opened a butcher's shop in the area. He enjoyed great personal popularity. When we arrived in the area together, the car crawling along at a snail's pace, all the windows down, along streets pitted by the lack of asphalt, stallholders and people engaged in repair or minor construction work in the streets gathered around his car to greet him or waved to him enthusiastically. Fruit sellers, women shopping, and adolescents playing soccer seemed equally pleased to see him. Muhsin greeted them all with the words *ezzayak habibi*? ("How are you, my dear?"). While he was still connected to various local charities, he said that his social work was more 'individual' than carried out with any association. He had built up a reputation for this work over many years, explaining its origin with some self-mythification.

> When I was seventeen years old, I heard a story about the Prophet helping some non-Muslim people and adjudicating between them. The Prophet never refused anyone anything. I said to myself then that I was going to live according to the same principle. I had heard the hadith in question in a mosque during Friday prayers . . . I was still young at the time, but I tried to apply the same principle to my own life among my group of friends. Today, whenever anyone has a problem he is always told to contact me because of my many years of experience.

A business-owner by profession, Muhsin was also a public works (*'amal 'amm*, that is, in social services) entrepreneur who possessed an extensive list of relations and contacts. The longstanding links between him and Sheikh al-Muhammadi's staff have already been mentioned. He was also a former member of the Labor Party and the 1992–97 LPC. Since 2005, he had been the sheikh's representative in the neighborhood, where his own office served as an additional constituency office. However, it is the other side of his activities—his identity as a non-Brother—which is of interest here and allows us to describe him as an associated personality. He was thus acting at the intersection between the local MB group and the neighborhood social networks.

As the official person in charge of the Labor Party office in 'Izbat al-Qibliyya from 1997 to 2003, Muhsin had been close to both the Brotherhood and the NDP MP at the time, Mohamed al-Ghamrawi, a former minister and a member of the People's Assembly until 2000. His comments illustrate how party networks could fluctuate and intertwine at the local level and highlight the role played by associated personalities like himself within these networks:

> Al-Ghamrawi used to work with us, and we used to send cases to him for help. He would do this because he was a good man, and he didn't care about the political allegiance of the people who would come to see him. We didn't care if people said that it was the NDP that had helped them in the end. Al-Ghamrawi has been replaced by Sayyid Mish'al now, who does nothing for anyone. He only has one office in Helwan, and he never visits it.

Starting in 2005, Muhsin had been carrying out a double role, doing some of his work in his own name and some in the name of Sheikh al-Muhammadi. While he drew a distinction in his own mind between these two areas, he seemed to be well aware of the confusion that could reign in the minds of others:

> The people who come to see me might have been sent by the sheikh, or they might have come to see me in a personal capacity and not as the representative of the sheikh, as they know that I can also be of service. They know that I support the sheikh. They can see the posters up in my office and the signs stuck on my car mentioning the sheikh's name. When he comes for a visit, I accompany him and introduce him to "important" people in the area, such as businessmen, the owners of large stores, pharmacists, and so on.

Muhsin described the benefits both men drew from their relationship. His position as a relational entrepreneur was strengthened by his cooperation with the MP, and the latter also benefited from his extensive contacts. Muhsin also said that he had a personal team that helped support poor families by paying them monthly benefits (shahriyyat) or paying for medical treatment. The team was made up of an engineer, the owner of a metal factory, the owner of some shops in Sharm al-Sheikh, a small shop owner, a spare-parts dealer, and the head of a company providing transport to one of the cement plants in the area. I interviewed the latter.[26] He had met Muhsin through Muhsin's brother, who was a mechanic in the neighboring area of 'Izbat al-Bahariyya, where the man's own company was also located. Like the other individuals making up Muhsin's team, he had no connection to the Labor Party or the Brotherhood, and he was also quite critical of them, although he knew that Muhsin worked with Sheikh al-Muhammadi. However, he saw Muhsin above all as a trustworthy person and as someone he had known for a long time, a neighbor belonging to the same social networks in the area. As a result, he did not set great store by the Brotherhood side of Muhsin's activities. Yet the zakat he passed onto Muhsin might have been seen by the recipients as coming from the Brotherhood providing they identified Muhsin as a Brother, though this would have been non-intentional on Muhsin's part.

I noted another example of Muhsin's dual identity during an interaction between him and a former independent candidate in the Helwan elections, businessman Isma'il Nasr al-Din, who had extensive networks in 'Izbat al-Qibliyya (Muhsin's area). Nasr al-Din had been an ally of the sheikh during the election campaign thanks to a tarbit, and he had subsequently reentered the NDP hoping to be the party's candidate in the following elections. Muhsin knew him through acquaintances the two men had in common, and he used to work with him from time to time in a local charity of the 'Izba. Muhsin introduced me to him in summer 2009. It was the middle of the month of Ramadan when we met Nasr al-Din in his office. Every day people were breaking the fast with iftar, and charities would organize collective meals. Muhsin asked Nasr al-Din whether he would pay for the iftar meals that "we want to organize" on the premises of the 'Izba charity in which they used to work, the "we" here being ambiguous. Nasr al-Din promised to pay for forty or so meals and called one of his staff on the phone to organize them. When Muhsin then left, leaving me alone with Nasr al-Din, the latter turned to me and said, "You know he is a Muslim Brother?" This meant that he had agreed to pay for a charitable activity organized by a person that he thought of as both an occasional work colleague in the area and a Brotherhood activist, on the premises of a charity with which he was himself connected. Who would the beneficiaries of the iftar meal think had provided it? Would they think of a vague group of residents of the neighborhood, or would they think of the charity, Nasr al-Din, Muhsin, or even, indirectly, the Brotherhood? The true identity of the donor of the meals would probably remain indistinct, and who would get credit for this action would depend on how people variously perceived Muhsin's identity (MB or not) as well as those of the other actors involved.

Far from being simply anecdotal, such details testify to an important aspect of the Brotherhood's grassroots' influence, which was its non-strategic character. It is true that the techniques the Brotherhood used to ensure its informal spread—techniques such as individual social action and the control of positions by Muslim Brothers in disguise or non-Brotherhood sympathizers—were all part of a certain strategy. However, these techniques also relied upon complex and largely uncontrolled mechanisms of identification. In fact, the multiple identities that the actors possessed were the condition that made it possible for the strategy to succeed, but that also made it impossible to control.

It was not only Muhsin whose identity was vague. His closest colleagues were also only vaguely identified, often without their even knowing it. Apart from the team of businessowners he mentioned, Muhsin's extended network also included two women. The first was his own wife. She was a housewife, but she also worked as a *da'iyya*, or preacher, giving religion classes in a mosque in Helwan and in the informal women's groups that met regularly in one another's houses. She was also a volunteer in an Islamic charity that one of the Brotherhood staff working for the sheikh told me "belonged to them" *(heyya beta'na)*, in other words, that it was probably run by a disguised Muslim Brother. However, when I broached the subject with Muhsin's wife, she seemed very surprised and insisted that the charity had nothing to do with the MB. Muhsin himself, present during this discussion, kept quiet. It seems that his wife was therefore working for a charity 'held' by the Brotherhood through the 'control of positions' strategy without knowing it. She herself had no control over the possible attribution of her work to the Brotherhood.

Muhsin's second female co-worker, Ruh, was a very active young woman in her twenties who was a resident of 'Izbat al-Qibliyya and worked professionally as a secretary in a real-estate agency in a well-off district of Cairo. She was also a *da'iyya* working with groups of women or children in Helwan, and though she was not a Muslim Sister she wore the niqab (the full face and body veil). She belonged to the 'mosques movement' studied by Saba Mahmood, as did the wife of Muhsin. Ruh told me that she "carried out social surveys for Sheikh al-Muhammadi," adding that her advantage in this regard was that she could "enter the houses of the poor, whereas Muhsin can't, except if he is invited to." Ruh also worked as Muhsin's deputy in the intermediary activity of collecting *zakat*.[27]

> He introduces people, donors, who want to give their *zakat*. Then people start to come to me directly as a result of word of mouth. I also collect money from people I know through the real-estate agency. I meet a lot of rich people that way. Some of them trust me to find poor families that they can help support.

Thus Ruh, chaperoned by Muhsin, had been able to build up her own personal network that was subtly connected to those of Muhsin and Sheikh al-Muhammadi. She was a lesser notable in the making (Menza 2012), just as was Wafa' in Madinat Nasr, whose case is described below. Muhsin's wife, Ruh, Wafa', and other women who will be discussed below showed the crucial importance of female neighborhood social networks in building the extended networks of the Brotherhood.

### Wafa,' a lesser notable in the making in Madinat Nasr

When we first met at an English course that she had organized in one of 'Isam Mukhtar's offices in Madinat Nasr in summer 2009, 'Madame'[28] Wafa' introduced herself as a "donor" *(mutabarri'a)*.[29] However, it turned out that her role lay less in giving money than in identifying people who needed help in her neighborhood and putting them in contact with organizations that could assist them. When I asked her whether she was a sort of popular leader *(qiyada sha'biyya)*, she burst out laughing. She probably thought that this term, usually only used for men, sounded comical when used by a European, but she may also have thought that her involvement in this type of action had been too recent to warrant so grand a title. It would thus be better to describe Wafa' as a lesser notable in the making in her 'Izba, a tiny district of narrow streets and cul-de-sacs in the area behind the MP's office building. This was a *sha'bi* (popular) area in the full sense of the term, since it was a mixture of informal housing, old buildings, and shops belonging to carpenters, mechanics, *makwagiyyin* (someone who irons clothes), barbers, locksmiths, and grocers.

Wafa' still lived in the building belonging to her grandfather in which she had been born in the 1960s and where she had brought up her two children. Her husband, whom she described as an "automobile engineer" in order to lend him social prestige, was in fact a mechanic in a small garage on the building's ground floor (the "garage" was actually just a tiny office, as all the work took place on the street). She had studied accounting at a vocational institute, but she did not have a job. The first time that she had come into contact with the Brotherhood, she said, had been during the 2005 parliamentary elections when "they appeared *[zaharu]* in the neighborhood." It was only later, during a clothing sale, that she had first entered the Brotherhood MP's office.

> Wafa': I had seen a clothing sale at MP 'Isam Mukhtar's office announced on a banner in the street. So I went and was warmly welcomed . . . Then I registered my mother for the Exemplary Mother Day in 2007, and she won the *'umra* prize [the minor pilgrimage to Mecca that can take place at any time of the year]. My mother is sick and has heart problems. My father died when I was small. Last year, I registered my sister-in-law, my two uncles, and my aunt for the *ta'shirat al-higg* [pilgrimage] draw. My sister-in-law [who also lived in the 'Izba] was one of the winners. . . . Then I saw that there was a medical caravan visiting the area from leaflets distributed in the street. I took my daughter and my husband for a medical examination, since it was free.
>
> Me: But isn't that only for very poor people?
>
> Wafa': No, everyone can go, but the poor don't pay for medicine, as it is very expensive. I paid for the medicine. It was only the consultation that was free.
>
> Me: But why didn't you go to a doctor in his office?
>
> Wafa': Because they were not regular doctors [at the medical caravan]. They were specialists. My daughter had a problem with her eyes, and my husband and I had problems with our stomachs. Sometimes I go to see a doctor, but private doctors are very expensive.

The case of Wafa' indicates the way in which the usual division between the middle classes and the poor did not in fact describe the many intermediary levels contained within these two categories. While she did not clearly identify herself as poor, she nevertheless experienced financial vulnerability that did not allow her to cover her family's healthcare needs, for example. She was "sufficiently well off economically to escape from precariousness and even achieve a certain relative well-being" (Schwartz 2011), but she was not able to meet unexpected or unusual expenses—she could afford to pay for a regular medical consultation, but she could not afford specialized treatment—and her social advancement had been fragile and had not allowed her to leave the 'Izba in which she lived. The different strata of the popular classes identified by Schwartz are useful for situating Wafa' in the social structure: the "most dominated of the dominated," the "poorly off," "subaltern groups with room to maneuver," and the "lower middle classes." Wafa' could be situated in the category of the "subaltern groups with room to maneuver, those who enjoy intermediate material living conditions and lifestyles, presenting a certain form of social mixing, combining attachments that could remain very strong with the popular classes with traits that relate them more to the middle classes" (Schwartz 2011). Wafa' had first come to the MP's office not only because she was looking for help to pay for big or small extras to everyday life (such as, in addition to medical costs, new clothes and her mother's pilgrimage), but also because she aspired to a higher social status. The role she had found had allowed her to realize that ambition, and she had become an essential intermediary between the MP and her neighborhood as a result, all the more so as it was one where the Brotherhood did not enjoy a strong grassroots presence. She described her role as follows:

> When I see someone among my neighbors who's ill or needs help, I call Hagg 'Isam and tell him the problem. He then decides what should be done. The other day, there was a young couple. The wife had given birth in the seventh month of pregnancy and so the baby needed to be put in an incubator. But in the hospital they were at, the incubator was very expensive, and as the baby had been very small when he was born, he was going to have to stay in hospital for several weeks at le2,500 a week. So Hagg 'Isam got in touch with al-Gam'iyya al-Shar'iyya, as they have a clinic that specializes in babies like this. They sent an ambulance because the baby could not be taken out of the incubator, and they transferred him to their clinic for free. What else? Oh yes, there was a girl whose mother had been a widow practically since she was born and who had never remarried. The girl wanted to get married, but she didn't have any money for the wedding. So the Brothers bought her a stove and other domestic appliances and organized her wedding for her. . . . Also, the other day, there was a man who was very sick and very poor who had lost his left leg. He called me and asked me for help, as he was in a lot of pain. I called Hagg 'Isam, and he sent

a doctor he knew, and together they arranged for the man to get an artificial leg. When you see him now, he is walking normally.

Wafa' appears here as a link in the chain between the social networks of the area and the MB or semi-MB networks described earlier, once again including al-Gam'iyya al-Shar'iyya. During the years that followed her first contact with Mukhtar's team, she completely adopted this role of intermediary, so much so that she spent most of her time in the narrow streets of the 'Izba or calling up people in search of individuals needing help. While the role of intermediary helped her to climb the social ladder, it should be emphasized that Wafa' was never acting alone. Instead, she was part of a network of neighborhood social relations whose structure shows how

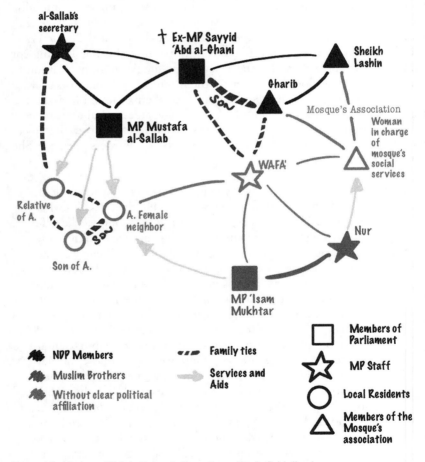

Figure 16. Madame Wafa's Network (from the author's field diary).

tightly interrelated were the local networks of political actors who at the national level were considered to be in competition with each other, or were even outright opponents.

Wafa' said that in some cases, for example when the MP was away, she would approach a neighborhood woman, Nur, who was "just below Mr. Husayn," the manager of Mukhtar's office in the area. She did not use the term 'Muslim Sister' to describe Nur, but that was what her words suggested. Nur was an enigmatic character who, according to Wafa', "does not go out much" (*matezharsh ketir*). However, she organized charitable activities on Mukhtar's behalf, and she also helped identify people in need. S., for example, a widow who needed an operation and whom I met with Wafa' , had been able to obtain the treatment she needed at the Gam'iyya al-Shar'iyya hospital thanks to Nur's intervention. S. also received LE100 a month from Nur that she said came from "the Brothers." But was it really coming from the Brothers? Or did Nur give out part of the non-official *zakat* funds that she collected from donors who were not necessarily members of the Brotherhood? Whatever the answer to this question might have been, the important thing was that S. believed it to be the case.

Wafa' said that Nur also organized a free meal for thirty or so people every Friday at one of the mosques in the 'Izbat area. This detail was interesting, since the meals were provided by the charity managing the mosque in question and in particular by the woman in charge of its social services. However, they were paid for through Nur, who was also in charge of delivering meals to people not able to collect their meals from the mosque. Wafa' said she thought the money came from the MP's office, as the meals were served "in the name of Hagg 'Isam." Her role was again that of identifying people who were eligible to receive the free meals in collaboration with Nur and the woman in charge of the charity's social services. Wafa' was well informed about how the meals were provided behind the scenes because she also had close links with the charity running the mosque in question. Wafa' was a relative of the former director of the charity, who was none other than Sayyid 'Abd al-Ghani, a 'son of the 'Izba,' a member of the NDP, and the predecessor of Mustafa al-Sallab as MP. After his death in 2002, the charity had remained closely linked to the NDP. It had at least two members of the NDP on its board who were also members of the Cairo Governorate Local Popular Council, in the persons of Sheikh Lashin and Gharib, the son of 'Abd al-Ghani, who was determined to become an MP in his turn. During a brief conversation that I had with Wafa' and Sheikh Lashin at the charity on "social work in the area," the sheikh praised the work being carried out by Mustafa al-Sallab, while half admitting that "I've heard that 'Isam Mukhtar does the same thing." Wafa' talked up al-Sallab's generosity and added that "both are good men." As we were leaving, she laughed and said,

Sheikh Lashin is pretending not to know that the Brothers and Hagg 'Isam pay for the Friday meals because he is a member of the NDP, and he doesn't want to admit it in public. But of course he knows.

Figure 16 is a graphic representation of part of the welfare network examined above. Though incomplete, it shows the close relationships between the Brotherhood networks and those of the NDP in the social networks of the area. Individuals like Wafa' or the female manager of the mosque's social services office were not part of either group, even if Wafa' could be seen as an associated personality working with Mukhtar's staff.

The diagram also shows a group of three residents belonging to the same family who were more closely linked to the NDP network but whose mother, A., a neighbor of Wafa', took weekly literacy classes at Mukhtar's office and also regularly received food aid. However, when I met her, she told me that she had a greater loyalty to Mustafa al-Sallab, who paid her a monthly sum in aid and had also helped her son to find a job. These two types of aid, monthly payments and jobs, were particularly important. Wafa,' criticizing what she saw as A.'s ingratitude (she had registered her for the class), commented, "between ourselves, A. receives a sum of money every month . . . but her husband is alive." She criticized the favoritism that A. was benefiting from and suggested that this was breaking the ethical rules associated with social work, a crucial point examined in more detail below.

## The Social Construction of Ethical Conduct
Despite her close relationship with the local NDP, Wafa' needed no prompting to emphasize the ethical conduct that characterized the Brotherhood.

> There are only the NDP or the Brothers here, and I voted for the Brothers. They work for the good *(khayr)*, and they don't look down on you *(mabeyetkabbarush)*. If you go to them with a request, they will look into it with care *(beyehtamu bih, bye'addaruh)* and above all in a selfless way *(bidun maslaha)*. This is because what they do is done for God *(li-wagh Illah)*.

In what follows, these comments by Wafa' will be taken as a starting point for an investigation into the 'ethical conduct' that the MB aimed to embody. The expression is placed in quotes because there is no intention here to make a judgment about the actual morality of the actors concerned, which does not concern a sociological inquiry. Instead, reference is made to works by Max Weber and Michel Foucault. For Weber, the concept of "conduct of life' *(Lebensführung)*, which is central in his *Sociology of Religion*, designates "a systematization of practical actions formed from an orientation to certain unified values" arising "out of religious motivations" such as the quest for salvation (Weber 1993: 149). For Foucault, the notion of 'conduct' is joined to that of 'governmentality,' defined as the "techniques and procedures which govern and guide people's conduct"(Foucault 1997:81). But it is also related to "ethical techniques of the self," or the ways in which individuals seek to fashion themselves as "ethical subjects" by adjusting their behavior to conform to principles that they consider should govern human existence (Foucault 1997: 81). Mahmood has said of Foucault's conception of positive ethics, inspired by the Aristotelian tradition, that it "conceives of ethics not as an idea, or as a set of regulatory norms, but as a set of practical activities that are germane to a certain way of life" (Mahmood 2005: 27). Here, I use the notion of 'ethical conduct' drawing on both Weber's approach, which emphasizes the manner in which practices are directed toward the quest for salvation, and Foucault's, which sees the ethical as being located in the techniques one uses to shape and govern oneself.

## Charity Days: Doing and Ways of Doing
### Mabeyetkabbarush! (They don't look down their noses at people)
The verb *takabbara*, which means being full of pride and looking down with disdain from a great height, cropped up again and again in what my interviewees had to say, with the opposite being said of the Brotherhood. Wafa' used this basic contrast between, on the one hand, notions of consideration, welfare, and piety and, on the other hand, ideas of contempt and self-interest, to structure what she had to say in comparing the Brotherhood and the NDP. Naturally, such a discourse also needs to be placed in the context of the relationship between researcher and interviewee: it is true that I first met Wafa' in Mukhtar's office. Yet the many other informal conversations I had with her in the street or at her house all had the same content. Let us listen to how she described the clothes sale that first led her to the Brotherhood MP's office.

> Wafa': There were loads of beautiful things there for just a few *gineh*. What was also good was that there were also separate areas, with the office over there being for women and this one being for men. That way, there was no "contact." And there weren't any lines either. People didn't have to wait. You got here, and people were on hand to welcome you. If someone very poor turned up who wanted to buy something but couldn't afford to pay for it, even LE2, they would say, "Go on, take it."

> Me: Things like that, the clothes sale, the award for the exemplary mother, is it only the Brothers that do them?

Wafa': No! Everybody does—the Party [NDP], Suzanne Mubarak, everyone. But what can I say? If you go over there to the party for the clothes fair, you'll see people lining up for a long time and then fighting each other, because it's entirely free, and they fight to get the same pair of shoes. Here, it's not free, but prices are very low. For example, a *gallabiyya* like this one costs LE5. Will you find that anywhere else? No. Everything's nice and clean and not expensive. And they give the money to orphans. Over there at the party they won't speak to you. They don't take the time to speak to you because the only thing that counts is what's in it for them. Everything is done in their interest *(kullu maslaha)*. . . . But here, for Mother's Day, when the Brothers give out the prize they talk about the person and her problems in front of everyone and congratulate her, and everyone claps. Over there, they say, "Take your gift," and then they throw it at you.

She sat back in the chair, stuck her stomach out, and put on an unpleasant voice and a haughty expression while making a disdainful gesture with her hand. Then she burst out laughing.

The difference did not lie in the kind of help that was being given, but in the *way* it was being given. Wafa' thought the MB's attitude was a good one because they respected people's dignity and flattered the cultural aspirations of the middle classes, with which Wafa' wished to be identified. The clothes they distributed were clean, even "chic," and the distribution was done without any pushing and shoving or contravention of the moral code that segregated men from women, something that Wafa' seemed to appreciate. The fact that the Brothers gave a ceremonial character to the awarding of the Exemplary Mother Prize was also appreciated by Wafa' ("They talk about the person and her problems in front of everyone and congratulate her"), because this was seen as a way of valorizing the beneficiaries.

The terms used to describe the NDP events, on the other hand, signaled a perception of humiliation ("They don't take the time to speak to you . . . they say, 'Take your gift,' and then they throw it at you"). She considers the NDP agents' attitude as haughty and deplores their lack of care in organizing the event, which was evidenced in the lines and the absence of gendered spaces. Wafa' was shocked by the fighting that went on between the beneficiaries, which she saw as being caused by the general atmosphere of contempt, and the fights were all the more shocking in that they were about items that were free.

However, at the same time Wafa' did not reject everything that was linked to the NDP. She did not hide her personal relationships with certain local NDP agents, and she described MP Mustafa al-Sallab as a well-off, charitable, and pious man.

Hagg Mustafa al-Sallab is a good man *(ragil tayyeb)*. He is good *(huwa kwayyes)*. He has money. . . . However, he wants to be an MP. He wants *wasla* [good relations with the regime]. He is not available for the people *(huwa mesh fadi li-l-sha'b)*. . . . It's impossible to see him. Have you ever seen him? You can't. You go over there, and the man who lets you in says *[she adopted a contemptuous manner and a hostile voice]*, "No, he's not here. Tomorrow." The people working in the office look at you like that *[she brought her hand up to her face, pressed her thumb against her chin and spread out her fingers, miming an attitude of contempt]*. "Later!" *[She laughed and called out to Ahmed, the young jack-of-all-trades in Mukhtar's office]*. Can you imagine if Ahmed received you like that? In Ramadan, for example, al-Sallab gives out bags, but he asks his employees to take charge of the distribution and they do it like this: three bags for the people they know, and one bag for the poor. What can I tell you? It's not fair, there is no equity *(mafeesh sawaseya)*.

According to Wafa,' Hagg Mustafa's personal qualities and the size of his personal resources did not make up for the attitude of his employees, whom she depicted as administrative staff flawed by personal interests, favoritism, and nepotism. In her view, as opposed to the NDP system that was based on *wasta* (personal relations) and corruption *(fasad)*, the Brothers were motivated by religious faith, which guaranteed fairness and equity. Religious morality combines here with the register of civil rights and citizenship. According to Wafa',  the moral qualities of individual members of the Brotherhood, whether MPs or others, compensate for their lack of material resources.

The Brothers give out of sincerity *(beyeddu bi-ikhlas)*. They don't think of themselves as superior *(mesh mutakabbarin)*. They behave with mercy *(beyet'amlu bi-hasana)*. The party, on the other hand, will give the *'umra* to a young woman who does not wear the veil rather than to a poor and sick woman.[30] What I mean is that the Brothers are good souls even if they lack resources *(al-ikhwan humma 'anduhum madda ulayyela, bass ruh-hum kwayyes)*.

What was particularly interesting here was that Wafa' derived this ensemble of qualities, values, and norms from the concrete gestures and body language that she observed and experienced during her charitable activities. The stories that she told as part of her arguments presented gestural oppositions, such as the Brothers talking about the person concerned and the audience applauding as opposed to the NDP agents throwing gifts at those attending their events and people fighting over them. They also referred to physical practices, such as the young, unveiled woman and the older, poor, and sick woman. She even felt the need to mime the behavior she had seen. Another example illustrates the importance given to the concrete forms of action in the constitution of the moral character of the Brotherhood.

> Here [among the Brothers] relations are good. There's nothing like that here [*she was implying favoritism*]. Things are the same for everyone. During the drawing for the pilgrimage, for example, they put all the tickets in one big transparent box, and then a child pulls out the winning ones. It's the best way to deal with people and the most respectful.

The morality of a given action thus seems to stem from its "morphology," to use Mahmood's word, that is, the specific form that constitutes its substantial content. In the example quoted, it was the hand of the child that guaranteed the ethical character of the action. However, this ethical morphology also depended on certain concrete dispositions that allowed the beneficiaries of a charitable action not only to benefit from it, but to *take part in it*. The use of symbolic prices at the clothes sale described by Wafa,' for example, was a form of concrete disposition that allowed the beneficiaries of the action to become donors to it as well, since their symbolic contributions would then help those who are more in need than them, namely orphans. In addition to its economic justification (since it helped to reduce costs), this practice also contributed to the formation of those involved as ethical subjects since it allowed them to take part in moral actions. Wafa' talked about this kind of self-understanding of beneficiary-becoming-donor in a vocabulary that was also physical, such as in her use of the verb 'to take' and in her description of very ordinary acts.

> I want to do something good for the future, and when I am helping others I am doing it for God (*li-wagh Illah*) in order to take my *sawab* [spiritual reward], and that makes me happy and comforts me. If I buy rice, meat, and vegetables during Ramadan, for example, and take them to my friend and say, "Cook these and put them in boxes to give to the poor," then my friend is also taking her *sawab*, and the person who comes to get the boxes and give them out also takes his *sawab*. Anyone who does something to help other people takes his *sawab*.

Thus, the ethical morphology of the action depended not only on physical behavior and the ways in which it was done, but also on the assemblage of these forms of behavior and 'ways of doing' things in a cumulative and collective process that involved the beneficiaries. It was precisely this that could be observed when looking in detail at the charitable events organized by the Brotherhood MPs: making a virtue out of necessity, in the exact sense of these terms, they very often drew upon popular participation.

## Celebrations and group weddings: staging mutual aid

According to a report in the September 2007 edition of the local newspaper Abna' Helwan, 'Ali Fath al-Bab had organized an awards ceremony for students, his sixteenth, and celebrated the group wedding of fourteen young couples, while the NDP MP for the neighboring constituency, Sayyid Mish'al, had organized "his second medical caravan specializing in ophthalmology, after the success of the first." There was obviously a competition going on between the MPs in organizing charitable events of this type. Activists working for the Brotherhood MPs prided themselves on having been the first ones to initiate and organize such events, in particular in 15 Mayo City owing to the longstanding position of Fath al-Bab as the local MP. Salma, a leading activist, said that they had been the first in the whole of Egypt to organize awards ceremonies for students under the patronage of the local MP. Ordinarily, such events were organized by charities, and their organization by an MP had been an innovation by the Brotherhood that its competitors had felt obliged to copy. This argument was often advanced by my interviewees from the three staff teams concerned, and it undoubtedly drew attention to their activities. However, even beyond the rhetoric, it did seem to correspond to reality, as some residents living in the 15 Mayo constituency told me that Mustafa al-Bakri had not organized student ceremonies before 2009 and that Fath al-Bab had been the first to do so.[31]

Yet at the same time Fath al-Bab's staff was having increasing difficulty accessing public space. While the student awards ceremony had taken place at the Tibbin steel factory club in 2007, attended by the president of the factory board and other managers, in 2009 the MP's staff could not find a public hall to rent and the event had to take place in the small garden located behind the MP's office. In spring 2008, the staff had to face new obstacles when repression intensified during the elections to the Local Popular Councils.

> Fath al-Bab: Obviously we can't hold the ceremony in the office, as it's far too small. We used to be able to hold it in a public building, in a youth club, for example. But now we can't, and it has been off-limits to us for the last two to three years. It's a symbol. They want to make things difficult for us by stopping the MPs from carrying out their activities. If we do something in the street, they come and take away the chairs. If we want to use a club and ask for

authorization to do so, then the club will call State Security, which will tell them to stop us from doing it. But what the regime doesn't understand is that all this will help us win. Whatever happens, the events have to take place. Another time, during the Mother's Day event, they refused to give us the authorization to use a room. So what we did was to visit each mother who had received an award at her home. The neighbors came to see what was happening and joined in the party. Sometimes the events even took place in the offices where the women worked.

Salma: We did it all day long between ten in the morning and eleven at night. It was really tiring. But we did it. There was a group of women, and a few men. We were in three cars. [At this point, I asked whether this group had been members of the Brotherhood.] No, not only Brothers . . . not even mainly.

Fath al-Bab: So, what happened? If we had had the event in a club, we would have attracted, say, one hundred people? But this way, by visiting people in their homes, we reached perhaps a thousand people if you include the neighbors and others. The government thinks that when it stops us from using public facilities we won't make the effort to get around the ban. But in fact we will.

Salma: We are always innovating and looking for new ideas.

Fath al-Bab: If I were Mubarak and I wanted to get rid of the Brotherhood, I would let it use the clubs and the public facilities. [Laughter].[32]

Both Fath al-Bab and Salma very often took up the idea that a constraint could give rise to stimulating new ideas *(tanshit)* and creative innovation *(ibda')*.[33] However, the success of such strategies designed to get around the ban on the Brotherhood was not always as great as the MP suggested. When the student event was held in the small garden, for example, many of the residents of the area whom I met complained about the noise and inconvenience of an event being held outside and said they wished it had taken place in a club. The activists were also unable to find a public hall in which to hold the group wedding ceremony in 2007, and so it had to be held in a private facility close to the Nile. Salma admitted that this was too far from 15 Mayo for comfort, but she added that "people lent their cars or we rented cars for each bride and her family, and we hired buses to bring in the guests. People could see the procession of cars going down the streets."

This form of action that depends on the use of limited means in a restricted context has also been noted by Ben Néfissa in an article on the Gam'iyya al-Shar'iyya in which she looks in detail at one of the charity's most popular programs. This program, the Kafalat al-Yatim, was designed to provide support for orphans, and it was introduced by the Brotherhood when it had most influence within the charity. It consisted of the identification of individuals, called "godfathers," who wished to sponsor one or more orphans in their neighborhoods. The godfather paid a monthly sum to the GS, which passed it on to the mother[34] of the child, who knows nothing of the godfather's identity. Quoting from the charity's internal documents, Ben Néfissa explains:

> This sponsorship is a form of contract between the GS and the godfather .... The aim is to "correct the relationship between the orphan and his or her entourage. Instead of having relationships with individuals who assist him, he must have a relationship with Muslim society at large, which becomes directly responsible for him." The unknown godfather is therefore a kind of "symbol" or representative of this Muslim society (Ben Néfissa 2003: 244).

The GS also contacted members of the local community and asked local craftsmen, merchants, doctors, pharmacists, bakers, hairdressers, butchers, and so on to provide food, medicine, educational materials, clothing, and other items as well. Such people were solicited for help according to their means, consciences, and convictions. As a document presenting the program explained, the latter is in itself an act of preaching, a link between the members of society, both rich and poor, and a revitalization of the solidarity and mutual aid promoted by Islam. *The goal is not only to support the orphans concerned, but also to involve other people in that support.'* (Ben Néfissa 2003: 245).

A similar pattern based on local aid, solidarity, and individual involvement was also at work in other charitable projects run by the MB, such as medical caravans (doctors gave their services for free), or the group weddings for poor or orphaned young people who otherwise would not have been able to marry. The latter were a case in point, consisting of help in organizing a festive ceremony, including clothing, hairdressing, makeup, a party with music, buffet and a photography session, and in furnishing the newlywed couples' new homes. Two categories of donors financed such events, the first being individuals, members of the Brotherhood or not, who would pay for everything that needed to be paid for in monetary terms and in general were unknown to the beneficiaries. The second category of donors consisted of small shopkeepers selling clothes, furniture, and domestic appliances, restaurant owners, hairdressers and so on, all of whom would contribute what they could by donating goods or services.

Salma gave an example.

> One hairdresser in Helwan takes care of all the hair and makeup needs
> of all the brides without exception. All of them. And she isn't a mem-
> ber of the Brotherhood or anything. She's just an ordinary woman.
> She does it all in a salon that is clean and air-conditioned . . . she even
> refuses to take a tip. Nothing—she does it all for nothing.

Figure 17. Recto and Verso of a postcard published by Fath al-Bab's office, calling people
for help in organizing a wedding ceremony.

Salma said that people in the area who had found out about the program
wanted to become involved in the next group wedding, for example by lending their cars or canvassing local shopkeepers. As in the Kafalat al-Yatim

project described earlier, this popular participation was one of the aims of the activity. In an interview posted on his personal page on the nowabikh-wan.com site, Fath al-Bab reportedly said:

> The efforts that have been made are not due to my own personal action, but are those of a whole mass *(ustul)* of donors and volunteers who want to take part in actions designed to build solidarity *(takaful)* and cooperation *(ta'awun)* with the community [since] the longer period of singlehood because of the high costs of marriage and the preparation of the marital home are concerns for all young people, especially those who are poor or in need. So, we are working with them so that they can build families.[35]

Just like the GS in the orphan project, the activists working for the Brotherhood MP acted here to link young married couples in danger of marginalization because of their poor or orphaned status with various elements of the local community in order to build social cohesion. They helped to reintegrate those who risked being pushed to the margins and fought against the danger of remaining unmarried. This danger would destabilize society as a whole since it threatened one of its main pillars, the family. This perception of the danger of singlehood was shared by broad sections of the population and was not specific to the Brotherhood. Other MPs and charities also organized group weddings. However, the particularity of those organized by the Brotherhood MPs lay in their emphasis on popular participation, constituting at once the ethical form of the event and an effective way of financing it. One female activist explained that such methods were used because of the lack of means available to the Brotherhood MP when compared to those available to his competitors.

> I don't believe that Mustafa al-Bakri, for example, needs to ask anyone for help when he wants to organize something or other, as he has plenty of scope and comfortable means. He can pay for things without needing people to participate in them.[36]

The Brotherhood's comparative lack of means was thus turned into an advantage, since it was used to enlarge the scope and meaning of an activity by mobilizing a self-help network based on the principle of collective participation to bring about well being *(khayr)*. This could be seen as a reinterpretation of the practice of *maghud al-dhati*, the spontaneous effort encouraged by the state. However, this particular form of *maghud al-dhati* aimed to be ethically exemplary in a particular way. Through the morphology of his practices and interactions, a Muslim Brother fashions himself as an example of 'ethical conduct,' in other words both as a paragon of virtue (someone who conducts himself well) and as a model for imitation (whose conduct can serve to lead others).

## Conducts of the Exemplary Self

The starting point of this section is the careers and discourse of two residents of 15 Mayo City, Zaki (fifty-three years old) and his daughter Hayat (twenty-one), who had become regular participants in the activities organized by the offices of MPs 'Ali Fath al-Bab and Sheikh al-Muhammadi. This will allow us not only to depend on the description that the Muslim Brothers themselves gave of their 'ethical conduct,' but also to see how this was perceived from the outside and how such perceptions could contribute to the construction of durable loyalty between residents of the districts in question and the Brotherhood.

### Ta'amul (way of dealing with) and loyalty

I had already noticed Zaki on a visit to the sheikh's office in Helwan Center. He was a social science teacher in a private school in the popular area of Muqattam in Cairo, and he gave extra lessons at the sheikh's office during the school holidays. I met him again at the 15 Mayo student event in summer 2009, when his daughter Hayat and his niece were members of the group organizing the event. The first time Zaki had come into contact with Fath al-Bab's staff had been in 1999 when Hayat, then aged eleven, had been one of the students to receive an award during the Brotherhood student event.

> When they saw that I was a teacher, they asked me if I would work with them. I didn't accept immediately. The regime was making people frightened, and it was putting out hostile propaganda about the Brothers. Then came 1995 and the first time that Fath al-Bab had stood in the elections. I wanted to vote, but I didn't know who to vote for. Everyone said that I shouldn't vote for him because he was against the state. But I didn't see that. What I saw was that he was providing social services. I am originally a man of al-Azhar [he had trained in the al-Azhar curriculum] . . . so I watched how the Brothers acted, and I thought they behaved in accordance with Islam. At first, I didn't really want to do voluntary work, as in Egypt we are not encouraged to do it. But I was a primary school teacher at the time, and I started to give free lessons in orphanages. As a result, I slowly got closer and closer to the office and I took part as well from time to time.[37]

Starting with the parliamentary elections in 2000, Zaki became involved with Fath al-Bab's election campaigns by distributing leaflets and above all by taking part in neighborhood discussions. He was still "a bit frightened," but had "got used to it." He laughed about the way people would react by warning him ("Take care—the Amn al-Dawla [State Security] will come and get you") or when they did not believe that he would do it without being paid ("They used to ask me how much I earned and were very surprised when I said 'nothing'"). In 2006, he started giving history lessons in Sheikh al-Muhammadi's office. In his view, "The office of Fath al-Bab in Mayo is a bit small, let's say. There aren't a lot of activities of this type." This latter remark chimed with my own observations about the lack of regular activities in 15 Mayo, and the fact that the ones that existed were largely ignoring boys.

It was therefore hardly surprising that it had been Zaki's daughter Hayat who had continued to be involved with the staff in the 15 Mayo office, and not his son, who had been recognized at an earlier student event. After she had celebrated her eleventh birthday, she took part in a course to learn the Qur'an organized by the office. When she was fifteen (in 2003), she joined a group of female students who had received awards in previous years and who were put in charge of organizing the annual event (it was in that year that her brother received his award). The group decided to put on a show.

> It was the first year that there was a "show." Before that, there had been the distribution of prizes, but there had been no singing, no children reciting the Qur'an, no performance. We went to see Mr. 'Ali and said, "Why don't we put on a show?" We wanted to put something on for people . . . something like singing or a performance, something that would show them that *they were there in our Islam and that they would feel well about it*. The sketch we did was about interference in the media [they staged a play about media propaganda by showing the unplanned effects of changes in radio frequencies]. People liked it, because it was new for them to see young people like us putting on something that didn't talk about the usual sort of things, things like love and so on, but that talked about the country.

Hayat then went on to take part in organizing the event every year. After she entered al-Azhar University as a student in 2007, she had more time, and she started to become involved in regular activities at the office of Sheikh al-Muhammadi in Helwan like her father. She said she was not a Muslim Sister in much the same way as her father had said he was not a Muslim Brother, and she added that she was not the only one to be in this situation. Of the group of female students who had organized the annual event in 15 Mayo, only one or two were members of the Gama'a, she said. However, she clearly described herself as a sympathizer of the Brotherhood.

> 'Ali Fath al Bab, the Brothers, their ideas are good. I am pious (*mutadayyina*) and also an Azharite like my father, and I want to see

my religion applied. Who will apply Islam as it is without changing it? The Muslim Brothers. The thinking of the Brothers is the
thinking of Islam *(fikr al-ikhwan huwa al-fikr al-islami)*. When
you deal with them *(lamma tet'amel ma'hum)* and you discuss
things with them . . . I began dealing with them *(at'amel ma'hum)*,
and I saw that their ideas were exactly what I was studying at
al-Azhar.

Hayat emphasized what she saw as differences in intention between the activities organized by Fath al-Bab and those organized by others. "The others
started to organize events because they saw that the Brothers were doing so,"
she said, adding that "the NDP organizes events in order to get votes in elections, while Mr. 'Ali doesn't do that. He does what he does in order to reward
the students and encourage them." As proof of this she cited the fact that the
students themselves had decided what they wanted to do at the event and
that there were always other activities besides just giving out prizes. Hayat
said that these specific practices stemmed from the more general fact that
the Brothers "correctly" applied Islam. She saw the Brotherhood's version of
Islam as being close to what she had learned at al-Azhar, and she emphasized
its practical side. It was the "application" *(tatbiq)* of religion that was most
important to her, and it was through the *ta'amul*, or manner of dealing with
or working with, that she had become convinced that the application of Islam
by the Brotherhood was the application of Islam, period.

However, if one were to choose an a priori definition of what is and
what is not Islamic, it would not really be possible to say that what I saw
of the content of the student event I attended demonstrated the correct
application of Islam by the Brotherhood. The format was very ordinary,
and it would have been easy to substitute Mustafa al-Bakri for 'Ali Fath
al-Bab on the podium. The sexes were not segregated, the choice of music
was not unusual, and the speech the MP made was not particularly religious, since all he did was to congratulate the students and emphasize
the importance of success and excellence.[38] Only the recitation of verses
from the Qur'an by two children could be seen at first glance as a distinctive sign of MB influence. However, this only lasted for fifteen minutes
or so, and the MP did not use the occasion to deliver a speech referring
to Islam, even briefly, even though the context would have allowed him
to do so. Instead, he only tried to make the audience laugh as a way of
appearing accessible and appreciating the children. "I can't compete with
him. I only make speeches in the People's Assembly, and standing next
to him I can't compete," he said. The recitation from the Qur'an was
also variously interpreted by those present. Two female high school students who had been recognized at the event told me that the difference
between this occasion and an event organized by the NDP was that "there

is a more religious atmosphere" because of the recitation of the Qur'an and the presence of the women organizers, who were wearing outfits that signaled that they were *multazimin* (committed to Islam), such as veils that came down to cover the bust *(khimar)* in brown or pastel colors. On the other hand, another group of male high school students told me that there was no difference, and that the event was "usual" *('adi)*.

The remarks made by the female students echoed something Hayat had said about the sketch that had been an important step in her own decision to become involved in the MP's staff. She said that the aim had been to show people a manifestation of "our Islam" and to make them feel that this could be a source of well-being. However, the sketch itself had had no direct connection to religion. I asked her to explain.

Me: Was there a religious dimension to the sketch?
Zaki: Mostly in the form of behavior *(sulukiyyan aktar)*.
Hayat: Yes, behavior.

It was thus the behavioral aspect *(al-suluk)* that for Hayat and Zaki constituted the Islamic dimension of the sketch, in the same way that the female high school students had detected a religious dimension to the clothing worn by the female office workers, saying that "this is good because it encourages us to be more religious"*(mutadayyinin aktar)*. Even though there was no explicit instruction to be more pious, the message could still be sent and perhaps temporarily accepted and its bearers credited with a certain esteem. Hayat, for example, tried out a form of behavior by working with the Brotherhood, and this in turn fashioned a particular way of working with them (a specific form of *ta'amul*).

It was also in these terms that Hadi, the secretary of MP 'Isam Mukhtar in Madinat Nasr who was not a member of the Brotherhood, expressed his perception of the *ta'amul* or *mu'amala* (way of dealing—a term derived from the same root) that was particularly good about the Brothers.

The good way of treating people *(husn al-mu'amala)* is what makes the difference between here and the NDP office. Over there, it's just an employee, someone who isn't himself the bearer of a message *(sahib al-risala)*. . . . Bearing a message means behaving in a way sanctioned by Islam. Here, there is a quality of behavior that I haven't seen anywhere else, including between employer and employee. Mr 'Isam doesn't behave like my boss, I think because he is a Brother.

These comments echoed those made by Wafa' regarding the moral distinction between NDP employees and 'assistants' working for the Brotherhood.

However, hearing it from the lips of Hadi was all the more significant in that he was an employee of the Brotherhood not a member of it. Prior to being hired by the office in 2006, Hadi had worked as a chair upholsterer, even though he had a degree in Spanish translation from al-Azhar University. He had gotten the job in Mukhtar's office through a friend who was a member of the Brotherhood, and he explained that it was what the job represented in terms of opportunity and social advancement that had motivated him to take it.

> Hadi: I was working very hard, and I wasn't making very much money . . . The job here paid a better salary, and so I immediately accepted it. I wasn't afraid [to work for the Brotherhood]. I didn't think about that. It was only later, when I knew more about it, that I began to think about it more.
>
> Me: If the job had been with an NDP MP, would you have taken it?
>
> Hadi: Yes, because it is a job. My friend didn't tell me that it was 'Isam Mukhtar exactly. If it had been Mustafa al-Sallab [the NDP MP], I would have taken the job without any problem.

However, Hadi had earlier come across the Brotherhood several times in his career. An orphan from a village in the Minufiyya governorate in the Nile Delta, he had been influenced by an MB schoolteacher who used to give him private lessons and then give him back his money at the end when the other children had gone home. When he arrived in Cairo to attend the university, the first person he met who helped him out was the friend who some years later recommended him for the post of secretary to the Brotherhood MP. He had never been pressed to join the organization, but that had not stopped him from sympathizing with its principles. "I am not a member of the Gama'a, but I am a Brother in terms of my way of thinking. I believe in their thinking (mu'min bi-fikrat-hum)," he commented. When asked to say what, in his opinion, marked out MB thinking, Hadi answered:

> The Muslim Brothers seek goodness (khayr), and I love khayr and strive for khayr. They are virtuous citizens (muwatinin salihin), and I hope to be a virtuous citizen as well. I want to be like that. I am not a member of the Gama'a, but I am just like them. I love Islam, and I understand Islam like them. They did not bring me a new religion. They make people discover religion in the field of ethics (fi-magal al-akhlaq) in a valuable way (bi-sifa hamida). . . . From primary school, I was in the Azhar system. And al-Azhar thought is the same as Muslim Brotherhood thought. We have learned the correct understanding of Islam. Islam, as a religion, is a form of behavior (mu'amala).[39]

It was thus no coincidence that Zaki, Hayat, and Hadi had all attended al-Azhar and that they had drawn a more or less explicit connection between their conception of good *ta'amul* and their earlier al-Azhar teaching. The loyalty they felt toward the Brotherhood had been built up through their experience of this *ta'amul*, and the experience had had a strong emotional affect. Hayat, for example, had felt valued as a pupil recognized by the Brotherhood and later as an organizer and a performer, whereas Hadi remembered with gratitude the experience of being taught by an MB schoolteacher. However, *ta'amul* was something that went beyond inter-actions between individuals; it also related to Islamic law *(fiqh)*, in which *al-mu'amalat* lays out the principles that regulate the relations between human beings and the rules of human behavior. Speaking more precisely, *ta'amul* relates to the Islamic notion of virtuous action *(al-'amal al-salih)*.

### Virtuous action: Historicity and intertextuality of a code of conduct
The history of this notion is a complex one (Mahmood 2005: 92), and since it includes and transforms elements coming from various contexts and involving different actors at different periods, the idea of virtuous action is probably best described as forming a "discursive tradition"[40] (Asad 1986) that is reinvented by various actors over time. As a result, the idea of virtu-ous action needs to be understood in terms of intertextuality. First of all, it is connected with the doctrinal principle of *amr bi-l-ma'ruf wa-l-nahi 'an al-munkar*, the obligation to "enjoin the good and forbid what is wrong" (Cook 2000). The interpretation of this principle has changed over time, however. While the radicalized Islamist groups argued for an interpreta-tion of it from the 1970s in which forbidding evil could entail the use of force, it has been other movements, insisting instead on the need to *amr bi-l-ma'ruf* ("enjoin the good"), that have established the core idea of vir-tuous action.[41] These movements trace their origins back to the reformist Salafism of the Islamic Renaissance *(al-nahda al-islamiyya)* that appeared at the end of the nineteenth century and the beginning of the twentieth. It was at this time that the writings of the Egyptian thinker Muhammad 'Abduh and his follower Rashid Rida played an essential role in defining this doctrinal principle as a religious duty incumbent on all virtuous Muslims. However, it was Hassan al-Banna, a pupil of Rida, who opened the way to its implementation in practice and on an everyday basis. For al-Banna, the "shaping of [individual] souls"[42] was the necessary point of departure for social transformation. He described a method *(minhag)* referred to as the "guidance of society" *(irshad al-mugtama')*, according to which the moral transformation of the self through faith and virtuous acts was instrumental in building a good, sound, and strong society and that this in turn would ensure the moral preservation of human souls. At the same time, other Islamic actors such as the Gam'iyya al-Shar'iyya also emphasized the

individual responsibility of *amr bi-l-ma'ruf* and the importance of social reform through the "formation of virtuous citizens" (Uways 1985). From its foundation, al-Gam'iyya al-Shar'iyya had had "two objectives of equal importance in view: *da'wa*, or preaching, and *al-'amal al-salih*, or virtuous acts" (Ben Néfissa 2003: 238). It was this similarity of objectives, according to Ben Néfissa, that made the entry of Brotherhood influence into the GS so important a cause for the organization in the 1970s. However, in the 1930s, the difference between the two movements lay in the willingness of al-Banna to put pressure on the government and in his criticisms of the official religious establishment and *ulama* (clerics), which he said had separated religion from the daily lives of individual Muslims. Al-Azhar was an early target of such criticisms, and they were repeated ever more insistently from the 1970s onward (Zeghal 1996).

Al-Azhar responded by actively promoting a conception of Islam as virtuous behavior that should be carried out in all human activities. At the same time, the 'mosques movement described by Mahmood was promoting the idea that piety consisted of an ensemble of obligatory acts *(al-fara'id)* and acts of charity denoted by the term *al-a'mal al-saliha* (in the plural) that appealed to God and that could be achieved in even the smallest of daily tasks. The educational material that the women of the movement used included a major work, *Fiqh al-Sunna* by Sheikh Sayyid Sabiq,[43] a colleague of Hassan al-Banna (who wrote the preface). The aim of this work was to provide a "simplified version of Islamic jurisprudence" *(fiqh)*, according to the author, and it presents itself as a highly accessible handbook providing guidance on virtuous behavior in everyday life.

The emphasis on virtuous behavior has also found a new and powerful formulation since the late 1990s. The mantra of development through faith has been promoted by Egyptian "superstar' preacher 'Amr Khaled[44] and his Life-Makers (Sunna' al-Hayah) association that has spread dramatically in Egypt and across the Middle East and North Africa. Calling on "Muslims to become pious and entrepreneurial subjects," Khaled "uses management science and self-help rhetoric to promote entrepreneurial activities as religious, with an emphasis on the role that voluntary work plays" (Atia 2012: 809). He has thus been able to build on the idea of piety as a source of social positivity.

Although they have not focused on productivity and economic success, the Brotherhood and al-Gam'iyya al-Shar'iyya have also emphasized that an individual is defined by an inner moral positivity *(igabiyya)* latent in each believer. Every Muslim possesses the seeds of this positivity because of his or her faith, and these seeds may be encouraged to grow. The individual is responsible for developing this latent disposition to virtue through the accomplishment of virtuous actions that are the products of an inner strength, which itself can be developed precisely by engaging in virtuous actions.

Interestingly enough, Sheikh al-Muhammadi, the founder of the Helwan branch of the GS, imported this conception of virtuous actions into the Local Popular Council he headed in the 1990s. Internal documents from the LPC insisted on a code of conduct for elected members based on the promotion of such virtuous acts. A member of the council was thus encouraged to "act as an example by promoting the image of a virtuous citizen."[45] "He should be the last to benefit from decisions [of the council], should ensure that public interests are safeguarded and set aside his private ones, and should be honest in his work and carry out the latter to perfection." He should also seek to "immerse himself in Helwan society, building close links with the local population, encouraging 'natural leaders' who have the characteristics of virtuous citizens, and . . . help them to take part" and "develop a positive spirit throughout society and encourage *al-maghud al-dhati*." Lastly, particular attention was paid to the local civil servants who worked with the LPC. Its members should "gain their trust through serious arguments, visit them and remind them of God and their professional responsibilities, and honor and thank those who work properly." A set of precise instructions was also issued to ensure that this ethical code was carried out in practice, including handing out self-help books to civil servants encouraging them to follow virtuous ways, privately advising those who were not acting properly in order to help them to improve, always replying to every citizen request, even if no help could be offered, and so on.

The role of the Brother, as a member of the LPC, was thus to provide a good model to follow and to encourage people toward virtuous action by having them take part and allowing them to experience their own positivity in so doing. According to the sheikh, this positivity existed within every believer. In an interview, he referred back to the doctrinal principle of *amr bi-l-ma'ruf* in order to emphasize the connection between religion and positivity.

> Religion says, "take part in society." It is not possible to retreat into yourself, whether you are Christian or Muslim. Religion in Egyptian society pushes individuals into enjoining the good and forbidding the wrong, and it encourages people to improve the relations between them (*al-din muharrik li-fi'l al-khayr wa mani' li-fi'l al-sharr wa-dafi' li-tahsin al-'ilaqat bayn al-nas*). Religion says, "treat other people in the best possible way."[46]

While I was not aware of the existence of the documents setting out a code of conduct for the sheikh's staff in 2005–10, it was clear to me that instructions of this sort were at work. The teacher on the staff, 'Abd al-Rahman, explained that the prize-giving ceremonies (for students, exemplary mothers, and so on) were very important to "encourage the 'positivity' of society." It was also this that lay behind the search for associated personalities, according to Akram:

> In the Wadi Huf office, for example, there is a person who is not a member of the Brotherhood but who takes care of popular justice (sulh) in the area. He does this because he loves the good (byehebb al-khayr), and since he had seen us doing it, he wanted to join in with us, and we said "itfaddal" (with pleasure). There are a lot of non-Brothers who work with us. The management team is made up of Brothers, but the people who do the work are often non-Brothers.[47]

Akram saw the MB activists as guides leading non-Brotherhood members toward the accomplishment of the good (al-khayr) that the latter loved spontaneously owing to their latent disposition toward virtue. Associated personalities such as Muhsin, Ruh, Wafa', and Zaki were thus neither anomalies nor exceptions. Their participation was an integral part of the staff's mode of action, not only because it was a way of gaining support, but also because this participation was an end in itself. It was therefore virtuous action itself which constituted, on a daily basis, the main form of political action, because it led to other virtuous actions and spread a kind of moral orthodoxy throughout society. The obligation of ethical conduct was thus one bearing on all members of the Brotherhood in all their everyday social interactions. Moreover, here one touches on another important aspect of ethical conduct, which was that outside of office activities it did not really function as a way of differentiating members of the Brotherhood from members of the NDP, but rather as a way of identifying MB members. This is crucially important because it resolves the paradox of the existence of the Brotherhood as a public secret.

### Singling out without showing off

The understanding of ethical conduct helps to answer the question of how the social activities of the Brotherhood could be effective in gaining political support when the Brothers themselves mostly acted without making public their identities as members of the organization. Even the activities of the Brotherhood MPs were often carried out without promoting explicitly the mark of the Brotherhood. However, it was this ethical conduct that allowed a Brother to be identified as such in his neighborhood community. Hamdi, a businessman working as a member of the Helwan staff, said, for example,

> Hamdi: Before I came here, I went to the house of a recently deceased neighbor. His children had organized a wake, and they were all very sad. I didn't know the neighbor concerned, but I went

anyway. Why? Because it is a religious duty. They know that I am a member of the Brotherhood. And even if they don't know . . .

Me: How do people know you are a member of the Brotherhood?

Hamdi: Perhaps someone has seen me at the mosque or engaged in social services. Perhaps I invited them to attend the elections, or a soccer match, or an event dedicated to memorizing the Qur'an, or I suggested they work with me on a business project . . . Anyway, they see that I behave well toward them, and they say, 'Why are you doing that? Why are you honest, not like those who aren't honest? Why don't you lie, not like those who do?' So I say, 'It's because I am a member of the Brothers (*ana min al-ikhwan*).[48]

In fact, Hamdi did not explicitly say that he was a member of the Brotherhood, and the situation he described here was more hypothetical than real. Most of the time, Brotherhood membership is something that is not stated, and only the ethical conduct is made obvious. According to Hamdi, a Muslim Brother can be recognized because he is the model of a virtuous citizen.

Some people know that I am a member of the Brotherhood, and others don't know. . . . There are Brothers that people don't know are Brothers, but they know they are good people, people who are virtuous models of the Muslim citizen (*namuzag salih li-l-muwatin al-muslim*).

It was also this identification by ethical conduct that provided the key to the strategy of the control of positions by Brothers in disguise. How could this strategy be useful for the Brotherhood if the services provided were not known to be provided by the organization? According to Hamdi, the Brotherhood's interest in this case was in the activity itself and the service it provided to people, and not in taking the credit for it.

There would be a problem if people knew that such and such an organization belonged to the Brotherhood. One doesn't just write "Brothers" on it. The idea is that if I, Hamdi, set up an organization, if I say that it belongs to the Brothers, they will close it. They don't know that Hamdi is a Brother. They only know that Hamdi is a good man, someone who is respectable and likes to help people. But if I write on it that it is linked to the Brothers, *they will close it clac-clac the second day* [spoken in English]. I do welfare work, but I don't say that it is on behalf of the Muslim Brotherhood, because this work is part of my religion.

Because of its illegal status, the Brotherhood could not directly indicate its responsibility by putting its logo on such activities. However, this limitation could easily be transformed into a virtuous action, since the impossibility of displaying a logo could be turned into a refusal to profit from carrying out such an action. The performance of ostensibly disinterested ethical conduct could thus be used to be identified as a member of the Brotherhood without saying it. In sum, this strategy of ethical distinctiveness worked precisely because it did not advertise itself as such. For the MB, discretion was core to distinctiveness.

This discretion was in striking contrast to the way the NDP Islamic businessmen described by Patrick Haenni (2005b) flaunted the good works they carried out. It should not be thought, in fact, that charitable activities were an exclusive feature of the Brotherhood or of the other Islamist movements, since the new classes associated with the *infitah* also used their wealth and munificence to make inroads into the welfare sector in Egypt, happily demonstrating, in Haenni's words, "the triple alliance between religious ethics, class interest, and the dominant international ideology, i.e. the promotion of the liberal social model" (Haenni 1997). While the disposition to perform acts of charity indisputably came from religious motives, it was also related to a desire to display social standing and the right to wealth on the part of those who had it. Thus, the generosity of the businessmen studied by Haenni was only rarely unconnected to a desire to display extravagant wealth, something that was not in itself stigmatized in Egypt in the years after 2000. However, it did walk a fine line between an emphasis on the good deeds of the donors (*ahl al-khayr*) and the "suspicion of wealth that had been 'dishonestly acquired'" associated with the figure of the *infitahi*, that is, the nouveau riche with all that term's associations of corruption and profiteering (Haenni 1997).

While the largesse of such philanthropic entrepreneurs was ostensible and unmistakable in Egyptian public space, the MB's charitable activities sought to situate themselves above any suspicion of private economic or political interest by a discretion that was at once necessary and deliberate. However, in the same way that an ethical element cannot be ruled out in the motivation of the generosity of the businessmen, a hard-headed understanding of the use of such a strategy of discretion cannot be excluded in the case of the Brotherhood. While the mark of the Brotherhood was not explicitly written on the frontage of such and such an association, the connection could just as well be made known by rumor. In other words, it was as if the security services were imposing the rules of a game on the Brotherhood that in reality took nobody in. It might still be doubted whether such and such an association was in fact held by the MB, but all the authorities were interested in was that this should not be explicitly known and that this form of public secret should not be made (too) public.

Rumors were thus an essential part of the Brotherhood's strategy of distinctiveness and a natural result of its emphasis on disinterested ethical conduct. It was a strategy that depended on discreet ostentation, something that by its very nature was paradoxical and deeply uncertain. While discretion was the best way of achieving distinctiveness for the Muslim Brothers, *uncertainty* was also the price that had to be paid. It was for this reason that this discreet ostentation was also the object of conflicting reactions on the part of the Brotherhood and the security services. The latter would tolerate it up to a certain point depending on the political situation at the time on local and national levels. Indeed, it could be said that State Security responded to the Brotherhood's strategy of uncertainty by adopting its own policy of uncertain repression, meaning that it could not be known in advance whether a given organization would or would not be targeted. As a result, some members of the Brotherhood were unexpectedly thrown out of their associations even if they had not publicly revealed their identity as Brothers. Others, on the other hand, were allowed to continue their charitable activities even though they were publicly known to be members of the Brotherhood. The son of Sheikh al-Muhammadi was arrested in front of his father's office on suspicion of belonging to a banned organization (the Gama'a), for example, at the same time that the sheikh himself was left alone to continue his work as an MP just a few floors above.

Muslim Brothers did not necessarily want to make their activities explicit, since the context of vagueness within which they operated meant they could soften a political identity, which otherwise might potentially be stigmatizing, in order to facilitate a hushed contact with the wider population. The aim was therefore somehow to become identified as a Muslim Brother while not appearing to do so, while at the same time also managing to distinguish oneself precisely through that discretion. It was a matter, in brief, of distinguishing oneself while seeming not to be doing so. As a result, most of the time people would not say "he is a Brother" about such individuals and would only say "*I think* he is a Brother."

Rana, a professor of education at Helwan University and an intermittent member of Fath al-Bab's staff in the 15 Mayo office, explained this in more detail when talking about collecting *zakat* in an informal fashion.

Me: You collect it on behalf of the Brothers?

Rana: No, not on behalf of the Brothers, as I am not known to be a Brother[49] ... since I have a university job, it would be a bit difficult (*fi diqa*) for me. So, I go to see my colleagues, for example, and say, "I am a member of an association collecting donations to help orphans get married" [related to the group weddings organized by the staff], and they contribute because they trust me.

Me: Do they know that you are with the Brothers?

Rana: Some yes, some no. I don't tell them. . . . But they know anyway because we have certain characteristics (*sifat*) in common, such as in appearance (*fi al-shakl*) and in the way we behave with them (*ta'amul*) . . . baggy clothing, the *'abayya*, the *khimar*, the fact of collecting *zakat*, our behavior (*suluk*). . . . And if someone talks to you about the situation in Palestine or the upcoming elections, you know he is a Brother [laughter]. But you can't say so directly, especially if you are a woman.[50]

Rana's final remark about the constraints weighing particularly on women indicates the ways in which such discretion could allow social interactions to take place despite the security restrictions. Since (female) political activities could still appear shocking to some in Egypt, they needed to be introduced tactfully through an approach that relied upon suggestion. Belonging to the Brotherhood was indicated through bodily gestures, behavior, virtuous actions, and, when the time was right, by more directly political comments (in this example, when speaking about Palestine Rana was referring to the war in Gaza in 2008–2009, when she had helped collect donations for aid convoys). Ethical conduct here was thus a way of fashioning the self and of incorporating the material forms of religious belief.

## Conclusion

The *khayr* sector in Egypt was thus characterized by networks that depended upon blurred identities and crisscrossing patterns of affiliation. The pervasiveness of these networks, permeating many spheres of life, and the low-profile nature of Brotherhood identity made connections easier between MB activists and other pious individuals willing to take part in *khayr* activities, whether or not for reasons of personal interest. Some of the latter might also be members of the NDP. For much of the time, people would simply describe a Muslim Brother as a good person who served God and engaged in welfare services. However, the politics of goodness were not immune from conflicts. Security services did not hesitate to use repression by capitalizing on uncertainties. There were also struggles with political rivals for recognition, and while the MB activists interviewed repeated "we have no problems with the NDP trying to imitate us and stealing our ideas," in fact they strove to distinguish themselves by the manner in which they delivered their social services. They intended, though discreetly, to make people understand that the aid they were receiving had come from the Brotherhood, even if it had actually come from an association in which a Muslim Brother was only active on an individual basis. Conversely, in local associations in which leading figures from the Brotherhood and the

NDP were both active, the latter would deny that any of the members was a Muslim Brother.

Such blurred identities and crisscrossing patterns of affiliation at once facilitated the Brotherhood's strategy of distinctiveness and prevented it from being fully controlled. It was a distinctiveness that depended upon random processes of identification. For the activists, being recognized as a member of the Brotherhood meant being distinguished in a double sense: being seen as different, being set apart from others as morally superior. Ways of acting, behaving, dressing, presenting oneself in social situations all contributed to the ethical conduct that not only allowed a Brother to be identified as such, but also to be identified as a model to be imitated by others. Ibrahim, in the Hadayek Helwan office, said, for example, that "good manners and behavior are the most important things at the Brothers' disposal to get their message across. When people see someone behaving well, they want to imitate that person and to take that person as a guide."[51]

Ethical conduct thus constituted the foundation of the Brotherhood's politics. It was a basic building block in creating loyalty to the Gamaʿa among the wider population, even if this process was one that in the main could not be precisely controlled. But beyond the question of strategy, this ethical conduct in the end constituted the very essence of the Brotherhood's action. In presenting themselves as ethical individuals, it was not enough for MB activists simply to manage their behavior in a way that seemed virtuous to them. Instead, it was also necessary to encourage others to behave according to the rules of virtuous action as well, thus bringing about the desired social reform through the moral transformation of individuals. Such techniques of self-regulation and of ensuring that one's own behavior and that of others conformed to certain rules of ethical conduct was a form of the government of the self and of others identified by Foucault. We shall now turn to the ways in which this conduct of conduct was acquired and embodied by the Brotherhood members, and to the political effects of such a form of government.

# 5

# The Double-Edged Sword of Brotherhood

How did Brotherhood activists acquire the ethical conduct by which they sought to distinguish themselves in their social relationships? Much has recently been written on this subject (Kandil 2015; al-Anani 2016; Ben Néfissa and Abo El-Kasem 2015; Ben Néfissa 2017) thanks to the circulation of various pieces about the Gama'a, including autobiographical accounts, memoirs, and internal documents, after the 2011 revolution. It was also easier to carry out fieldwork in Egypt in the 2011–12 period, since interviews, focus groups, and observations were hedged around by fewer constraints than had been the case during the Mubarak years, until repression dramatically returned with the clampdown in the summer of 2013.

These new studies have reignited an important debate on how MB activists were ideologically indoctrinated and have particularly questioned the role of religious faith. They show how the Gama'a, through specific methods of recruitment and cultivation *(tarbiyya)*, strove to fashion a distinctive Muslim self, one that would embody "Ikhwanism" (al-Anani 2016: chapter 8). This literature has insisted on the sectarian dimension of the Gama'a, that is to say, on the intense religious and ideological indoctrination the organization spread among its members and through which it isolated them from wider social life. In this way, the Gama'a produced a closed and total inner circle in which only distinctive *ikhwani* selves could develop. While Kandil recognizes that, "like any other organization (and, indeed, like any individual), the Brotherhood is the sum total of its interior and exterior facets" (2015: 4), he nevertheless exclusively focuses on the "interior facet" in his work and insists that the Brotherhood formed "a largely independent community, living alongside rather than with [other] Egyptians" (Kandil 2015: 79). Conversely, al-Anani considers that Brotherhood membership did not "require individuals to break with previous social ties" (2016: 70) and stresses the importance of social networks for

189

recruitment and mobilization (al-Anani 2016: 79). He does not, however, provide an in-depth analysis of the articulation between the interior and exterior facets of the organization. It is this nexus that I intend to identify in this chapter.

So far, I have placed much emphasis on the external facet of the Gama'a and on how embedded it was in Egyptian society under Mubarak. But it would be wrong to think that the Gama'a was only that. It consisted also of a secretive, internal inner circle closely connected to the *tanzim*. However, the production of this inner circle was the other side of the coin of the Gama'a's social embedding. In fact, these two facets formed a system, by which I mean that there was a common mechanism for the external social spread of the Brotherhood and the internal formation of its closed inner circle. The mechanism was the embodiment of the ethical conduct referred to in the previous chapter that was both the product of the Gama'a's inner cultivation and the vehicle for its social entrenchment.

However, this system was under considerable tension. As we shall see, it encapsulated the paradoxes and challenges of constituting the self and community in ethical terms while simultaneously seeking to use those terms to maintain identity boundaries and enforce internal discipline. How was it possible to claim that one was both an integral part of the social fabric *(dimn nasig al-mugtama')* and a member of an ethically defined community that was somehow morally superior to the rest of society? How was it possible to fashion a distinctively *ikhwani* self while also relating to other selves who bore competing understandings of the ethical? Such paradoxes I call the "double-edged sword of brotherhood."

This chapter explores the ways in which this double-edged sword generated tensions inside the Gama'a and constrained its external relations, shifting the focus onto the individual. It builds on the work of Kandil, al-Anani, and Ben Néfissa, as well as on my own empirical research, to explain the processes of recruitment, cultivation, and promotion that took place inside the Gama'a. It explains how distinctive *ikhwani* selves were shaped in the innermost circles of the Gama'a embodying ethical conduct. The chapter then shows the ways in which the hypothesis of an independent community confining its members within sectarian patterns of socialization nevertheless did not hold true. I make an original argument: that margins were central to the Gama'a. I intend to explain how Brotherhood members felt that they were distinctive individuals united by distinctive bonds while they were, at the same time, anchored in wider social life. My point here is that belief and behavioral contradictions were constitutive of the Muslim Brother self, just as they are for any other self.

# Becoming a Brother: The Embodiment of Ethical Conduct
## Methodological Remarks
While the focus and main contribution of the present work lies in its original analysis of the social embedding of the Gama‘a at the grassroots level, this analysis cannot be complete without a more detailed investigation of the internal workings of the organization. It is interesting to note that the descriptions of its workings offered by Kandil, al-Anani, and Ben Néfissa agree with each other and are in line with my own observations. They bear witness to an ensemble of procedures, norms, practices, visions of the world, and values that was characteristic of the ways in which socialization took place among the Brothers. However, significantly different interpretations arise from these otherwise similar descriptions regarding the role of ideology and religious faith within the organization as well as on the impacts that this had on its social and political positioning. After summarizing the descriptions found in the works of others, I offer my own analysis based on interviews with the activists described in this book and my own interpretation of them. In essence—and this is the major difference between the present work and those cited earlier—it was my repeated visits to these activists, the systematic reconstruction of the social characteristics of my interviewees, and the analysis of their group relations that has allowed me to put forward a more sociologically informed interpretation of their discourse.

Thus I have sought to look at these examples as sociological case studies and not as straightforward illustrations of a preexisting hypothesis. In my view, the main problem with the studies cited above is that they attempt to provide evidence by amalgamating fragments of speech produced under a variety of different discursive situations. Thus they do not clearly distinguish different levels of discourse, and they treat them equally, considering fragments of speech as self-contained pieces of information or illustrations of a particular fact. In these studies, the writing mode mixes up quotes taken from interviews, autobiographical accounts in book form, and essays written by leading figures in the organization.[1] Moreover, most of the time the activists concerned are presented as individuals without any particular social background and about whom one is told very little. Lastly, their words are often used simply as illustrations of a more important text, which, because it comes from a leader of the group or an ideologue, is assumed to be authoritative. My view, on the contrary, is that it is crucial to situate such discursive fragments in the context of the trajectories, positions, and social situations of the actors who express them.

Simply put, the fact that al-Banna once wrote that the Gama‘a was pursuing such and such an objective and should be organized in such and such a way does not constitute proof that this objective and this principle of organization determine the behavior of activists today. The fact that a given individual claims that the organization is applying the recommendations of al-Banna also does not constitute proof that in fact it is doing so. It is more relevant to ask what uses this individual and others are making of the words or texts of al-Banna and to observe the ways in which he and others may be departing from them. It is then possible to understand such differences sociologically and to put forward interpretations concerning the relationships between the activists and the organization to which they belong.

By analyzing different sociological cases in depth, one is also in a better position to explore such relationships in all their complexity and ambiguity. Apart from ideological and educational texts produced by the Brotherhood, Kandil and Ben Néfissa base their analysis on statements coming essentially from oppositional members of the organization or from former members who have broken with it and often have strong feelings of resentment toward it (as well they might). My point here is not that these activists' resentment necessarily biases their statements, but only that were one to look at a larger sample and to consider the statements made by individuals who have had less painful and happier experiences as activists, we would be able to arrive at a fuller understanding of what the Gama'a is or was about. However, the fact remains that these authors have made valuable contributions to our understanding of the Egyptian Muslim Brotherhood.

### Shaping Orthopraxy: Islam, *Tarbiyya*, and Discipline
According to Ben Néfissa and al-Anani, the production of MB activists starts with recruitment processes that depend on the Individual Call method. This method of preaching, supposedly unique to the Brotherhood and not used by other Islamist movements, was set out in the writings of Hassan al-Banna and above all in the book *al-Da'wa al-fardiyya* by Mustafa Mashhur, the organization's fifth supreme guide, who died in 2002. It consists of six steps:

1. Selecting an individual who seems likely to respond to Brotherhood preaching and creating a strong relationship between him and the MB preacher

2. Convincing the potential new recruit of the importance of religion

3. Encouraging him to take part in group readings of religious texts, to distance himself from his former friends and acquaintances, and to apply Islam to all aspects of his personal and social life, including ways of dress, marital, professional, and sports habits, and so on

4. Explaining to him his obligation to engage in his social and political life and activities in order to defend Islam and restore the Caliphate

5. Convincing him that this duty must be accomplished in a collective manner

6. Convincing him that the Gama'a is the only organization able to lead the Islamic movement in the right manner, since its aim is to "lay the foundations (of this movement) through the education of Muslims and through their unification" (Ben Néfissa and Abo al-Kasem 2015: 113)

Al-Anani explains that the progression from one stage to the next is gradual and takes place over months or even years. "In many cases, potential members do not know about these stages until they are fully-fledged members. In fact, they move from one stage to the next without realizing the difference between them" (al-Anani 2016: 79). The progression also takes place through a multi-tiered membership system that has several levels. The first are not, strictly speaking, part of the membership system; they include individuals who are *muhibbin* (sympathizers) and *mu'ayyidin* (supporters). My informants often mentioned a third level of membership, which consisted of *mu'ayyidin qawiyyin* (strong supporters). It is during these first levels of the membership system that the various stages of the Individual Call are achieved. Once these have been completed, a new recruit is required to take an oath of allegiance to the leadership of the Gama'a *(bay'a)*,[2] after which he becomes a member *('udu)*. He then goes through several other levels, including *'udu muntasib* (associate member), *muntazim* (organization member), and *'amil* (active member). According to Kandil, there are two further levels of membership, the first being *musa'id* (assistant) and the second *mujahid* (warrior) (Kandil 2015: 185).[3] He also insists that "promotion from novice to full member is subject to a complicated set of monitoring mechanisms centered on the process referred to as cultivation *(tarbiyya)* . . . Practically speaking, cultivation requires frequent group meetings in which an experienced prefect *(naqib)* guides members through a detailed cultivation curriculum *(manhaj tarbiyya)* under the careful gaze of the cultivation committee and with regular interventions from the higher administrative circles" (Kandil 2015: 7).

He gives details of the forms of indoctrination and control used by this cultivation committee or education committee *(lagnat al-tarbiyya)*, which is made up of "staunch loyalists," most of them retirees able to dedicate themselves full time to the activity.[4] First, these senior cultivators have put together a curriculum "composed of several edited volumes, running from basic to advanced levels," Kandil says (2015: 8), with *nuqaba'* (prefects or delegates) following them in the lessons they give during weekly meetings of the *usar* (basic units of the Gama'a). Second, according to Kandil, the delegates would administer questionnaires on a weekly or monthly basis designed to measure the "spiritual condition and religious performance" of members, as well as their "emotional presence," psychological state, and feelings and relations toward other Brothers (Kandil 2015: 7, 11, 15). Other questionnaires would be self-administered by the members themselves. Some of these aimed at evaluating religious observance: twice a day a Brother would monitor his own behavior toward God, questioning his deeds and thoughts and recording the results in questionnaires handed back to delegates. Others sought to check up on the submissiveness of members toward the delegates and encourage them to measure the modesty, respect, and veneration they have toward the latter (Kandil 2015: 16, 23). A third method of indoctrination used by the cultivation committee takes place in different kinds of group meetings: in addition to the weekly *usar* and monthly *shu'ab* gatherings, there are also *kata'ib* (sing. *katiba*), *rahalat* (sing. *rihla*), and *mu'askarat* (sing. *mu'askar*) meetings aimed at providing spiritual and physical training, preparing members for life's hardships, strengthening their allegiance to the Gama'a, and nurturing relationships of solidarity between them.[5] Kandil and al-Anani do not report the same things about the content and regularity of these meetings, however. The former says that the *rihla* is a biannual fieldtrip on which Brothers bring their families for recreational purposes to forge a sense of community. The latter explains that it is a monthly trip of fifteen members (or potential members) walking together in the desert or the countryside without eating or drinking from dawn to dusk, with the goal of achieving self-purification and reinforcing commitment.

Ben Néfissa similarly emphasizes the importance of the evaluation and training procedures used in this form of education. She says that these procedures were paired with an intensive program of religious indoctrination, including supererogatory practices and physical exercises that can put considerable strains on the body. Commenting on this mix of religion and group discipline, al-Anani explains that organizational rules and behavioral norms are blended with "Islamic teachings and principles to preserve their symbolic power and influence." Ikhwanism, she argues, is "not a rigid set of sacred ideas but a constellation of social norms and organizational values that stems from the internal dynamics and interactions within the movement" (al-Anani 2016: 120). This code of conduct is sourced from the most widely read text by al-Banna, the *Risalat al-ta'alim*, which describes the ten *arkan al-bay'a* (pillars of allegiance) of the Brotherhood. These include core values such as obedience *(ta'a)* and trust *(thiqa)* that are translated into organizational rules (obedience to the leadership and trust in its virtuousness) and also framed in Islamic terms such that submissiveness to the organization and its leadership is conflated with religious devotion and a commitment to act not only for the Gama'a but also for Islam. This conflation leads to the sacralization of the organization and its leaders alike. As

Kandil puts it, "it is as if the movement itself is the ultimate goal," one which "is sacred because what it represents is sacred—that is, Islam" (Kandil 2015: 48). Hence, members should never be in any doubt that the Gama'a, while it may sometimes make mistakes, remains the "better-equipped movement" to expand Islam, unify the community of Muslims *(umma)*, and restore the caliphate that was abolished shortly before al-Banna created the organization (Kandil 2015: 51–52).

This sacralization paves the way for a whole set of disciplinary techniques that prevent internal criticism or dissent. Kandil places great emphasis on these, identifying four ways in which the leadership attempts to tame possible disputes or indiscipline (Kandil 2015: 22–31). The first is the preempting of argument, since deflating debates before they arise is one of the main tasks of the delegates, who make sure that members see any criticisms as an unnecessary source of dissension. The second is disinformation, to which the leadership frequently resorts in order to conceal any disagreements that may occur among the ruling bodies of the *tanzim* or to justify controversial decisions. The third is organizational pressure, by which restive members are referred to investigation committees that have the power to punish or expel them. Ben Néfissa also remarks that punishment is part and parcel of the training during the *mu'askarat* and *rahalat*, though the sanctions target delegates rather than ordinary members, in order to drive home the lesson of the equal submission of all the Brothers to the Gama'a, whatever their age, status, or position (Ben Néfissa 2017). Disinformation and organizational pressure can also combine to spread malicious rumors or gossip about "argumentative Brothers," as Kandil calls them. The fourth method is more positive and consists of constantly praising the harmony among members. While arguments are considered to be a cause of *fitna* (division within the *umma*), harmony and consensus are manifestations of *fahm*, or the proper comprehension of Islam, which is one of the ten pillars of *bay'a*.

The preemption of argument is also rooted in the Brotherhood's specific understanding of Islam. As Kandil rightly argues, this does not lie in its theological positions or original interpretations of dogma but relates to the "pervasive stress on practicality" (Kandil 2015: 12) found in the organization's ideology. This is in line with the importance of *mu'amala* and *ta'amul* that was pointed to in chapter four. Members of the Brotherhood are continuously urged to shape and normalize their behavior, by following ethical instructions such as talking politely and calmly, showing modesty, patience, and punctuality, observing hygiene, avoiding loud laughter, abstaining from smoking, attending burial ablutions, and so on. Some of these instructions are given in the *Risalat al-ta'alim*, and, according to Kandil, they would be checked up on through various questionnaires. The latter even states that Brotherhood delegates and leaders often discourage members from reading religious texts other than those recommended by the organization, in order to preempt any theological debate and to focus on praxis alone.

Lastly, the sacralization of the Gama'a generates, and is generated by, the strong interactions between the Brothers. Discussions within the *usra* are intended to help an individual member to improve his behavior in his daily interactions or to deal with difficulties in his own daily life, including in the professional and marital spheres. This makes the *usra* a space of trust that is conducive to the establishment of strong links between individuals, who will share personal problems, give advice, and encourage each other in solving them. While they are engaged in advising their peers, members are also encouraged to monitor and shape the behavior of others as well as their own attitudes. They are expected to conform to specific ethical rules toward each other that include shaking hands with affection, telling each other how much they have missed them, showing concern about those who are absent, being cheerful, and the like (Kandil 2015: 12, 27). In so doing, while each member is entrusted with the task of being the guardian of the orthopraxy of his peers, the *usra* also aims to produce a powerful affective bond between its members: the socialization that takes place in the *usra* is intended to make the *ikhwani* circle the primary circle of each individual, on the same basis as family and friends, or even given priority over them. In order to enlarge this *ikhwani* circle, members are redistributed among new *usar* on an annual basis with new delegates put in charge, so that they can become intimate with a larger number of individual members throughout their careers. The powerful emotional links created by the *usra* are the key to the tight-knit structure of the organization and to the members' belief in its sanctity. Indeed, through the love that members feel for their peers, they are supposed to experience love for the whole community of Brothers and for the Gama'a as such. This feeling, called *ukhuwwa* (the sense of brotherhood), is assimilated to the pure and authentic love that should bind all Muslims together.

Kandil and Ben Néfissa argue that the flip side of this love among the Brothers is an antipathy toward others: the "attachment to your Brothers entails separation from others," Kandil says. Non-Brotherhood Muslims, even close members of your own family or your former best friends, will then appear to you as sinners (Kandil 2015: 49). By shaping the orthopraxy of its members, the Gama'a imbues them with the belief that they are good, true, virtuous, and exemplary Muslims. The aim of *tarbiyya* is "not to win over more believers, but to produce a new kind of person— a Muslim Brother. This is a person striving for a new world through a spiritual struggle that reproduces the experience of the early Muslims" (Kandil 2015: 6). Ben Néfissa explains that this ambition refers to Sayyid Qutb's conception of the "vanguard of believers," and she identifies a rise in Qutbism during recent decades due to the hegemony of *tanzimiyyin* leaders. Kandil adds that the vibrancy of Qutbism inside the organization has been sustained by two other structural dynamics: the ruralization of the leadership, entailing a higher level of conservatism, and the Salafization of many members because of the influence of Saudi Wahhabism.[6] Lastly, the self-perception of the Brothers as distinctive and ethically superior Muslim selves is reinforced by the social networks inside the Gama'a. According to both authors, Brothers would get married to the sisters or daughters of their peers, send their children to schools controlled by Brothers, find jobs in MB-owned companies, go to MB doctors and hospitals, and so on. They would also distribute money to members in need, including to prisoners' families. All of this would only accentuate the gap between the Brotherhood community and the outside social world, with almost any need being satisfied within the MB's internal social networks. As a result, Ben Néfissa concludes that the Gama'a in many ways resembles a religious sect more than a political organization (2017: 204).

Al-Anani takes a different stance on the matter of sectarianism, though he agrees that the main purpose of the Gama'a is to produce "a sense of differentiation and distinctiveness within its members" (al-Anani 2016: 118). The Brothers are shaped by a unique code of identity (Ikhwanism) and live according to the specific subculture created by the regulations and interactions inside the organization: "to be an *ikhwani* is to think, live, and behave as a committed and obedient member" (al-Anani 2016: 119), he says. However, al-Anani also suggests:

> *Ikhwanism* does not negate the fact that the Brotherhood's members can maintain their personal, social or professional identities; being an *ikhwani* does not mean that one cannot work as a lawyer, doctor or teacher, for example. Indeed, what distinguishes the Brotherhood from other Islamist movements is the *multiple layers of identity that facilitate the dissemination of the Brotherhood's ideology in the wider society* (al-Anani 2016: 120).

Yet al-Anani does not provide a thorough examination of how these multiple identities are articulated. This is because he does not examine the social trajectories of those whose testimonies he quotes. I argue that exploring the various processes of socialization inside and outside the Gama'a, and, most importantly, on its margins, is needed to understand the complex formation of *ikhwani* selves. Such an exploration also calls into question Kandil's hypothesis of the Brothers' antipathy toward outsiders.

## Socializing the Brothers: The Centrality of Margins
### Locating the *Ikhwani* Self
When describing the ethical conduct of a Brother, what al-Anani calls the *ikhwani* code of conduct, the activists that I have interviewed often used the

expression "*shakluh kwayyes*," literally meaning his form is good, or, in other words, he seems good, straightforward, and correct. This is an everyday expression in Egypt used by people from different social backgrounds, and not only by members of the Brotherhood, to refer to someone who appears charitable, honest, pious, or modest. The term "*shakl*" (form or manner) expresses the importance of behavior and bodily disposition but leaves the content of the morality thus described somewhat vague. Forms of ethical conduct similar to the *ikhwani* code could also be described as *shakluh kwayyes*, for example, even if the person manifesting them had nothing to do with the Brotherhood. Salwa Ismail has brilliantly analyzed the complex effects of the drive for both homogenization and pluralization in the construction of Muslim selves in Egypt. She shows, on the one hand, that "personal quests and accompanying individualization find expression in a pluralization of the languages and registers of being Muslim (a *heteroglossia* of sorts, to use Mikhail Bakhtin's terms)." Yet, on the other hand, "the desire to identify a fixed Islam fuels homogenization efforts (*monologisation* in Bakhtin's terms)" (Ismail 2007: 11). The public sphere in Egypt has been configured by these two driving forces. This collective transformation has paradoxically been achieved through projects of individual self-transformation focusing on how Muslims should "conduct themselves in a manner consonant with Islam in their daily lives"—that is to say, on *mu'amalat* (Ismail 2007: 14).[7] Although they share a common focus on ethical self-fashioning, these projects are multiple and often in competition, Ismail argues. They are also deeply entangled in material conditions and power relations grounded in social contexts.

How, then, are we to locate the *ikhwani* project of self in this variety of possible conservative Muslims selves? How is the *ikhwani* distinctiveness different from other Islamic self-fashioning patterns if all of them equally emphasize ethical conduct in daily life? A complete comparison of the behavioral and bodily practices promoted by the different Islamic and Islamist movements has yet to be fully fleshed out. It would require taking into account the dynamics of political and socioeconomic transformation in national and local settings alike, in order to make sense of why, for example, Salafism in one location does not shape exactly the same Muslim selves as Salafism in another. However, in the local settings explored in this study, one distinctive feature of *ikhwani* selves when compared to Salafi or *tablighi*[8] ones can be identified.

While the latter are recognizable at first glance because of certain distinctive elements relating to dress code—the niqab for Salafi women and the shape of the beard and the short *gallabiyya* for men, or, for Tabligh members, the half-length white tunic, for example—*ikhwani* selves cannot be identified so easily. Some male members of the Brotherhood have very short, carefully trimmed beards and mustaches, while others shave off their mustaches and allow their beards to grow quite long in the Salafi fashion. Others still are clean-shaven. Most of the time, the men wear shirts and pants and for the most part look like any other Egyptian man. Brotherhood women tend to wear the *khimar*, though I have also met young women wearing the simple *hijab*, in a style that comes down quite low at the front. Others wear the niqab. As a result, a wide range of dress and behavior can be observed in general because the Brothers do not seek to imitate the Prophet in these aspects.

It is therefore in the *mu'amalat*, the interactions that Brotherhood members have with others, that efforts at distinctiveness are to be found. It starts with a kind of systematic bodily restraint, supposed to express modesty. It includes not shaking women's hands or looking them in the eye (although lowering the gaze happens mostly at the time of greetings) as well as keeping at a physical distance from female bodies. It also includes standing up straight, moving in a measured way, speaking quietly, not bursting out in laughter, and so on. Second, there is the use of multiple religious formulas and polite expressions in speech. Third, efforts are directed toward displaying virtue in everyday relations, with the *ikhwani* self typically showing compassion, assistance, and service within his immediate social environment. This attitude may be accompanied by a tendency to admonish people for what an MB individual considers to be non-Islamic practices or dress. However, it is difficult to know whether this practice of admonishing is widespread or not. There is no single answer to this question since, as Ismail notes, it depends on the power relations at play in local social contexts.

The systematic character of these behavioral traits—the bodily restraint, the religious language, the display of virtue (sometimes hectoring), and the self-conscious altruism—when combined with an ordinary style of dress, aims at producing a Muslim self that is both ordinary and extraordinarily intense. It is intense because of the systematic character of such behavior that is the product of the *tarbiyya ikhwaniyya*. And it is ordinary because nothing in it allows an observer to say with any certainty that this behavior must be that of a Muslim Brother. A non-Brother who is highly pious and works actively for charity could very well exhibit the same systematic form of behavior, for example. There is, therefore, a kind of resonance, or a monochrome gradient of practices, between the *ikhwani* model of the self and other pious models of Muslim selves that are also publicly available.

It is this resonance that is signaled in the expression *shakluh kwayyes*, which indicates that *ihkwani* modes of conduct could be common to other, broader ethical sensibilities and could cross social boundaries. They could be perceived—or not—as being those of a Brother. As a result, the internally produced *ikhwani* sense of distinctiveness, which also produces a systematic external modesty, is very noticeable to observers. But it is connected to broader Islamic practices of self-fashioning that make it only unpredictably recognizable.

The merging of the *ikhwani* self into the wider frame of *shakluh kwayyes* was very operative in the recruitment process to the Brotherhood, and it was mentioned in all the accounts of entering the Gama'a that I heard from the activists interviewed.

In Helwan, 'Abd al-Rahman (the teacher), Gamal (the shopkeeper), Hamdi (the businessman), and Salah (the technician in the cement works) all talked about a similar pattern of recruitment, though adjusted to their differing social backgrounds. For all of them, the first contact with the Brothers had been made after leaving high school, in a small group of young people from the neighborhood and usually in the local mosque. Only 'Abd al-Rahman, whose family, unlike those of the others, did not live in Helwan but in a village in the Delta, had had his first contact at al-Azhar University, where he had gone to study, and not in his family neighborhood. All of them explained that at first they had not fully realized that this small group of young people were Muslim Brothers. Their relations started as friendship, built on common interests like playing sports. Soccer games were particularly important in establishing friendly relations and experiencing for the first time the *ikhwani* code of conduct. Salah remembered the admiration he felt at the time.

> When I was nineteen years old and at the technical institute, I used to go to pray. 'Ala', a Brother, used to do the preaching. He was younger than me. People said he was a Brother because he used to talk about Hassan al-Banna in his sermons, but there were not many Brothers at the time who would admit to being one. It was a case of word of mouth. 'Ala' also used to organize sports events in the mornings after the *fagr* prayer. He used to gather the young men in the mosque, and then they used to go off to the soccer field. During the games, they never swore, never behaved badly . . . I used to watch them. I was impressed by their good behavior. I wasn't really very observant at the time, but I liked this guy 'Ala' who was doing the preaching. He invited me to the soccer matches. I admired him. Everyone appreciated him. He also practiced kung fu, which lots of people were interested in at that time.[9] I liked the soccer games so much that I started organizing them myself as well. I got closer to 'Ala', and then we started to meet with others at his place as well. We started to read about religion and the life of the Prophet.[10]

Salah's participation in the soccer matches thus led to his own adoption of the *shakluh kwayyes*, or good behavior, that had attracted him to them in the first place. Moreover, this physical activity, clearly involving some disciplining of the body, also led to more regular religious practices, since it was part of a fixed program that included getting up at dawn, praying, and engaging in sports for the rest of the morning until midday prayers (or sermon on Fridays). A short while later, Salah started working at the cement factory, where he began his social and religious activities with some coworkers. He also attended classes at a local Preaching Institute of the Gam'iyya al-Shar'iyya to train to become a preacher.

Hamdi's story was much the same, and he noted that soccer was "the means [wasila] by which I met the Brothers."[11] While he did not identify them as such, he was also at first impressed by their behavior, which contrasted with that of his other friends at the time ("some of them picked up girls, which is haram, but no one told us, and some used to smoke drugs"). Expecting to find "people who never laughed, never went out, always stayed in the mosque," he was amazed to meet young men who were "kwayyesin [good, well-intentioned] who would play soccer and crack jokes like everyone else" and who knew how to encourage him in his other passion, which was singing. Hamdi had been a member of the choir in the Scouts Club of the Arab Socialist Union ("We sang to celebrate the peace with Israel"), and his new friends proposed setting up a new choir that would chant Islamic songs at weddings. This was later very successful. Hamdi then started his "career as a businessman," he said jokingly, by selling books of sermons and cassettes of preachers to raise money for Qur'an lessons and children's schoolbooks.

This capacity to detect a new recruit's interests and to encourage him to take part in new social relationships was also notable in Gamal's account. When he was twenty years old, Gamal had "few friends," and he spent a lot of his time reading books as part of his study of Islamic law at al-Azhar while also working in his father's grocery shop in 'Izbat al-Qibliyya. Yet being the son of the local shopkeeper made him well known in the neighborhood, and two young men from the area started to visit him on a regular basis.

> Of course they didn't tell me who they were. . . . They would spend a little time with you: "How are you doing, take this cassette, take this book," things by Imam Hassan al-Banna, Sheikh Sabiq, and Sayyid Qutb. I started to listen and to read, and I liked it a lot. I particularly remember the "Letter on Jihad" by Hassan al-Banna. At the time I liked jihad a lot. I was very upset by what was going on in Palestine, by the Jews . . . and I really wanted to travel, to leave the 'Izba and to emigrate. So, when the Brothers saw this love of jihad in me, they thought, 'He is the right type. Let's try with him.' There was an empty apartment in our building (upstairs—it was intended for when I got married), so we used to stay there reading

books. . . . They would arrange for me to meet the *ulama* that I admired. For example, Dr. 'Abd al-Hadi,[12] that was great, it really encouraged me to enter the Brotherhood.[13]

Gamal was more observant than Salah or Hamdi before he met the Brothers. He had also been interested in other Islamist currents such as the Salafists and the Tabligh, but he said, "they didn't correspond to the Islam I had in mind." The latter form of Islam he had learned about since primary school through al-Azhar teaching, just like Hamdi and 'Abd al-Rahman, and he found it again in books by al-Banna, al-Sabiq, and even Sayyid Qutb. Reading this material had led him to channel his thirst for heroic action into everyday virtuous action, Gamal observed. "The Salafists don't observe the whole of Islam. They don't embrace it as a totality. They only apply it in the mosque. . . . They don't direct it to action outside." However, it was exactly in this "action outside," in the external relationships with others, that Gamal located his own subjective experience of ethical transformation. He maintained that "if I weren't a Brother, people wouldn't like me as much as they do." According to him, it had been the Brothers who had "begun to give him a very good education in the love of the good, far from egoism and from the love of the self." Gamal then started to become involved in a charity in the 'Izba, in which several Brothers, who were not known to the State Security, were also working.

'Abd al-Rahman described himself as having been a "difficult" child. He had quarreled with his father and left his home in the countryside for Cairo when he was still in high school. He had then found a room in the al-Azhar University dormitories thanks to a student grant, and had been shocked to see other students being thrown out of their rooms because they were members of the Brotherhood. "It was unfair. Why stop them from having a room if they deserved one as much as anyone else? That was how I came into contact with the Brothers." He started to take part in a small group focusing on everyday activities, mostly soccer again, and he found that "they were very open-minded about meeting others."

> They would come to talk to you about "how much tomatoes cost today," a very ordinary subject of discussion, so relations would start naturally. Then the more in-depth discussions would begin. . . . We didn't belong to the Brothers at the time. But we would engage in activities with the Brothers as fellow students and friends. *We were neither Brothers, nor not Brothers, that wasn't the question.* We would do things together as a group of friends, going to summer camp, playing soccer, going to pray together, things like that, lots of things, but nothing related to the question of Brother or not Brother. . . . I used to say to myself that perhaps the one who

was organizing all this was a Brother, but all the others around him, they weren't necessarily Brothers.[14]

As in the other cases mentioned, the MB identities of those young people he was interacting with were unclear to him at first. Over time the activities in which he was involved became more intense. He was encouraged to become interested in public work and to take part in social and political activities. Before long, 'Abd al-Rahman was standing in the student elections on a mixed list, and then he took part in Mahdi 'Akif's campaign in Madinat Nasr for the 1987 parliamentary elections ('Akif became the Brotherhood's supreme guide in 2004). Of course, all this could be seen as simply the implementation of the Individual Call strategy of recruitment described above.

However, what would be missing from such a strategic reading is that the process did not necessarily involve severing the new recruit from his outside social networks and enclosing him in Brotherhood circles alone, or plunging him into a life of austere asceticism. Indeed, the activists interviewed for this study often referred to their sense of personal fulfillment and their attainment of denser social relationships, including outside the organization, compared to what had been the case before they met the Brothers. The question of what was inside and what was outside the Brotherhood was in any case a complicated one, since the boundaries of the Gama'a, here as elsewhere, were revealed to be porous.

## To Be or Not to Be *Ikhwani*—Is That the Question?

During this first phase, the new recruits did not really know whether they were part of the Gama'a. All those interviewed had difficulty precisely dating their entry into the Brothers. Hamdi and Gamal believed that they had entered immediately. Salah had given more thought to the question and figured out that the process must have taken a dozen years or so. "At the beginning [1982], I thought I was already a Brother," he commented, but it was only quite a while later, when he was already privy to the secrets of the organization, that he realized he had actually entered during his last summer camp in 1991. "I understood that much later when I was myself organizing this type of camp!" he exclaimed. For 'Abd al-Rahman, the question of when he had entered the organization was not relevant to his experience. He was visibly annoyed when I asked him "How did you join the Brotherhood?" But his answer was fascinating.

> Listen, I had made the decision, that's all there is to it. I had known the Brothers, I knew now, at university—this activity and that one, it was the Brothers . . . they carry a print, a particular form . . . there is a distinctive image . . . you would know the image, recognize it

immediately, by the form, the behavior . . . it's as if you were to see a picture of me, you would recognize it right away. Well, it is the same thing.

This image *(sura)*, form *(shakl)*, and behavior *(tasarruf)*—in brief, this *shakluh kwayyes* that earned the recruiter–friends so much admiration—was what attracted new recruits and what made ordinary activities quite distinctive in the latter's eyes. It meant that participating in such activities became both ordinary and special, and therefore both natural and specific. They were experienced as a rite of passage through the shifting margins of the Gama'a—that is to say, between the latter understood as an 'institution spreading meaning and ideas' and the organization itself (that is, the *tanzim*).

This aspect draws attention once again to the boundaries of the Gama'a, since the institution's area extended beyond its formal organization. Another way of putting this would be to say that cultural belonging to the Brotherhood extended far beyond organizational belonging. It began at the point where the adoption of ethical conduct seemed to begin in the subjective experience of the individuals concerned. In this liminal area between the Brotherhood as institution and Brotherhood as organization, the categories of *muhibb*, *mu'ayyid*, and *mu'ayyid qawi* were to be found.

It was only once they had entered the organization that the activists discovered the existence of these categories, such that they only really became members, so to speak, when they realized that they hadn't 'really' been members all along. Some might even have believed themselves to be members while not actually being anything of the sort. 'Abd al-Rahman once let slip, for example, that this was the case of one member of Sheikh al-Muhammadi's core staff who was also in charge of one of the offices. Suddenly remembering himself, he swiftly added:

> I don't want to say anything more. It doesn't much matter whether or not he knows that he isn't a Brother. I don't make a difference *(mesh 'awiz afraq)* between him and us since he does exactly the same thing as us. From the point of view of thinking, he is a Brother *(fikriyyan huwa ikhwan)*, and from the point of view of practice, he serves people, he does the best he can for them, there's no difference . . . I don't want to hurt his feelings . . . if I say to him "you are a bit far from us, you are not a member of our family," that could hurt him . . . what counts is the thinking and the action *(al-fikra wa-l-haraka)*. This is a popular movement, which means that it includes anyone who wants to help people, to act, and to share in ideas and action. Anyone who does this is good *(kwayyes)*, and that's the important thing. The *tanzim* is a secondary thing *(al-tanzim haga thanawiyya)*.[15]

'Abd al-Rahman was emphasizing the gap between organizational belonging and cultural belonging here. He was affirming the greater importance of the latter while at the same time using the image of the family (*'a'ila*) for the former. This point of view may not have been shared by all the activists interviewed, but it was repeated by Muhsin (the associated personality and entrepreneur), who also used the comparison with the family.

> People say I am a Brother, but I'm not. I like the Brothers, but I am not a Brother. The Brothers inherit an ideology. They are Brothers from the time they are very young (around fifteen years old). I got to know them when I was an adult, and the Brothers don't let someone of adult age join them. They are like a family. They don't reveal everything to their sympathizers. They have secrets about their family. It's not because they don't trust me that they are not going to share their secrets with me, for example. It's just because they are family secrets. . . . They are the affairs of their *tanzim*, and I am not part of those things. If I cooperate with you, is it your political affiliation or your behavior that strikes me? . . . I am a practicing believer. I perform the prayers. But I don't have a beard, and I dress in a modern way. Islam is more about behavior than about appearance.[16]

Muhsin had begun working regularly with the Brothers when he was around thirty years old, during his time on the Local Popular Council. He had already been a member of the Labor Party for many years, and this made his entry later into the Gama'a unlikely. However, Muhsin nevertheless felt included in the Brotherhood's circle of trusted individuals, and he shared with the Brothers the emphasis on behavior, considering this to be the most important thing for a Muslim.

He was probably one of those who believed that they were not Brothers but in fact were to a certain degree. This was the case for Hadi, MP Mukhtar's secretary in Madinat Nasr, who, using his own terms, was not "from the Brothers" *(ana mesh min al-ikhwan)*. However, when I repeated what Hadi had said to another member of Mukhtar's staff, the latter burst out laughing, saying, "No, who told you that?" He then refused to say anything else.

Most probably, Hadi fell into one or the other of the categories on the margins of the Brotherhood as organization, and therefore he did in fact 'belong' to it. Even though he felt that he was not a member of the Brothers, not being aware of the existence of such categories, Hadi also felt that in a way he was a Brother by his way of thinking and behavior.[17] In his view, he had acquired this ethical conduct through his involvement with the Brothers, but also through his al-Azhar training, which emphasized the same understanding of Islam as virtuous conduct. Hadi was a perfect example of the close attachments that the *ikhwani* code of conduct was supposed to lead to, and he had retained emotionally charged memories of his first encounter with the Brothers when he was a child.

> I'm going to tell you something. . . . I was an orphan, and orphans have to make more effort in order to succeed. So when I was at preparatory school I used to have private lessons in English, and the teacher was a Muslim Brother. We had to pay LE8 per lesson, and there were five of us in the class. He would collect the money at the beginning of the lesson, but I was an orphan . . . [and] at the end of the class when my friends had left he would call me back and would give me back the money. That impressed me a lot. When you are living in poverty and you are treated like that, it really stays with you.[18]

It was a childhood relationship of another kind that led Abu al-Qasim to become a helping hand at the Helwan Center office as an extra job in addition to his main one in a local government office. Abu al-Qasim was a childhood friend of 'Abd al-Rahman from the same village in Minufiyya. He did not ask himself any questions regarding his belonging to the Brothers or his relationship with them.

> Abu al-Qasim: I could have found another job, for example working for a lawyer or something. Let's say that I could have found a job paying LE500. But I wouldn't have been as happy as I am here, where, say, I only get LE200 or LE300, because I feel happy doing what I do here. It's good work *('amal khayr)*, and I feel . . . [he made a gesture with his hand, moving it from the top to the bottom of his body and not completing the sentence]. This work helps me to understand people's poverty and to feel empathy *(ta'atuf)* for them. Is it shameful to be engaged in cleaning the office and feeding the cat here, when I am an employee of the Ministry of Tourism? No . . . what do you think? It's good?

> Me: Yes . . . and what do you think of the Brothers and what they do? What do you think of their ideas?

> Abu al-Qasim: I don't have an opinion. I don't know what their ideas are, and I don't even want to know. I'm not interested. I avoid talking about them. I'll tell you something—politics is not for me. I am an ordinary man, you see. I wear a *gallabiyya*. I don't think about anything else.[19]

It would be tempting to interpret Abu al-Qasim's recourse to this bodily gesture expressing the sense of acting for the good as a sign of his physical incorporation of *ikhwani* conduct. Was Abu al-Qasim in fact already a *muhibb*, even if he might not have considered himself to be? Was he a *muhibb* from the point of view of the Brotherhood as an institution? Was it not necessarily the case that someone in his position would be put in a specific category? Did the education committee actually intervene at every stage of the relationship between an individual and the institution? While the various categories of membership seemed to be well defined for the older activists I met, where did they in fact begin? And were they as well defined as these activists seemed to think?

It was striking that the activists used to talk about the membership categories as if they were objectively given, even as there were wide variations between the descriptions they gave when recounting their own experiences. The boundaries between the categories were in fact often vague and fraught with various assumptions. Bassim, the young accountant working on Mukhtar's staff in Madinat Nasr, said, for example:

> I joined the Brothers in 1988 when I was eighteen years old. Before that, I used to take part without being a member, from the time I was sixteen years old. I used to give Qur'an lessons to small children in the mosque. When I started going, it had been to learn the Qur'an myself. There were a dozen or so people giving Qur'an lessons in the mosque, of all ages and different religious backgrounds (Salafists, Brothers, and Tabligh). Three of the teachers were Brothers. I was friendly with one of them, but at the time I didn't know that they were Brothers. Then we decided to continue reading the Qur'an together, and one day he told me that we were going to be joined by two other people. We became a sort of *usra*. I was in a Brotherhood *usra* without knowing it, but the question was never asked. I thought it was a matter of religious education and that's all. The two others didn't know either. The teacher never said anything. That lasted nearly a year-and-a-half. . . .
> We started to talk about social matters (what to do about young people who smoked, for example), so I felt in my element. That's what I liked doing, so I wanted to continue. One day, during the summer holidays just before I was due to go back to university, I went to the *usra*, and there was a person from the education committee (*lagnat al-tarbiyya*) there. He didn't say officially that I was part of the Brothers, but I *felt* it. He said, "We want you to join such and such a committee," which meant that I was from then on part of the organization.[20]

Bassim's account illustrates well the progress that could take place (over two years) between entering the Brotherhood as institution and entering the Brotherhood as an organization. The formation of the *usra* probably corresponded to his passage from *muhibb* to *mu'ayyid*, and the arrival of an outside member at the *usra*, identified as being in charge of the Gama'a's local education committee, probably marked his entrance into the organization, though the word was never used. Yet the fact that Bassim also mentioned a "feeling" or "sensation"—a subjective bodily experience—as marking the crossing of the threshold into the Gama'a was also not an accident. It underlined the fact that "bodily experience is the main mechanism by which the ambient power of the institution establishes itself over those who belong to it" and that belonging to the institution is a process achieved "through the body and the mind" (Lagroye 2009: 101) before it is objectified through a formal procedure, title, or function.

Moreover, it was noticeable that very few of the activists mentioned the *bay'a*, even though this is emphasized in the literature. This might have been because when they talked to me, some of them wanted to put forward a non-authoritarian image of the organization. But it cannot have been the reason that caused Mustafa, the young dentist working on the Madinat Nasr staff who was also a friend of Bassim's and an influential and critical Brotherhood blogger, not to mention it more during the lengthy interviews and many informal conversations we had together between 2007 and 2010. At this time, he was reviewing his situation in the lead-up to leaving the organization. Despite the criticisms he made of the latter, he still insisted on the fulfillment that his meeting with the Brothers had given him, the autonomy that he had experienced as a member, and the external social network he had been able to develop thanks to his adoption of the *ikhwani* code of conduct.

### Brothers and Others: When *Tarbiyya* Encourages Social Interaction

Mustafa had begun to attend events organized by the Brothers in 1986 when he was seven years old. That year, he took part in a summer camp in his home district of Alexandria, most of the residents of which came from the middle classes, like his own family. Mustafa described his family as educated and quite politicized, with different political sympathies. Some of the family members were leftists, while others were Nasserists, and others still were Brothers, including his grandfather. His parents had been quite close to the Islamic movement that was gaining momentum in the 1970s, though they had not been members of any particular group. Most of Mustafa's sisters and brothers, on the other hand, had joined the Brothers, like him, in the 1980s. However, it had been his schoolfriends and friends in the neighborhood who had encouraged him to take part in the 1986 camp, emphasizing that it offered a full range of activities including swimming, soccer, and religious education through games and Qur'an-recitation competitions. After that, Mustafa used to go regularly to the mosque in his district with a small group of friends to continue learning the Qur'an from a twenty-five-year-old MB sheikh who was also an engineer.

> Alexandria had an open feel at the time. There wasn't any propaganda against the Brothers. There were a lot of charities in my area that organized a lot of activities in the mosque. . . . The activities were attractive, and the educators (*murabbiyyin*) worked for free without getting paid. They used to come after work. . . . There was a real atmosphere of friendship and cooperation, and the teacher used to help us with schoolwork and show us how to behave properly at home.[21]

In the summer of 1995, when Mustafa was sixteen years old, the teacher from the mosque called him and a dozen or so of his friends together and suggested that they join the Gama'a. This teacher said that becoming a Brother carried certain risks that one should be aware of, as well as certain obligations, such as meeting every week in the *usra*. Mustafa was given a month to think about it, and he asked the teacher about aspects of life as a member of the Brotherhood. What would happen if he wanted to leave? Did the Brothers check up on a member's private life? What did the concept of 'listening and obeying' mean for the Gama'a?

> The teacher told me that the Brotherhood was a civil institution (*mu'assasa madaniyya*), that I would be free to leave if I wanted to, and to manage my private life in the way I wanted, choosing to listen to or ignore any advice that they might give me . . . Obeying was not a matter of "come here, do that." It was the idea that one should respect decisions that had been taken collectively according to the principle of *shura* [collective consultation]. . . . I felt reassured by what he said, and I agreed to join. . . . They have always given me advice, without in any way obliging me to do anything.

There was a small celebration among friends to mark Mustafa's entry to the organization, and then there was the beginning of the weekly meetings in the *usra*, always facilitated by a teacher. Mustafa then began to get more involved in the administrative work (*shughl idari*) in the schoolchildren's section of the organization, and he joined various charitable and cultural associations that did not necessarily have formal links with the Brotherhood, or had no links at all, such as the Russian Cultural Center in Alexandria. These years of adolescence, followed by those as a student at the Faculty of Dentistry at Cairo University, were "happy ones on a personal level" for Mustafa. It was also a "period of intense reflection," in which he read a lot, and not just the religious materials studied in the *usra*. He also read books by Marxist authors lent him by his uncles. "I felt that I was supplying the motivation myself," he said, and while the "school wasn't teaching me anything," the Gama'a was providing a space in which he could "learn how to think, to organize [his] ideas, and to think about [his] future" with the help of educators to whom he became strongly attached (he wrote a long text in memory of one of them on his blog).

Mustafa's commitment to the Brothers thus grew over time, softly, in the exact sense of that term, and he would speak about it with remarkable emotion. His becoming a Brother changed the way others saw him, at first for the worse, though Mustafa fought against the image of austerity often associated with the Brotherhood. This stereotype perceives the Brothers as people who are saintly, who don't know how to have fun, who don't listen to music, and who don't go to the cinema. However, Mustafa was also seen for the better by those around him, since a Brother is also considered to be someone to whom one can go in case of problems and someone who will defend the rights of the community as a whole. At university, the other students would ask Mustafa to represent them to the dean, and later, when he was working in a public hospital, his colleagues would ask him to do the same thing, though this time to the head of the department. He became a spokesman in student demonstrations and a candidate in elections to the student union, where he had to deal with fraud, repression, and court cases that were won but whose verdicts were never carried out. However, while the experience of student activism undoubtedly opened up opportunities for Mustafa, it was only when he began to practice as a dentist on his own account that he really became involved in political activities. These were years of widespread political contestation in Egypt, when thousands of people turned out to demonstrate against the war against Iraq in 2003. With the beginning of the preparations for the flagship parliamentary elections to be held in 2005, Mustafa was promoted to the position of head of the communication committee of the campaign team of 'Isam Mukhtar and Makarim al-Diri in Madinat Nasr (his home district). He was twenty-six. He was then made a member of the political committee of the Gama'a for the East Cairo region, as well as of the national media committee.

In 2007, when Mustafa recounted his story to me, he was well aware of the disciplinary techniques being used in the organization and also critical of them. However, this did not stop him from emphasizing the personal fulfillment he had obtained from belonging to the Brotherhood during a formative period of his life (from seven to twenty-eight years old) or the "outward-looking" attitudes he had acquired from it.

In Helwan, 'Abd al-Rahman (drawing on his own expertise as a teacher) also emphasized the link between the "religious and moral education" the Brotherhood offered and what he called its "social education."

As a Brother, you receive many types of education. There is the education of faith *(al-tarbiyya al-imaniyya)* that gives you a good understanding of Islam, and there is moral education *(al-tarbiyya al-akhlaqiyya)* that teaches you not to betray others, not to reveal a secret, not to lie, and so on. These two forms of education give you a social education *(tarbiyya igtima'iyya)*, in other words, how to deal with other people *(izzay bi-tet'amil ma' al-nas)*. As a Brother, I am required to know my neighbors, my relatives, my friends, and so on, and also to meet and behave with them in a natural fashion. . . . It's true that the Brothers encourage you to be open toward society, but that depends on the nature of the personality of each person and his way of life. Someone who works very late or who is ill will have fewer opportunities to engage in social relationships. I can deal with anybody, anybody at all. Every group in society uses a language I know. I can even make friends on the metro going from here to Cairo. I also know a lot of people because I have taught whole generations of children since 1991. The relations I have created with these young people are strong, because I am not the sort of person to stay at home. . . . As far as he is able, a Brother should aim to have relations with different people in different places. This is one of the Brothers' written instructions. It is also a hadith of the Prophet: "*Khayr al-nas anfa'hum li-l-nas*" ('The best people are those who are of the greatest benefit to others').[22]

While 'Abd al-Rahman emphasized his ordinary and even natural capacity to socialize with others, in reality this was in part the result of the techniques used to encourage Brotherhood activists to socialize. Moreover, it seems that the Gama'a would aim to detect a sociability potential among its recruits and then to develop this in order to increase its grassroots influence. Recruits like 'Abd al-Rahman and Gamal would be targeted on the grounds that they had the psychological profiles of isolated adolescents as a result of their backgrounds (one was a migrant to the city from a rural area and the other was solitary by nature). But their social situations (in this case a student living in a university dormitory and the son of a grocer) could allow them to develop a range of social relationships. The fact that many Brothers became teachers or doctors in their professional lives was also related to this logic of social detection and development.

In the frame of activist training, the encouragement toward sociability played a major role. It encouraged the adoption of *shakluh kwayyes* from a very early stage in an activist's career, and at the *mu'ayyid* stage, recruits were encouraged to involve themselves in one or more welfare activities, such as working for charities or developing informal activities that included collecting *zakat* contributions, distributing food aid, or engaging in cleanup campaigns. This was the case in the examples taken from Helwan above, as well as in the case of Bassim in Madinat Nasr who swiftly became disenchanted with simply taking classes in the Qur'an and was invited to deliver them instead. He later became involved in the local administrative council of al-Gam'iyya al-Shar'iyya. Learning about virtuous action could thus lead an individual to appreciate his own 'altruistic self' that had been fashioned by processes of *tarbiyya*.[23]

Yet, even beyond its educational virtues, having Brotherhood recruits work in charitable activities also helped to spread the informal affective power of the Gama'a throughout society by using the services of the nascent activists. They were non-Brothers from the organization's point of view, and therefore they were also still not known to be Brothers by the security services and the wider public. However, they were already Brothers in another sense, in that they were already partly socially captured by the Brotherhood as an institution. Their behavior in delivering welfare activities, undertaken in conformity with the *ikhwani* code of conduct, was intended to signal their identity as Brothers and thus discreetly to publicize the actions of the Brotherhood in the ways described in chapter four. However, as the activists adopted more and more of the *ikhawni* code of conduct they advanced in the organization and began to take part in more sensitive activities, such as elections. The risks increased as they became publicly known to be Brothers in their turn and began to draw the attention of the security services.

We can thus conclude this section by pointing to a paradox, which is that the informal spread of the Brotherhood happened, in part, thanks to the work of individuals who were not in fact full members of the organization. This helped to protect the *tanzim*, since the nascent activists, neither absolute beginners in the organization nor full members, were trained in the field in a step-by-step fashion without their knowing enough about the Gama'a itself to put it in peril. This technique also reinforced the ethical distinctiveness of the Muslim Brothers, since the disinterestedness of these individuals in their charitable work was the result of two things: the way the Brotherhood as an institution worked, and a genuine ethical disposition on their part, whose strategic character was at least temporarily not noticeable to them. This was because at this stage, at least, they were not working directly in order to promote the objectives of the organization.

## When 'Good' Is Not 'Right': 'Us' vs. 'Them'

Understanding the centrality of the Gama'a's margins should not lead us to think that the intensity of the relationships that linked the activists together, along with their subjective perceptions of being in some sense distinctive, has been overestimated by researchers. The intellectual challenge that we need to meet is to think about these two aspects together, understanding that even if they are contradictory, they are also equally fully present. Our task is to analyze the resulting tension between them without underestimating the importance of one aspect at the expense of the other.

This tension was made apparent in the criticisms made by a group of young Brotherhood activists who became increasingly disapproving of the organization from 2006 onward. Their words are particularly valuable because they can help us to understand the ambivalent aspects of the relationship between 'us' and 'them' for the Brotherhood and their organizational and political consequences.

## The Emergence of Public Dissent: Listening to the Bloggers

The development of such criticisms within the Brotherhood took place within the paradoxical context of a political clampdown and social liberation that has already been described several times in this book.[24] As a result of the wider proliferation of the media, and particularly social media networks, Internet activism flourished during this period, especially after the call for a general strike made on Facebook on 6 April 2008 by a group of young activists.[25] It was within these growing virtual networks of Internet activism that the young MB bloggers appeared. For them, the connective social media sphere, with its relative freedom and possibilities for unrestrained public expression, contrasted sharply with the hierarchical, opaque, and highly disciplined world of the Gama'a. The appeal of social media was even greater because the state's intensified repression of the Brotherhood in this era had also encouraged the hegemony of organizationists (tanzimiyyin) within the organization itself who argued for a strategic lockdown. However, it was precisely this isolationist attitude that was most contested by the young bloggers,[26] who pioneered forms of speech that were at once public, personal, and highly critical and that broke decisively with the Gama'a's traditions of opaqueness.

Their first act was to engage in a process of self-criticism. For them, the internal organization of the Gama'a had led not only to the organizational stagnation of the Brotherhood, most notably in the shape of its aging leadership and hierarchical rigidity, but also to its political stagnation. The Gama'a's incapacity to bring about a change of regime (taghyir al-nizam) was the result of the ineffectiveness of its political activities, the young bloggers said. This was due to a lack of political professionalism among its activists and a failure to specialize its activities. This meant that they were criticizing the way in which the Gama'a was organized internally. Such dissenting views were not favorably received by the leadership, since this process of self-criticism increasingly targeted the hierarchy and had within it demands for revisions to the organization's ideology. Many of the young bloggers became strident in their denunciation, and several of them eventually left the organization. However, it was remarkable that those who eventually sought to "exit" developed, for a time, paradoxical forms of "loyalty" toward the organization, even as they were "voicing" their criticisms of it and despite the very palpable weakening of their ideological convictions.[27]

The paradoxical loyalty of the young activists to the Gama'a, despite their ideological disarray, was due to their powerful emotional attachment to it. However, this attachment, called *ukhuwwa*, or the feeling of brotherhood, could also be used against a dissident member as a way of reminding him of his duty to the organization. *Ukhuwwa* in fact was a double-edged sword: it was the foundation of the attractiveness of the Brotherhood and of the loyalty it engendered among its members, but it could also be used to exclude or to exercise violence against those same members. Techniques of *tarbiyya ikhwaniyya*, precisely because they could produce this double-edged feeling of affection and exclusion, could in the end result in lowering the costs of possible defection.

Two of the activists I met on the MPs' staff became bloggers over the course of my fieldwork. The first was Mustafa, the young dentist working in the Madinat Nasr constituency, and the second was his friend Rafiq, who was an activist working for another Brotherhood MP in the Cairo constituency of 6 October.

Both young men were much less reticent in talking about the affairs of the *tanzim* than the other activists I interviewed, and they provided me with valuable information about the internal workings of the organization. However, the most valuable thing of all I obtained from them was the possibility of closely following their "moral careers" as activists (Goffman 1959; Becker 1973) by conducting multiple interviews with them on biographical matters over several years, as well as numerous informal discussions.[28]

This approach, focusing on the "moral careers" of the activists, allowed their MB identity to be seen not as something that was detached from the rest of their lives but, insofar as this was possible, looked at it in the changing context of the lives of the individuals concerned, as well as the strategies of the organization to which they belonged and the wider sociopolitical environment.[29] The series of interviews that I conducted with both of them at different times also combined comments on either the recent or the more distant past with observations on the course of contemporary events. Thus they allowed me carefully to monitor the "going-back points" (Fuchs-Ebaugh 1988) that had punctuated the exit trajectories of both Mustafa and Rafiq.

Mustafa had become one of the main dissident MB bloggers by the end of 2007. He ended up leaving the organization in 2009 after a long and gradual process. After the revolutionary uprising in 2011, he became a well-known figure on the wider political scene. In what follows, I compare the contents of the interviews conducted with him with what he wrote on the two Internet blogs he set up when he was still a member of the Brotherhood. The first of these, "Waves in a Sea of Change" (*Amwag fi bahr al-taghyir*, cited as *Amwag*), Mustafa ran from 2007 to 2009, and hosted contributions from most of the other influential bloggers. Its contents are a prime example of the critical ideas mentioned above. The second, which Mustafa ran from 2007 to 2010, called "I Am with Them" *(Ana ma'ahum)*, was dedicated entirely to personal material, some political and some more private, for which he received a prize from the UN Human Rights Council in 2010. Comparing the two sets of materials can be used to qualify the "biographical illusion" (Bourdieu 1986) that the narrative of a life can produce. In this analysis, I am situating what appears on a blog within the larger context of a career and the thick network of affective ties that link an activist to the group to which he belongs.

Rafiq's case was different from Mustafa's in the manner and timeframe in which he left the Brotherhood. He had progressively become ideologically dissatisfied with the organization around the same time as his friend, and he had vocalized this just as clearly. Yet Rafiq had also managed to renegotiate the terms of his belonging for a longer time, with only the experience of the revolutionary uprising in 2011 finally leading to a violent break and his subsequent expulsion from the Gama'a. Even so, while Rafiq's 'paradoxical loyalty' to the Brotherhood had lasted longer than Mustafa's, the two young men's experiences were sufficiently similar to make the comparison relevant.

From a theoretical point of view, the comparison allows me to examine the question of affection more carefully and to show how in each case it worked differently. First of all, Rafiq, like Mustafa, was a member of two different activist worlds that were in tension with each other. On the one hand, there was his political and social work as a Brotherhood activist in a middle-class suburb of Greater Cairo, and on the other hand, there was his blogging. Even though his smaller blog was not as successful as his friend's (Mustafa's blogs enjoyed a much greater visibility), Rafiq was nevertheless well integrated in the emerging cyberactivist sphere and in revolutionary networks. After he cut ties with the Brotherhood, thanks to his relationships with many various political activists he managed to convert into new forms of action and became a key figure of the party created around Abd al-Mun'im Abu al-Futuh, the Strong Egypt Party (Misr al-Qawiyya).[30] Like Rafiq, Abu al-Futuh, a top-level leader, had recently been expelled from the Gama'a.

Second, both Rafiq and Mustafa had been members of the Brotherhood since childhood, and both came from mostly MB families and were married to Muslim Sisters. They were thus both similarly psychologically dependent on the Brotherhood, but independent of it in material terms, since both were skilled professionals working in structures (hospital, company) not linked to the organization. Yet in the end it was the differences in their immediate environments as activists and private individuals that accounted for the various conditions in which they preserved their affective ties with the Brotherhood and renegotiated their identities as activists. Their respective families, friends, and peers had reacted differently to Brotherhood techniques aiming to absorb "significant others and generalized others" (Mead 1934). In other words, the two men shared a belief in the idea that any criticism of the organization as a whole was necessarily a criticism of each of its members, and vice versa.

From a methodological point of view, the two young men's profiles are also interesting because, unlike some former members of the Brotherhood who have since gone on to publish their memoirs, Rafiq and Mustafa did not go on to become professional enemies of the organization. They did not seek to capitalize on their experiences as former MB members even when the media's anti-Brotherhood discourse accelerated virulently over the course of the revolution, eventually reaching the apogee it has achieved today. The particular character of their experiences gave them the opportunity to think more deeply about their relationship to the organization.

## Ideological Defection and Emotional (Dis)affection
### Mustafa's moral career[31]

In May 2007, Mustafa was fully engaged in his work as a member of MP Mukhtar's staff in Madinat Nasr, where he was in charge of the social services and communications committees. He was also working in Gama'a committees at the national level. However, during that time the regime's policies toward the Brotherhood became considerably harsher, and the impacts of these policies on the internal equilibrium of the organization began to be felt.

On 2 May, Mustafa wrote his first post on the personal blog he had just set up. *"Why am I with them?"* he asked. This "them" was not just the Brothers, for as Mustafa wrote, it included *"every honest heart, every conscious mind, and every respectable human being who loves this country and wants to do something for it. These people are the young who are dreaming of the future and are not afraid."*[32] Mustafa was thus calling on young people from every background—Muslim Brothers, communists, leftists, Nasserists, nationalists, and liberals—to join together in dialogue and to go beyond the quarrels that were dividing the country's political elites and thus serving the system presided over by the regime. Mustafa was operating here on multiple fronts, working directly for the Gama'a and also wanting to open it up to other political currents.

However, at the end of August 2007, this early enthusiasm was significantly stunted by the leak to the press of the draft program of the political party that the Gama'a was planning to create. The program caused a scandal in the wider society, notably because it ruled out the possibility of a Copt or a woman ever becoming president. Mustafa, deeply disappointed, published a post on his blog on 18 September in which he denounced without reservation *"those who are addicted to a single way of thinking"* in the Gama'a, who practiced *"intellectual terrorism"* and were clinging to a *"stagnant boat that won't move on the current of change, development, and reaction to the facts"* that was sweeping the country. These people thought that *"anyone opposing them was a troublemaker and ill-disciplined and needed reeducation."* He warned the leaders whom he trusted in the *tanzim* that if they *"do nothing to try to calm those people, out of their own fear, incapacity, or indolence . . . [they] will expose the 'ranks' [of the organization] to the risks of collapse, division, and disobedience."* A few days after this, Mustafa started his "Amwag" blog which was designed to be participatory and soon made him a prominent figure on the Egyptian web. But he also *"excused himself"* (a euphemism meaning that he resigned) from the regional political committee of the Brotherhood, since it was considered to have played a major role in drafting the MB party's program. He then spent a lot of his time working on his blog and promoting it among activist networks from a variety of backgrounds that were then being set up with a view to defending human rights and denouncing the use of torture. His involvement in the MP's staff diminished, and he resigned from the social services committee.

In the blog posts that Mustafa uploaded, he shared his reservations about the activities carried out by the Brotherhood MPs, seeing them as being vitiated by a lack of political professionalism. In interviews, however, Mustafa was less severe, and what he had to say about the MP he worked for remained positive: "He knows what I am writing about and he doesn't agree with me, but that's OK because we're friends. He doesn't criticize me. He just jokes with me, and we have a laugh." The reason for these friendly relations, rather surprising if we rely on the reading of Mustafa's blog, was the principle of *shura*, used as the basis of all decisions taken.

> The Gama'a brings together people who have different ideas, but that does not mean that we can't work together. I often don't agree with the MP, and we have opposing ideas. But that doesn't stop us from working together in concrete ways or from having a good relationship. If we don't agree in the team, we organize a vote in order to arrive at a decision, and the group that has the majority of the vote wins. Everything we do in the Brotherhood relies upon democratic procedures.

Throughout our conversations, Mustafa insisted that these procedures were actually applied, meaning that, for him, the organizational problem in the Gama'a did not lie in the procedures but in the mainstream conservative ideas circulating within it.

Mustafa's trust in the principle of *shura* also had a deeper explanation related to the nature of the Gama'a as he perceived it. In an interview on 4 April 2008, he explained that belonging to the Brotherhood was something that was more social than political, and that its members were bound together by strong affective bonds. "You feel that the Gama'a is your family," he said. These bonds were felt primarily toward those members of the organization whom one saw most frequently, like, in Mustafa's case, his very close friend who had been in prison for several years and whose wife and children Mustafa was financially supporting. However, this bond could also be present among Brothers who met for the first time. In this regard, Mustafa said that when he had gone to Mansoura in the Delta to observe the voting in the 2005 elections, he had been met by Brothers for whom "in a few days [he had] felt such a love *(hubb)* that he didn't want to leave." This love was the emotion of "fraternity" *(al-ukhuwwa)*, one of the ten *arkan al-bay'a* described by al-Banna,[33] that Mustafa had experienced throughout his membership of the Brotherhood. "You grow up with that as part of your education—that you love your Brother more than yourself. . . . When we were kids and used to play soccer, no one would be the first to take water to drink. Everyone would give it to someone else first." He also described the extraordinary feeling he had of being at home that had struck him on arriving at a Brother's house in Upper Egypt (who was putting him up). He was surprised by this feeling because the "people there are really different from how they are here."

For Mustafa, it was this emotion that explained the remarkable organizational links *(tarabut al-tanzim)* that prevented the implosion of the Brotherhood. Despite the range of divergent opinions in the organization, the *ukhuwwa* was a fundamental principle of Islam and was shared by all members of the Gama'a. They were held together, he said, by "an extremely important attachment of hearts" *(rabita qalbiyya)* that was reinforced by various symbolic rituals. There was, for example, the "oration of the Brothers" ritual *(du'a' al-ikhwan)*, he recounted, when at dusk each day every Brother in Egypt and the rest of the world was called upon to produce a mental image of all his brothers in religion all performing the evening *(maghrib)* prayer and to deliver this oration, the words of which were written by the organization's founder, al-Banna.[34] This feeling of attachment, experienced subjectively and objectively in common practices of socialization, meant that it was unthinkable for Mustafa to consider leaving the Gama'a at that time. This *ukhuwwa* always caused him to believe in the "project" of the Brotherhood, at least. "Even if today only a hundred or so of us have these ideas, I know that the true project of the Gama'a is in fact our project. Our interpretation is the correct one. We need to reform ourselves from within . . . little by little. . . . What counts is not the people who talk. It is actions that will make the difference."

Yet Mustafa did not have a monopoly on action. Between 4 April 2008, when he was still confident about the possibility of internal reform, and 16 April, when we met again, two events took place that had disturbed the unstable balance between the temptation to leave the organization on ideological grounds and to stay within it because of his powerful affection for it. On 6 April, the leadership of the Brotherhood had indeed refused to take part in the movement for the general strike launched on Facebook. On 15 April, the military courts passed heavy sentences on forty Brotherhood leaders arrested at the end of 2006. "I was frightened about what might happen," Mustafa confided, and in fact the sentences corresponded to the tightening of the *tanzimiyyin*'s grip on the Brotherhood.

During the second half of 2008, Mustafa was seriously ill for several months. While this was due to personal reasons, it is not unreasonable to think that this physical illness could have been the result of the turbulence he was experiencing in his life as an activist as well. When he had become well enough to return to work, Mustafa concentrated on his professional activity as a dentist. He only occasionally went to Mukhtar's office, and eventually he stopped going altogether. He also resigned from the Brotherhood media committee at the national level and refused all proposals to become involved in any other form of organizational work. However, he continued with his educational work in the *usra* once a week. At the same time, when his health permitted he continued to take part in activities organized by various human rights networks in Egypt. He took part in events organized by the Kefaya and 6 April movements as well. He also organized conferences with them at the Journalists' Syndicate in Cairo. Writing on his blog became his main form of commitment. In 2008, he wrote a third of the material that appeared on "Amwag," leveling his criticisms at the stagnant state of the Brotherhood. He also posted more personal thoughts on his own blog that testified to his growing emotional suffering. In October of that year, for example, in a post titled "And What Happens Then? The Closest People Are Not Those around You," he wrote:

*While you are rearranging your ideas to remap your brain, things are changing around you and some of those who are living with you and with whom you are living are changing their opinions about you, doubting your intentions, looking at you in a hostile way, and forgetting who you are. Despite the fact that they have known you for a long time, they have a bad opinion of you. They see you as someone who is a loose cannon, someone who is more destructive than constructive, someone who is a danger to the Idea itself, even when they know how much you were convinced by the Idea, how much you worked to apply it, spread it, see it grow, and how much you believed in it to the point of preparing to die for it and to pay whatever price was necessary for it.*

It was thus the deterioration in his personal relations with his immediate Brotherhood entourage that was most important at this stage. The criticisms that he was making of the Brotherhood leadership were perceived by his peers as direct attacks on the organization, as well as on the "project" or convictions that it represented (the 'Idea') and thus as attacks on each one of them as well. The general self (the Gama'a) and the individual self (the members of his entourage) thus merged, and the emotional power of *ukhuwwa* began to be mobilized against Mustafa. He reacted in an extremely emotional manner to the violent treatment inflicted on him by his Brothers, in the double sense of the term. For him, it was they who were betraying him by accusing him of betraying a cause to which he had given so much of himself. In the same blog post in October 2008, Mustafa expressed something of the anxiety and feelings of madness that were assailing him.

> *You turn around and around, you ask yourself what you should do; what is the simplest and the least tiring? Should you go back on what you said? Should you shut up and relieve those around you? . . . You love and respect them, but shouldn't the love you have for the Idea be greater than any other love? Will the Idea forgive you one day for going off the rails and ceasing to find a way forward? . . . Will [your children] forgive you, when they have grown up and see the faults of those who, like you, preferred peace of mind to the difficulties of the road and its suffering and anxiety?*

The psychological pressure continued to build in 2009. At first it came from the middle ranks of the *tanzim* and, according to Mustafa, it verged on harassment. There were no formal sanctions against him, but there was an atmosphere of repeated emotional blackmail: "Why did you write this or that? I am angry with you because, in writing like that, you are damaging the Gama'a. You are causing *fitna* [division of the community], and you are annoying your friends," Mustafa remembered being told. Higher-level leaders of the organization only intervened occasionally and one of them, Khayrat al-Shater, gave Mustafa his personal support. At this point, Mustafa's immediate circle became the arena for more violent criticisms. He started to go to only one meeting of his *usra* out of every two, and the majority of those present kept their distance from him. Finally, he stopped going altogether, as he "wasn't able to do it anymore," he admitted. Then part of his own family seemed to disown him. Mustafa stopped writing on "Amwag," a sign of his feelings of paralysis, though the debate about the future of the Brotherhood persisted on the site without him.

What Mustafa described as a "major psychological crisis" led him to leave the organization at the end of 2009. Remarkably, exiting from the Gama'a seemed even less formalized than entering it, and much was left unsaid. "I went to see my superior, and I told him that I didn't want to continue organizational activities. I didn't say that I was resigning or that I was leaving, but he understood. If you stop at the organizational level, there is nothing left," he said. Mustafa thus did not leave in response to any new event, and there was no relationship between his leaving and the controversy over the internal Brotherhood elections in December 2009. There was no slamming of doors or taking up of positions against the Brotherhood. Instead, he simply left without any particular drama.

> I felt that my continuing presence was going to cause a shock. And that wouldn't have satisfied me. It wouldn't have allowed me to do what I wanted. . . . A period came when I felt that that was it, that I couldn't go on, that it would be better to go like that. If I hadn't, I would have had to accept ideas and positions that I didn't agree with. People around you ask, "Why did the Brothers do such and such?" and you have to defend what they did even when you don't agree with it yourself. So, what's the point?

What was the point when the brotherly love that had connected Mustafa to the Gama'a had turned into daily suffering? After months spent in trying to reform the Gama'a from within, Mustafa realized that it was not so much reform *(al-islah)* of the Brotherhood or of the wider society or of the political system that was necessary, as total change *(al-taghyir)*—in other words, revolutionary change.

Three months after this, his political aspirations and his ambitions as an activist were fulfilled by a man who seemed to symbolize the hope that such change would take place. As a result, and gathering up what was left of his energies, Mustafa, still only thirty-one, became one of the most committed supporters of Mohamed ElBaradei in the latter's National Campaign for Change. A year later, Mustafa wrote a moving text in praise of ElBaradei on his Facebook page that bore witness to the emotional and personal changes that he himself was living through. Lastly, it was the revolutionary uprising of 2011 that gave him the opportunity to bring his thoughts to fruition. In May 2011, Mustafa founded his own al-'Adl (Justice) Party, whose manifesto emphasized ideological pluralism and cooperation among all political currents.[35] In the parliamentary elections in the winter of 2011–12, Mustafa was the only candidate on the party's list to be elected, winning one of the two seats in the Madinat Nasr constituency. While Mustafa was not in direct competition with the former MP Mukhtar—since he was standing for the fi'at seat and Mukhtar was standing for the workers' one—he nevertheless beat the Salafi candidate with whom Mukhtar had entered into an alliance. The campaign was cruel. Mustafa's former comrades tried to have him disqualified even though he had been the manager of their own campaign in 2005, accusing him of paying bribes and working for Christian missionaries. However, Mustafa incarnated something of the youthful spirit of Tahrir Square and was able to draw on his experience in electoral mobilization and on his personal networks in the constituency.[36] Did Mustafa's previous comrades lack such contacts? Did they miss Mustafa's personal efforts? Whatever the answer to these questions might be, Mukhtar also lost his seat in these elections.

Mustafa's speaking out did not in itself make his departure from the Brotherhood inevitable. He had very early on demanded the right to express his own ideas, and the trust he had placed in his peers did not, for him, entail the surrendering of self *(fides implicita)*[37] to the organization. On the contrary, the trust he felt toward his peers and the ties of mutual affection that bound them together led him to believe that he would be able to keep his place among them in spite of their disagreements and ideological differences. He tried to renegotiate the terms of his commitment several times by modifying his activities, trying temporary withdrawal, seeking to gather with other dissidents, and searching for support among part of the leadership. But the intransigence of those immediately around him (the usra, the middle-rank leaders) rendered all such attempts futile, since it was precisely this rigidity that undermined their mutual affection.

The case of Rafiq, on the other hand, showed that in other circumstances—characterized by different immediate relationships, a different regional section, a different constituency, a different *usra*, and a different family history—the coexistence of individual voice and group loyalty was possible for longer. While Rafiq had ideologically left the Brotherhood at the same time as Mustafa, his departure from it as an activist was forestalled thanks to the preservation of a binding affection within his immediate entourage.

### The tortured love of *ukhuwwa*
In November 2010, the campaign for the parliamentary elections was in full swing against a background of intense frustration. The heavy cloud hovering over the country, especially when compared to the brighter mood before the 2005 elections, showed that the long-promised democratic reforms that had been postponed on successive occasions by the regime had finally failed. For Rafiq, a twenty-seven-year-old engineer working for a multinational automobile company, what Egypt needed was not so much reform as total transformation. Like that of his friend Mustafa, Rafiq's view of the Brotherhood was a disenchanted one, and he now had no faith that it could change from within. The timeframe of his disillusionment with the

capacity of the Gama'a to renew itself by listening to internal criticisms had followed Mustafa's. At the end of 2009, when Mustafa himself had left the organization, Rafiq stopped contributing to criticisms of the Brotherhood through the personal blog he had been writing. However, although he was disillusioned, Rafiq did not withdraw from his activities with the Brotherhood, and he actively took part in its 2010 election campaign in the 6 October constituency.[38] While he was vehemently opposed to the idea of taking part in the elections, he nevertheless considered that he needed to follow the organizational line during the campaign period.

This sense of loyalty did not come from any residual hope of reestablishing some degree of ideological resonance with the organization. Instead, it was motivated by a desire to still 'feel with' the Brotherhood, to act along with it, bonded to "his" Gama'a that he said he did not want to abandon. He also expressed a fear that he himself would feel deserted if he were constrained to leave the Gama'a, even though he was also a member of other activist networks whose political opinions he shared. He feared the sense of solitude that might come with leaving the Brotherhood. If "a single [Gama'a] is missing, everything is unpeopled,"[39] one might add, and this would not be too far from the truth, since Rafiq never attempted to hide the fact that for him this was a loving relationship. In order to understand this more fully, it is necessary to read Rafiq's account closely, delivered with a broken voice when his ideological disagreements with the Brotherhood were at their height.

> Why do I stay? Because I am emotionally bound to the Gama'a. I grew up . . . this is a very strong reason, you know . . . I grew up in a Brotherhood family—my parents, my brothers and sisters, everyone was a Brother. But despite this, when I was fourteen years old I told my father that I didn't want to be a Brother. So my father, who was a leader of the Brotherhood (we were living in Saudi Arabia at the time, where he was director of public relations in a company), my father brought me some books and said, "There you are. Read them and choose what you want to be." I read different things, and books by Hassan al-Banna, and I said to myself, "That's it." So the result was that I entered the Brothers out of conviction. Later, I became connected to them, I liked them, and I lived with them, and in order for me to go away from them, I would have to break those bonds. I am linked to them emotionally. . . . When you meet a person who holds the same values as you do, you like him, and the more you live with that person the more you like him. But it's not just that I like a person, it's also the Gama'a itself. I feel related to it. I am used to belonging to the Gama'a, and over time I became emotionally connected to it. . . .

I have lived with them, eaten with them . . . we grew up together, went to prison together, lived through difficult times and happy times together . . . it's like your childhood friends, friends from school . . . but I used to see them at school and outside school, at high school and outside high school, at university and outside university. I saw them all the time, I liked seeing them. It became a habit. . . . If I left, I would still see them, but what can I say? It's a habit. I like to stay with them . . . . It's like in a couple, when you love someone, but the person makes mistakes and does things you don't like, but you don't just go, you love them anyway. . . . I have very close friends who are not Brothers. I don't love Brothers more just because they are Brothers. My best friend is a member of the NDP. He would come to warn us, when we were at university, what time the police would arrive and what they would do to us and so on. But with the Brothers, we have lived together, had all sorts of experiences together. Of course, the group has changed. I am not with the same people I was with when I was small. When I say that we lived together, that was perhaps for a short time, maybe four years. But that was enough to connect me very strongly to them, to make me love them and them to love me, as I have a strongly emotional and affectionate personality.

In this account, Rafiq gave a psychological explanation for the powerful affective bonds that connected him to the Brotherhood. However, in doing so he was at least partially mistaken, since *ukhuwwa* was in fact a feeling that was deliberately produced by techniques of socialization *(tarbiyya)*, as well as by the daily meetings of fellow Brotherhood members and the common experience of repression.

We can see in his account, for example, the emphasis placed on the fact that the Brothers were not only peers in the organization. They were also childhood friends, friends from school and university, then friends in adulthood, and very often also friends from prison. Rafiq mentioned his arrest and later imprisonment for a month in 2007 when he was on a trip to Alexandria with MB friends from university, with whom he had traveled to have a holiday while also revising for exams. This trip away was as much an educational *rihla* (journey), as designed by the *tarbiyya* program, as it was a holiday with friends, which shows that in practice the Brotherhood activists did not always have the impression that they were being acted upon by techniques of *tarbiyya*. This confusion could mean that a comrade in the Brotherhood was also a close friend in everyday life, and it shows the extent to which Brotherhood *tarbiyya* was not necessarily experienced as a matter of discipline and limitations. It was a fluid process of pedagogical socialization.

Rafiq said that the control procedures used by the Brotherhood, such as the questionnaires, were also not as formalized as the account given by Kandil might suggest. "We would simply take some bits of paper at the beginning of an *usra* meeting and just write down, as a mark out of ten, for example, what we thought about our behavior and our actions that week. You would write down six, seven, or eight according to how you felt that week, and that would be it," he said. Moreover, Brotherhood discipline rarely meant formal sanctions; it mostly took the form of the same kind of practices that strengthened relationships between individual Brothers—in other words, *ukhuwwa*. This was an informal mode of discipline that worked by the practice of spontaneous emotional blackmail by peers. But it could end in a violent backlash against the activist who had been labeled as not conforming.

Rafiq was protected for longer than Mustafa against this kind of sanctioning, however, and several factors explain the preservation of his affective bonds with those around him. First of all, his family circle and his marital relationships were different. Rafiq had been born into a family in which all the other members were also members of the Brotherhood. He explained that his father's open-mindedness had been such that disagreements could exist without leading to breakdowns in relationships. He also married within the Brotherhood in January 2010, and this reinforced his affective bonds to the organization at a time when his ideological disagreements with it were already well advanced. Furthermore, there had been the conciliatory attitude of his peers. At the time when he experienced ideological defection, Rafiq had been the official delegate of his *usra*. As such, he had had to put up with criticisms, or even quarrels, by members of his group. Yet he described how he had the good fortune to be in an environment in which such disagreements were acceptable. The Brotherhood official responsible for the 6 October region was a reformer *(islahi)*, and he encouraged debate and discussion within the *usar* in his area. As a result, the expression of criticisms did not necessarily lead to the kind of opprobrium or ostracism that Mustafa had suffered in Madinat Nasr. Lastly, this relatively open environment had allowed Rafiq to redeploy his activist commitments in arenas where he had some margin of maneuver. He spent most of his time on the 2010 election campaign engaging in raising political and cultural awareness among the citizens, for example. He also organized internal brainstorming and debating sessions for his local group to spread the idea of the need for greater political professionalism.

Just a few months later, the 25 January 2011 revolution upset these fragile internal balances. Rafiq found a substitute for Brotherhood *ukhuwwa* in the emotional intensity of the occupation of Tahrir Square, which he experienced with a new circle of peers, even as the oft-remarked absence of the Brotherhood from the first days of the uprising sickened him. He then refused to join the new political party formed by the Gama'a, the Freedom and Justice Party (FJP), as the latter's subordination to the former was at odds with his belief in political specialization. On 3 July 2011, he was expelled from the Gama'a along with four other activists from the 6 October region. The rift also led to the sudden breakdown of his marriage and the faltering of various friendships, although his close family remained supportive of him and respected his decisions. The psychological reprisals carried out against him by many Brotherhood members (even people he didn't know personally) over a period of two years bore witness to its capacity to produce a sufficiently powerful state of mind among its members that the betrayal of one deviant individual with regard to the Gama'a was also felt by each of its member as an act of personal treason. Among the techniques used, one can point to the deployment of defamatory rumors claiming that the individual in question was immoral in various ways (addicted to alcohol or hashish, or involved in sexual scandals). These rumors were then widely circulated on Facebook. Rafiq's Facebook wall filled up with insulting messages over the next few months from people who had previously considered themselves his brothers.

## The Ambivalence of Virtue

Returning to the end of 2010, Rafiq's reflection on his own situation then and on that of his friend Mustafa led him to identify two problematic aspects of Brotherhood socialization. The first was what he called the "tube" (he used the English word), meaning the tendency of some Brothers to perceive themselves as living their lives inside of a Brotherhood society and engaging in personal relationships only within this closed group. The second aspect was that criteria associated with *shakluh kwayyes* were the most important factors when deciding on internal promotions. What linked these two aspects together was the ambivalence of "virtue," insofar as it was intended to regulate relationships outside and inside the Gama'a.

### "Tube" and SIM card

Even though he considered it to be "the most beautiful feeling there is," the *ukhuwwa* had led to palpable misgivings on the part of Rafiq. In his criticisms of the "tube" mentioned above, it was actually *ukhuwwa* that he was denouncing, although without being fully aware of it. It was a form of love "that was both real and particular to the Muslim Brothers," he asserted, because they did everything possible to cultivate it through the methods of *tarbiyya*. *Ukhuwwa* also "came from Islam and should be felt toward every Muslim and every other person as well," Rafiq elucidated. Using the image of the "tube," he thus identified a crucial tension at the heart of Brotherhood socialization—praising the fact that feelings of fraternity were *particularly* cultivated among members of the Gama'a as well as deploring the fact that they were only felt among the Brothers in *particular*.

"I have very close friends who are not Brothers. I don't love the Brothers more because they are Brothers, [and] my best friend is a member of the NDP," he elaborated in his long account of himself. For Rafiq, the difference between his relationships with his MB friends and his other friends was a matter of the number of "things we have experienced together" and not a matter of an a priori assumption that the MB friends should be closer than the others. However, he also recognized with some embarrassment that *ukhuwwa* conveys ideas of moral superiority and exclusion. This is particularly visible in the following passage, where Rafiq is remembering his trip to Alexandria with other Muslim Brothers.

> Me: How was Amn al-Dawla (State Security) able to recognize you when you were on the beach?
>
> Rafiq: First of all, we were known to be Brothers because of our activities at 'Ain Shams University. And then there was a difference between us, because of the way we were behaving, and the other young people on the beach, who were smoking and drinking. They were running around, not focusing. . . . It wasn't because of the tobacco and the alcohol. I know lots of people who indulge in these things who are very respectable *(muhtaramin)*. . . . But you can see it in the behavior . . .
>
> Me: So, they arrested you because you were identifiably Brothers?
>
> Rafiq: No, when people see us, they just think that we are respectable people. . . . But I don't want you to think that I am saying that we are better than other people. That's not what I am saying at all.

Rafiq emphasized the good behavior of his peers, their *shakluh kwayyes*, but refused to accept the idea that there was any suggestion of moral superiority attached to it, thereby rejecting any notion of exclusivity. However, while relationships with others, and a fortiori variances from others, might be met with tolerance by many Brothers, that tolerance could often stop when it came to accepting such differences. Tolerance tended to be understood in its first meaning of "admitting with a certain passivity or often condescension," and it rarely extended to the second meaning of being "open to other ways of thinking and behaving." Another person could be passively tolerated even as he or she was being judged to be immoral, according to a single-minded conception of virtue. It was this kind of relationship to others that Rafiq was criticizing through the image of the "tube" or of a "society within society."

> Being a Brother does not prevent one from living in society or from being among everyone else at work or among friends, for

example. I don't live closed off in Brotherhood society *(al-mug-tama' al-ikhwani)*. I used that word, but I don't like it, and it is not correct. Unfortunately, some Brothers do live as if they've formed a [separate] society within society and that's a problem. First, when you read the texts written by Hassan al-Banna, you don't find that there is ever any obligation for Brothers to marry only within the Brotherhood and only to do things with other Brothers and so on. This idea has been invented by other people. Also, at each stage in history there are different tools. The opening up to the public in the 2005 elections was a way of getting out of Brotherhood society and of living fully in the society as a whole.[40]

Rafiq regretted that the opportunity to make one's affiliation public during the 2005 election campaign had not been taken by all the members of the Brotherhood as a way of getting out of their "tube"—or, to speak more exactly, of accepting all the consequences of doing so. It was true that social embedding and the extension of the borders of the organization were fundamental aspects of Brotherhood action; the argument that "we are part of the texture of society"*(ihna dimn nasig al-mugtama')* was often heard from activists working for the Brotherhood MPs. But these activists had been selected to work for the MPs exactly because of their local social embedding. Second, even those activists who worked most engagingly on the local level were capable of excluding non-Brothers from their personal or intimate lives. "Many only invite fellow Brothers to their marriages and the circumcisions of the children, and so on," Rafiq further clarified.

However, it is difficult to know how many Brothers lived their entire social lives within the "tube" identified by Rafiq, how many only lived their personal lives within it, and how many were prepared to live outside the confines of it in every area of their lives. We have no way of knowing with any degree of certainty what the proportions might have been, or which group was the predominant one. In Egypt, 'mixed' families are socially ubiquitous; many families have a brother, a sister, or an uncle who is a member of the Brotherhood, and the rest of the members have other religious and social affiliations. I met many people who also passed through the organization at one point or another in their lives. One female resident of an informal area of Tibbin, a fervent supporter of President Abdel Fattah al-Sisi, told me in 2014, for example, that "the solution is reconciliation. We need peace, because in the end who are the Brothers? It is one person in this house, another one in that, and so on. We are all Egyptians, all brothers. My neighbor, for example, who supports Morsi, we have normal relations in everyday life, and she looks after my children."[41]

What gave the impression that there were mostly 'Brothers in the tube,' however, was the subjective feeling found among many activists that they were living in Brotherhood society even when objectively they actually had a variety of social relationships. The case of a friend of Rafiq, whom I met in December 2012, illustrates this phenomenon. This young activist was a member of an MB family, who had married a Sister and was now an organizer in the local branch of the Freedom and Justice Party. We were sitting in a café in 6 October, and he was telling Rafiq about his own doubts regarding the direction of the Brotherhood (he knew that Rafiq had been expelled from the Gama'a more than a year before). Though they were very critical of the strategies employed by the Gama'a and the party, the activist and his wife were hesitant about leaving the organization. "I'm afraid of leaving the Muslim Brotherhood," he said. "What will happen to us? What will happen to our daughter? How will she grow up?" I asked him where his daughter went to school. The answer was to a state school. I asked him where he worked. The answer was as an engineer in a private company not connected to the Brotherhood. I asked him where he lived. In a rented apartment, was the answer. I concluded by asking, "I don't understand. What will change in your situation and that of your daughter if you leave the Gama'a?" He thought for a moment, and said, "Nothing . . . I must have a SIM card inserted somewhere here [he put his hand to his neck] that is making me think otherwise. Can you get it out somehow?" We all laughed.

This SIM card bears witness to the methods of subjugation used by the Gama'a in the double meaning that Foucault has given to the term. On the one hand, the *tarbiyya* used by the Brotherhood inculcated a mode of conduct into its members (being subjugated), and on the other, it also provided the resources by which the self was morally constituted (becomes a subject), if only because it led that self to reflect on his or her complex relationships with others. Indeed, "Who are we?" was a recurrent question asked by the MB activists. And it was for this reason that the friend of Rafiq was able to reflect on the way he had been 'formatted' by techniques of MB socialization, even joking that he had been given a "SIM card." Whether he recognized it or not, the ability to reflect on his own self-constitution was the expression of the plural pattern of socialization through which he was morally constituted and which combined different elements coming from the *tarbiyya ikhwaniyya* and from other spheres of socialization.

I build on the theoretical framework established by Bernard Lahire (2011) for describing the sociological mechanisms of individual socialization. It sets aside the assumption of the general coherence of individual behavior, and instead looks at the complexity of the ways in which a given individual has been socialized, in order to explain the variations and contradictions in the behavior, ways of thinking, and preferences of that individual (the intra-individual behavioral variations). In Lahire's view, the plurality of dispositions and competences on the one hand and the variety of the contexts in which these are actualized, on the other, are what can sociologically speaking explain the variation in the behavior of a given individual or a given group of individuals, depending on the areas of practices, the particular features of the context of action, or the unique circumstances of a practice. (Lahire 2006: 27)[42]

Bearing this in mind, our task here should be to explore the complexity of the ways in which individual members of the Gama'a were socialized—whether this is recognized or not—not reducing them to simply being members of the Brotherhood but developing, even if marginally, in plural spheres of socialization. It is also necessary to place MB practices of socialization within the larger processes of socialization in order both to understand the social conditions of Brotherhood commitment and to recognize that the particular features of *tarbiyya ikhwaniyya* are not extraneous to the general dynamics of moral and political subject formation in Egypt. As Rock-Singer has put it in comments on al-Anani's book:

> *Tarbiyya* . . . can hardly be understood in isolation, and the Brotherhood's model of *tarbiyya* is itself derived from, and shaped by, nationalist education efforts spearheaded by the Ministry of Education. While current Muslim Brothers might not acknowledge the influence of such alternative projects, their silence does not mean that scholars should ignore the role played by the state in shaping Islamist ideological claims. This critique is only strengthened by al-Anani's argument for the importance of daily practice, as members of the Muslim Brotherhood, like all Egyptians, generally attend state-controlled primary and secondary educational institutions and often work within state institutions. Without taking seriously the influence of this broader intellectual and social world, including experience within state institutions, it is difficult to discern the broader social formation of the Muslim Brotherhood's rank-and-file. By extension, al-Anani also neglects to emphasize the ways in which values of nationalist allegiance could possibly make Egyptians more receptive to the call of the Brotherhood. (Rock-Singer 2017)

In other words, the fact that an individual Brother considered himself to be cut off from the wider society did not mean that he was completely isolated, objectively speaking. To put this more starkly, the Brotherhood did not have the resources to behave like the kind of sect created by David Koresh in Waco, Texas—that is to say, a group that can control all the socialization experiences of its members. As a result, it would be very misleading to think about the internal mechanisms of socialization of the Brotherhood in isolation from the wider social world, and to think that MB activists were not effectively subjected to the plurality of spheres of socialization that exist in Egypt (familial, marital, educational, and professional circles as well as friends and neighborhood social groups, media socialization, etc.). The fact that the Brotherhood's leadership, especially the *tanzimiyyin*, wanted to produce a belief of this sort among the organization's activists does not mean that we as sociologists should reproduce this belief uncritically in our analysis—even if the activists themselves were happy to accept it. Reconstructing the meaning that a given group of actors attach to their actions is one thing (in this case, reconstructing the sense those actors have of living in Brotherhood society). But taking those actors at their word in their understanding of social reality (by accepting that a parallel Brotherhood society in fact exists) is quite another.

Yet this does not mean that the Gama'a's leadership did not seek to make the *tarbiyya ikhwaniyya* the most important form of socialization experienced by the activists. Even if its leaders were mistaken in thinking that they could ever completely control the members' socialization experiences, this characteristic mode of education did have real and observable consequences on the way the organization was run, with the ethical overshadowing any emphasis on competence. This was the second problematic aspect identified by Rafiq.

### *"Matshoqqesh al-saff!"* ("Don't break ranks!")
"Don't break ranks" was an order the *tanzim* regularly gave to the organization's activists, and one that was made much fun of by a young MB actor, 'Abd al-Rahman al-Shafi'i, in a hilarious video he uploaded on YouTube in 2014.[43] Not breaking ranks, not creating division, being modest and respectful, and avoiding arguments and conflicts were all considered to be ethical virtues, or what were called Brotherhood qualities (*al-mazaya al-ikhwaniya*) in the organization's jargon. They were also the criteria used to select officials at different levels of the *tanzim*. As a result, it was not possible for members of the Brotherhood to seek to exercise any particular function within the Gama'a by identifying a position and then applying for it. For 'Abd al-Rahman, the teacher in Helwan, this way of appointing Brotherhood officials had positive aspects.

> It doesn't much matter to us whether we are in a leading position or not. I may be put in charge of a specific job, but tomorrow I could be asked to drop it and be put in charge of something else. It's not like in political parties. We are not like them: we are committed (*multazimin*) to a shared idea. It does not matter who the

president is, as it does in parties, because he is not the one who is at the top and makes the decisions. We commit ourselves to the principle of *shura* [consultation] instead, by which we agree on who is suited for which role. Nobody is above anybody else. I play my role because I am committed to *shura*, but I am not the *sahib al-qarar* [the boss].[44]

This emphasis on *iltizam* (commitment) and *shura*, both echoes of Islamic ideas, was recurrent in the discourse used by MB members I spoke with. It was why they were not supposed to ask or apply for a leadership position, since this would go against the Islamic principle that "the one who asks to rule does not rule" *(talib al-wilaya la yuwwala)*, which was the same principle used when selecting Brotherhood candidates for parliamentary elections. However, beyond the moral justification, the mechanism also had a disciplinary function. For Rafiq, promoting individuals internally by the criteria of *shakluh kwayyes* had the unfortunate consequence of damaging the overall competence of the Gama'a.

The main problem is with the middle management [of the *tanzim*]. These leaders do not have any political experience, and they only have experience of working in Brotherhood action, that is, in social work *(al-'amal al-mugtama'i)*. . . . In the end, when the internal elections take place, when the leader of a section or region is to be elected, they choose him by saying, "Ah, yes, that one is *shakluh kwayyes! Multazim, kwayyes, beta' rabbena*" [He has a good appearance. He seems to be committed to Islam, a good man, close to our Lord], when normally each candidate should stand on an electoral program that would say what he proposed to do to develop the Gama'a and improve the way it works. I've told them that this is the way they should do things. We should choose the person by what he proposes. . . . The MPs are chosen according to their popularity, not their political experience but their social experience. It's the same thing: "Ah! *shakluh kwayyes!*" The same criteria. The result is MPs like 'Isam Mukhtar, who mostly does things for charity. He would be able to do more in terms of services by using parliamentary means to put pressure on the government and to bring about real change *(al-taghyir al-haqiqi)*. Just having more clothing sales doesn't bring results.[45]

If an individual member mentioned his particular desire or personal competence in relation to a certain post, this would be a sign for the Gama'a hierarchy that he thought he was more qualified than the rest of the Brothers and that he had an elevated notion of himself. It could be considered as signaling the sin of pride and calling into question his ethical qualities. It could also be a sign that the individual in question was trying to move out of his proper rank and to move higher up, potentially initiating conflict. Political skills in particular, including the ability to debate, to present contradictory arguments, and to discuss strategy were regarded with suspicion as a source of polemic and therefore a lack of discipline. Those who were politically incompetent, on the other hand, and who did not make criticisms or engage in discussion, were seen as loyal and moral members. This explains the Gama'a's opposition to the specialization and professionalization of competencies, as this would have led to the sin of pride, moral deterioration, and the breakdown of ranks in the organization. Yet for Rafiq, whose attitudes and ideas of what constituted legitimate political action were strongly marked by his professional training as an engineer for a multinational company, such specialization was indispensable for effective action.

> The problem of the Gama'a is that it aims to grow quantitatively rather than qualitatively. It needs to recognize and to promote specialized skills and good governance ('amaliyya idariyya), in order to develop a clear and more efficient strategy.... Over the eighty years of its existence, it should have been able to achieve more results than it has. But they don't know how to engage in politics, not just participate in it, but to engage in it. The local tanzim leaders who vote for decisions like whether to boycott elections or not don't know anything about politics. They are not competent. Trained leaders, not local managers, should be responsible for these kinds of decisions and be allowed to apply for political positions.[46]

This argument did not emerge only from the dissident experience of Rafiq and the bloggers, however. I also heard it from two other activists, Wissam and Farid, who, when the bloggers were beginning to make their voices heard, were descended from the opposite archetype of Brothers from the ranks (ikhwan al-saff).

In 2006, Wissam and Farid were the organizers of the 'al-Azhar Militias,' that is to say, the kung fu demonstration that MB students carried out on al-Azhar University's campus.[47] They were more generally in charge of the MB students at al-Azhar (some five hundred or so students). The 'al-Azhar Militias' affair had significant repercussions. Some saw it as proving the existence of a Brotherhood army. Others took it to mean that the organization's youth was under the firm control of its hierarchy and that the principle of listening and obeying (al-sam' wa-l-ta'a) was very strongly applied within the ranks. Several students were arrested after the demonstration took place. Wissam was put in prison for three months, where he was tortured. "Farid ran away, dropping me right in it," he said jokingly. However, Farid and Wissam were in fact inseparable. Originally from Buhayra, both had been born in 1988 to Brotherhood families from the rural bourgeoisie (shopkeepers), and Wissam was from a prominent MB family in Buhayra. His grandfather on his mother's side had been a companion of Hassan al-Banna and one of the founders of the organization's local branch. His father was a leader in the *tanzim* at the governorate level. Wissam and Farid had gone to Cairo together to study medicine at al-Azhar and they graduated together in 2010.

When I met them in Istanbul in September 2014, they had been living in exile for eight months, and they had been through a lot since the 2006 events. Both Wissam and Farid were experimenting with taking up dissident positions. It was while they were in exile that they developed their criticisms of the mechanism that, as they saw it, linked together the Brotherhood's refusal to develop professional competences, its refusal to listen to individual criticisms, and its maintenance of internal discipline through *shakluh kwayyes*. They acknowledged it. It was only after they themselves had experienced the harmful consequences of this mechanism that they allowed themselves to state criticisms publicly. However, did this mean that before they had not had anything critical to say about it? Had they accepted it and approved of it without reservation when they had been simply Brothers from the ranks?

Farid and Wissam tried to remember. It is worth quoting at length from what they had to say, since the dynamics of the dialogue are interesting. It was the first time they had ever spoken about such matters to someone so far removed from their usual networks, but even so we swiftly developed a relationship based on close understanding and trust. I knew a close friend of theirs, I spoke to them in Egyptian Arabic in an Istanbul café where everyone else around was talking in a language that we could not understand, and I came with considerable background experience of the Brothers and expertise in their social mores and traditions. I understood the diversity of the movement and knew many activists, ordinary members, leadership figures, and young dissidents. Although I was considered a foreigner, I was lending them a friendly ear. I asked them what they had thought of the young bloggers and their criticisms of the Brotherhood.

> Farid: It needs personal experience or concrete organizational experience *(tagriba idariyya 'amaliyya)*. Otherwise, you will just think that it's Mustafa, or 'Abd al-Mun'im Mahmud, or 'Ayyash who is wrong.[48] It's not the methods used by the Gama'a that are at stake *(manhag)*. It's not their definition. The problem is their application.

Me: So, the Gama'a was right at the time?

Farid: No, it was wrong, but I couldn't see that. Why not? Because we were making decisions according to the procedure of *shura*. So, when the majority was in agreement, like in a party, I had to follow what they said even if I personally didn't agree.[49] But when the decisions were not made in that way, and when the majority was not being respected, then no, I could not accept it.

Me: But the bloggers said the same thing, that the *shura* was not being respected, for example during the vote on participating or boycotting the local elections in 2008. . . . It's true that at that time you were with the al-Azhar militias, so . . . [laughter, as they knew I was teasing them].

Wissam: [laughing] But I'm going to tell you something—the militias, the leaders didn't know anything about that. They didn't have anything to do with that. There was a problem with the management of the university. Some students had been suspended in an arbitrary way, and we wanted to make a show of force to compel the administration to readmit them.

Farid: There were huge numbers of MB students at al-Azhar at that time, and so we thought the administration would be afraid of causing too many problems. We were also young and enthusiastic. So we held that demonstration, but it wasn't a big deal—there were less than 10 of us. Then it was blown out of all proportion in the media. But to return to the bloggers, at the time we thought that it was just the problems of the people involved. It was one, two, three people. We thought they had personal problems or psychological problems.

Ironically, the al-Azhar martial arts demonstration, the event that was taken as a sign of the *ikhwan al-saff*'s ideological indoctrination and submission to the *tanzim* hierarchy, was in fact the result of a decision made by Farid and Wissam to confront the arbitrary rule of the state. Farid said that the leadership would probably have disapproved of their decision had it known about it. He also mentioned another episode when he was summoned by his peers to explain a polarizing position he had taken in 2009.

I was put in prison in 2009 because I had had an altercation with an officer from Amn al-Dawla. He was harassing my brother, who was only a high school student at the time and anyway he wasn't doing anything. I intervened and he took me away. Then the Brothers in my village in Buhayra didn't support me. They were annoyed and said, "Why did you go and cause a problem with that officer?" even though it was my right to do so. But they didn't understand what had been at stake. Even in human terms it was difficult, as there wasn't any support from their side. They simply saw us, me, Wissam, and the others, as young guys causing problems or as people doing things that weren't very clear in Cairo.

Yet Farid also explained why he would not turn his disagreements into opposition. This had not been out of submissiveness, indoctrination, consent, or an inability to think for himself. It had instead been due to two forms of relationship within the Gama'a. The first was the *shura* that Farid—but also Mustafa, as we saw earlier, or 'Abd al-Rahman in Helwan—considered as a guarantee of respect and equality among members of the Brotherhood. Even so, that *shura* could mask the fact that if everyone seemed to be agreeing with each other, it was because no one wanted to cause an argument. No one said a word in opposition to the opinions of the dominant figures in the Gama'a. But not saying a word is not necessarily the same as being in agreement.

The second form of relationship, *ukhuwwa*, accounts for this reluctance to cause an argument since no one wanted to contradict a Brother or cause him harm, all the more so when that Brother may have been older, had suffered repression, and had experienced years of self-sacrifice, as had been the case for the older leaders. *Ukhuwwa* led each Brother to excuse 'his Brothers' even when one of them may have been doing something with which he disagreed. Such affection also remained even in the presence of disagreements, as long as these were not understood to represent opposition between one member and others. If this line was crossed, however, then the full force of *ukhuwwa* could be mobilized against the members in question, as in the cases of Mustafa and Rafiq. For Farid and Wissam, this only started to happen during their exile in 2014, even though earlier significant disagreements had begun to cause fractures in their relations of *ukhuwwa* with certain leading figures in the Brotherhood, most prominently with Morsi. Farid reflected:

> When I think about it in retrospect, it's good to realize what you understood rightly or wrongly. You know, very often you don't judge people immediately, not the first time there is a problem, not the second time, and not the third time either. You make excuses, you see. I remember that when we used to organize student elections [during the Mubarak era] we were sometimes told [by the *tanzim*] not to let the person we had chosen as our candidate stand, but to pick another one instead. They used to come with their criteria and say, "Look, he is better, *shakluh kwayyes*, his morals

are good, he comes from an MB family, he listens to us [*beyesma'*
*al-kalam*, or 'he listens and obeys']," even if the person in question was not interested in being a candidate. You know the story,
*talib al-wilaya la yuwwala*. And this is applied to everything, even
to political work. But I don't want to see someone be president of
the student union and be completely timid, be afraid of speaking,
not be interested. . . . Even in the case of Dr. Morsi, he was chosen
[to be president], but he wasn't liked within the Brotherhood. He
was very aggressive, very curt with other people when he spoke.
So, at the beginning we tried to say to ourselves, "It's OK, perhaps
he'll do all right. We'll see." But he didn't have any charisma, and
he didn't know how to govern. I remember that after the Conference of Young Brothers I met Morsi and he told us that "*sekkinat
al-ikhwan hamya*" ('the Brothers' knife is sharp'). It was a way of
warning us in case we wanted to cause any problems.

Farid was referring to a meeting called the Brotherhood Youth Conference: New Visions from Inside that was held in Cairo on 26 March 2011.
It was the initiative of some young activists who were not intending to leave
the Gama'a but were trying to reform it.[50] Some four hundred members of
the Brotherhood from different regions attended the meeting. The participants tried to define what the nature and the role of the Gama'a should be
in the post-revolution political sphere, calling for it to focus on religious
and social activities. Politics, they argued, should be left to the fully independent political parties and should not be the affair of the Gama'a. This
stance was strongly at odds with the view of the leadership, who disapproved of the conference. The tanzim leaders were preparing to launch
the Freedom and Justice Party and ordering members of the Gama'a to
join.[51] While neither Farid nor Wissam attended the Brotherhood Youth
Conference, they were nonetheless shocked by Morsi's reaction, which
contradicted the idea of *ukhuwwa*. They also refused to join the Freedom
and Justice Party, as Wissam explained.

Let me tell you how the party's founders were chosen. Each local
section of the Gama'a chose four or five persons from among its
members and said, "Here they are, the party's founders." They registered them, and that was it. They didn't say, "Listen, guys, we
are going to create a party, who wants to be in it?" They didn't
choose the founders according to their political experience or
skills. They took the ones who did whatever they were told to do.
That's why I didn't want to be a part of it, because it was not properly thought out. After all, why should it have been just one party,
and not two or three or four? My own brother, who like me was

quite conservative,[52] had the idea of creating a party with some Brotherhood friends. He had started to think about that in 2007 and then tried to do it after the revolution, but he dropped the idea because the leadership launched attacks against him and threatened to expel him.[53]

Unlike Rafiq and the other young activists who left the Gama'a after this meeting and founded their own parties, Wissam and Farid decided not to join any political party and to continue with their commitment to the Gama'a. They even took on new administrative roles in the *tanzim* and expanded their activism. After his graduation in 2010, Farid became one of the heads of the MB student committee at a national level. He started working as a physician in a public hospital as well as in a *khayri* hospital belonging to the Brotherhood-affiliated Islamic Medical Association (al-Gam'iyya al-Tibbiyya al-Islamiyya). He was also active on the relief committee of the Doctors' Syndicate (*lagnat al-ighatha*), which had been controlled by Brotherhood members since the 1980s and had remained operative even in the decades when the syndicate was frozen.[54] Wissam was also a member of the relief committee but he did not work as a physician. Instead, he took up media work, joined the national media committee of the Gama'a, and completed a further degree in administration at the American University in Cairo. He then set up a media company with his brother, and in 2012 he joined President Morsi's media and public relations team.

However, as the extracts above clearly show, none of this meant that either Farid or Wissam agreed with all the leadership's decisions, including important ones such as the creation of the Freedom and Justice Party or the decision to stand in the presidential elections. Wissam recalled his strong opposition to the leadership's choice of Morsi as the Brotherhood's candidate, even though he later became one of his media advisors.

I was against our having a candidate in the presidential elections. I thought we should have been supporting Abu al-Futuh, as the Brothers were not sufficiently prepared to take on both the parliament and the presidency. It wasn't possible. When they decided to put forward Khayrat al-Shater as the candidate, I was very annoyed, and I was very annoyed that Morsi was his replacement. Then, when al-Shater was pushed aside and it was Morsi, I wasn't in agreement at all. But by then it was done, so *khalas*. They said they wouldn't put forward a candidate, but they were afraid that the parliament would be dissolved and so on. . . . Later, when I was an advisor to Morsi, they would often tell me to do this and not do that, but I liked my job and I used to spend all my time with journalists and public media figures.

Farid and Wissam also said that they had participated in most of the demonstrations following Mubarak's fall in 2011–12, including those which the Brotherhood hierarchy had officially opposed (starting in September 2011). "We went to everything—the *milyuniyyat*, Mohamed Mahmoud I and II,[55] and the Maglis al-Wuzara'[56]—not as *ikhwan*, but as individuals," Wissam said. The November 2012 clashes in Mohamed Mahmoud Street marked the moment when they started to lose confidence in the Brotherhood leadership's respect for *shura* and when their disagreement began to turn into outright opposition.

> Wissam: We started to lose confidence just after Mohamed Mahmoud and the events outside the cabinet office [silence].
>
> Me: Mohamed Mahmoud I or II?
>
> Wissam: The second . . . in the first we asked ourselves why the Brothers had stayed with the army and hadn't gone down into the streets. I mean, we had doubts and questions . . . After that, it changed into a lack of confidence. When the Brothers had been in power. Because Morsi was unable to control things *(mesh 'arif yesaytar)*. Because the Brothers who were running things were choosing people according to their allegiance *(wala')* and not their competence. . . . But I want to add that we have remained Brothers up to now *(ila al-an ma zilna ikhwan)*.

Some days later a related event, the clashes at the Ittihadeyya Palace,[57] marked another turning point. Farid was also directly involved. Wissam recounted:

> Farid was in charge of the al-Azhar students. There were five hundred people following his orders. He got a phone call from a leader who said, "Go at once, all of you, to Ittihadeyya, immediately. There is a revolution. They are trying to overthrow Morsi." But Farid heard the accounts of the students, who said, "There are clashes, gunfire, people being wounded. We don't understand what's going on." So he called the Brothers back and asked for clarification. "Why do we have to go over there? What's going on exactly? We are hearing of people being wounded, people dying. If we have to die, at least tell us why, so that I will know if I am dying for a good reason or not." They said, "Just go." But Farid refused, and he told the students not to go.

These tragic events led to a profound deterioration in Farid's and Wissam's perceptions of the Brotherhood leadership and the decision-making processes of the Gama'a. The mask of *shura* had unceremoniously fallen. Even so, as Wissam noted, they still remained "always Brothers," as the *ukhuwwa* had managed to survive the strain. It only began to fragment during their exile in 2014. How can one explain the fact that the many disagreements that Wissam and Farid had with the Brotherhood leadership took so long to turn into outright opposition? A comparison with the cases of Mustafa and Rafiq may clarify the experiences of Wissam and Farid. Three phases can be distinguished.

1. *Occasional disagreement not turning into opposition (2006–11)*: Despite occasional periods of disagreement, they stayed loyal in the sense that they remained ready to "excuse" the Brotherhood leaders, as Farid put it. Their trust in the *shura* within the Gama'a was maintained thanks to the political and social circumstances in which they had begun their adult lives. They started out as students at al-Azhar at precisely the moment when the political situation was becoming more restricted and the repression of the Brotherhood was beginning once again (for example arrests of MB members during the demonstrations supporting the judges in summer 2006, obstruction of MB candidates in the student union and syndicate elections in the fall, and so on). They had not experienced the period of relative openness from 2000 to 2005—unlike the cohort of Mustafa, Rafiq, and other figures like Mohamed al-Qassas, who were at least five years older and had been university students during the period when political pluralism had been more marked (especially at Cairo University). This cohort had cooperated with other movements, among them the revolutionary left and the liberals, and they had shared a number of intense experiences, including on the committees in support of the Palestinian cause in 2001, the rallies against the Iraq War in 2003, and the Kefaya Movement in 2004–2005.[58] In contrast, since their first steps in adult life, Farid and Wissam had been in the eye of the storm of repression because of the 'al-Azhar Militias' affair, and they thus saw the necessity for greater group solidarity to face the attacks waged on the Brotherhood from every direction.

   Why should they want to attack it from within as well, in the way the bloggers were doing, from their point of view? The bloggers' *voice*, isolated and expressed during a period of external repression, appeared to them as a form of deviance. They actually lived through periods of disagreement with the Brotherhood hierarchy when they were faced with decisions that they perceived to be unjust, but they did not experience these things alone. Instead, they experienced them among friends (Wissam and Farid together against the decisions made by the *tanzim* regarding the student unions) or in the framework of family (such as Farid and his younger brother in 2009 when they clashed with the officer, or Wissam and his elder brother in 2007 concerning the idea of creating a political party). As a result, the feeling of *ukhuwwa* in their immediate family circle and in that of their friends was maintained, if not reinforced.

2.  *Widespread disagreement and multiple opposition (2011–13):* The organizational routines of the Gama'a were thrown into disarray during the revolutionary period. Activist schedules were rewritten to match the exceptional timeframe of this period that was so charged with major events. Less time was spent with the *usra* and more with groups of close friends from the Brotherhood, such as those with whom Wissam and Farid spent their time in Tahrir Square after 28 January 2011 and with whom they later took part in demonstrations in a personal capacity. This was an exceptional period that felt qualitatively different and was politically and emotionally intense. Feelings of *ukhuwwa* became stronger among groups of friends who shared viscerally unforgettable experiences. Discussions became more general, and endless debate took place touching on the party, the proper strategies to follow, what was happening, and what would happen or could happen in the future. Meetings took place with activists from other movements and debates as well. Several senior figures in the Brotherhood went from disagreement to open opposition to the *tanzim*, in some cases leaving the organization and slamming the door behind them. This was the case with Abu al-Futuh, of course, but also with Ibrahim al-Za'farani, who founded another party, al-Nahda, and was soon joined by Mohamed Habib, the former deputy guide[59] of the Gama'a.

*Voice* was no longer a marker of deviance,[60] since in this period of generalized political effervescence in Egypt, *voice* was everywhere around the Gama'a and was imbricated into all social levels and interstices. Farid and Wissam started their adulthood and working lives at the time of this euphoric change, and it was an opportunity to discover a range of exciting new roles and new social worlds. Farid discovered what it was to be a hospital doctor, made new professional friendships, engaged in humanitarian convoys for Syrian refugees with the Doctors' Relief committee, and attained a higher position in the *tanzim* as a member of the student committee.[61]

Wissam entered the new world of the American University in Cairo (a sharp contrast with al-Azhar's world) as well as the official media world, which he scaled to the top as an advisor to the president while launching his own company with his beloved elder brother. As a result, their relationship to the leadership deteriorated, as did their perceptions of *shura*, but the *ukhuwwa* and the feeling for debate were reinforced in their immediate entourage. While disagreements turned into opposition vis-à-vis the Brotherhood hierarchy, they were collective and numerous enough not to drive those expressing them into isolation.

3. *Exile, fragmentation, and opposition (2014–)*: As we will see in the following chapter, the conjunction of Morsi's historic failure in power, then massive repression launched against the Brotherhood, its political withdrawal, and its organizational dislocation led to deep internal breaks, with *voice* being once again seen as a marker of deviance and a direct cause for rupture. It also ushered in a wholly new period in the relationship between the inside and the outside of the Gama'a.

## Conclusion

There are, generally speaking, three arguments supporting the idea that the Gama'a can be seen as a sect. The first, an ideological one, points to the mental stranglehold exercised by the organization over its members, leading to a loss of autonomy on their part and, in consequence, a loss of the freedom to choose whom they meet, what they believe in, and their ways of behaving, consuming, dressing, and so on. The second argument, this one sociological, states that in order to be effective this mental stranglehold must confine its activists in a closed and homogeneous environment hermetically sealed off from the wider society. The third argument, religious in character, says that this psychic grip is made all the stronger by the fact that it is fed by theological beliefs, or eschatological ones, derived from the thinking of Sayyid Qutb. This holds that the Brothers are God's elect and that they have a unique mission and destiny to fulfill. Kandil calls this theological belief "religious determinism" (2015: 81ff), and argues that the

Muslim Brothers had accomplished an ideological innovation "amount[ing] to no less than an inversion of the conventional understanding of sharia' by reversing the interpretation of the verse *'If you support God, He will support you'* (Qur'an: 47:7). He explains that while "traditional Muslim scholars understood this verse to mean that if someone undertakes a task, with the intention of supporting God, then God endows him with confidence and composure," Brotherhood ideology "holds that, if someone becomes pious, God guarantees his victory in various worldly endeavors," including politics, economics, and war. This "solve[s] the paradox of why an ideological movement of the size and experience of the Brotherhood has no concrete program for political, socioeconomic, and geopolitical transformation" (Kandil 2015: 107) and explains its inability to anticipate and react to failure in 2013, he concludes.

However, the individual cases I have examined in this chapter largely qualify or even contradict such arguments. It has been shown, for example, that even when the Gama'a used significant techniques of indoctrination on its members (and here I agree with Kandil, al-Anani, and Ben Néfissa), these members nevertheless experienced other forms of socialization besides those deployed by the *tarbiyya ikhwaniyya*, and the latter were simply unable to wipe them away.

Like any other individual, a member of the Brotherhood could have had heterogeneous experiences of socialization during his or her childhood and adolescence ('mixed' family, state school, different friends in the neighborhood, and so on), along with significant changes in lifestyle and living conditions (rising or declining social status, movement to and from the city, and so on). In addition, there will likely be the effects of different educational and professional careers, leading to encounters with a wide variety of other people and to the acquisition of diverse skills and professional ethos. As with any other individual, a Brother could develop ambivalent relationships to his family circle, and be variously affected by changing social and political contexts during the course of his life.

All these composite forms of socialization might produce an entangled web of different practices and beliefs, in spite of the *tanzim*'s effort to standardize the members' thoughts.[62] The variations are to be found not only between individuals, but also *inside* one individual, making him act and think in heterogeneous scripts according to the specific social situations in which he is mired. In a nutshell, being in the ranks did not mean having identical thoughts or sharing a unified outlook on life.

It could be contended that Farid and Wissam only agreed to speak to me in the first place because they were no longer in the ranks of the Brotherhood in 2014, and therefore they could not be seen as representative of the mass of Brotherhood members. Yet those who make such arguments are equally unable to show that the cases they know best correspond to the statistical norm. In-depth examination of individual cases has allowed me to understand the multiplicity in which the MB activists have engaged in their practices and beliefs. Depending on the context, they could act with strong or weak conviction, believe intensively or more moderately, and undertake other incongruent practices or develop contradicting beliefs and preferences.

The myriad of socialization forms experienced by Brotherhood members constituted different "programs of truth" (Veyne 1988) in their minds. While the activists in Rab'a al-'Adawiyya Square in Cairo might well have said, as Kandil writes, that they believed the Angel Gabriel would come to save them (Kandil 2015: 81), this does not mean that in another context they would say the same thing. Neither does it mean that they did not think that their actions were not hugely dangerous and could expose them to imminent repression. Invoking divine intervention in such circumstances could in fact have been a way of reinforcing their belief in what they were doing and of strengthening their resistance. More generally, what is argued for here is a conception of belief that does not necessarily mean believing with complete conviction, but instead one that covers an expansive gamut of cognitive attitudes from quasi-certainty to quasi-skepticism (Piette 2014).

Lastly, the argument that the Brothers would believe in religious determinism, besides not being empirically demonstrated, also reveals a move often made when labeling a group a sect. This classical move involves defining a belief as contrary to what the official religious institutions discursively authorize (in this case, the Sunni tradition) in order to accuse those who continue to believe in it of being somehow the victims of brainwashing. In the next chapter, a different interpretation of the fall of the Brotherhood after the 25 January revolution will be put forward.

# 6

# Goodness in Dire Straits

I n the previous chapter, we crossed the Rubicon of revolution. Although this book is mainly about the Mubarak era, I have deliberately chosen to mix periods and not to confine discussion of the post-2011 period to the final chapter. All too often, the 2011 uprising is considered as an absolute break, whereas some dynamics, which have their own rhythm and timeframes, have been neither interrupted nor created by the uprising. The internal dissent in the Brotherhood was one such dynamic, as was the Gama'a's ambiguous positioning vis-à-vis the regime (Pahwa 2017). This final chapter will deal with both the before and after of the 2011 revolution, examining the complex power effects of the politics of goodness.

The politics of goodness under Mubarak's rule had three defining features. As was shown in earlier chapters of this book, it consisted, first, in the relocation of state developmentalist policies onto the micro-terrain of social services carried out by local elites. Second, it was made up of overlapping networks of public work and charitable activities in which political identities were often blurred. Third, it was defined as a conflictual consensus in which political antagonisms were, for most of the time, watered down. I argue here that this politics of goodness was challenged by the radicalization of conflicts that took place between 2011 and 2013 and that this explains much of the Brotherhood's failure to entrench its rule.

## The Politics of Conflictual Consensus

The power dynamics of the politics of goodness were complex because, depending on context, it could help to sustain the neoliberal authoritarian order, catalyze the development of latent conflicts, or promote potentially subversive models of subjectivity. The Brotherhood did not openly struggle against the system, but it did not *only* collaborate with it either. Instead, it operated within a conflictual consensus—a consensus that was characterized by at least latent conflict—in which politicization was mainly limited to the adoption of ethical distinctiveness. There were only a few occasions on which such politics led to the development of clear-cut divides on the local level.

## Authoritarian Co-production and Latent Conflict
### Tacit cooperation

My interviewees did not think of their activities as being designed to establish a counter-society opposed to the existing order. Hamdi (the entrepreneur in Helwan) explained that the social activities of the Brotherhood were part of the governing order, since the latter relied on the gradual takeover by the population and private intermediaries of the state's social responsibilities (what was called *al-maghud al-dhati*).

> Why has the government left us the job of running schools and hospitals? Why didn't it just stop us at the beginning? Because it knew that we were running them. Because it is incapable of running them itself. If they closed these establishments down, their incapacity would be obvious. For example, if they closed the al-Azhar Institute or the secondary school [in Helwan], other state schools in Helwan would have to take the students. There aren't enough schools or hospitals, so they let us run them instead.[1]

State Security largely tolerated the Brotherhood's running of such services, though always on the condition that it was not widely known. 'Abd al-Rahman (the teacher in Helwan) commented that,

> Their main goal, their number one, is not to stop the Brothers doing what they want. It is to make sure they do it among themselves *(ma' nafsuhum)*. They don't have any problems with the Brothers in themselves. They know that they are good people who don't represent any danger for the interests of Egypt. So, what is the danger [for the regime]? It is that the regime wants people to need it and to choose it, so if they choose us instead, it's "bye-bye" to the regime. If people choose the Brothers, where is the regime? It will disappear. Their second goal is to make sure that no one talks to people about this situation.[2]

In 'Abd al-Rahman's view, neither the Brotherhood nor its activities were repressed as such. What was instead looked at closely by the authorities was the effect that such activities could have on the citizens' perceptions of the capacity, or lack of it, of the regime to respond to their needs. However, he added that while the Brotherhood did not seek to show its explicit opposition to the regime in its everyday activities, and even helped it in a way by taking care of certain social services, this did not mean that it did not see these forms of cooperation as actually being forms of political competition. Another example may help to bring out this ambivalence, which is based on the interdependence of the actors involved.

If I cooperate with them [state officials] to help them to reform the country, the first thing is that I am carrying out the role that is required of me by my religion, my ethics, and my love for my country. The second thing is that I am helping with reforms that help people, and the third is that I am smoothing relations between the system and the people. During the bread crisis, people started to block the roads. It happened in Helwan, and State Security called Sheikh al-Muhammadi to ask him to disperse the demonstrations, since he is respected and people listen to him. . . . State Security would not have been able to resolve the problem alone. They would have used force, and there would have been people hurt, and that would have affected the regime. So they called someone who could resolve the problem without doing any damage. But the State Security man who called the sheikh didn't tell his superiors what he had done. He couldn't. He saw that there was an urgent problem, and he wanted to bring it under control. The superior might have thought that the sheikh had come of his own volition, but the man who called him knew that the sheikh would be able to solve the problem.

This account shows the way in which the public secret represented by the Brotherhood could be used by the authorities, at least on the local level, to help resolve social conflicts. However, such tacit cooperation (since the State Security officer had had to hide his approach to the sheikh) nevertheless opened up spaces of latent conflict. The fact that Sheikh al-Muhammadi had been asked to intervene by the authorities in this case put him in the position of exactly the kind of ethical model and intermediary that the Brotherhood wanted, even though such roles were not officially recognized and were only known about through rumor. Letting such rumors spread, cultivating ambiguity, denying any intention to reap political benefits, hushing up any explicit conflict—all these things that were apparently part of a strategy of depoliticization could in fact be part of a deliberately ambiguous political strategy. By not denouncing the incapacity of the authorities publicly, the sheikh was setting himself up as precisely the kind of ethical model he was more generally aiming to incarnate. He was counting on the indirect conflict possibly caused by his own ethical distinctiveness. However, these indirect effects were not, strictly speaking, intended by the sheikh or under his control, since they depended upon the way his actions were seen by their intended audience. More specifically, they depended upon a certain sequence of cognitive reactions.

## Cognitive mechanisms of conflict

The cognitive sequence that the activists sought to generate in the beneficiaries' minds typically proceeded as follows: perceiving the ethical distinctiveness displayed by the activist involved, identifying it as a sign that this activist is a Muslim Brother, then generalizing from this individual case that all Brothers are good persons, and lastly forming an oppositional consciousness favorable to the Brotherhood.

> Me: Does an event like a student award ceremony influence people?
>
> 'Abd al-Rahman: Of course! First of all, there was the joy of the families of the students concerned. They all came to the office to ask for a CD of the event that they could show to their friends. So the impact of the event does not stop with the students and their families. What do they want to do, after all? They want to show how happy they are with their children, to make people understand how well they have brought them up, and to show that their son and daughter are at the top of their classes. So, when they do that, what do they actually do? They spread the Idea—they know the Brothers, and the Brothers do things and take care of people and provide educational services. What is the point of celebrating valedictorian students? It's to encourage everyone to aim for excellence. And who is it that helps you to arrive at excellence? A good person. And what about someone who gives you medical services? He helps people to preserve their health, doesn't he? Anyone who aims to give out medical services to help preserve health is a good person.[3]

This potential conflict with the regime remained latent, however, since it mostly depended on cognitive processes whose chances of success remained uncertain. First, the identification of the 'good persons' as Brotherhood members might not take place. For example, I met one old man, both poor and sick, whose medical and financial needs were being met by Muhsin from aid provided by Sheikh al-Muhammadi. However, the old man did not know whether the sheikh was a member of the NDP or of the Brotherhood. Second, even if the ethical conduct in question was recognized as a Brotherhood mark by the recipients, this did not necessarily mean that they would forget its strategic function. This can be seen by looking again at a discussion with Rawda and Hisham at a small local charity in Helwan during the 2008 local elections.

## "It's Not Obvious. It's Not Proven."

Hisham had just said that the only reason the Brothers distributed goods and services was to win votes.[4]

Rawda (angrily): Yes, but it's not obvious, and it's not proven. I mean, someone who sees a neighbor in need and who wants to help him . . .

Hisham (cutting her off): But it's bigger than that . . . they bet on every house. Everyone knows that.

Me: Every house?

Hisham: Yes, it's like that in this area. They know who is with whom on every street (beya'rifu fi-l-shari' kul wahed ma' min).

Rawda: Listen, I'll tell you something. In every country, there are rich people and poor people, right? Even in European countries? So, here we say that . . .

Hisham: No, there are only poor people here.

Rawda: There are rich people as well. Here, the rich help the poor. They don't want to see them wrecked. They don't want to see them begging or stealing. No, they say, "Don't beg, don't steal, and if we have something, we will give it to you." So, someone who has gives to someone who hasn't. And this is something that has nothing to do with government politics . . . high politics, I mean. We are talking about neighbors, about people who live in the area. All that. Me, for example, a veiled woman and a widow. I can't go out to work, and the Brothers want to help me so that I don't have to go out to work. So they help me, so that I can raise my children and give them a good education. So they do that.

Me: What do you think of it?

Rawda: They do good work, good work.

Hisham: Yes, good work.

Rawda: They say, "Don't steal, don't beg, don't do anything wrong in relation to our Lord." So, is that the good? That's all; that's it. That's their idea.

Me: You don't think they do that to get the support to win elections? The NDP offers services as well . . .

Rawda: I'll tell you. The elections, they're about government politics and about the . . . leaders. We, as individuals, we don't know anything about that (malenash fih, mane'rafsh haga). The leaders talk about it among themselves. You understand? Me, as an individual, or as a woman in society, I have no influence (malish ta'thir). I have no influence.

Me: What's the difference between a Brother who provides services and a member of the NDP who provides services?

Rawda: I swear that we, as the people, we want the Brothers to carry out their services and the NDP to carry out theirs. We need the services of both. Welcome to both, no? That's all. But in politics, we want the one who gives us services, as people. Me, as a widow, after the death of my husband I got a pension of LE345 . . .

Me: The Brothers don't provide services with a political end in mind?

Rawda: No, I don't think they do anything for political reasons. Me, when someone talks politics to me, I say that it's nothing to do with me.

Me: And do the NDP do it with a political end in mind?

Rawda: They don't do anything, that's all.

Hisham: They don't do anything at all—*khalas*.

Me: Even during elections?

Hisham: No, or if they do, it's because of orders. They are paid to do it.

Rawda (replying to Hisham): No, they don't give anyone anything, why are you saying that? No, their money never gets out.

Hisham: Yes, it does. But it's not like with the Brothers. The Brothers [banging on the table to imitate someone knocking at the door], they knock on people's doors.

Rawda: I'll tell you something. The NDP, those people up high, they're full of themselves. But they are "watermelons," they don't understand anything.

Me: If there had been Brotherhood candidates in these local elections, would you have supported them?

Rawda: I support the good one *(al-kwayyes)*. I would have supported the good one. Look, I voted for the Tagammu' candidate because she was the only one I knew. Rather than go and give my vote to someone I don't know, I knew that she was good, and like that I kept my vote. At least I knew that my vote was "with her" *('andaha)*.

Me: But you could vote for the Brothers?

Rawda: That's if I were to vote . . .

Hisham (cutting her off): Don't give your vote to the Brothers.

Rawda: Why not?

Hisham: Because . . . They are good, but they can't do anything *(humma kwayyesin, bass mabeya'rafush ye'melu haga)* . . .

Rawda: They can't?

Hisham: Because they are not the sort of people one should associate with. If they were elected, the government would close every door to them so that they wouldn't be able to win again or get people to support them.

Rawda and Hisham did not describe themselves as MB sympathizers (it will be on the record that I had met them in a charity that was connected to both the NDP and the left), but they both appreciated the ethical distinctiveness of the Brothers ("They do good work"), which they compared to the practices of the NDP, judged to be corrupt. Their disagreement concerned the strategic character, or alternatively the disinterestedness, of the actions carried out by the Brothers. Hisham said they were a matter of strategy and Rawda disagreed with him. They also disagreed about their own strategy—as voters, did they have an interest in voting for the Brothers? While Hisham thought that any such vote would be wasted because, even if elected, the Brothers would be blocked by the regime, Rawda emphasized what she considered to be important for those who, like her, "speak as neighbors and as residents of the neighborhood." She was not interested in "high politics," though in fact, while she refused to use the word, she spoke informedly on political matters. But she talked about politics from below, the kind of politics which affected the grassroots and which the "watermelons" (her own vivid expression to name the foolish big guys on top) did not understand. At this level, the important thing was to serve others, to be decent (kwayyes), to make sure the poor were not humiliated, and to behave virtuously.

This dialogue allows us to understand the importance of the virtuous citizen, the figure which the Brothers claimed to incarnate. This figure is even better grasped when reformulated, as Rawda did here, by talking about the virtuous neighbor. Salah, the member of Sheikh al-Muhammadi's team in Helwan, got it right when he said that "the regime tries to push us into a corner [fi zawiya] . . . but it can't stop us from seeing our neighbors." This "seeing the neighbors" was almost the quintessence of political work for the Brothers. First, because "seeing the neighbors" could lead to votes. Rawda did not think along the strategic lines set out by Hisham, since the latter were for her simply the "politics of the watermelons." The important thing to her was the politics of the grassroots, that is to say, the mutual aid among neighbors, and so she voted for those who seemed to be closest to her. If they were the Brothers, so be it. However, "seeing the neighbors" was also part of another form of politicization not related to the question of voting: the process of 'intimate attachment.'

### The challenge of intimate attachment

The content of our social activities has nothing specific; for example, when we set up an IT workshop, that's a universal thing. The difference is not in the content, it is in the feeling that young people get when they come here. They feel more respected here than elsewhere. There is an atmosphere of respect. If it's time for prayer, I excuse myself and say I'm going to pray. . . . There is no smoking or anything like that. That's the difference. When we organize a soccer match, it is both to offer young people leisure activities and to protect them from running risks doing nothing, such as from drugs and alcohol. There's no cup, as everyone shares in winning. At the same time, people who come to the soccer match know that I am organizing it to serve them. They will be bound to me by affection *(fih irtibat biya widdiyyan)*, whatever they do later at the university or in politics. They know that I did something good for them.

This is how Akram, the coordinator of the Helwan offices, described the way in which the ethical conduct potentially generated political conflict. Through experiencing 'ethical conduct,' people could differentiate the Brothers from others, then generalize from a particular feeling to larger opinions (for example, the respect felt during an IT workshop or a soccer match could give way to the idea that the Brothers in general 'do good'), and finally they could possibly build a cognitive opposition (the Brothers 'do better than others'). But Akram also emphasized something else, which was that the 'ethical conduct' created emotional, intimate, attachments. These attachments could be deep and long-lasting, even if they did not necessarily translate into obvious political support (Akram suggested that a young person affected early on by the Brothers might go on to develop other political orientations). He gave another example while commenting on the supposed disadvantages that the Brothers would have suffered from if compared to the NDP.

The other MP, the minister Sayyid Mish'al, has greater access to state resources. . . . But we have more of the resources of the streets. He has the military factories that are under the authority of his ministry. During Ramadan, he distributes hundreds of bags of food containing oil, flour, sugar, and so on in the factories. How is he able to do that? Because he uses state money. But the difference with us is that his employees distribute, say, five hundred bags to the poor and five hundred to themselves, while those who receive food from us know that it comes from the Brothers and from Sheikh al-Muhammadi. We distribute it to the people directly, and they prefer that. Why? Because they care about the intentions behind the act. People like those who do them service but do so out of the love of goodness. The government doesn't understand that.

Even if actions designed to create intimate attachments did not necessarily lead to a vote or political support for the Brothers, they could make people say that 'the Brothers are different and want to do things for society' (see the box below), make them dislike 'the Brothers in general' but like 'the Brothers they personally know,' or lead skeptics to think that 'the Brothers are the best of the worst' *(ahsan al-wehshin)*. Thus, the residents of an informal area of Tibbin interviewed during the 2008 local elections were mostly loyal to media star Mustafa Bakri who 'held' their area, but they nonetheless formulated complex judgments about Brotherhood MP 'Ali Fath al-Bab. Two examples follow.

---

### Adham and Karim—The Complexities of Ordinary Judgment

*Adham was twenty-four years old when I interviewed him. He had started to study law at the University of Helwan, but he had had to stop, he said, because "my main concern was how I was going to live." He voted for the first time in the 2005 elections, casting his two votes for Bakri and Fath al-Bab. He was preparing to vote for the NDP candidates that he knew well when I spoke to him on the eve of the 2008 local elections.*

I voted for Bakri because the candidate before him didn't do anything for us. So I wanted to see someone new being elected. Bakri had also provided people in the area with social services during the election campaign (by finding them work), and he is an opposition figure. 'Ali Fath al-Bab is a respectable religious man. I voted for him because he doesn't do anyone any harm, and he doesn't go in for cheap publicity. He helps people out in factories. He also helps people to get pensions and social security coverage. I knew about him during the election campaign because he used to hold meetings where he talked about his ideas, and also about religion and the Qur'an. I was convinced by his words because he is a religious man. He's better than the other candidates who make promises during the elections but don't do anything once they are elected. We didn't see 'Ali Fath al-Bab after he was elected either, but people said he had done a lot for the workers in factories. . . . He won because of the Brotherhood vote. I don't like the Brothers because they want to take power quickly. They use religion as a way of taking power because they know that religion is important to Muslims. But 'Ali Fath al-Bab is "the best of the worst" *(ahsan al-wehshin)*. . . . My father told me that. He said, "Vote for Bakri and Fath al-Bab."

*Karim was also twenty-four years old. He had a degree from the Faculty of Commerce at Cairo University, but he was unemployed. He had never voted, as he said that "there's no point. Six months before the elections the candidates make promises, and then they don't do anything once they have been elected."*

People here vote for the candidates who are close to them. I don't vote, but I know the different candidates. Mahgub [the former minister] did nothing for sixteen years. Bakri runs every year, but he lost against the NDP up until 2005. He made promises before the elections, and some of them he kept.

Me: Do you know the other MP?

Karim: No.

Me: 'Ali Fath al-Bab . . .

Karim: Ah, yes, that one is a member of the Brotherhood. The Brothers are different. They want to do things for society, but they are marginalized by the government. They have lots of activities. When I was a child, they used to come to our district and organize sports competitions on Fridays from morning till night. The government has banned them for the last six years, and so we have been deprived of these activities. The government doesn't recognize them as a political party. But they are the best at organizing activities. The government couldn't stop 'Ali Fath al-Bab from being elected, because they know he is popular and that he does a lot for people. He's always here. He has offices in Helwan to receive people.

Me: Is he the only one who has offices?

Karim: No, Bakri has offices as well. I am not against Bakri, but I don't think he has done anything.

Me: What do you think of the Brothers?

Karim: It's new [that they are in parliament]. They could be the best of the worst (ahsan al-wehshin). We don't know what they will be able to do yet. We don't know whether they will do what they said they would.

Me: 'Ali Fath al-Bab has been there for a long time. . . .

Karim: Yes, but even though he is an MP, the government doesn't give him the financial or human resources to do what he promises. If they had, I think he would have been able to do something. The Brothers do what they can with what they have. People say there are twenty-five thousand Brothers in prison. I saw them myself when I went to visit someone in prison.

Me: You have friends who are Brothers?

Karim: No, but I know that certain people are Brothers. I've guessed as much. But some Brothers, you don't even know they are Brothers.

Me: How do you guess?

Karim: Because I know them. . . . They were the Brothers who organized the activities when I was little [the sports matches, religious competitions, and general knowledge quizzes].

These accounts indicate the ways in which emotional attachments to the Brothers could affect political judgments. Adham, for example, said that he did "not like the Brothers because they use religion for political purposes as a way of taking power." But at the same time, he also said that he liked Fath al-Bab because he was "religious and respectable," "didn't go in for cheap publicity," and was said to have "helped the workers," only to conclude by saying that he liked him above all because his father told him to! One could interpret this confusion as an indicator that Adham was not politicized, but I would argue instead that politicization operates precisely through this entanglement of judgments. Karim thought of the Brothers as being apart from a certain way of doing politics, though he was skeptical about their ability to get things done and refused to give them his vote. However, at the same time he had childhood memories that he talked about as if echoing Akram's comments. His account also draws attention to another politicizing mechanism: triggering the oppressed figure, or *mazlum* (pl., *mazlumin*).

## *Mazlumin* and Virtuous Neighbors: Activating Political Divisions

The idea of *mazlum* was related to a model of subjectivity that had both moral and political dimensions, and that in certain circumstances could activate the latent conflict into outright divisions between the Brotherhood and the regime. Contrary to what might have been thought, the Brothers did not always seek to present themselves as *mazlumin*, and in fact my interviewees more often sought to qualify the idea that they were necessarily the targets of repression. Instead they insisted on the time they spent negotiating with the authorities and the different government agencies on a daily basis, which required them to minimize their status as opponents. As a result, when they did choose to mobilize the figure of *mazlum* it was only at particular moments. On one occasion, for example, State Security arrived at the student award ceremony organized by the MP in Helwan, and took away all the chairs. "We stood up and continued without chairs . . . and the next time we held the award we arranged to meet on the Nile Corniche and then held the ceremony on a boat we had hired for the occasion," Hamdi said, proud to draw attention to the Brothers' capacity to resist oppression. In Madinat Nasr, MP 'Isam Mukhtar gave another example.

> The important thing when you're organizing an event is not to say where it is being held. The first year of the mandate, we had announced that we would hold the student award in the wedding hall at the al-Salam Mosque. But State Security arrived and closed the hall. Then we had to organize the event at the office, but we had to divide it into two sessions because the office was too small. Now, we announce that the meeting point is here and we don't disclose in advance the place where we hold the event so that we

don't have problems. They don't interfere during the event itself, because they don't want to do it when people are present, as that could cause problems. There are families and children . . . and it would be good publicity *(di'aya)* for me. People would see who is being oppressed *(al-mazlum)* and would understand that we are the oppressed ones.

In these examples, the epitome of *mazlum* was activated by default, because of the State Security's interference and without the activists explicitly wanting to do so. In the electoral context, on the other hand, the Brotherhood media constantly tapped into this theme, comparing arrested activists to "fighters" sacrificing themselves in order to defend the rights of the Egyptian people from the "corruption of the rulers." During the April 2008 local elections, for example, the MB's official Internet site published lists of the organization's members and their families who had been arrested by the security forces every day for nearly two months, along with lists of people whose houses had been raided. These lists were then repeated, often in full, in the local independent and international press.

However, electoral periods could be just as favorable to an emphasis on another figure, the virtuous neighbor. I observed this on a particularly striking occasion, during canvassing carried out by Salah, the cement-factory worker who succeeded Sheikh al-Muhammadi as Brotherhood candidate in Helwan, during the campaign for the fall 2010 parliamentary elections. Even though these seats were lost in advance, the Brothers in Helwan mobilized in force almost as if they thought there was something genuinely at stake.[5] Salah had inherited the sheikh's popularity, but he also had his own legitimacy to draw upon thanks to his union work, and this enabled him to win the support of local left-wing activists. The real aim of the canvassing was not to win the election, however, but to activate the political divide between the Brotherhood and the regime, by associating the former with the image of the virtuous neighbor in the eyes of local voters.

### Canvassing in Madinat al-Huda (Helwan)

Night is falling in the unpaved streets of Madinat al-Huda. The core activists of Sheikh al-Muhammadi's staff are leaving the mosque in which they have just been performing the *maghrib* prayer, and where they had planned to meet to start canvassing. Salah, dressed in a black suit and a blue shirt, is joking with his colleagues, who for the most part are dressed more soberly in light-colored sports shirts or striped polo shirts and shapeless brown or gray trousers. Other activists join the group: some of them are intermittent participants of the team whom I recognize, and others I do not know. Six other young men are present, most well dressed. Two of them, wearing black suits, are particularly elegant, very tall, and look like bodyguards. Their task is to introduce Salah to local voters. Some of the young men tell me that they are from the *tanzim*'s communication committee. There are also five other men in their forties or older. They look more ordinary, rather like the core activists. These men are neighborhood Brothers. They hug each other affectionately and begin to walk in groups of two or three, occasionally grasping each other's hands or putting their arms around one another's shoulders and using the occasion to catch up on news or other things.

The group starts to move down the busy street, which, in addition to the mosque, is also lined with dusty café terraces. Men of all ages are sitting there, playing backgammon or watching the group of Brothers. The streetlights overhead provide some pale illumination, drowning out the strings of colored bulbs and glowing shishas below. A 'body-guard' positions himself at the head of the group next to Salah, and we go to meet the men in the café. "Salah X, Brotherhood candidate for the workers' seat," the 'bodyguard' declaims, his voice powerful and his body slightly to one side to make way for Salah, who seems much smaller in comparison. As good-humored as ever, Salah goes around the plastic tables of the café shaking hands and exchanging the kinds of jokes that he never seems to be short of. The activists do the same thing, some of them embracing one or two of the customers. The air rings with salutations and casual greetings.

Some of the young men stand a bit to one side. They turn toward a group of teenagers dressed in *riwish*, hip fashion, with gelled hair and wearing cheap jeans and T-shirts. They are leaning against a group of parked cars and smoking while they watch. The conversation starts with questions about registering to vote. The boys ask questions, and the young Brothers answer, seemingly both serious and friendly. The boys take the leaflets they are given and watch the group leave. The same scenario repeats itself at each café, shop, and building entrance where local residents are taking the air, most of them men, though sometimes there are a few women. However, the two 'bodyguards' take turns accompanying Salah, and depending on the street where we are, one or two of the older Brothers from the area also introduce Salah, as they will likely know the shopkeeper or residents concerned. A younger member of the group takes photographs of each encounter to post on Salah's Facebook page, which has been created as part of the campaign. After the opening salutation by the 'bodyguard,' Salah and the Brothers from the area take over, saying, "we are going to continue on the trail blazed by Sheikh al-Muhammadi." Some of the residents ask about him, and the Brothers make reassuring sounds. Other residents start explaining the problems they have been facing, sometimes angrily. Often it is an activist from the core team that responds, taking the person's contact details and inviting him or her to an appointment at the office.

As we enter the labyrinth of dimly lit streets that makes up the heart of the area, we are joined by other individuals, older men, some in white *gallabiyyat* with heads uncovered, others in black *gallabiyyat* and white-and-red *taqiyyat* (traditional Islamic hats) that indicate their status as sheikhs, most probably of the Gam'iyya al-Shar'iyya. Their presence next to the younger men wearing contemporary clothes adds an unusual aspect to the group. And when we meet another sheikh in the street or a well-known old inhabitant, hugs burst forth and the greetings exchanged take a more solemn turn.

At the other end of the local male social hierarchy, teenagers from the area watch the spectacle and try to get close to one or another of the younger MB activists. They seem to admire the model of success, both social and moral, that the latter display through their behavior and appearance: they don't have beards, don't show off, and don't condescend to the boys around them, who for the most part are simply leaning against the walls. Even though they also live in this working-class area, their careful dress, their modern look that is oddly combined with a modest code of bodily behavior, their calm, friendly voices, and their capacity to appear at their ease in any situation, including when an old woman starts heckling them, make them stand out from those around them. They do not march in the street as a compact block like demonstrators, but instead they walk quietly in intertwined pairs and mix with local residents with obvious affection. This group gives the reassuring and exciting impression that anyone could join, be part of this inclusive community, and benefit from both the protection and the power that it seems to offer.

This staging of a respectable self and of a protective group makes sense when one thinks of the young males' social conditions in this working-class neighborhood. Here, as in other such areas, young men were often trying to "regain lost positions of authority," having been affected by political exclusion, social stigmatization, police repression, unemployment, and the emergence of women as competing actors in the labor market (Ismail 2006). The model of the self that these young Brothers embodied carried with it the signs of social success[6] and was at the same time well adapted to the local cultural codes of this popular urban space, while also embodying certain Islamic virtues such as altruism and modesty. Moreover, it was a model that valued the collective, aiming to occupy public space by making a promise of empowerment: the group ran into a police patrol car, but instead of reacting, the police merely greeted the group and accepted the leaflets that were given to them.

On another occasion, I observed an event during which the figure of *mazlum* was brought together with that of virtuous neighbor. It took place during the April 2008 local elections when there were significant demonstrations happening across the country. Two days before election day, the 6 April general strike was announced in support of workers in one of the factories in Mahalla al-Kubra, marking a kind of culmination of the innumerable strikes and other protests that had been taking place in different sectors since 2006. These had been caused in part by rampant inflation and in part by shortages of subsidized bread that had plunged the country into the depths of a bread crisis. While the Gama'a did not officially support the protest movements or the calls for a general strike, it had nevertheless been taking advantage of the election campaign in order to make its presence felt in the streets. I attended an election rally for women *(mu'tamar nisa'i)* organized by activists in the al-Raml constituency in Alexandria on 3 April 2008.

---

### A Women's Electoral Rally in Alexandria

A popular area, its streets paved in parts and full of donkey carts, panel trucks, fruit sellers, and men smoking water pipes in cafés. The offices of the constituency's two Brotherhood MPs, elected in the 2005 elections, were on the first floor of a building on the main street, which consisted of two lanes divided down the middle by a median strip. The offices were serving as the logistical base for the rally. Fifty or so activists, mostly men, were preparing material, including the stage, loudspeakers, banners, and leaflets, all of which was being set up in record time on the pavement outside the building. In a side room, the two female candidates standing in the local elections were practicing their speeches. One of them was the wife of a local Brotherhood leader.

---

She had degrees in Islamic law and Arabic language and was used to speaking in public. The other, a housewife, was more worried about giving her first speech in public. Both of them were very active in local welfare work, including work among neighbors and for charities as well as activities set up by the MPs' staff. They were watching the arrival of the audience from a window overlooking the street. They told me that "two-thirds of it was made up of Muslim Sisters and the other third of sympathizers," which they referred to as *murtabitin*.

The street was transformed in just a couple of minutes. Police cars a hundred meters or so from the stage were directing the traffic into the right-hand lane, and policemen were, strangely, standing apart at distance. In front of the stage, and filling the sidewalk and the left-hand lane, were hundreds of women, girls, and children (seven hundred, I was told), standing in ranks and forming a mass of brown or pastel-colored *akhmira* (a veil covering the head, arms, and top of the body). They were carrying banners bearing slogans like "The Brothers are coming to help with life" and "Fight against corruption in the Local Popular Councils," and were chanting the slogans and songs coming from the stage, also occupied by women. Following a brief introduction by one of the activists working in the MP's office, the first female candidate gave a lively demonstration of her oratorical skills, emphasized by a powerful echo from the loudspeakers. Girls whose fathers were in prison then chanted songs. Male activists stayed on the margins of the meeting. While the organizing group stood behind the stage, the other men present hung around the edges where there were fewer women, or stayed with the cars and pickup trucks parked along the median strip as if to protect the rows formed by the women. "It's a women's meeting," one activist told me. "The men who are present are only here in case there are problems with the police. The ones sitting in the cafés or watching from the sidewalk aren't Brothers. If they were, they wouldn't be standing just behind the women. They are picking up on the slogans because those are simple phrases that are easy to remember." Other passers-by only stopped for a minute or two. I started to talk with two girls whose style of dress contrasted sharply with that of the activists. "We're not staying because we have the baby with us," they said. "But it is very important that people express themselves. What's happening is very harsh [alluding to the bread crisis]. . . . But there are not enough people. There should be more." I asked them if they were going to vote in the upcoming local elections: "What elections? Ah, yes, of course. When are they?" they answered back.

This interaction suggested a shift in what was at stake in the meeting, away from the elections. The rally turned into a sort of protest against the catastrophic economic situation and the policies of the regime. The staging bore all the hallmarks of the Brotherhood: the fact that it was taking place in front of the MPs' offices, the use of slogans and chanting, banners and leaflets with the name and logo of the Brotherhood, and the gendered segregation of space. There was also the uniform clothing of the participants, and the way in which they were arranged in orderly rows. In the general atmosphere of protest that was prevailing at the time, this kind of meeting enabled the Brotherhood to take part in street demonstrations, while ensuring that they were strictly controlled. The image of protesting women also suggested various ways of looking at the event, as was made clear by a leaflet distributed at the meeting and entitled "Women of Egypt . . . Crying Out against Corruption."

> Confronted by the high prices that are closing the door on any hope of a life of dignity (*hayah karima*) for Egyptian women;
>
> Confronted by the absence of security and protection and attacks on the dignity of women in the street, on public transport, and in bread lines;
>
> Confronted by the suffering of a spouse whose husband or son is in prison, not for a crime or an act of wrongdoing, but for having protested against corruption and high prices;
>
> Confronted by the corruption that imperils the humanity of Egyptian girls and women, we, the women of Egypt, must cry out and say with force:
>
> No . . . to the high prices that are depriving us of food for our children every day (bottle of oil LE12, wheat LE4.5, rice LE4.5);
>
> No . . . to the unemployment that has become a threat to our young people's future;
>
> No . . . to corruption in the education and healthcare systems;
>
> No . . . to increased divorce rates that have forced women to leave the house to work and have made them support their families both outside and inside the household;
>
> No . . . and we, the women of Egypt, demand a halt to the suffering of those who have been unjustly and harshly imprisoned. [We demand] their freedom so that they can return to their spouses and families. We call upon all the women of Egypt to fight against corruption and to refuse every sort of violation to which a woman

is exposed. We say to all those involved in the oppression of the people in general and women in particular, "Enough of your injustice!" Soon we will eliminate this injustice by force of law, and Egypt will be free and proud (*abiyya*), and Egyptian women will be dignified (*shamikha*) and virtuous (*karima*). We cry out against corruption, saying like the Prophet Shuʿayb, "I only intend reform as much as I am able. And my success is only through Allah. Upon him I have relied, and to Him I return."[7]

The leaflet thus referred to different depictions of females: 1) urban women exposed to danger in the streets and on public transport, 2) mothers waiting in vain in front of bakeries to buy subsidized bread to feed their children while trying to protect them against the corruption of failing education, health, and social security systems, 3) divorced women left to their own devices, implicitly described as victims of the general deterioration in moral standards, and 4) the mothers or wives of Muslim Brothers who were the victims of the tyranny of the regime. By mentioning all these female figures in the same breath, the leaflet and the meeting at which it was handed out linked ordinary female citizens to Muslim Sisters. All women share in the daily suffering and have the same aspirations, it seemed to be saying, but the case of the Sisters drew greater attention to the injustice of the regime while investing them with exemplary moral virtue.

However, the meeting also indicated something of the ambiguity of this type of mobilization. The appearance of women in public space and their demands for the freeing of prisoners, a more dignified life, the improvement of living standards, and more general reform had an undeniably oppositional content, and they presented the Brothers as being opposed to the regime in the tense run-up to the elections. There was a strong element of protest against repression and corruption. The evening before the meeting, the immediately identifiable sirens of Amn al-Dawla cars had been heard throughout another area of Alexandria while another meeting, this one smaller and involving only men, was being prepared at the local Brotherhood MP's premises. They were a signal that the meeting should be called off or those involved should be prepared to risk the consequences.[8] Therefore, turning to women to hold meetings was part of a strategy to defuse police repression, while at the same time adding greater protest potential to the event because of its unusual character.

But, this gendered content also gave the meeting its conservative and consensual character. It reinforced the "politics of respectability" regarding women that the regime used to control public space (Amar 2011). As Paul Amar explains, under Mubarak the presentation of protesters, including women, as thugs ("thugification") had been a way of breaking up and discouraging demonstrations. Working-class women were humiliated or sexually harassed by the police, arrested on suspicion of being "prostitutes," judged to be "sexual delinquents."[9] They were presented as being troublemakers who deliberately flouted the behavior expected of respectable women, which emphasized modesty, discipline, and reserve. As a result, the mobilization of women in public space in the Brotherhood meeting who were "clearly identified as being pious and respectable through their appearance and their class background" was "politically powerful" in that it subverted the policy of "thugification" (Amar 2011: 309). Yet it also reinforced existing norms of respectability for women, and thus, at least in part, supported the policing of public space.

In concluding this section, it can be said that in the framework of the politics of goodness and at the local level, conflict was latent most of the time. Only on specific occasions were clear-cut divides activated through the mobilization of subjectivity models that identified the Brothers as virtuous heroes resisting a corrupt regime. However, this whole framework was challenged and eventually transformed in the post-2011 social and political context, when the preexisting 'conflictual consensus' turned into open and radicalized conflict. We should now try to understand why and how.

## Breaking Down and Falling Out: The Radicalization of Conflict

The 2011–13 period was highly charged with important and multiple events, and it is not the intention here to describe all of them. It is not the intention, either, to enumerate all the factors that account for the electoral success of the Brotherhood and the election of Mohamed Morsi as president,[10] or those that caused the latter's sudden fall in July 2013, the harsh repression of his supporters in the Rab'a al-'Adawiyya and al-Nahda Squares between 14 and 18 August, or the later banning of the movement. In order to do so, one would need to describe the role of the army and police in detail, as well as the actions of different political actors and the country's media, judicial, and economic elites. One would also need to look at the economic factors, notably the deterioration of the energy sector, and at the interference of foreign powers. It would finally be necessary to scrutinize the ambiguous reactions of the Gama'a to the revolutionary developments of these years, as well as the violent and authoritarian practices of the Morsi regime vis-à-vis the protest movements, and the policies carried out during Morsi's year as president.

Without denying in any way the importance of such considerations, my intention here is to look at what was happening at the local level in the social embedding of the Brotherhood and in its internal dynamics, in line with the method of this book as a whole. Because I was finishing my PhD dissertation at the time, I was not able to continue intensive ethnographic fieldwork with the Brotherhood in Madinat Nasr, Helwan, and Tibbin during the Revolution period. However, I was able to interview some of my informants again in December 2012 and to conduct new interviews in December 2013 in Cairo and a nearby village. Then I carried out a survey of groups of voters in Tibbin in 2014–15, and interviewed various MB members in exile in Istanbul between 2014 and 2017.

My main argument is that a dramatic shift took place in the local landscape in these years that destroyed the earlier 'conflictual consensus.' The previous environment of overlapping networks and mixed identities unraveled, giving way to more polarized divisions. We will start by examining the case of Mansour, a former low-ranking NDP official, as a way to illustrate this change. Then we will analyze the Brotherhood's significant contribution to this shift.

## Mansour, a Low-ranking *Feloul* in the Breakdown of Local Politics

December 2013: When asked to introduce himself, Mansour does not hesitate to say, a smile on his lips, that "I am what could be called a *feloul* [a 'remnant' of the former regime]. I was assistant secretary of the NDP office on the village level."[11] Born in 1964 in a small village in the Banha governorate to the north of Cairo, where he still lives, Mansour had grown up in the ruins of the Nasserist dream of national grandeur and social progress, some of which he still retained within him. "My heart is on the left and for socialism and social justice, I mean, my heart is Nasserist," he said. He had started his involvement in politics at the age of thirteen by supporting one of the Free Officers behind the 1952 coup d'état, Kamal al-Din Husayn, who was also originally from Banha. In the 1980s, he grew closer to the leftwing Tagammu' Party, founded by another former Free Officer, and then to the Labor Party, which he actively supported in the 1987 parliamentary elections. However, five years after that, he decided to join the NDP. "I knew that it was in my own best interests to become closer to the NDP in order to get on in life and get easier access to things," he commented. It was also necessary for his work, since he was an employee of the Ministry of the Interior at the local level.

Thus Mansour's career in the political and administrative system started, and he became a member of the NDP local section's assembly before being appointed assistant secretary in 2003. At the same time, he applied for, and obtained, a seat on the Local Popular Council, which he held from 2000 to 2011. He set up a youth center in his village as well as a local development association (*gam'iyya li-tanmiyyat al-mugtama'*) that provided various social services to the population. As a result, he became someone to listen to and a popular local leader. It was said in his village that no MP had ever managed to get elected over the previous fifteen years without first getting the support of Mansour. Even the Brotherhood MP Mohsen Radi had needed his support to win the seat in 2005.

I decided to support Mohsen instead of the NDP candidate, and I persuaded 80 percent of the section to do the same. I had a personal problem with the candidate, as he had opposed my standing for the Local Popular Council some years before. And I knew the Brothers well through my wife's family . . . I trusted them.

This trust was first confirmed, and then shattered, between 2011 and 2013. While Mansour claimed that he had "obviously supported the 2011 revolution because there were too many abuses and too much corruption," after the January–February 2011 uprising he spent about one year in the wilderness. He lost his post in the NDP section and his seat on the Local Popular Council, since both were dissolved in spring 2011. He became fearful, burned his archives, withdrew into charity work only, and kept a low profile for some months before the parliamentary elections came along in the fall to open up new perspectives. The sanctions against the agents of the NDP that had earlier been threatened were not imposed, and Mansour began to regain his optimism and his hopes for a boost to his career thanks to the Brotherhood's electoral success.

> I supported the Brothers again in 2011, and I knew they were going to win. This was because Mohsen Radi had set up a "system" in 2005 that had impacted people a lot. He was always around in constituency surgeries, where he could be seen every day. He welcomed people in person, and he helped them himself in carrying out administrative procedures. He used to take them with him in his car wherever they wanted to go. He was working day and night. He never slept. This is why he was elected again in 2011, and the Freedom and Justice Party also won the seats reserved for the party-list vote.[12]

> However, he was soon disillusioned.

> As soon as the elections were over, things were finished. I immediately understood that. The MPs' offices were closed, or only kept open for form's sake, and there was only a secretary there who would just send people back home. Mohsen Radi had disappeared. He wasn't there anymore. His car, it was now a chauffeur who drove it and he would sit in the back. . . . We had a meeting attended by some leading figures from the village, and we asked him what had happened. We told him that people were unhappy and that they didn't understand. He told us that now he would have to concentrate on his role "under the dome" [in parliament] and that he couldn't continue in the way he had before. The role of an MP was to make laws, he said.

This sudden change was a serious error that cost the Brothers a good deal of support. Yet the fact that Mansour, like many others, was so quick to turn against his former allies can be explained by the fact that the terms of that alliance seemed to have been broken. Despite his hopes, Mohsen Radi and his colleagues did not thank Mansour for his support in the past. No new position was offered to him. The elections for the Local Popular Councils were postponed indefinitely. Mansour commented bitterly that "thanks to my position on the council I used to get two days off work per week and receive a stipend. Now, I'm obliged to go to work every day, and that doesn't suit me." While he made no attempt to disguise the convenience of the previous arrangement, he swiftly fended off accusations of personal benefit by presenting facts in a favorable light and building a narrative in which the Muslim Brothers were the bad guys.

> I thought they were devoted to God, but in fact they are only devoted to their positions. They're hypocrites. They said they didn't want the presidency, and then they took it. They've got their fingers everywhere in every institution in order to take control of everything. In the justice system, in the police, in the army, in places where even Mubarak didn't dare go. They have caused shocks everywhere, and these have destabilized the country.

In 2012, Mansour and his friends began a long campaign to undermine the Brotherhood's hegemony. Previous members of the local NDP section regrouped and started to hold meetings again. In the 2012 presidential elections, Mansour officially supported Ahmed Shafiq, the candidate who was a senior commander in the Egyptian Air Force and a former minister in Mubarak's era, though in the first round he voted for the Nasserist Hamdin Sabbahi. Mansour began to go around the village telling anyone who would listen that the Brothers were "liars" and spreading rumors about them, such as that there was a plot between the Brothers, the United States, and Israel, or that Morsi had sold parts of Egypt to Palestinian Hamas or to Sudan, and so on. In February 2013, when the Tamarrod movement took off in Cairo,[13] Mansour and his friends enthusiastically supported it in Banha. They prepared for the 30 June demonstrations calling for Morsi to resign, and when the day came the center of the village was crammed full of people. "It took me more than three hours to get up the main street. It was crazy! That was a great revolution of the people and the Egyptian nation." Mansour was clearly very happy to take his revenge on the Brothers, and ironically for this supporter of the former regime, his newfound political legitimacy relied on his appropriation of the capacity for protest in the streets.

Mansour's career draws attention to the significant changes in the sociopolitical configuration that had taken place and illustrates how the foundations of local politics had been upset by the revolutionary turmoil. Following the dissolution of the NDP, the parliament, and the Local Popular Councils in early 2011, tens of thousands of local agents like Mansour were deprived of their positions and stopped acting as the everyday faces of the state. As a result, the micro-level spirit of service broke down as a substitute for the state, something which was cruelly felt by large parts of the population who were suffering from growing poverty and were now without even informal access to patronage through those local agents. With the Local Popular Councils still dissolved and with no new elections in sight, all expectations of patronage and demands for services were transferred to the MPs elected in late 2011. For many people struggling for survival on a day-to-day basis, a new parliament seemed to mean the return of a potential source of material aid, which, although also seemingly minimal, mattered in an economy based on everyday survival.

It came as no surprise that the Brothers, seconded by the Salafists and perceived as being able to answer these popular expectations, won the 2011 parliamentary election and that the parties who embodied the spirit of the Revolution did not. However, during the short duration of the parliament, sitting between February and June 2012, the Brotherhood MPs abandoned the "system" referred to by Mansour that had emphasized small symbolic differences that have great effects, among them MPs being present in their local offices and picking people up at home by car. Instead, the Brotherhood MPs now turned their backs on the local offices and dedicated themselves instead to legislative work, even though most of them had had no experience of it and in any case mostly lacked the necessary skills for lawmaking. Moreover, the parliament itself got caught up in an institutional battle, as the Higher Constitutional Court, supported by the interim military government, threatened for months to dissolve it, which duly took place in June 2012.[14] Since they had anticipated the dissolution, the Brotherhood MPs were eager to pass laws guaranteeing their presence in the Constituent Assembly that was to be formed. They also focused on a political isolation law that banned officials who had served in top posts under Mubarak from running in new elections. While this law was canceled when the parliament was dissolved, a related article was included in the constitution introduced by Morsi in late 2012.

This move from *khidma* (service) to legislation seems to have caused much disgruntlement among voters, who were angry at the Brotherhood's neglect of local issues. As Mansour's case shows, it also sparked anger among former NDP officials, who considered the political isolation law to be a potential threat. They were especially concerned about the fate of the Local Popular Councils, previously their strongholds, since new elections to these were constantly being postponed while parliament drafted new legislation to rule them. Many believed this to be a sign that the Brotherhood sought complete hegemony, and they began to mobilize against it.

The breakdown of the previous local politics (that is, the ending of former patronage relations, the increasing distancing of the Brotherhood MPs from their constituencies, and the growing potential for conflict over political identities and divisions) was therefore caused partly by the institutional turmoil that came in the wake of the Revolution, partly by *feloul* strategies, and partly by the incoherent actions taken by the Brothers themselves. Why would the Brotherhood MPS halt the very system that had been the basis of their past success? One of the reasons was the Gama'a's failure to extricate itself effectively from its previous condition of open secrecy.

## How *Not* to Get Out from Secrecy

The Brotherhood's failure to come fully out into the open and abandon its previous condition of open secrecy involved several stages that I summarize here.

### Step 1: Remain illegal, prevent the party from developing, and change the parliamentary strategy

The fact that the Gama'a did not transform itself into a genuine political party after the 2011 revolution has been much commented upon. But what was most striking in the case of the Brotherhood was not that it did not dissolve the Gama'a when the Freedom and Justice Party was created. This was quite a standard move among the other Islamist parties. More striking was the fact that the Gama'a resisted any kind of legalization after the lifting of the previous regime's ban, and that even though it was no longer compelled to exist clandestinely, it refused to enter any regular legal category. Instead, the Brotherhood leadership simply asked for the lifting of the 1954 ban. As a result, several lawsuits were filed against the Gama'a, contesting its insistence on remaining illegal now that nothing prevented its official registration. Yet it was only in March 2013 that the Brotherhood officially registered itself as an association, under pressure from the Supreme Administrative Court that had threatened to order its dissolution. Even so, the Gama'a did not actually become a legal association, and instead a legal association was created *in addition* to the Gama'a, which therefore remained in a legal vacuum. This is proved by the fact that the declared president of the new association was not the then supreme guide of the Gama'a, Mohamed Badi', but its former one, Mahdi 'Akif, who had resigned in 2009.

This resistance to legalization was linked to the historical ambition of the Gama'a to be recognized as a unique, ad hoc, and non-defined organization. As seen in chapter one, this lack of clear definition had been part of the Gama'a's identity since its foundation, and even more so since its reemergence in the 1970s. However, it was a lack that became less and less acceptable to the changing rules of legitimacy that grew up in the emerging political configuration after the Revolution, which required greater transparency and conformity with the law. The undefined nature of the Gama'a was also questioned by other political actors, the media, and parts of the population, as well as by an increasing number of Brotherhood members beyond the small circles of earlier dissidents. It was to address such issues that younger members of the organization decided to hold the controversial Brotherhood Youth Conference in March 2011.[15]

In the meantime, the organization's leadership, which disapproved of this event, dealt with the creation of the Freedom and Justice Party (FJP) as a mere formality, seeing it as being wholly controlled by the *tanzim*. This was obvious in the first official act setting up the new party that took place on 30 April 2011: a press conference was held in front of the Gama'a's new headquarters in the Muqattam Hills in Cairo, after the 109-member General Consultative Assembly (Maglis al-Shura al-'Amm), the legislative body of the Gama'a, had gathered for its first plenary session since 1995. While it affirmed the independence of the FJP, the assembly declared that it had appointed Morsi president of it. 'Isam al-'Iryan was to be vice-president for political affairs and Saad al-Katatni secretary-general. All three men were members of the Brotherhood's Guidance Bureau, and although they announced they would formally resign, this was a clear signal of the *tanzim*'s grip. The Maglis al-Shura al-'Amm also sketched out the party's bylaws and organization chart. According to Wissam, Farid, and other young activists critical of the way the party was being shaped, FJP officials' positions in the governorates and districts were awarded to *tanzim* leaders of the same level.[16] As Wissam commented, the same policy of promoting virtue over specialized political competence, just as in the *tanzim*, prevailed in the selection of party leaders.

> To be frank, what is the composition of the Gama'a's Maglis al-Shura al-'Amm? Among the one hundred leaders sitting in it, eighty or so do not understand anything about politics. They just listen to the handful of powerful people inside the *tanzim* and vote as they do. Debate and discussion are looked down upon in the Gama'a's ranks, and the same thing is true of the FJP. An individual must not take part in polemics if he wants to be favored by the Brotherhood.[17]

The *tanzim*'s grip on the new party thus prevented the latter from serving as a vehicle for any greater openness of the organization vis-à-vis the wider society. It may also partly explain the sudden drop of the system of local work that the Brotherhood MPs had put in place between 2005 and 2010 and that they seemingly abandoned during the 2012 parliament. The *tanzim* had indeed been in charge of selecting the FJP candidates for the 2011–12 parliamentary elections (Trager 2016: 188), and this had entailed two surprising consequences.

First was the fact that Brothers who had already had experience as candidates or even as MPs were not favored in the selection. This is apparent if one looks at the careers of the 166 Brotherhood candidates in the 2005 elections examined in chapter one.[18] Almost half of them (seventy-eight) were absent from the new selection despite their previous experience. Aside from the two who had left the Gama'a, twelve of them were redeployed to stand as candidates in the less important elections for the upper house of parliament (the Shura Council). But most of them (sixty-four) simply did not take part in the 2011–12 elections. What is even more surprising is the fact that among these sixty-four absentees there were twenty former MPs from the 2005–10 parliament, even though their political experience would have been a clear advantage for the FJP over the candidates from other parties. The second surprise was that leading figures from the *tanzim* were elected to parliament in 2012 as part of the cohort of new MPs, while the Brotherhood had not selected *tanzim* leaders as candidates in previous parliamentary elections, as we have shown in chapter one.

These changes in the selection of the MB parliamentary elections candidates suggest two hypotheses. The first is that the *tanzim* was seeking to check the increasing power of the MPs by preventing them from using the new party as a means to gain both autonomy and additional political expertise through reelection. This would explain the rejection of the twenty former MPs and their replacement by *tanzim* appointees. The marginalization of MP Mohamed al-Beltagy, who had a political reputation, during the FJP internal elections in Cairo can also be understood in this light. The second hypothesis, which can account for the different logics of selection, is that the main aim of the Gama'a during the 2012 parliament was no longer to entrench its existing social embedding. Instead, it was to create the legislative conditions that would allow it to control the country's political institutions and to overcome any obstructions from the state apparatus. In short, a strategy of institutional embedding had now replaced the strategy of social embedding, the latter being considered as something that had effectively been achieved. However, by thinking this way the leadership was committing a serious error. It did not take into consideration that in a fast-changing and unpredictable environment, such as one caused by a revolution, the perceptions of all those involved, including the voters, are fluid and can change quickly and unpredictably.

## Step 2: Miscommunicate and destroy the symbolic economy of disinterestedness

It can be argued that voters' perceptions were thrown into disarray by the incoherent communication strategy adopted by the Gama'a. At the national level, its leading figures showed themselves to be incapable of responding to the calls for greater transparency that were coming from all directions as a result of the general opening up of the regime and of public space. Not only had they retained the Gama'a's opaque and illegal status intact, but they had also made a variety of self-contradictory declarations that had negatively impacted public perceptions of the Brotherhood. Their announcement that they would stand for only 20 percent of the parliamentary seats in the 2011–12 elections, then 50 percent, and finally 100 percent, had fed accusations of dishonesty and hypocrisy, as had a similar announcement that they would not be running for the presidency, before finally doing everything they could to support Mohamed Morsi's campaign. This opacity became even worse when Morsi was finally in power. The traditional distrust of the media entertained by members of the *tanzim*, along with their longstanding culture of secrecy, led them to see any opposition to their power as irrefutable proof of plots against them. In line with this way of thinking, they managed to turn every debate into a sterile round of accusations and counter-accusations of plots, with the Brothers denouncing the deep state and their opponents adverting to the Islamists' attacks against the state. Fears of the 'Brotherhoodization' of the state institutions were fed by the confused way in which Morsi and the Brotherhood members at large acted, notably during the dramatic clashes at the Ittihadeyya Palace in December 2012 when MB activists took on the role of the police in driving back the demonstrators. Morsi rapidly took on the appearance of a president governing in favor of his organization alone and not for the benefit of the Egyptian people as a whole. He even appeared to be a puppet whose strings were being pulled either by the supreme guide of the Gama'a or by its powerful deputy guide, businessman Khayrat al-Shater.

However, on the local level there was a communication strategy diametrically opposed to the national one, where the Brotherhood, far from behaving opaquely, was making its presence felt in a very extensive way through its neighborhood networks. There was now no longer any need for activists to hide their Brotherhood identity, and most of them, not only those working for the MPs, started to announce their membership in the Brotherhood in public. The Gama'a and the FJP began to open a large number of offices under their own names across the country in addition to the existing MPs' offices, and Brotherhood networks became far more visible on the local level as a result. This had two main effects. The first was that the sheer extent of these networks came as something of a surprise, and also cause for concern, among those who now discovered their existence in their own districts. The second was that this public emergence by the Brothers, seemingly so sudden and so obvious, was swiftly perceived as a sign of arrogance.

Comments made by one resident of Tibbin can be understood in this light. He was a lesser notable and someone well versed in religious practices, active in *sulh* (customary justice) and other activities in the area. He was also typical of the sort of associated personality wooed by the Brothers during the Mubarak years. In previous years he had voted for Fath al-Bab, but in June 2014, when my interview with him took place, he did not hesitate to express his strong support for newly elected president al-Sisi. Commenting on the past popularity and sudden collapse in fortunes of the Brotherhood (which his own changing political allegiances illustrated), he fell back in a more or less stereotypical way on a culturalist explanation that relies on the supposed mentality of the Egyptian population, even if he did so with a certain degree of irony. "Here, it's a case of *ma'ahum ma'ahum, 'alayhum 'alayhum* [when everyone's with you, I am with you; when everyone's against you, I'm against you]. . . . If you are a minister, you will get everyone's support. If you are nothing, people will turn their backs on you. It's just how it is. People used to like the Brothers. But now they like al-Sisi." Then he added,

> But we didn't really know who the Brothers were. We knew them, but we didn't see a lot of them. They were like fish you see when you look down into the water. And then suddenly there they were on the surface. Neighbors, relatives . . . You suddenly discover they are Brothers. They appeared everywhere all of a sudden, saying, "We are here, and we are strong."[19]

The Brotherhood's failure to emerge convincingly from its previously clandestine existence was thus characterized both by its persistence in practices more suitable to a secret organization and by its broadcasting of the existence of extensive Brotherhood networks in a way that was judged by many to be overdone. Moreover, the sudden publicization of the MB networks at the local level also went hand in hand with the direct politicization of their activities, something that contradicted the former symbolic economy of disinterestedness, described in chapter two.

It will be remembered that this economy had six main aspects: (1) the religious motivation behind the provision of social services, understood as a gift from the self; (2) the detachment of these services from the electoral calendar, providing them within a long-term timeframe; (3) the dissimulation of the identity of the Brotherhood as the actual provider of such services; (4) the effacement of the individual self; (5) the collective mediation, that is to say the involvement of others in the provision of services, including non-Brotherhood members and local notables; and (6) the symbolic staging and public display of consideration and respect for citizens. However, following the revolutionary uprising, one of the major changes in the MB social activities was their explicit politicization; they were now directly labeled as having been organized by the Brotherhood, as Steven Brooke has rightly remarked. Brooke has examined the major campaign of mobile medical clinics and other social services, called "Ma'an nabni Masr" (Together We Build Egypt), organized by the Gama'a and the FJP, that took place across the country between January and May 2013. This campaign was explicitly linked to the June 2013 parliamentary elections planned by the Morsi regime, as Brooke makes clear. "For decades, the Brotherhood strove to keep social service provision and politics separate, but the high stakes of these crucial elections made it difficult to maintain the firewall" (Brooke 2019: 124). As a result, despite the huge amount of services dispensed as part of this campaign, making up, perhaps, for the abandoning of the system earlier used by the Brotherhood MPs, the religious motive behind it was occluded and replaced by a primarily political one. Moreover, the services were now being provided to meet the needs of the electoral cycle, not separate from it as had been the case before, and the Brotherhood's responsibility for the campaign was made everywhere apparent. There was now no longer any sign of the involvement of non-MB members or local notables, who were replaced by Brotherhood activists and supporters, and the residents of the areas concerned were treated as the simple beneficiaries of the aid.

When seen in the context of the growing polarization that was taking place on the national political scene at the time, this politicization of the Brotherhood's social activities called into question the blurring of identities that had taken place in the past and hardened various divisions. Under Mubarak many voters had not seen any obvious contradiction in voting at the same time for the Brotherhood and the NDP, because of the general confusion of political identities in which the ethical distinctiveness of the Muslim Brothers was expressed subtly. On the contrary, the new emphasis on clear political identifications led many to reject such vague loyalties and to join one or the other camp. Even regular sympathizers of the Brotherhood were disturbed by the Gama'a's sudden strategic reversals and incoherent public presentation.

## Step 3: Neglect changes in perceptions, demands, and norms

The importance of step 3 can be understood by listening to a female resident of Tibbin, "A.," who had previously been a loyal supporter of the Brotherhood. She had voted for Fath al-Bab in the 2005 elections, and after the redrawing of the constituencies in the 2011 voting system, she had voted for Salah, the successor of Sheikh al-Muhammadi. In June 2014, she said she was against al-Sisi and the coup d'état, but at the same time she also criticized the Brotherhood.

> A.: The Brothers are good people, and they help people without advertising what they are doing. They don't do things just for the publicity. But they made a mistake in wanting to become involved in politics. They should have contented themselves with the parliament, where they could have done amazing things. Their first decision was to renounce the LE500 that MPs get every time they turn up for parliament. But first they said they would only take 20 percent of the seats, and then 50 percent, and finally 100 percent, and then they took part in the presidential elections after they had said they wouldn't. I really liked the decision they made not to take part, which I thought was very respectable. I was disappointed that they then decided to participate. But I voted for Morsi anyway on the second round, though on the first round I voted for Abu al-Futuh, because I liked his manifesto and what he had to say. Morsi was a good guy, but it was predictable that the Brothers would not be able to play a properly political role because they had been excluded from politics for decades. It was a way of going too quickly from the darkness into the light and into politics. They weren't ready or capable of managing the country at that moment.

> Me: But the Brothers had been taking part in politics and elections for a long time . . .

> A.: Yes . . . but . . . how can I put this . . . parliament is different. It has a service role *(khadami)*. That's why the Brothers would have done such good work there . . . as they were the oldest and the most widespread organization in Egypt, and they had been serving people for a long time. They would have done very good work if they had been given the time and if they hadn't gone into politics.[20]

The Brotherhood had lost its legitimacy by wanting to leave behind the politics of *khidma* and *khayr*, areas in which it had previously excelled through charities and parliament, she said. She criticized the Brothers for wanting to assert their hegemony and, in so doing, for getting involved in politics in the sense of fighting for power. She also criticized them for lacking management skills, in other words for failing to do politics properly in the sense of operating in a professional way with specialized competence. It was this kind of professional political competence that was needed to fill the post of head of state, she said, and for this reason Abu al-Futuh, more politically experienced than Morsi, had seemed to her to be the more suited. What this woman voter had to say speaks volumes about how the norms of political activity were being questioned and redefined in the post-revolution context. She drew on two definitions of political legitimacy. One of them had to do with political expertise and relying upon speech-making skills and management abilities. This was where the president should excel. The other was the politics of *khayr*, which depended on a commitment to service, and this was where parliament should take over. From her point of view the Muslim Brothers had lost their credibility both because they had not been able to adapt to the demands of the first kind of politics, so that they failed to manage public affairs transparently and communicate properly, and because they had neglected the second kind of politics, giving up their previous policy of social embedding.

However, this point of view, held by part of the electorate, was not the only possible one, and the ways in which political norms were changing was certainly not one-directional. Thus, for other voters, including some who had previously supported the MB, it was the politics of *khayr* that they rejected. The 2011 uprising had made it obvious that *khayr* in itself was not enough to make up for the state's failure to provide social protection. And the relocation of welfare into goodness was called into question as a result of rising demands for genuine social justice (*'adala igtima'iyya*) and radical changes in the policies of redistribution. After two decades of privatization policies, the expectations that people had of the state were high. In Egypt, expectations of the state had historically been related to security and social protection, and they had focused on the two major symbols of state-led development, that is to say, the army and the president. This mixture of social protection and security has recently been supported by a significant international trend reasserting the need for strong state leadership to prevent the collapse of state institutions while at the same time deregulating the economy.

It was in this context that Morsi came to embody the state when he was elected president, and he did not fit with the image of the president as the *za'im* (leader) and savior of the nation, which was being revived by expectations of increased state protection. Some saw Morsi as a good man but *fashil* (a loser) in terms of being unable to govern "a state that is too big for him," as one former Morsi voter told me. Yet, in addition to his lack of charisma, absence of a coherent economic program, and overriding neoliberal agenda, it could be argued that this was also because the politics of *khayr*, of which the Brotherhood had previously been the champion, did not fit the new demands for genuine state intervention. Meanwhile, others saw Morsi as a threat to the state. Behind the irreverent nickname of *al-kharuf* (the sheep) given to him by the press, there was more than the hostility of the country's journalists toward the MB. There was also the idea that the Brotherhood was weakening the autonomy of the state and making it submit to the needs of its own *tanzim*.

However, what is at stake in post-Mubarak Egypt also goes far beyond the political failure of the Brotherhood. Instead, it lies in the total breakdown of the politics of goodness and the challenge to the relocation of state welfare services onto the terrain of local practices of service and charity, a form of governmentality in which the Muslim Brothers, like the former NDP notables, had excelled.

As for the MB, this breakdown meant that their entire system of action had been challenged. The massive repression that they had been enduring since the bloody dispersal of the Rab'a sit-ins was of course the first cause of the Gama'a's collapse. Indeed, there is a case for saying that for the first time in history the regime had endeavored to uproot the Gama'a completely from its social anchoring (Brooke 2019). Yet the Brotherhood's relations with society were also profoundly transformed by these two short but crucial years in which it failed to make the transition to open political action and lost its aura of moral disinterestedness.

Finally, in order to conclude this book, we need to address how internal relations within the organization were impacted by this failure.

## Exiles and Exits

This final section reintroduces Wissam, Farid, and other anonymous members of the Brotherhood in exile in Istanbul. Their fortunes since 2013 have been highly revealing of the fates of the various exile groups dispersed across Turkey, Qatar, Sudan, Malaysia, Lebanon, and Europe that we still call the "Egyptian Muslim Brotherhood" even if the group no longer exists as it used to. In the aftermath of the waves of arrests of leading MB figures in the summer of 2013, the Gama'a itself largely broke up, such that it now no longer exists as a single organization. There are now two Gama'at al-Ikhwan al-Muslimin, each of which claims to be the legitimate heir of the organization initially created by Hassan al-Banna.

### From Rab'a to Istanbul: The radicalization of internal conflict

August 2013: Wissam and Farid are in Rab'a al-'Adawiyya Square in Cairo. The repression has taken place, and Farid is looking after the wounded. Wissam is responsible for media coverage, along with his elder brother. But the latter is quickly arrested, and since he is widely considered to be one of the leaders of the sit-in because of his frequent interviews on Al Jazeera, he is harshly tortured. His health declines dangerously over the months that follow, and his life is felt to be in danger.

Wissam and Farid both fled their homes, and both lost their jobs. Farid was fired from the state hospital in which he worked, and the IMA hospital in which he had had a second job was confiscated by the authorities. Wissam's media company was closed down, and his family's stores were attacked and then also closed. His entire family was obliged to flee to another governorate.

In January 2014, Wissam and Farid left for Istanbul accompanied by their wives and children. They were able to travel to Istanbul and then to survive once they got there thanks to their savings and the contacts they had made in Turkey with aid organizations working with Syrian refugees through the Relief Committee of the Doctors' Syndicate. However, to their considerable surprise, they received no help from the leadership of the Brotherhood in Istanbul that was set up on the orders of Mahmoud Hussein, the secretary-general of the Gama'a in exile in Qatar. Wissam and Farid estimated that some eight hundred Muslim Brothers were in exile on Turkish soil at the time, a figure that is said to have risen to three thousand in fall 2014 and five thousand in August 2016. While those who leave Egypt have enough money to travel and take care of their needs during at least their early weeks abroad, many of the young men and women concerned are then left to their own devices.[21] They do not know the language, cannot find jobs, experience financial and administrative problems in obtaining a residence permit, and are often forced to live in small and overcrowded apartments.

However, the Brotherhood's leadership had swiftly reorganized at least a semblance of the *tanzim*, notably by setting up *usar* and *shu'ab*. It also set up a legal framework for regularizing its activities in Turkey in the shape of an NGO, named Rab'a, registered with the authorities in January 2014 and directed by the leaders of the *tanzim*. However, this NGO has remained singularly inactive and hasn't organized any political (no conferences or demonstrations), humanitarian, or judicial activities. Wissam, Farid, and four other activists (two of them young women), along with about sixty other young exiles, then demanded that internal elections be held in order to replace the NGO's executive board. The leadership gave way to the pressure and accepted the idea of internal elections in principle, but then did everything it could to control them, including by announcing the holding of the elections on the same day that they were to take place. It withheld information and engaged in various acts of dissuasion. However, against all predictions, the young people managed to win the elections, chiefly by being able to mobilize their supporters at the last minute. But the victory proved illusory, and while the youth were successful in selecting the head of the NGO, they accepted a compromise in allowing the former president of the board (a *tanzimi* leader) to retain his position. Hakim, the young coordinator of the NGO who had been educated at the American University in Cairo and had experience of running such associations, remembered that,

> The president never approved any decision made by the board, so much so that we asked ourselves whether he was president of the association or the Brothers' man in the association. He was always referring everything to the apparatus and distorting what we wanted to do. The premises of the association was located on the

outskirts of Istanbul, for example, in quite an inaccessible area. You had to walk through an area of wasteland in order to get there. We asked for the premises to be relocated to Fatih and for an apartment to be found to lodge new arrivals. He totally refused. He did everything he could to put a spoke in the wheels. He was opposed to my appointment as head of the association at first, but as the board insisted, he had to give in in the end. But he never wanted to give any information, for example on the number of Egyptians who were here in Turkey, or on the requests that were being made by families, and so on.[22]

When Wissam, Farid, and their colleagues decided to organize a sit-in to commemorate the military coup d'état from 3 to 7 July 2014, the leadership of the *tanzim* boycotted the initiative and instructed its members that they should not attend. This was the only act that had been jointly organized by the MB exiles and their Turkish partners until that moment. The fact that mobilizing the latter was not straightforward can be explained by the poor relations that the MB leadership had with them, as Hakim explained.

One proof of their incompetence was that there were no contact files with Turkish organizations. Things went very badly between the former board of the association and the IHH Humanitarian Relief Foundation,[23] for example. The leadership did not respect established rules, and they did not send a person of the same rank as the one who received them. They boasted about being "the Muslim Brothers" and thought that would be enough. When we took the association over, everything had to be done again on the level of relations with Turkish organizations. Yet when we got onto the board, the *tanzim* leaders started to tell people that we were incompetent and that we weren't good people. They even said that they weren't entirely sure that we were really Brothers at all and that they hadn't known us before. These were the same people who had been with me in my *shu'ba* in Egypt who were now saying that.

When I met Wissam, Farid, and Hakim at the beginning of September 2014, they were ready to resign from the association, exhausted and overwhelmed by the conflicts they had experienced. It was the first time that they had had to endure such harsh and personal attacks.[24] Wissam expressed himself with sadness and anger.

The leaders are not capable of setting up a *tanzim* and managing the situation. They are *'agza* (powerless) and *fashla* (in failure) and incapable of adapting themselves *(ghayr gedira)* to the place they find themselves in. They are failures because they have no vision, no strategy, no willpower, and no proper reflection. There are plenty of people here who have ideas and skills and are ready to make them available. But they don't want them. . . . They don't want anyone making criticisms, going back over the past, or analyzing what has happened. It's not possible with them. They are the foot soldiers of the *tanzim*. And I am saying this even though my grandfather was a Brother, as were my father, my mother, and my brothers. I'm not saying it as someone who has only been in the Brothers since yesterday, as I have spent my whole life in the Brothers *(fi-l-ikhwan)*. But little by little, things have been getting clearer. It's clear that our system is not right and that our way of running things is not right *(tariqat idaritna ghalat)*. There is no development. When we had to run Egypt, we did it like we ran the Gama'a. In the Gama'a, when an individual was told to do something, he said *hader* ('right away'). Do this, do that, and it was always *hader*. But it's not possible to run a state like that. Not a state the size of Egypt. . . . Even the smallest small company produces reports and looks at what works and what doesn't. But here, no, that's not possible. They tell you it's not possible at the moment because of the security pressures and the people who are in prison, and so on. But all that is false. We have been here a year, and we are still living from day to day. There is no proper reflection. And our experience in the association makes this very obvious.

What struck me most in this account was the way in which Wissam continuously compared the internal problems of the Gama'a to the failures of Morsi's presidency. Sometimes, this comparison, running in the direction of 'Gama'a>failure,' allowed him to identify the reasons behind that failure ("they wanted to run the state in the way they ran the Gama'a"). But when it ran in other direction of 'failure>Gama'a,' the comparison was a way of denouncing the injustices committed by the leadership on the basis of arguments that the leadership itself would be obliged to admit to.

> They did everything they could to stop us from working. Normally, the former board should have told us what the situation was, what they had done, their contacts, information, and so on. But they didn't give us anything. They did exactly what the Supreme Council of the Armed Forces (SCAF) did with the Brotherhood when Morsi took power. The SCAF prevented him from having access to all the files.

Did they really think it possible that an executive board that had been elected did not have the right to appoint the head of the association? Are they kidding me *(yenfaʿ keda)*? I am elected. You are appointed [addressing the leaders with anger]. . . . Are we really going to do what Adly Mansour did [the interim president who replaced Morsi after the coup]? He was appointed, and he would go on to cancel the decisions made by Morsi, when Morsi was the one who had been elected!

What we can observe through this rhetorical device is a deeper process by which activists such as Wissam have started to disconnect the cause of the Brotherhood from the *tanzim* that claims to serve and represent it. This is something which I also saw among other exiled members. This process was initiated by the failure of Morsi's presidency, the reaction of the *tanzim*, and the specific experience of exile.

### *"Mesh lazim tanzim"*

As Stéphane Dufoix has noted, the experience of exile is characterized by a contradiction between the breaking off of relations that initiates it (with the physical and legal distancing it implies from the country of origin) and the political continuity that those experiencing it try to proclaim and preserve. Political leaders in exile still pretend their legitimacy and power is intact, "as if what is going on in the country at the same time is something that could simply be put between parentheses and those in exile could simply freeze the political order as it was when they left and simply wait for the fall of the incumbent regime" (Dufoix 2002: 65). The claim for political continuity leads to the suspension of the passage of time for the exiled group, with the result that previous "political titles are maintained and cannot be questioned. In this way biological age becomes an important factor in the organization [of the group]" (Dufoix 2002: 134). However, this fixing of titles and hierarchies is in striking contrast to the consequences of exile, since the latter does have the effect of "destroying the apparent solidity of the social world and objectively existing social constructions" (Dufoix 2002: 65). The exiles are plunged into a changing world characterized by a deep uncertainty about whether they can continue to exist, politically speaking. As a result, recognition of the leaders' legitimacy can evaporate during the course of exile. Activists who previously had perhaps never questioned the legitimacy of internal rules and practices might now find themselves confronted by a "critical reality test"(Boltanski and Thévenot 1991)—in other words, by a major revision of the given order of importance according to which individuals, rules, and ideas are arranged.

In the case of the Brotherhood, a critical reality test of this sort was all the more likely in that processes of revision had already started after the trauma of the failure of Morsi's presidency and the Rab'a massacre. There was a crying need to understand what had happened and how the organization had reached this point. The need for a period of reflection after a disaster of this sort appeared to the exiled activists to be as vital as the safeguarding of the cause *(al-fikra)* itself. Interestingly enough, while my interviewees had difficulty in defining exactly what this cause was, they had no doubt regarding its supremacy. What did the cause consist of? *"Hubb al-khayr"* (love of goodness), Hakim told me; *"manhag al-ikh-wan"* (the method of the Brothers), Farid said; or *"shumuliyyat al-islam"* (the comprehensiveness of Islam), according to Yousri, whom I also met in Istanbul. It was this supremacy of the cause that led them to justify their right to criticize what had happened under Morsi and gave them the right to try out new initiatives that might get them out of the subsequent mess. When the *tanzim* explicitly denied them that right, they felt it was an attack against the supremacy of the cause itself, contesting its grandeur and, in a way, setting itself up as somehow superior to it. As a result, this denial produced a reaction that appeared to justify criticisms of the *tanzim* among the activists, who now reread what had taken place in the light of these criticisms. It resulted in demands for the disappearance of the *tanzim* as a condition for the safeguarding of the cause. Farid put this well.

> We don't have a culture of disagreement in the *tanzim*, even though this is something that is natural for all human beings. People naturally get angry, argue, and criticize each other. When you try to kill that off, you threaten your identity itself *(al-kayan al-kebir)*. It's dangerous and it's bad, and it is not part of the thought of the Brotherhood or of Islam. God wanted us to be like that. The founder of the Muslim Brotherhood never said that the one who was at the top of the organization should be the best. He is the best because at his side he has competent people who can tell him when he is taking the wrong direction and to whom he should listen. But the present leaders, when someone criticizes them, they think that it's something that is out of order *(khurug 'an al haya')*, when that has nothing to do with the *tarbiyya* [the education of the Brothers]. That's my opinion.

While Farid, Wissam, and Hakim have gone on to uncertain destinies, I will give the last words of this book to Yousri. A lawyer born in Damanhur, he had worked for an international human rights NGO since 2009. He had stopped undertaking activities for the *tanzim* on the same date, he said, as he did not want its instructions to interfere with his work for the NGO. Yet, whether he recognized it or not, he had still been a member of the *tanzim*, since he had continued to take part in its educational activities, including the weekly meeting of the *usra*. This lasted until his departure for Istanbul in September 2013, which marked a clearer break with the *tanzim*. He continued his work with the same NGO in Istanbul, even though his wife was going back and forth between Istanbul and Cairo. She was herself a Brotherhood member, like all his family and his wife's family. During our long interview, Yousri firmly stated that "I don't want to have anything further to do with the Muslim Brothers," referring to the leaders of the *tanzim*. However, speaking of the cause, he said,

> I am a Muslim Brother. I believe in all the ideas of the Muslim Brotherhood. I have not changed any of my ideas. My ideological commitments are the same, and my convictions haven't changed one jot. But there's no need to be a member of the *tanzim* for that. Whoever said that it did? Renovation *(tagdid)* is not something that only concerns those who are members of the *tanzim*, but also and even more those who are outside of it. *Mesh lazim tanzim* (there's no need for a *tanzim*).

## Conclusion

> An important point is that no one, neither the regime nor the world system, can ignore the presence of the Muslim Brotherhood. . . . We cannot deny it, we cannot say "there is no sun." The Brothers are present as a reality. The members are present on the ground. What I mean is that if I take an organization, and we go out in the field and see who, of its members, is there, maybe I won't find anyone. While we are present in the fabric of society, present in the concrete, it is something tangible. ('Abd al-Rahman, core member of the Brotherhood MP's team in Helwan, September 2009)

Comparing the existence of the Muslim Brotherhood in Egyptian society with that of the sun, as if it fills a vital need. Defining it as a "reality," and characterizing it as "presence on the ground," "presence in the fabric of society," or "palpable and concrete presence:" All this was, for sure, a rhetoric used by this Brotherhood activist in order to affirm the legitimacy of the organization to which he belonged. But the metaphor also reveals many of the features of the political and social existence of the Gama'a until the fall of Hosni Mubarak. Its anchoring into society was the key to its long and paradoxical history as a major, albeit illegal, political actor. Like the rays of the sun, this social embedding was as tangible as it was diffuse, and elusive because it was shaped by the particular mechanisms of open secrecy and by the wider framework of the politics of goodness.

In local environments and in the context of social action, the networks of the Brotherhood and those of the NDP were largely intertwined, and there were multiple opportunities for connections between them, as for people sharing and exchanging loyalty. The difference between the Brothers and the local elites of the regime lay in small differences that had great effects. Despite their limited potential for conflict, these small differences could act to undermine the credibility of the elites as they reinforced that of the Brothers. "The most dangerous form of politics in Egypt is social work" *(akhtar ʿamal siyasi fi Misr al-ʿamal al-igtimaʿi)*, Muhsin, an activist in Helwan, said, his profile as an associated personality being typical of exactly these kinds of interrelations and exchanges.[25] However, all of this unraveled after the 2011 Revolution.

Even if nothing that has happened since 2011 has been inexorable, the end of open secrecy, and later the social uprooting undertaken by the current regime, have broken all these mechanisms. Is this rupture irreversible? Are we to conclude that the Egyptian Muslim Brotherhood has finally come to an end? Can we now say, against the opinion of the activist mentioned above, that "there is no sun"? In the late 1960s, Richard Mitchell had perilously drawn such a conclusion after the repression of the Nasser era and was talking about the Muslim Brotherhood as a bygone movement. Like him, I chose to write most of this book using the past tense. However, I will not jump to such a conclusion. First, because it is sociologically untenable: every movement leaves a legacy, continues in one way or another, as Abdullah al-Arian (2014) has brilliantly shown in his study of the Egyptian Muslim Brotherhood's reemergence in the 1970s. There is no end, just a reconfiguration. Secondly, because on a deontological level I cannot proclaim the "end" of the multitude of activists, dissidents, sympathizers, associated personalities, families, and neighbors who are briefly referred to as "Muslim Brothers. " If the current repression, so fiercely conducted by the al-Sisi regime, seeks to eradicate them, let sociology do its modest work by offering them a space where they can continue to discreetly and safely exist, even if under plural, complex, and perhaps even changing social identities.

# Notes

## Introduction

1   According to sources in the security services, there were some five hundred thousand Brothers in September 2005. In 2007, there were one and a half million, suggesting that the 2005 figure was an underestimate. It is possible that the Brotherhood itself did not know exactly how many members it had, since producing such figures would have risked publicizing the organization's secrets (Tammam 2006: 17).

2   A genre of TV soap opera in Egyptian Arabic.

3   One hundred twenty-four students and seventeen high-ranking leaders of the organization were put in prison and the leaders' possessions were confiscated. Several hundred activists were later arrested across the country (Shehata and Statcher 2007).

4   This label has now been replaced by *al-irhabiyya* ('the terrorist'), which is stronger and more pejorative.

5   For a similar approach applied to an Islamic movement in Turkey, see the pioneering work by Jenny White 2001.

6   See the box "'Brotherhood' or 'Brotherhood-ized' Associations" in chapter one.

7   I borrow this term from Saba Mahmood, who uses it to avoid the simple binary of resistance/subordination (Mahmood 2005: chapter 1).

## Chapter 1

1   An expression used by Massicard (2015).

2   Between 1954 and 1970, many members of the Brotherhood escaped repression in Egypt by fleeing to the Arabian Peninsula. Saudi Arabia welcomed many such Brotherhood refugees, with whom the Saudi royal family shared a common enemy in the pan-Arab socialism of then-Egyptian president Gamal Abd al-Nasser. These favorable conditions enabled many Muslim Brothers to start what later became flourishing businesses.

3   On such *"passeurs de scène"* or "brokers" in the context of the Islamists'
    relationship to the state, see Camau and Geisser (2003).
4   Examples include billionaire businessman 'Uthman Ahmed 'Uthman and
    the al-Sharif and Mar'i families (al-Awadi 2004).
5   The number of students registered in institutions of higher education in
    Egypt, already doubling in the 1960s, continued to rise in the 1970s, with
    the proportion of secondary school students going on to university ris-
    ing from 40 to 60 percent. One main reason was the fact that since 1964
    the state had guaranteed a public-sector job to all university graduates
    (Wickham 2002: 38–40).
6   Brotherhood members joined 'university clubs' *(nawadi hay'at al-tadris)*,
    the equivalent of professional syndicates for university teachers, in large
    numbers, along with the student unions that had been reestablished by
    Mubarak in 1984.
7   In 1995, around one hundred leading Brotherhood figures were arrested,
    including al-'Iryan (deputy secretary-general of the Doctors' Syndi-
    cate), Abu al-Futuh (secretary-general of the Union of Arab Doctors),
    Mohamed Habib (president of the Minya University Teachers' Club), and
    Ibrahim al-Za'farani (secretary-general of the Alexandria Doctors' Syndi-
    cate), who received sentences of between three and five years in prison. In
    the same year, businessman Khayrat al-Shater and some of his associates
    were also thrown into prison in the wake of the "Salsabil affair"—Salsabil
    being the name of an IT company run by al-Shater in which the security
    services had supposedly discovered files giving details of a plan to over-
    throw the Egyptian state and install an Islamic state in its place.
8   The Lawyers and Engineers syndicates were exceptions, as these had
    had their assets sequestered in 1995 following accusations of financial
    mismanagement. In the case of the Lawyers' Syndicate, state tutelage was
    lifted in 2001, leading to new elections.
9   Numerous assassinations and other acts of violence were carried out by
    Muslim Brothers belonging to the organization's paramilitary branch, the
    'Secret Apparatus' *(al-tanzim al-sirri)*, among other groups, in the 1940s.
    Historians still debate whether the establishment of the 'Secret Appara-
    tus' was planned or whether it was an ad hoc creation, raising questions
    regarding the responsibility for the violence. Little information is avail-
    able also about the 1965 Organization. For an account of alternative
    views, see Mubarak (1995: 34–42), Tammam (2011), and al-Arian (2014).
10  For a different view, see al-Awadi (2004: 38–39), who thinks that it was
    legal recognition, and not the existence of the *tanzim*, that was seen by
    the Brotherhood leaders as the sole guarantee of the organization's exis-
    tence. However, the fact remains that they saw the reconstruction of a
    powerful *tanzim* as essential to the growth of the movement, a condition
    needed to negotiate its legalization by the state.

11  The association grew from fifteen branches in the Suez and Delta regions in 1933 to around one hundred in 1936. By 1937, there were more than two hundred branches across the country, reaching a total of between one thousand and 1,500 by 1944 (Lia 1998: 295).

12  Lia 1998:107, quoting from al-Banna's memoirs and the association's 1934 constitution.

13  According to thinkers associated with the Arab Nahda, the "backward-ness" of Muslim societies when compared to the western societies that had colonized them was due to the rigidities that the traditional *ulama* had introduced into Islam. For such thinkers, it was therefore important to return to the original religious texts and to strip away later accretions, in order to modernize Islam. At the same time, they thought that Islam should not be something distant or remote from ordinary Muslim lives, and that it was therefore necessary for all Muslims to take part in the call (*al-da'wa*) for the rediscovery of Islam.

14  From al-Banna's "Epistle of the Fifth Congress" (al-Banna 2002: 101).

15  In October 1977, the Brotherhood's leader, 'Umar al-Tilmisani, a lawyer by profession, filed a lawsuit challenging the decision made by Nasser in 1954 to dissolve the organization, arguing that the government of the Revolutionary Command Council was unconstitutional and so were all its decisions. The lawsuit never reached a conclusion, and it was adjourned more than forty times between 1977 and 1990.

16  From al-Banna's "Epistle of the Fifth Congress," translated into English by Richard Mitchell (Mitchell 1969: 14).

17  Two electoral systems were used in 1987, with certain seats being reserved for candidates affiliated with the political parties and contested using a party-list system and others being reserved for individual inde-pendent candidates.

18  The decision to return to a first-past-the-post system was also the result of a ruling by the Higher Constitutional Court (HCC) judging the party-list sys-tem to be unconstitutional on the grounds that it disadvantaged candidates not belonging to a political party. While it was common for the regime to ignore the opinions of the judges, on this occasion Mubarak chose to follow the HCC ruling, twice dissolving parliament, in 1987 and 1990.

19  Independents made up 54 percent of the candidates in the 1987 elections and no fewer than 80 percent of those standing in the 1990, 1995, and 2000 elections. Of the 110 MPs elected from the 1,700 genuine inde-pendents who had stood in the 1995 elections, only thirteen remained independent afterward (Ben Néfissa 1996: 59).

20  This method of controlling the outcome of elections by using indepen-dent candidates reached its limits after 2000, however, when the NDP was only able to achieve a majority in parliament by co-opting such inde-pendents and when it was no longer able to manage the competition in

its own ranks. In 2010, the party introduced a system preventing NDP members from standing as independents. When this failed, it ended up fielding more than two candidates in each constituency.

21　In 2005, all voters born before 1982 were supposed to register themselves voluntarily with the police authorities, along with all those wanting to change the constituency in which they were registered for work or residence reasons.

22　The right and left platforms became the Ahrar (Liberal) and Tagammu' Parties after the introduction of the multiparty system in 1978.

23　The Sadat regime began attacking the Labor Party in 1981, causing many of its MPs to leave it. These either chose to forgo party affiliation or joined the NDP.

24　Four Labor Party MPs were elected as independents under the individual candidate system. The party achieved a total of sixteen seats, counting those it had won under the party-list system with the Islamic Alliance (which won sixty seats).

25　There are major differences in the sources concerning the outcome of these elections.

26　The Nasserist Arab Democratic Party, legalized in 1992.

27　The al-Ghad Party was founded by Ayman Nur, a candidate in the 2005 presidential elections. The Karama Party, Nasserist in inspiration, was not legal at the time of the elections, but it still managed to win two seats under the independent candidate system.

28　Twelve seats were filled in later by-elections.

29　Addition of sixty-four seats reserved for women.

30　The cooperation with the Labor Party, which lost much of its socialist coloring during the campaign, continued with the Islamization of the party and its important newspaper al-Sha'b. Both the party and its newspaper were temporarily banned in 2000 as a result of a decision by the Political Parties Commission.

31　'Ali Fath al-Bab, MP for Tibbin/15 Mayo City from 1995 to 2010, whose career will be described in detail later.

32　Article 88 of the Constitution was amended in 2007, taking away the judges' role in supervising the polling during elections.

33　In addition to the parliamentary elections in the fall, two other rounds of voting took place in 2005. On 25 May, there was a referendum on a constitutional amendment allowing the first multi-candidate presidential elections, which then took place on 7 September of the same year. Mubarak won the elections, receiving an official figure of more than 88 percent of the votes cast, as against 7 percent for Ayman Nur, president of the al-Ghad Party, who had been imprisoned from January to March 2005 and was again in prison from December 2005 to 2009. The Brotherhood did not field a candidate in the 2005 presidential elections, and it did not indicate to its supporters how they should vote.

34 The NDP won 97 percent of the fifty-three thousand seats contested in the 2008 local council elections and more than 86 percent of the seats in the 2010 parliament.

35 These documents were given to me by one of the managers of the Brotherhood campaign in the 6 October governorate. Those quoted from here were distributed to all the governorates.

36 www.ikhwanonline.net, which should not be confused with the Brotherhood's site at www.ikhwanonline.com. Other sources, such as personal Web pages, have also been used in some cases.

37 The proportion of non-Brotherhood MPs can be calculated from Rabi' (2006b), who reports 6 percent of MPs having professional medical backgrounds and 6 percent engineering backgrounds in parliament as a whole. However, there are also some significant differences of opinion: Soleiman gives estimates of 3 percent of MPs having medical backgrounds and 5 percent being engineers (Soleiman 2006).

38 As against just 9 percent in parliament as a whole.

39 These skilled workers had graduated from technical institutes. They generally see themselves as "the elite of the working classes" (Longuenesse 2001).

40 This was by virtue of their professional activities as state schoolteachers, doctors in state hospitals, and engineers holding senior positions in the public sector or in public-sector enterprises.

41 Only 15 percent of the MB candidates in 2005 had been members of student unions previously, and only 32 percent had been members of professional syndicates.

42 Interview with Mohamed Habib in Cairo in May 2007.

43 *al-Gam'iyyat li-tanmiyyat al-mugtama'* are specific kinds of associations that work in rural areas and are generally overseen by the local authorities (Yacoub 2009).

44 Operating under the direction of the Nasser Bank, a public-sector Islamic bank set up by Sadat and overseen by the Ministry of Social Affairs, *zakat* committees can be set up in any type of institution (though generally private or public mosques, government departments, companies, hospitals, and so on) on straightforward application to a branch of the Nasser Bank (Ben Néfissa 1991). Their spread went largely unnoticed until 2005, and it was in any case encouraged by the state in the 1980s to help reduce spending on social security. As a result, the committees constituted an obvious field of activity for the Brotherhood, which used them as a substitute for its own NGOs. However, this only continued until after the 2005 elections, when a report drew attention to the situation and led to the Ministry of Social Affairs suddenly reasserting its control in 2007. According to a report in the newspaper *Sawt al-umma* (no. 325, dated 26

February 2007), at the beginning of 2007 there were 5,500 *zakat* committees dealing with a total of LE3 billion on an annual basis, with thirty-two million beneficiaries. There are also many informal *zakat* committees operating without reference to the official regulations.

45 Among them was Sheikh Sayyid 'Askar, the MP for Tanta and a senior member of the Islamic Research Academy of al-Azhar that had played an important censorship role since the 1960s. 'Askar was also the founder and vice-president of the Ulama of al-Azhar Front (Gabhat Ulamaa al-Azhar), set up in 1947 and independent of al-Azhar itself, which brought together *ulama* who had more radical and conservative views than those closer to the political authorities. The Front was particularly opposed to the then grand sheikh of al-Azhar, Sayyid al-Tantawi (in office from 1996 to 2010), which eventually led to its formal dissolution in 1998. It nevertheless continued to make its voice heard, even issuing fatwas that led to wider controversies.

## Chapter 2

1   Twenty-two percent of MPs, according to Soleiman (2006); 15 percent, according to Rabi' (2006b).

2   The increase was an effect of the judicial supervision of the 2000 and 2005 elections, which had diverted electoral fraud outside polling stations. Since the *mandubin* (the agents of the candidates) could no longer collect voting cards and vote in the voters' place, they had to find a way of bringing in and marshaling groups of voters outside the polling stations. They then found themselves having to compete with other individuals (*samasir*) claiming to marshal the voters as well, including by distributing money (Haenni 2005a; Ben Néfissa and Arafat 2005: 232).

3   Biographical information taken from the PhD thesis by Bachir Benaziz, "The Private-sector Egyptian Press: A Sociological History of a New Venue for the Production of Information" (2018). I am indebted to Bachir Benaziz for his assistance.
Interviews and informal conversations with Tibbin residents, March–April 2008 and June 2014.

4   Interviews and informal conversations with Tibbin residents, March–April 2008 and June 2014.

5   Interview with Mahmud Bakri, May 2008, Cairo.

6   The Center for Trade Union and Workers Services (CTUWS). In 2005, another cofounder of the center and former EISCO worker, Kamal 'Abbas, took up the torch to represent the left in elections.

7   The NDP candidate and MP in the 2000 elections for the workers' seat was Ibrahim Lutfi Zanati, director of public relations at Military Factory 999, vice-president of the Military Production Workers' Syndicate, vice-president of the East Helwan Youth Club, member of the Local Popular

Council for Helwan and later for the Cairo governorate, and responsible for the local and regional section of the NDP. His profile was exactly that of a classically eligible candidate, particularly since he had extensive experience in local political and administrative organizations.

8　During the same period, this syndicate leader attempted to found the Wasat Party and left the Brotherhood shortly thereafter.

9　His words: his father was an employee of the Ministry of Defense. Interview, August 2009, Helwan.

10　Nasr al-Din received 10,897 votes versus 9,321 for Sayyid Mish'al in the first round, according to the newspaper *Nuhud Helwan* (14 November 2005). In the second round, Mish'al came out ahead with 18,977 votes to 7,677. According to observers, the elections were strictly transparent in the first round, with the security services observing the rules of neutrality. In the second round, there were multiple reports of fraud, which explain the large difference between the results of the first and second rounds.

11　He had to wait until the NDP was dissolved before being elected to the House of Representatives in 2015, the new name of the lower house of parliament under President al-Sisi.

12　The differences were even more remarkable in 2000: 9.3 percent in Madinat Nasr, 25.4 percent in Helwan, and 23.5 percent in Tibbin (Rabi' 2002, 2006a, 2006b).

13　See the reports on the 2005 and 2010 election campaigns by the Egyptian Association for Community Participation Enhancement (EACPE).

14　See the report by the EACPE from 9 November 2005 (available at http://www.anhri.net/egypt/cpe/2005/pr1109.shtml)

15　Interview with Mustafa al-Sallab, May 2007, Cairo.

16　In the 1995 elections, Fath al-Bab presented himself as the candidate "officially of the Labor Party, unofficially of the Muslim Brothers," and had a profile that was "deliberately moderate and wide-ranging" (Longuenesse 1997). Ten years later, Mohamed Habib, the deputy guide of the Gama'a, commented that "they [the regime] might have thought that Fath al-Bab was not really a Brother, so they let him through the net. They thought he was closer to the Labor Party than to the Brothers" (interview, May 2007, Cairo).

17　The 2006 workers' elections were characterized by a "witch hunt against the Brothers," raising suspicions that the state's intervention had something to do with his failure to be reelected even if his popularity had been going down among the voters (Clément 2007a).

18　"Summary of Fath al-Bab's Period in Office as Representative of Personnel at al-Hadid wa-l-Sulb Factory," circulated during his 2006 reelection campaign.

19　Interview with 'Ali Fath al-Bab, May 2007, 15 Mayo.

20　Interview with 'Ali Fath al-Bab, May 2007, 15 Mayo.

21 This section draws on several interviews with Sheikh al-Muhammadi conducted in April–May 2007, December 2008, and June–September 2009. It also draws on an interview conducted by Sarah Ben Néfissa at the end of the 1990s (Ben Néfissa 2003).

22 He was also a candidate for the Shura Council, the upper house of parliament, in 1989.

23 He was secretary of the Helwan branch in 1994, and then of the South Cairo section in 1995. At the same time, he became a member of the party's Higher Committee, before joining the National Executive Committee in 1998 until the 'freeze' of the Party in 2000.

24 14 November 2005. This newspaper was close to the Brothers, and of all the examples of the local press that I was able to gather from 2005, it was the one that most often quoted Brotherhood candidates. However, the emphatic tone used to refer to al-Muhammadi was not used in the same way for Fath al-Bab.

25 According to Mohamed Habib, the deputy guide in charge of selecting candidates, interview, May 2007, Cairo.

26 Interview with 'Isam Mukhtar, May 2007, Madinat Nasr.

27 Interview with 'Isam Mukhtar in the pro-Brotherhood newspaper *Afaq 'arabiya*, no. 11, 2005.

28 We will see that this was also a way of enforcing discipline within the organization.

29 Interview with Bassim, December 2008, Madinat Nasr.

30 Interview with 'Isam Mukhtar, May 2007, Madinat Nasr.

31 The smallest unit in the organization, the *usra* (pl. *usar*), brought together five or six individuals. The next level up, the *shu'ba* (pl. *shu'ab*), brought together four to eight *usar*, and was then included in turn in a *mantiqa* and then a *muhafaza*, the highest level before the national one. See chapter three for details of the organizational structure of the Gama'a.

32 Interview with Sheikh al-Muhammadi, May 2007, Helwan.

33 See leaflet in pictures 3 and 4: "The Voice of the Workers."

34 Terms used by a resident of one of the better-off areas in the constituency (conversation, April 2007, Cairo).

35 Interview with Mustafa, May 2007, Madinat Nasr. He was becoming one of the most important of the Brotherhood's young bloggers at this time. See chapter five for details.

36 Interview with M.G of *al-Masry al-youm*, April 2007, Cairo.

37 Unlike the Kefaya demonstrations taking place in the center of Cairo in 2005, the *masirat* did not avoid the popular areas and only rarely clashed with the security forces. This is important when one remembers that one of the most important reasons for voters to stay at home on election day was the threat of violence.

38 Interview with Salma, May 2007, 15 Mayo.

39 Interview with Sheikh al-Muhammadi, May 2007, Helwan. In the popular imagination, *'asabiyya* refers to the esprit de corps characterizing a major family, a tribe, or a group originating from the same place.

40 Interview with Mohamed Habib, May 2007, Cairo.

41 Arabic for pound.

42 Interview with Hagg Nabil, May 2008, Madinat Nasr.

43 Note that he gives the MP the title of 'doctor,' whereas in fact he had a secondary technical diploma.

44 Interview with Hagg Muftah, April 2008, Wardiyyan, Alexandria.

45 The Brothers also targeted areas where the NDP had formed electoral blocs by registering the inhabitants on the electoral roll. Mohamed Habib was quite frank in admitting that the presence of electoral blocs was a determining criterion in choosing which constituencies to contest in elections. "Take the example of a village or a suburban zone where there are ten thousand inhabitants but where only one thousand or so have voters' cards . . . this is very different from an area where there are only five thousand inhabitants but where four thousand of them have voters' cards" (Interview, May 2007, Cairo).

46 Verse 88 of the *Hud* sura, or chapter, of the Qur'an: *I only intend reform as much as I am able. And my success is not but through God. Upon him I have relied, and to Him I return.*

## Chapter 3

1 Ragab Abu Zayd and Sabri 'Amir, MPs for the Minufiyya governorate.

2 When I asked one Helwan activist in an interview how they were able to meet for *shu'ba* meetings, he said, "We are going to do so this evening . . . it's X's wedding." I looked blank, and he told me that weddings were one way of holding such meetings to make it look as if nothing was happening (interview with Hamdi, a businessman, July 2009, Helwan).

3 This parliamentary committee was set up as part of the *tanzim* after the 2000 legislative elections when seventeen Brotherhood MPs were elected. The committee was institutionalized in 2005 after an increase in the number of MPs to eighty-eight. Earlier, the Labor Party had been responsible for organizing the Brothers who had been elected to parliament or to the local popular councils.

4 Interview with Saad al-Katatni, August 2009, Cairo.

5 See chapter two for an explanation of this principle.

6 Interview with Akram, August 2009, Helwan.

7 *al-Masry al-Youm*, 8 May 2008.

8 There was another office on the ground floor of a building that also housed the medical office of the MP's son (a GP).

9 This section draws on interviews carried out with twelve of the core

activists. I also met several others, usually younger, who frequently worked in the sheikh's offices but were not responsible for the activities.

10 Interview with Gamal, December 2008, Helwan.

11 Interview with Akram, August 2009, Helwan.

12 See chapter one for more information about this charitable association.

13 See chapter five for an account of entry procedures to the Gama'a.

14 Interview with Muhsin, January 2009, Helwan.

15 One of them said that he was not a resident of Madinat Nasr but lived in Giza. He had been 'recruited' through a university professor in Madinat Nasr, who also lived in Giza and was a member of the Brotherhood, to man the local office during the election campaign and then to work in the al-Hay al-'Ashir office after the election. For him, the work was a paid job even though he was a Brother (interview, December 2008, Madinat Nasr).

16 Interview, July 2009, Madinat Nasr.

17 Interview with 'Isam Mukhtar in the presence of Bassim and Hadi, December 2008, Madinat Nasr.

18 Interview with Bassim, December 2008, Madinat Nasr.

19 Interview with Hadi, December 2008, Madinat Nasr.

20 There were five other offices in the former small towns of Tibbin, Kafr al-'Ilu, and Helwan al-Balad and in the 'Arab Ghunim and 'Izbat al-Walda informal areas.

21 Interview with 'Ali Fath al-Bab, Salma, and Farida, December 2008, 15 Mayo.

22 'Ali Fath al-Bab emphasized this point by saying that the office could never be used for Brotherhood meetings, as it was linked to his position as an MP, which had nothing to with his activities as a Brother.

23 These interventions were collected from publications of the Communication Center of the parliamentary bloc, as well as the leaflets produced by the offices of the three MPs studied. Internal reports of parliamentary activities were also used, as well as copies of some speeches.

24 *Report on the Activities of MP Maqsud 2008*, internal document, p. 13.

25 Ben Néfissa's article draws on an internal report of the LPC chaired by the sheikh.

26 Interview with 'Abd al-Rahman, January 2009, Helwan.

27 Interview with Akram, August 2009, Helwan.

28 Interview with 'Umar, a lawyer close to the Brotherhood and an observer of local life in 15 Mayo, September 2009.

29 Interview with 'Ali Fath al-Bab, Salma, and Farida, December 2008, 15 Mayo.

30 Observations in the field, January 2009, Helwan.

31 Interview with Hadi, December 2008, Madinat Nasr.

32 Interview, November 2010, Madinat Nasr.

## Chapter 4

1   According to a leaflet produced to mark the end of Mukhtar's term in office, these ceremonies recognized more than one thousand students, two hundred and fifty mothers, and four hundred workers in Madinat Nasr over a five-year period.

2   Annual quotas are established for different organizations by country in order to control the number of pilgrims.

3   An internal document from the Madinat Nasr office gives a figure of LE1,950 as the cost of organizing the exemplary mother event. For Hadayek Helwan, Ibrahim provided an account of the cost of activities over a period of thirteen months, showing that these had reached LE38,800, with LE14,000 being the fixed costs for each month.

4   For many Egyptians, Ahmed Ezz was an emblematic figure of the corruption of the Mubarak regime. A businessman and CEO of the largest steel company in Egypt, having illegally acquired control of three-quarters of national production, he was also an MP from 2000 to 2011, a member of the NDP's influential Political Bureau, and close to Gamal Mubarak. Ezz was sentenced to ten years in prison in September 2011 but was released on bail in 2014 and acquitted on certain charges.

5   Interview with 'Isam Mukhtar, Bassim, and Hadi, December 2008, Madinat Nasr.

6   It should be noted that sixteen of the accused lived in Constituency 5 in Madinat Nasr. See also the report of the Sawasya Center (no date, 314ff).

7   Interview with Akram, August 2009, Helwan.

8   Interview with Sheikh al-Muhammadi, May 2007, Helwan.

9   Interview with Akram, August 2009, Helwan.

10  Interview with Bassim, December 2008, Madinat Nasr.

11  Based on two interviews with Ayman in May and December 2008.

12  In addition to the works by Clark, Wickham, Bayat, and Masoud already mentioned, see also the approaches of Sullivan and Abed-Kotob (1999) and Siyam (2006).

13  See chapter one.

14  There were 1,208 *khayri* hospitals in Egypt in 2008 as compared to 1,187 public ones. Among the latter, various types of hospital need to be distinguished, including university hospitals, hospitals only treating patients covered by medical insurance or other categories, and hospitals run by the Ministry of Health. The latter are those understood to be *mustashfayyat 'amma* (public hospitals). There were 1,049 hospitals of this type, each having an average of seventy-five beds (al-Merghani: 2009). Al-Hadi Hospital was thus comparable to a hospital of this size.

15 Interview with Ehab, August 2009, Helwan.

16 An official at al-Hadi Hospital explained its rules during my visit, including not smoking, not talking or making noise in the corridors, and having good relations with colleagues. There was segregation of the sexes in only two departments, and then only if the patient wished it, these being dentistry and gynecology. He said that "this doesn't enter the minds of a lot of people, and we don't want to go in that direction."

17 State Security prevented him from standing as a candidate for the association's board and took away his membership in the GS. He filed a complaint with an administrative tribunal, which upheld his complaint on two counts. However, the judgment was only ever partially applied, and he was only able to keep his membership in the GS.

18 I observed dignitaries from the GS present during Brotherhood election meetings. Ibrahim, the manager of the MP's office in Hadayek Helwan, explained the details of the agreement between the sheikh and the GS to organize an aid convoy to Gaza during the war in the winter of 2008–2009. There were also other forms of partnership on a more everyday basis, including renting a room to organize an event, sending constituency residents who had asked for long-term help to the association, sharing information gathered from the GS's social surveys, and so on.

19 The former deputy guide of the Gama'a, Mohamed Habib, said that "the Brothers do not have a relationship with the GS. . . . They have their own principles and their own rules, their own financing, and their own personnel" (interview, May 2007, Cairo).

20 Interview with Akram, August 2009, Helwan.

21 See the continuation of the debate in chapter six.

22 Field observation and informal conversation, April 2008, Helwan.

23 Field observation, September 2009.

24 See chapter two.

25 Based on two interviews with Muhsin in December 2008 and January 2009, Helwan, along with several informal conversations.

26 Interview, January 2009, Helwan.

27 Interview with Ruh, December 2008, Helwan.

28 She introduced herself using this title in French, which is often used in Egypt to address a married woman from the middle or upper classes.

29 Based on an interview with Wafa' in July 2009, along with several informal conversations.

30 Wafa' was alluding to an episode that she went on to explain in more detail later in the interview. "In 2008, I went with a woman I know to the event for exemplary mothers [organized by the NDP], as she was taking part in the competition. They were giving out the best prizes to the people they knew! It was a young woman who didn't wear the veil who won the 'umra, even though there were older and sick women [ta'banin] and

widows there as well who didn't get anything. Is that right? It's always the same ones who win the prizes from one year to the next because they belong to them *[humma min-hum]*. The poor *[al-ghalbanin]* never win, and their [that is, the NDP's] friends win twice over."

31 Conversation with residents of the district met at the student award ceremony in 2009. All of them had been to other events organized by al-Bakri and the local section of the NDP that year. In order to stave off the competition, the NDP had also organized its event on the same day as the one to be held by the Brotherhood MP, forcing the latter to postpone the event. A journalist I met by chance in downtown Cairo who happened to have spent his childhood in 15 Mayo also told me how much he had been impressed by the student events Fath al-Bab had organized, alone at that time, at the end of the 1990s.

32 Interview with 'Ali Fath al-Bab and Salma, April 2008, 15 Mayo.

33 These terms (*tanshit* and *ibda'*) were used by the MP. He added, "We are always finding new ways to get our message out there. State Security starts running after us, and we start running as well. It's like that. There's no problem."

34 An orphan in Egypt is considered to be either a child who has lost both his parents, or one who has lost only his father, in which case he is left to be brought up by his mother, who often will not be able to find salaried employment.

35 "Fath al-Bab Weds Fourteen Young Brides in Tibbin and Mayo," 14 August 2007.

36 Interview with Farida (with Salma present), July 2009, 15 Mayo.

37 Interview with Zaki and Hayat, September 2009, Muqattam.

38 The only explicitly political speech made at the event was not made by Fath al-Bab or a member of the Brotherhood, but by a worker who declaimed humorous verses about increases in the price of bread.

39 Interview with Hadi, August 2009, Madinat Nasr.

40 For the anthropologist Talal Asad, what is called Islam is only ever one manner, among others, of understanding the sacred texts founding the religion, and of referring to them, using them for various purposes, and defining the values and practices that are regarded as fundamental within a given set of circumstances. However, when these things are reproduced, they form a tradition that reinforces the legitimacy of this one manner.

41 Even if there is of course a profound ambiguity in the idea of commanding the good, which can overlap with the moral and social control of other people. In his study of Sayyid's thought, Carré comments, "anyone who commands a virtuous society in the end is thinking of a [reign of] terror" (Carré 1984: 190).

42 Hassan al-Banna, "Aghrad al-ikhwan al-muslimin," *Jaridat al-Ikhwan al-Muslimin* 7(1352/1933), quoted by Brynjar Lia (1998: 67).

43 Imprisoned at the end of the 1940s for having defended the assassination by a Brother of then Prime Minister Nuqrashi Pasha, Sabiq was a senior official at the Ministry of Awqaf in the 1950s and 1960s before being moved to al-Azhar. He later emigrated to Saudi Arabia, where he taught at the Umm al-Qura University in Mecca and became famous throughout the Middle East as an Islamic legal scholar. He died in 2000.

44 'Amr Khaled is one of the new preachers *(al-shuyukh al-gudad)* who have been gaining momentum in Egypt since the late 1990s, and who have created a new form of preaching focused on inner spirituality, self-fulfillment, individual emotion, and efforts to create a successful life (Haenni 2002).

45 All quotations are from a document given to me by Ayman, one of the activists, and from other internal documents quoted by Sarah Ben Néfissa in her study from the late 1990s on the LPC in Helwan (Ben Néfissa 1999).

46 Interview, April 2007, Helwan.

47 Interview, August 2009, Helwan.

48 Interview with 'Abd al-Rahman and Hamdi, December 2008, Helwan.

49 The women activists used the words "I am with the Brothers" *(ana min al-Ikhwan)* and not "I am a Sister" *(ana ukht)* or "with the Sisters" *(min al-akhawat)*, which indicates that they saw the Brothers as an organization.

50 Interview with Rana, August 2009, 15 Mayo.

51 Interview with Ibrahim, September 2009, Helwan.

## Chapter 5

1 While Kandil explains his methodology as well as his different types of material in an appendix to his book (forty-two interviews, seventeen university studies, fourteen unpublished documents, and thirty-eight publications), these are mixed together in the text of the book itself and are analyzed in the same terms (completely going against the methods of Bourdieu, whom the author nevertheless cites). The following passage is just one example of this (I indicate the origin of the source material quoted in brackets): "Particularly restive Brothers are often loaded with administrative duties to absorb their excessive energy [interview]. Sameh 'Eid, for instance was saddled with 13 group meetings a month to the point where he had no time to think [published autobiography]. One way of keeping the Brothers' hands full is to oblige them to monitor their action scrupulously. General Guide Telmesani advised his followers to spend at least an hour before retiring to bed revising their actions during the day [published memoir]" (Kandil 2015: 15).

2 Al-Anani rightly mentions that "there is no fixed statement or formula for *bay'a*." However, he indicates that the "common pledge" consists of the following oath: "I pledge with God to abide by the rule of Islam and

jihad for Allah's sake, and to fulfill and commit myself to the conditions and obligations of the Muslim Brothers, and to listen to and to obey its leadership whether willingly or not as long as he succumbs to Allah. I swear by God on that and He is the witness on my pledge" (al-Anani 2016: 122).

3    Their meaning has changed over time. According to Mitchell, in 1935 there were four categories: *musaʻid*, *muntasib*, *ʻamil*, and *mujahid* (with no mention of *muntazim*) (Mitchell 1969: 183).

4    As explained in chapter three above, the *tanzim* has three dimensions: the administrative dimension (chain of command); the educational dimension (headed by the cultivation committee); and the corporatist dimension (including various committees, among them the cultivation committee). Like the other committees, the cultivation committee has regional branches, but it is by far the most powerful. Mohamed Badi,' the current supreme guide of the Brotherhood (elected in 2009), was formerly head of the cultivation committee.

5    These activities are described in an important work of reference on Brotherhood education, *Means of Education among the Muslim Brothers*, by Brotherhood veteran ʻAli ʻAbd al-Halim Mahmud, *ʻalim* of al-Azhar (1928–2014) (Mahmud, 1990).

6    Both ideas had been shown by Hossam Tammam in an earlier study (2011).

7    Ismail notes that "the share of *muʻamalat* (transactions) in collections of *fatwas* in the modern period declined because civil law regimes in many Muslim countries draw little on the Sharia. However, I suggest that there are reasons to think that this may be changing. There may be an increase in the recourse to *fatwas* dealing with transactions as individuals redirect their activities to the informal sphere which is not regulated by the state and as such would have little use for civil law to regulate their interaction" (Ismail 2007: 14).

8    The Tabligh is a Muslim missionary movement born in the 1920s on the Indian subcontinent. It is characterized by itinerant preaching and presents itself as non-political.

9    On the success of this practice in popular areas in Egypt, see Haenni 2005a.

10   Interview with Salah, January 2009, Helwan.

11   Interview with Hamdi, July 2009, Helwan.

12   Like Sheikh Sabiq (author of the guide to virtuous conduct mentioned in the previous chapter), Sheikh ʻAbd al-Hadi was an Egyptian Muslim Brother teaching Islamic history at the Umm al-Qura University in Mecca. He also presented Islamic programs on satellite TV channels.

13   Interview with Gamal, December 2008, Helwan.

14   Interview with ʻAbd al-Rahman, January 2009, Helwan.

15  Interview with 'Abd al-Rahman, January 2009, Helwan.
16  Interview with Muhsin, January 2009, Helwan.
17  See the extract from an interview on this point in chapter four.
18  Interview with Hadi, August 2009, Madinat Nasr.
19  Interview with Abu al-Qasim, July 2009, Helwan.
20  Interview with Bassim, December 2008, Madinat Nasr.
21  Interview with Mustafa, May 2007, Madinat Nasr.
22  Interview with 'Abd al-Rahman, January 2009, Helwan.
23  Gamal explained the importance of virtuous action as follows: "You go to work, you work, everything's fine, you're happy, but afterward you're not. It's not enough. I have to work for others better than I work for myself. The reason is that the more you work, the more God rewards you, and I am better, my wife is better, and my children are better. And that is what happens. Everyone likes us. The reason why people like us is the Gama'a, because it makes us better people." (Interview, December 2008, Helwan).
24  See chapter three.
25  This was how the 6 April Movement, which later played a substantial role in the 2011 revolution, first began.
26  It should be mentioned that a second type of Brotherhood blogs emerged at this time in order to denounce the repression, provide information about the military trials, and mobilize support for Brotherhood detainees. One example is the blog entitled *Ensaa* (Forget).
27  I refer to Hirshman's famous trilogy (1970) of "exit," "voice," and "loyalty."
28  I conducted five interviews and had numerous conversations with Mustafa between 2007 and 2010 and three interviews with Rafiq in 2009–10, together with numerous conversations up until 2017.
29  The romantic sphere was only explored to a limited extent. This was because of the circumstances of the fieldwork and the relationships I had with my informants, there being a certain social and religious modesty in evoking conjugal and love matters. It was also the result of my own choice, since I did not want to report on personal details mentioned in private conversations and outside the framework of formal interviews.
30  Abu al-Futuh was a Brotherhood member of the intermediate generation who developed from Salafist positions toward a reformist stance over the course of time. He joined the Brotherhood's Guidance Bureau in 1987 but was marginalized by the *tanzimiyyin*, with whom he had strong disagreements. He left the Bureau in 2009 but remained a member of the Brotherhood. These latent conflicts turned into an outright clash after the Revolution, when Abu al-Futuh decided to run as an independent candidate in the 2012 presidential elections and resigned from the Gama'a to be able to do so. While the organization had previously announced it would not be presenting a candidate in the elections,

it subsequently changed its mind and nominated Khayrat al-Shater. The latter was then prevented from running by a court order, which prompted Morsi's nomination as the Gama'a candidate (see El Sherif 2016; Wickham 2013; Trager 2016).

31  See the account of the beginning of Mustafa's career earlier in this chapter.

32  Extracts from blogs are given in italics and extracts from interviews in regular script.

33  *Ukhuwwa* was one of the five pillars that Gamal, the shopkeeper from Helwan, was able to remember from al-Banna's text, the others being *al-fahm* (understanding), *al-ikhlas* (sincerity), *al-tagarrud* (renunciation of evil desires), and *al-'amal* (work). He omitted (or professed to omit) *al-ta'a* (obedience), *al-jihad* (effort to improve the self and for Islam), *al-thabat* (constancy), and *al-tadhiyya* (sacrifice).

34  This practice, still called "the invocation of the link" *(wird al-rabita)*, is explained in the collection of prayers by al-Banna called *al-Ma'thurat*. An extract from the *wird al-rabita* had been framed and put up in the offices of Mukhtar and Sheikh al-Muhammadi.

35  A later disagreement caused Mustafa to leave the party fairly rapidly.

36  See his relationship with Hagg Nabil (as explained in chapter two).

37  As Bourdieu notes, "what the medieval theologians called in a wonderful phrase *fides implicita* [is] implicit faith, a faith that does not rise to the level of discourse but is reduced to a practical sense . . . All Churches love *fides implicita*. The idea of *fides implicita* contains the idea of entrusting oneself" (Bourdieu 1993: 164).

38  6 October is a satellite city outside Cairo.

39  Loose translation of a celebrated poem by Alphonse de Lamartine ("L'isolement"[Isolation], in the collection *Méditations poétiques*).

40  Interview with Rafiq, October 2010, Cairo.

41  Interview with Gehan, May 2014, Tibbin.

42  Author's translation.

43  al-Shafi'i, "Matshoqqesh omm es-saff," YouTube: https://youtu.be/J1FMs_dxdcg

44  Interview with 'Abd al-Rahman, December 2009, Helwan.

45  Interview with Rafiq, November 2010. He was still a member of the organization at the time.

46  Interview with Rafiq, November 2010, 6 October.

47  See the account of this event in the introduction.

48  Two other influential bloggers of the period.

49  Notice that Farid compared the *shura* in the Gama'a to the model of a political party, while in the previous quotation 'Abd al-Rahman criticized political parties precisely for their absence of *shura*. This is an example of the different uses and ways of understanding the same concept.

50 Interview with Badr (one of the main organizers of the conference), Cairo, December 2013. See also the blog "Wa'yuna nahdatuna," which describes the disagreements surrounding the conference from the inside: http://wa3yena.blogspot.com

51 The Brotherhood leadership also issued a statement forbidding all members of the organization from creating or joining any other party apart from the FJP.

52 Wissam's brother was later one of the main figures of the Rab'a al-'Adawiyya Square sit-in in summer 2013.

53 Interview with Wissam and Farid, September 2014.

54 On the Islamic Medical Association and the Doctors' Syndicate, see chapter one.

55 The SCAF (Supreme Council of the Armed Forces) put down demonstrations demanding compensation and justice for the victims of the Revolution in Mohamed Mahmoud Street in Downtown Cairo close to Tahrir Square from 19 to 25 November 2011, leading to the deaths of forty-one people. Further demonstrations were held a year later in the same street on 19 November 2012 to commemorate those who died and to protest against the presidency of Mohamed Morsi. On 22 November 2012, Morsi issued a constitutional declaration that gave him legislative powers and immunized his decisions against judicial review. This declaration triggered the demonstrations.

56 On 23 December 2011, demonstrations continued in front of the cabinet building in the form of a sit-in protesting against the appointment of Kamal al-Ganzuri as prime minister. The subsequent repression led to the deaths of seventeen people.

57 Demonstrations took place in front of the Ittihadiyya Presidential Palace to protest against the constitutional declaration issued on 22 November, in which Morsi had given himself full powers until the adoption of a new constitution and the election of a new parliament. A small number of demonstrators organized a sit-in during the night, and Morsi supporters dislodged them using violent means. The clashes led to the deaths of eleven people.

58 Interview with Mohamed al-Qassas, December 2013. On this period of cooperation, see Shehata (2010).

59 Habib had announced his resignation in 2010 after controversial internal elections that had resulted in Mohammed Badi' becoming supreme guide (see also chapter three).

60 I refer here to Howard Becker's labeling theory of deviance (Becker 1973), according to which the deviants are members of a group who are labeled as such because they have broken certain rules applied by the group. However, rules and their application can change under certain circumstances, which makes the labeling of deviants a dynamic process.

61  We can assume that the exit of dissident figures from the previous generation (such as Mustafa, Rafiq, and al-Qassas) had created space within the *tanzim* for the rapid promotion of younger activists who were less experienced but less polemical, such as Farid and Wissam.

62  I am paraphrasing Lahire (2006: 28). See also Lahire 2003.

## Chapter 6

1  Interview with Hamdi, July 2009, Helwan.

2  Interview with 'Abd al-Rahman, December 2009, Helwan.

3  Interview with 'Abd al-Rahman, December 2009, Helwan.

4  See the beginning of this dialogue in the box in chapter four.

5  Pressure from the security services had prevented them from carrying out certain activities, including the famous *masirat* that had marked the 2005 campaign.

6  One of them indeed told me that he was an engineer, another a representative for an IT company, and a third an employee in local government.

7  Note that this is, again, the eighty-eighth verse of the Hud sura, the same verse that was used on leaflets during parliamentary elections.

8  Observation in the field, 2 April 2008, Mina al-Basal.

9  See the reports produced by the al-Nadeem Center for the Rehabilitation of the Victims of Violence, an NGO: *Days of Torture: Women in Police Custody* (2004) and *Torture in Egypt: 2003–2006* (2006), available at www.alnadeem.org.

10  The Freedom and Justice Party, the political party of the Muslim Brotherhood, won 44 percent of the seats in parliament in December 2011–January 2012. In the presidential election in May–June 2012, Morsi won 25 percent of the vote on the first round and then just under 52 percent on the second round against Ahmed Shafiq, who was supported by the army and members of the former Mubarak regime, among others. For an analysis of the MB's electoral strategies during this period, see Pahwa 2017.

11  Interview with Mansour, village in the Banha governorate, December 2013.

12  The parliamentary elections were held between 28 November 2011 and 11 January 2012 in three phases, and were organized under a parallel voting system. Two-thirds of the seats were elected by party-list proportional representation. The remaining one-third were elected under the first-past-the-post system providing two seats ('workers' and 'fi'at' in each constituency).

13  The Tamarrod, or "Rebellion," movement grew up around a petition demanding the resignation of President Morsi that collected between 15 and 22 million signatures. The movement called for a demonstration against Morsi on 30 June 2013, with now well-known consequences.

14  In February 2012, the Higher Constitutional Court recommended the dissolution of parliament on the grounds that the law under which it had been elected was unconstitutional. The SCAF implemented this order by decree in June 2012 between the two rounds of the presidential elections.

15  See the reference to the event made by Wissam and Farid in chapter five.

16  General elections were held between October 2012 and February 2013 after Morsi was elected president and had resigned from the party. Numerous conflicts erupted, the most visible being one opposing the candidates running for the party's presidency, Saad al-Katatni (who finally won) and 'Isam al-'Iryan.

17  Interview with Wissam, Istanbul, September 2014.

18  There were one hundred and seventy in 2005, but four had died by 2011.

19  Interview with M., June 2014, Tibbin.

20  Interview with A., June 2014, Tibbin.

21  It should be emphasized that some of them were not members of the Brotherhood. I met a female student at al-Azhar, for example, who had been arrested for defending another student who was being harassed by the police. She left for Istanbul as soon as she could afterward, where she was living in difficult circumstances. Interview with I., August 2014, Istanbul.

22  Interview with Hakim and Wissam, December 2014, Istanbul.

23  IHH (in Turkish: İnsani Hak ve Hurriyetler, İnsani Yardım Vakfı) is one of the largest Islamic NGOs in Turkey, managing humanitarian programs in one hundred and twenty countries. It was founded in 1992 by the German branch of the Islamist and nationalist movement Milli Görüş, led by Necmettin Erbakan, to organize humanitarian missions in Bosnia during the Balkan war. It got involved in the Egyptian case after the July 2013 coup d'état by sending an observation mission and alerting the international community to the possibility of massive repression of Morsi's supporters. The IHH is also reported to have engaged in informal negotiations with the new military leaders in Egypt to find a solution to the crisis (Tabak 2015). After the Rab'a massacre, the NGO sent numerous letters to the United Nations and the International Criminal Court, filed a complaint with an Istanbul court against the new Egyptian leaders for crimes against humanity, and organized demonstrations in Turkey mobilizing its approximately 100,000 volunteers. However, my field research with this NGO showed that these demonstrations were organized by Turkish actors only and that the IHH had almost no connection with the exiled Muslim Brotherhood in Istanbul, at least between 2013 and 2016 (Vannetzel 2018).

24  See the account of their careers in chapter five.

25  Interview with Muhsin, January 2009, Helwan.

# Bibliography

## Primary Sources
### State Institutions
CAPMAS (Central Agency for Public Mobilization and Statistics). http://www.msrintranet.capmas.gov.eg

CAPMAS/OUCC. "One-century census 1896–1996." CD-ROM, EGIPTE, edited in cooperation with CEDEJ (Centre d'études et de documentation économiques, juridiques et sociales, French research center in Cairo).

Electoral Committee: http://www.elections.eg.

### Non-Governmental Organizations (NGOs)
Dar al-Khadamat al-Naqabiyya wa-l-'Ummaliyya (Center for Trade Union and Workers Services [CTUWS]). http://www.ctuws.com/

Democracy Reporting International, Egyptian Organization for Human Rights (DRI), 2007. *Assessment of the Electoral Framework: Final Report, Arab Republic of Egypt.* http://aceproject.org/ero-en/regions/mideast/EG/egypt-final-report-assessment-of-the-electoral/at_download/file

Egyptian Association for Supporting Democratic Development (EASDD) and Egyptian Center for Development and Democratic Studies (ECDDS). *Observation Campaign on the 2008 Local Popular Councils' Elections.* http://www.egyelections.com/primary_1.pdf

*al-Gam'iyya al-misriyya li-l-nuhud bi-l-musharaka al-mugtama'iyya* (The Egyptian Association for Community Participation Enhancement [EACPE]). *Observation Reports on the 2005 and 2010 Parliamentary Elections (Various Constituencies).* http://www.mosharka.org

Land Center for Human Rights. *Egypt's Workers' Demands for Change.* Cairo: Economic and Social Rights Series 82. http://www.lchreg.org/114/eco287e.zip

Sawasya Center (affiliated with the Muslim Brotherhood).

*al-Muʻarada al-mustabaha: taqrir hawla al-muhakama al-ʻaskariyya li-qiyyadat al-Ikhwan al-Muslimin 14/12/2006–15/04/2008.* Cairo: n.d.

### Websites of the Egyptian Muslim Brotherhood
2005 election campaign: www.ikhwan.net (CVs of candidates online).
Muslim Brothers' parliamentary bloc: www.nowabikhwan.com. Includes personal pages of Members of Parliament, in particular of 'Isam Mukhtar, 'Ali Fath al-Bab, and al-Muhammadi 'Abd al-Maqsud ("Parliamentary Activities," "News from the MP," "Achievements and Services")
Helwan MP: http://nwabhelwan.maktoobblog.com/ www.forhelwan.com
Biographical data on MPs and leaders of the organization: Ikhwanwiki.com
Video broadcasts: www.ikhwantube.org

### Documents Distributed by the Brotherhood MP's Teams
#### Documents related to elections
Electoral leaflets, press articles, and partial results of the 1995 elections in Helwan and Tibbin/15 Mayo (archives provided by Elisabeth Longuenesse).
Electoral leaflets related to the 2005 parliamentary elections in Helwan, Tibbin/15 Mayo, and Madinat Nasr (including archives provided by Nefissa Dessouki).
Partial detailed results of the 2005 elections in Helwan by polling stations.
Electoral leaflets related to the 2008 local elections in Helwan and Alexandria.
Thank-you flyers addressed to local residents.
Special issue of the newspaper *Afaq 'arabiya*, no. 11, November 2005, introducing the Muslim Brotherhood's candidates in Madinat Nasr.
*Idarat al-hamla al-intikhabiyya* 2010: Internal document preparing the electoral campaign of the 2010 parliamentary elections in 6 October.

### Publications issued by the MPs' offices (2005–10)
Several issues of Sheikh al-Muhammadi's newspaper *al-Muhammadi* in Helwan.
Several issues of 'Ali Fath al-Bab's newspaper *Li-kull al-nas* in Tibbin/15 Mayo.
Several issues of 'Ali Fath al-Bab's and Sheikh al-Muhammadi's newspaper *Ma' al-nas* in Helwan and Tibbin/15 Mayo.
Leaflet "Lamahat 'an al-rihla al-barlamaniya" assessing 'Isam Mukhtar's achievements in Madinat Nasr, October 2010.
Several newsletters and flyers issues by Brotherhood MPs in the Mina al-Basal and Raml constituencies in Alexandria.

CD-ROMs containing videos and pictures of activities and events organized by the MPs in Madinat Nasr, Helwan, and Tibbin/15 Mayo.

Greeting cards, invitations, and posters advertising events and activities.

## Internal documents of the MPs' offices (2005–10)

Partial reports of daily activities in Helwan and Madinat Nasr.

Budget documents for some activities in Helwan and Madinat Nasr.

Application forms filled in by local residents for the Exemplary Family Day in Helwan.

Archive of the Helwan Local Council ("The CPL in a Few Lines: Reform, Consultation, Construction").

## Documents relating to parliamentary interventions (2005–10)

Letters of individual and collective requests to the administration.

Partial assessments of Sheikh al-Muhammadi's and 'Isam Mukhtar's parliamentary interventions.

Brochure published by the Communication Center of the Muslim Brotherhood Parliamentary Bloc, entitled *Light on the Performance of the Muslim Brotherhood Parliamentary Bloc from 2005 to 2010*, published in autumn 2010 (96 pp.).

Texts of about thirty interpellations given by the permanent member of the parliamentary bloc.

CD-ROM containing an incomplete list of the main interpellations and texts of the spokesperson of the block (Hamdi Hasan).

## Secondary Sources

Abed-Kotob, Sana. 1995. "The Accommodationists Speak: Goals and Strategies of the Muslim Brotherhood in Egypt." *International Journal of Middle East Studies* 27 (3), pp.321–39.

Abélès, Marc. 1991. *Quiet Days in Burgundy: A Study of Local Politics*. Cambridge: Cambridge University Press; Paris: Editions de la Maison des Sciences de l'Homme.

Aclimandos, Tewfiq. 2010. "Splendeurs et misères du clientélisme." In "La Fabrique des élections," Égypte Monde arabe, edited by F. Kohstall and F. Vairel, 3rd series, no. 7: 197–219.

Albrecht, Holger. 2005. "How Can Opposition Support Authoritarianism? Lessons from Egypt." *Democratization* 12, no. 3: 378–97.

Amar, Paul. 2011. "Turning the Gendered Politics of the Security State Inside Out?" *International Feminist Journal of Politics* 13, no. 3: 299–328.

al-Anani, Khalil. 2007. *al-Ikhwan al-Muslimun fi Misr: Shuykhukha tusari' al-zaman*. Cairo: Maktabat al-Shuruq al-Dawliya.

————. 2016. *Inside the Muslim Brotherhood: Religion, Identity, and Politics.* Oxford: Oxford University Press.

Arafat, Alaa al-Din. 2009. *The Mubarak Leadership and Future of Democracy in Egypt.* New York: Palgrave Macmillan.

al-Arian, Abdullah. 2014. *Answering the Call: Popular Islamic Activism in Sadat's Egypt.* New York: Oxford University Press.

Asad, Talal. 1986. *The Idea of an Anthropology of Islam.* Occasional Paper Series. Washington, DC: Georgetown University Center for Contemporary Arab Studies.

Atia, Mona. 2012. "A Way to Paradise: Pious Neo-liberalism, Islam, and Faith-based Development." *Annals of the Association of American Geographers* 102, no. 4: 808–27.

'Awad, Huda Raghib, and Hasanayn Tawfiq. 1996. *al-Ikhwan al-Muslimun wa-l-siyasa fi Misr: dirasa fi al-tahalufat al-intikhabiyya wa-l-mumarasat al-barlamaniyya li-l-Ikhwan al-Muslimun fi zil al-ta'addudiyya al-siyasiyya al-muqayyada (1984–1990).* Cairo: al-Mahrusa.

al-Awadi, Hesham. 2004. *In Pursuit of Legitimacy: The Muslim Brothers and Mubarak, 1982–2000.* London: Tauris.

al-Banna, Hassan. 2002. *Majmu'at al-rasa'il.* Cairo: Dar El Shorouk.

Bayart, Jean-François. 1985. "L'énonciation du politique." *Revue française de science politique* 35, no. 3: 343–73.

Bayart, Jean-François, Achille Mbembe, and Comi Toulabor. 1992. *La politique par le bas in Afrique noire.* Paris: Karthala.

Bayat, Asef. 2005. "Islamism and Social Movement Theory." *Third World Quarterly* 26, no. 6: 891–908.

————. 2007. *Making Islam Democratic: Social Movements and the Post-Islamist Turn.* Stanford, CA: Stanford University Press.

Becker, Howard S. 1973. *Outsiders: Studies in the Sociology of Deviance.* New York: Free Press.

————. 1998. *Tricks of the Trade: How to Think about Your Research While You're Doing It.* Chicago: University of Chicago Press.

Ben Néfissa, Sarah. 1991. "Zakât officielle et zakât non officielle aujourd'hui en Égypte." *Égypte Monde arabe*, 1st series, no. 7, 105–20.

————. 1995. "Les ligues régionales et les associations islamiques en Égypte: deux formes de regroupements à vocation sociale et caritative." *Revue Tiers-Monde* 141: 163–77.

————. 1996. "Les partis politiques égyptiens entre les contraintes du système politique et le renouvellement des élites." *Revue du monde musulman et de la Méditerranée* 81–82: 55–87.

————. 1999. "Morale individuelle et politique: L'expérience d'un conseil municipal islamiste dans le quartier de Hélouan." *La Lettre d'information de l'Observatoire urbain du Caire contemporain* 49: 20–29.

————. 2000. "Pluralisme juridique et ordre politique urbain au Caire: les faux-semblants des majâlis 'urfiyya." In *Un passeur entre les mondes: le livre des anthropologues du Droit, disciples et amis du Recteur Michel Alliot*, edited by E. Le Roy, 207–26. Paris: Publications de la Sorbonne.

———. 2003."Citoyenneté morale en Égypte: Une association entre Etat et Frères musulmans." In *ONG et gouvernance dans le monde arabe; L'enjeu démocratique*, edited by Sarah Ben Néfissa et al., 213–70. Paris: Editions Karthala et CEDEJ.

———. 2009. "Cairo's City Government: The Crisis of Local Administration and the Refusal of Urban Citizenship." In *Cairo Contested: Governance, Urban Space and Global Modernity*, edited by D. Singerman, 177–97. Cairo: The American University in Cairo Press.

———. 2017. "La production du 'vrai musulman' par l'organisation des Frères musulmans égyptiens: Fidélité et dissidences." *Revue internationale des études du développement* 229: 185–207.

Ben Néfissa, Sarah, and Alaa al-Din Arafat. 2005. *Vote et démocratie dans l'Égypte contemporaine*. Paris: Karthala-IRD.

Ben Néfissa, Sarah, and Mahmoud Hamdy Abo El-Kasem. 2015. "L'organisation des Frères musulmans égyptiens à l'aune de l'hypothèse qutbiste." *Revue Tiers Monde* 222: 103–22.

Berman, Bruce, and John Lonsdale. 1992. *Unhappy Valley: Conflict in Kenya and Africa*. London: James Currey.

Bernard-Maugiron, Nathalie. 2010. "Les juges et la supervision des élections de 2005." In *La Fabrique des élections*, edited by F. Kohstall and F. Vairel, Égypte Monde arabe, 3rd series, no. 7, 129–56.

Bianchi, Robert. 1989. *Unruly Corporatism: Associational Life in Twentieth-century Egypt*. New York and Oxford: Oxford University Press.

Blaydes, Lisa. 2009. "Women's Electoral Participation in Egypt: The Implications of Gender for Voter Recruitment and Mobilization." *Middle East Journal* 63, no. 3: 364–80.

———. 2010. *Elections and Distributive Politics in Mubarak's Egypt*. New York: Cambridge University Press.

Boltanski, Luc, and Laurent Thévenot. 1991. *De la justification*. Paris: Gallimard.

Bourdieu, Pierre. 1986. "L'illusion biographique." *Actes de la recherche en sciences sociales* 62–63: 69–72.

———. 1993. *Sociology in Question*. London: Sage Publications.

———. 1998. *Practical Reason: On the Theory of Action*. Stanford, CA: Stanford University Press.

Brooke, Steven. 2015. *The Muslim Brotherhood's Social Outreach after the Egyptian Coup*. Brookings Institution Working Paper. Washington: Brookings Institution.

———. 2019. *Winning Hearts and Votes: Social Services and the Islamist Political Advantage*. Ithaca, NY: Cornell University Press.

Brumberg, Daniel. 2002. "The Trap of Liberalized Autocracy." *Journal of Democracy* 13, no. 4: 56–68.

Camau, Michel, and Vincent Geisser. 2003. *Le Syndrome autoritaire: Politique en Tunisie de Bourguiba à Ben Ali*. Paris: Presses de Sciences Po.

Carré, Olivier. 1984. *Mystique et politique: le Coran des islamistes. Lecture révolutionnaire du Coran par Sayyid Qutb, Frère musulman radical*. Paris: Presses de Sciences Po.

Clark, Janine. 2004. *Islam, Charity, and Activism: Middle-class Networks and Social Welfare in Egypt, Jordan, and Yemen*. Bloomington: Indiana University Press.

Clément, Françoise. 2007a. "Elections ouvrières: entre fraude et chasse aux Frères masqués." In *Chroniques égyptiennes 2006*, edited by C. Hassabo and E. Klaus, 59–86. Cairo: CEDEJ.

———. 2007b. "Réformer l'assurance en Égypte pour résorberson déficit? Enquête sur un alibi." *Égypte Monde arabe*, 3rd series, no. 4: 303–41.

Cook, Michael. 2000. *Commanding Right and Forbidding Wrong in Islamic Thought*. Cambridge: Cambridge University Press.

Crozier, Michel, and Erhard Friedberg. 1980. *Actors and Systems: The Politics of Collective Action*. Chicago: University of Chicago Press.

De Certeau, Michel. 1980. *L'invention du quotidien*. Vol. 1, *Arts de faire*. Paris: Gallimard.

Denis, Eric. 1995. "Le Caire, aspects sociaux del'étalementurbain: entre spécialisation et mixité." *Égypte Monde arabe*, 1st series, no. 23: 77130.

Depaule, Jean-Claude, and Galila El Kadi. 1990. "New Settlements: une réponse à la surpopulation?" *Égypte Monde arabe*, first series, no. 1: 187–97.

Dessouki, Nefissa. 2010. "Représentations du rôle du député chez les électeurs égyptiens: le cas des circonscriptions 24 et 25 de Hélouane." In "La Fabrique des élections," edited by F. Kohstall and F. Vairel, Égypte Monde arabe, 3rd series, no. 7: 47–67.

Dufoix, Stéphane. 2002. *Politiques d'exil: Hongrois, Polonais et Tchécoslovaques en France après 1945*. Paris: Presses universitaires françaises.

ElShobaki, Amr. 2009. *Les Frères musulmans des origines à nos jours*. Paris: Karthala.

Elyachar, Julia. 2003. "Mappings of Power: The State, NGOs, and International Organizations in the Informal Economy of Cairo." *Comparative Studies in Society and History* 45, no. 3 (July): 571–605.

Fahmy, Ninette. 1998. "The Performance of the Egyptian Muslim Brotherhood in the Egyptian Syndicates: An Alternative Formula for Reform?" *Middle East Journal* 52, no. 4: 551–62.

———. 2002. *The Politics of Egypt: State–Society Relationship*. London and New York: Routledge.

Fakhoury, Hani. 1972. *Kafr al-'Elow: An Egyptian Village in Transition*. New York: Holt Rinehart and Winston.

Farag, Iman. 1992. "Croyance et intérêt: réflexion sur deux associations islamiques." In *Modernisation et nouvelles formes de mobilisation sociale, 2, Égypte-Turquie. Actes des Journées d'Etudes tenues au Caire, les 8, 9, 10 juin 1990*, 127–40. Cairo: CEDEJ.

Ferrié, Jean-Noël. 2003. "Les limites de la démocratisation par la société civile en Afrique du Nord." *Maghreb-Machrek* 75: 15–33.

Foucault, Michel. 1997. *Ethics: Subjectivity and Truth*. Vol. 1 of *The Essential Works of Michel Foucault 1954–1984*, edited by P. Rabinow. New York: New Press.

———. 2004. *Naissancedelabiopolitique: Coursau Collège deFrance, 1978–1979*. Paris: Gallimard/Seuil.

Fuchs-Ebaugh, Helen. 1988. *Becoming an Ex: The Process of Role Exit*. Chicago: University of Chicago Press.

Geertz, Clifford. 1973. "Thick Description: Toward an Interpretive Theory of Culture." In *The Interpretation of Cultures: Selected Essays*, 3–30. New York: Basic Books.

al-Ghobashy, Mona. 2005. "The Metamorphosis of the Egyptian Muslim Brothers." *International Journal of Middle East Studies* 37, no. 3: 373–95.

Ginzburg, Carlo. 1989. *Clues, Myths and the Historical Method*. Baltimore: Johns Hopkins University Press.

Goffman, Erving. 1959. "The Moral Career of the Mental Patient." *Psychiatry* 22, no. 2: 123–42.

———. 1974. *Frame Analysis: An Essay on the Organization of Experience*. London: Harper and Row.

Haenni, Patrick. 1997. "Gérer les normes extérieures: Le penchant occidental de la bienfaisance islamique en Égypte." *Égypte Monde arabe*, 1st series, no. 30–31: 275–91.

———. 2002. "Au-delà du repli identitaire: Les nouveaux prêcheurs égyptiens et la modernisation paradoxale de l'islam." *Religioscope*.

———. 2005a. *L'ordre des caïds: Conjurer la dissidence urbaine au Caire*. Paris: Karthala; Cairo: CEDEJ.

———. 2005b. *L'islam de marché: l'autre révolution conservatrice*. Paris: Seuil/La République des idées.

Harrigan, Jane, and Hamid El-Said. 2009. *Economic Liberalisation, Social Capital and Islamic Welfare Provision*. Hampshire and New York: Palgrave Macmillan.

Hasan, Ahmed H. 2000. *al-Su'ud al-siyasi li-l-Islam dakhil al-naqabat al-mihniya*. Cairo: al-Dar al-Thaqafiya li-l-Nashr.

Hirschman, Albert O. 1970. *Exit, Voice, and Loyalty: Responses to Decline in Firms, Organizations, and States*. Cambridge: Harvard University Press.

Ibrahim, Solava. 2007. "The Role of Local Councils in Empowerment and Poverty Reduction in Egypt." *Cairo Papers in Social Science* 27, no. 3.

Ismail, Salwa. 2000. "The Popular Movement Dimensions of Contemporary

Militant Islamism: Socio-spatial Determinants in the Cairo Urban Setting." *Comparative Studies in Society and History* 42, no. 2: 363–39.

———. 2003. *Rethinking Islamist Politics: Culture, the State and Islamism*. London: I.B. Tauris.

———. 2006. *Political Life in Cairo's New Quarters: Encountering the Everyday State*. Minneapolis: University of Minnesota Press.

———. 2007. "Islamism, Re-Islamization and the Fashioning of Muslim Selves: Refiguring the Public Sphere." *Muslim World Journal of Human Rights* 4, no. 1: 263–86.

Jossifort, Sabine. 1995. "L'aventure des villes nouvelles." *Égypte Monde arabe*, 1st series, no. 23: 169–94.

El Kadi, Galila. 1990. "Trente ans deplanification urbaine au Caire."*Tiers-Monde* 31, no. 121: 185–207.

Kandil, Hazem. 2015. *Inside the Brotherhood*. Cambridge and Malden: Polity Press.

Kassem, Maye. 1999. *In the Guise of Democracy: Governance in Contemporary Egypt*. Reading: Ithaca Press, Garnet Publishing.

———. 2004. *Egyptian Politics: The Dynamics of Authoritarian Rule*. Boulder, CO: Lynne Rienner.

Kepel, Gilles. 1985. *Muslim Extremism in Egypt: The Prophet and Pharaoh*. London: Al Saqi Books.

Kienle, Eberhard. 1998. "More than a Response to Islamism: The Political Deliberalization of Egypt in the 1990s."*Middle East Journal* 52, no. 2: 219–35.

Kohstall, Florian, and Frédéric Vairel. 2010. "Introduction: Les élections législatives et présidentielles en Égypte de 2005 à 2010." Égypte Monde arabe, 3rd series, no. 7: 1-18.

Lagroye, Jacques. 2003. "Les processus de politisation." In *La politisation*, edited by J. Lagroye, 359–72. Paris: Belin.

———. 2009. *Appartenir à une institution: Catholiques en France aujourd'hui*. Paris: Economica.

Lahire, Bernard. 2003. "From the Habitus to an Individual Heritage of Dispositions: Towards a Sociology at the Level of the Individual." *Poetics* 31, no. 5–6: 329–55.

———. 2006. *La culture des individus: Dissonances culturelles et distinction de soi*. Paris: La Découverte.

———. 2011. *The Plural Actor*. Cambridge and Malden: Polity Press.

Leila, Reem. 2010. "Plastic Smiles."*Al-Ahram Weekly*, no. 1015, 16–22 September.

Lia, Brynjar. 1998. *The Society of the Muslim Brothers in Egypt: The Rise of an Islamic Mass Movement 1928–1942*. Reading: Ithaca Press.

Linz, Juan J. 1975. "Totalitarian and Authoritarian Regimes." In *Handbook of Political Science*, vol. 3, *Macropolitical Theory*, edited by F. Greenstein and N. Polsby, 291–328. Reading, MA: Addison-Wesley.

Longuenesse, Elisabeth. 1997. "Logiques d'appartenances et dynamiques électorales dans une banlieue ouvrière: le cas de la circonscription 25, Helwan." In *Contours et détours du politique en Égypte: Les élections législatives de 1995*, edited by S. Gamblin, 228–64. Paris: Karthala; Cairo: CEDEJ.

———. 2001. "Constructions professionnelles et luttes de classement en Egypte: L'exemple des 'professions techniques appliquées.'" *Sociétés contemporaines* 43: 121–45.

Longuenesse, Elisabeth, and Abd al-Masih Felly Youssef. 1999. "Affaires et politique au Caire: L'exemple du quartier de Sayyeda Zaynab." *Maghreb-Machrek* 166: 53–69.

Lust-Okar, Ellen. 2005. *Structuring Conflict in the Arab World: Incumbents, Opponents, and Institutions*. Cambridge: Cambridge University Press.

Mahmood, Saba. 2005. *Politics of Piety: The Islamic Revival and the Feminist Subject*. Princeton, NJ: Princeton University Press.

Mahmud, 'Ali Abd al-Halim. 1990. *Wasa'il al-tarbiyya 'ind al-ikhwan al-muslimin*, Mansura: Dar al-Wafa'.

Makram-Ebeid, Dina. 2012. *Manufacturing Stability: Everyday Politics of Work in an Industrial Steel Town in Helwan, Egypt*. London: London School of Economics and Political Science.

Mannheim, Karl. 1952. "The Problem of Generations." In *Essays on the Sociology of Knowledge*, edited by P. Kecskemeti, 276–320. London: Routledge.

Masoud, Tarek. 2014. *Counting Islam: Religion, Class, and Elections in Egypt*. Cambridge: Cambridge University Press.

Massicard, Elise. 2015. "The Incomplete Civil Servant? The Figure of the Neighbourhood Headman (Muhtar)." In *Order and Compromise: Government Practices in Turkey from the Late Ottoman Empire to the Early 21st Century*, edited by M. Aymes, B. Gourisse, and E. Massicard, 256–90. Leiden: Brill.

Mead, George H. 1934. *Mind, Self, and Society from the Standpoint of a Social Behaviorist*. Edited by C.W. Morris. Chicago: University of Chicago Press.

Menza, Mohamed Fahmy. 2012. *Patronage Politics in Egypt: The National Democratic Party and Muslim Brotherhood in Cairo*. New York: Routledge.

———. 2019. "Cairo's New Old Faces: Redrawing the Map of Patron–Client Networks after 2011." In *Clientelism and Patronage in the Middle East and North Africa: Networks of Dependency*, edited by L. Ruiz de Elvira, C.H. Schwarz, and I. Weipert-Fenner, 98–117. Oxford and New York: Routledge.

al-Merghani, Elhami. 2009. "Khaskhasat al-khadamat al-sihhiyya." Unpublished.

al-Messiri, Sawsan. 1978. *Ibn al-balad: A Concept of Egyptian Identity*. Leiden: E.J. Brill.

Mitchell, Richard P. 1969. *The Society of the Muslim Brothers*. New York: Oxford University Press.

Mitchell, Timothy. 1991. "The Limits of the State: Beyond Statist Approaches and Their Critics."*The American Political Science Review* 85, no. 1 (March): 77–96.

Mubarak, Hesham. 1995. *al-Irhabiyyun qadimun! Dirasat muqarana bayn mawqif al-Ikhwan al-Muslimin wa-jama'at al-jihad min qadiyyat al-'unf (1928–1994)*. Cairo: al-Mahrusa.

Pahwa, Sumita. 2013. "Secularizing Islamism and Islamizing Democracy: The Political and Ideational Evolution of the Egyptian Muslim Brothers 1984–2012." *Mediterranean Politics* 18, no. 2: 189–206.

———. 2017. "Pathways of Islamist Adaptation: The Egyptian Muslim Brothers' Lessons for Inclusion Moderation Theory." *Democratization* 24, no. 6: 1066–84.

Piette, Albert. 2014. "An Anthropology of Belief and a Theory of Homo Religiosus." *Archives de sciences sociales des religions* 167: 277–94.

Prestel, Joseph Ben. 2017. *Emotional Cities: Debates on Urban Change in Berlin and Cairo 1860–1910*. Oxford: Oxford University Press.

Qandil, Amani. 1994. "L'évolution du rôle des islamistes dans les syndicats professionnels égyptiens." In *Le phénomène de la violence politique: Perspectives comparatistes et paradigme égyptien*, edited by B. Dupret, 281–93. Cairo: Dossiers du CEDEJ.

Rabi', 'Amr Hashim, ed. 2002. *Dalil al-nukhba al-barlamaniyya 2000*. Cairo: al-Ahram Center for Political and Strategic Studies.

———, ed. 2006a. *Dalil al-nukhba al-barlamaniyya 2005*. Cairo: al-Ahram Center for Political and Strategic Studies.

———, ed. 2006b. *Intikhabat maglis al-sha'b 2005*. Cairo: al-Ahram Center for Political and Strategic Studies.

———. 2009a. "al-Ikhwan fi al-barlaman (12/2005–01/2007)." Unpublished.

———. 2009b. "al-Wafd wa-l-Ikhwan fi al-barlaman." Unpublished.

Richards, Alan, and John Waterbury. 1996. *A Political Economy of the Middle East*. Boulder, CO, and Oxford: Westview Press.

Rock-Singer, Aaron. 2017. Review of Khalil al-Anani, *Inside the Muslim Brotherhood: Religion, Identity and Politics. Sociology of Islam* 5: 95–98.

Sabry, Sarah. 2009. "Egypt's Informal Areas: Inaccurate and Contradictory Data." In *Cairo's Informal Areas between Urban Challenges and Hidden Potentials: Facts, Voices, Visions*, edited by R. Kipper and M. Fischer, 29–34. Egyptian–German Participatory Development Programme in Urban Areas. Cairo: German Technical Cooperation.

Sadowski, Yahia M. 1991. *Political Vegetables? Businessmen and Bureaucrats in the Development of Egyptian Agriculture*. Washington, D.C.: Brookings.

Sa'id, Karam. 2005. *Muhafazat al-Qahira*. Cairo: al-Ahram Center for Political and Strategic Studies.

Schwartz, Olivier. 2011. "Peut-on parler des classes populaires?"*La Vie des Idées*.

Schwedler, Jillian. 2006. *Faith in Moderation: Islamist Parties in Jordan and Yemen.* Cambridge and New York: Cambridge University Press.

———. 2011. "Can Islamists Become Moderates? Rethinking the Inclusion-Moderation Hypothesis." *World Politics* 63, no. 2: 347–76.

Sfakianakis, John. 2004. "The Whales of the Nile: Networks, Businessmen, and Bureaucrats during the Era of Privatization in Egypt." In *Networks of Privilege in the Middle-East: The Politics of Economic Reform Revisited*, edited by S. Heydemann, 77–100. New York: Palgrave McMillan.

Shehata, Dina. 2010. *Islamists and Secularists in Egypt: Opposition, Conflict, and Cooperation.* London and New York: Routledge.

Shehata, Samer, and Joshua Stacher. 2006. "Brotherhood Goes to Parliament." *Middle East Report*, no. 240: 32–39.

———. 2007. "Boxing in the Brothers." *Middle East Report Online*, 8 August.

El Sherif, Ashraf. 2016. "The Strong Egypt Party: Representing a Progressive/Democratic Islamist Party?" *Contemporary Islam* 10: 311–31.

Singerman, Diane. 1995. *Avenues of Participation: Family, Politics, and Networks in Urban Quarters of Cairo.* Princeton, NJ: Princeton University Press.

———. 2003. "Réseaux, cadres culturels et structures des opportunités politiques: Le mouvement islamiste en Égypte." In *Résistances et protestations dans les sociétés musulmanes*, edited by M. Bennani-Chraïbi and O. Fillieule, 219–42. Paris: Presses de la FNSP.

Siyam, 'Imad. 2006. "al-Haraka al-islamiyya wa-l-jam'iyyat al-ahliyya al-islamiyya." In *al-Jam'iyyat al-ahliyya al-islamiyya fi Misr*, edited by A.G. Shukr, 83–150. Cairo: Dar al-Amin.

Soleiman, Samir. 2006. *al-Musharaka al-siyasiyya fi al-intikhabat al-niyabiyya 2005.* Cairo: Egyptian Association for Community Participation Enhancement.

Springborg, Robert. 1982. *Family, Power, and Politics in Egypt: Sayed Bey Marei—His Clan, Clients, and Cohorts.* Philadelphia: University of Pennsylvania Press.

Sullivan, Denis, and Sana Abed-Kotob. 1999. *Islam in Contemporary Egypt: Civil Society vs. the State.* Boulder, CO: Lynne Rienner Publishers.

Tabak, Hüsrev. 2015. "Broadening the Non-Governmental Mission: The IHH and Mediation." *Insight Turkey* 17, no. 3: 193–215.

Tammam, Hossam. 2006. *Tahawwulat al-Ikhwan al-Muslimin.* Cairo: Madbouli.

———. 2011. *The Salafization of Muslim Brothers: The Erosion of the Fundamental Hypothesis and the Rising of Salafism within the Muslim Brotherhood; The Paths and the Repercussions of Change.* Alexandria: Bibliotheca Alexandrina (Marased, 1).

El-Tarouty, Safinaz. 2015. *Businessmen, Clientelism, and Authoritarianism in Egypt.* London and New York: Palgrave Macmillan.

Thompson, John B. 2000. *Political Scandal: Power and Visibility in the Media Age.* Cambridge: Polity Press.

Trager, Eric. 2016. *Arab Fall: How the Muslim Brotherhood Won and Lost Egypt in 891 Days*. Washington, DC: Georgetown University Press.

Uways, Sayyid. 1985. *L'Histoire que je porte sur mon dos: Mémoires*. Cairo: CEDEJ.

Vannetzel, Marie. 2012. *2005 Parliamentary Elections Brotherhood Candidates Database*. unpublished.

———. 2017. "The Party, the *Gama'a* and the Tanzim: The Organisational Dynamics of the Egyptian Muslim Brotherhood's post-2011 Failure." *British Journal of Middle Eastern Studies* 44, no. 2: 211–26.

———. 2018. "Sous le signe de Rabia: Circulations et segmentations des mobilisations (trans)nationales en Turquie." *Critique internationale* 1, no. 78: 41–62.

Veyne, Paul. 1988. *Did the Greeks Believe in Their Myths? An Essay on the Constitutive Imagination*. Chicago: University of Chicago Press.

Waterbury, John. 1983. *The Egypt of Nasser and Sadat: The Political Economy of Two Regimes*. Princeton, NJ: Princeton University Press.

Weber, Max. 1993. *The Sociology of Religion*. Boston: Beacon Press.

White, Jenny B. 2002. *Islamist Mobilization in Turkey: A Study in Vernacular Politics*. Seattle and London: University of Washington Press.

Wickham, Carrie R. 1997. "Islamic Mobilization and Political Change." In *Political Islam: Essays from Middle East Report*, edited by J. Beinin and J. Stork, 120–35. London: I.B. Tauris.

———. 2002. *Mobilizing Islam: Religion, Activism and Political Change in Egypt*. New York: Columbia University Press.

———. 2013. *The Muslim Brotherhood: Evolution of an Islamist Movement*. Princeton, NJ: Princeton University Press.

Wiktorowicz, Quintan. 2001. *The Management of Islamic Activism: Salafis, the Muslim Brotherhood, and the State Power in Jordan*. Albany: State University of New York Press.

———, ed. 2004. *Islamic Activism: A Social Movement Theory Approach*. Bloomington: Indiana University Press.

Yacoub, Milad. 2009. *Le développement local en Egypte: Rencontres associatives dans un village*. Paris: Editions L'Harmattan.

Zahran, Farid. 1996. *al-Intikhabat al-barlamaniyya fi Misr 1995*. Cairo: al-Mahrusa.

Zeghal, Malika. 1996. *Gardiens de l'Islam: les oulémas d'Al Azhar dans l'Égypte contemporaine*. Paris: Presses de Sciences Po.

# Index

Page numbers in *italics* refer to tables, figures, and maps.

preaching and virtuous acts 180
Guidance Bureau (Maktab al-Irshad) 3, 43, 98, 99, 101, 269; 2009 elections 100; MB headquarters 12; *see also* Supreme Guide; the *tanzim*

Habib, Mohamed 46, 87, 100, 241
al-Hadi al-Islami Hospital 148–51; *khayri* status of 149
Haenni, Patrick 29, 184
'half-Brothers' 11, 148
healthcare paid by the state 134–5
Helwan 12, 16, 18, 56; candidates in 60–1, *60*; canvassing in Madinat al-Huda 257–8; Constituency 24: 56, 60; craft and industrial workers by subdistrict *67*; demographic disparities between subdistricts *67*; electoral constituencies of *66*; employees in the public sector by subdistrict, all occupations *69*; MB candidates in *39*, 49, 65–6; professionals in technical and scientific occupations by subdistrict *69*; services and sales workers by subdistrict *68*; stable relationship networks 56, 57; technicians and clerks by subdistrict *68*; *see also* al-Muhammadi 'Abd al-Maqsud, Sheikh
Helwan, MP staff/office *105–107*, 254; face-to-face meeting with residents 125, 126–30, 131–3, 144; Helwan Center office 126, 130–1, 206; Labor Party offices 110; local court of justice in the MP's office 131–3; a network of networks around Sheikh al-Muhammadi 103–10, 114, 136; relationship with Sheikh al-Muhammadi 108–10; social work 104, 108; the *tanzim* 110
Heshmat, Gamal 25, 48
Husayn, 'Adil 65
Husayn, Kamal al-Din 264
Hussein, Mahmoud 277

ideology: developmentalist ideology 28; *see also* MB ideology
Ikhwanism 189, 194, 197; Brotherhood qualities *(al-mazaya al-ikhwaniya)* 231; *ikhwani* circle 196; *ikhwani* code of conduct 197, 200, 206, 208, 212; *ikhwani* self 189, 190, 197–208; *see also* MB recruitment, cultivation, promotion; *tarbiyya*
IMA (Islamic Medical Association, al-Gam'iyya al-Tibbiyya al-Islamiyya) 48, 149, 150, 238, 276; as 'Brotherhood-ized' association 48; MB and 8, 48; mobilization of voters 48
'Imara, 'Abd al-Mun'im 64, 90
*infitah* 29, 30, 184
Internet 27, 41, 96, 256; Internet activism 213, 215; young MB bloggers 11, 12, 96, 213, 214
Iraq War (2003) 210, 240
al-'Iryan, 'Isam 25, 42, 44, 48; FJP 43, 269; incarceration 43; a misleading 'ideal-type' career 43, 46
Islam: 'discursive policy' 93; election candidates and 93; ethical conduct and 175–7, 180, 198; 'Islam Is the Solution' slogan 72, 102, 130; Islamic jurisprudence *(fiqh)* 179, 180; MB MPs' politics of goodness 139, 142, 175–7, 183; MB and politics 70, 72, 79, 80–1, 83, 92–3, 253, 255; MB recruitment, cultivation, promotion 194–5; MB social services 70, 72, 93; Mubarak, Hosni 93; NDP 93; in politics 22; symbolic economy of disinterestedness and religious motivation of service 76, 77, 92–3, 272
Islamic Alliance (al-Tahaluf al-Islami) 37, 38; MB candidates in Helwan *39*; al-Muhammadi, Sheikh 73–4, 109
Islamic social movement: institutions of 7–8; scholarship on 7–9
Islamism 23, 24; shari'a as main source of Egyptian legislation 36, 37
Ismail, Salwa 6, 198
Ittihadeyya Palace clashes (2012) 9, 239, 271
'Izbat al-Haggana (Madinat Nasr) 62, 87–91; housing in 116; medical caravan in 152, 154–5

Al Jazeera 126, 276

Kandil, Hazem 189, 190, 191, 192, 193–7, 225, 242–3, 244
al-Katatni, Saad 101–102, 269
Kefaya Movement 38, 96, 219, 240
Khaled, 'Amr 180
*khayr* (goodness, charity) 10, 139–40; *see also* MB MPs' politics of goodness; politics of goodness
*khidma/khadamat see* social services

Labna, Thurayya 63, 64
Labor Party (Hizb al-'Amal) 59, 65, 156, 264; Helwan 110; MB/Labor Party alliance 37, 65; al-Muhammadi, Sheikh 75, 108, 109; Tibbin/15 Mayo 114
Lahire, Bernard 229–30
LECs (local executive councils) 30, 117
Liberal Party (Hizb al-Ahrar) 37
Lonsdale, John 6
LPCs (Local Popular Councils) 30, 50, 74, 264–5; 2011 dissolution 265, 267; ethical conduct 181; al-Muhammadi, Sheikh 74, 108–109, 117, 118, 181

Madi, Abu al-'Ila 27, 60
Madinat Nasr 12, 16, 62; candidates in 63–5, *64*; Constituency 6: 62–5; craft and industrial workers by subdistrict *67*; demographic disparities between subdistricts *67*; electoral constituencies of *66*; electoral turnout 82; electoral volatility 56; employees in the public sector by subdistrict, all occupations *69*; fragmented electorate 62, 113; MB in 65–6; MB MP staff and the *tanzim* 110–13, 114; professionals in technical and scientific occupations by subdistrict *69*; services and sales workers by subdistrict *68*; technicians and clerks by subdistrict *68*; *see also* Mukhtar, 'Isam
*al-maghud al-dhati* (self-effort) 119–20, 136, 181, 246

Mahgub, Mohamed 58, 59, 60, 70, 254
Mahmood, Saba 142, 159, 165, 168, 180
al-Malt, Ahmad 48
Mashhur, Mustafa 25; *al-Da'wa al-fardiyya* 192
Masoud, Tareq 8, 53
al-Matrawi, Muhammad 65
MB (Muslim Brotherhood) 1; 1970s reemergence 22–4, 26, 27, 268–9, 283; 1970s–1980s new generation of activists 23, 24; 2011–12 reemergence 2; 2013 registration as association 268; collapse of 8, 11, 276, 283; hierarchy 11, 17, 26, 213, 232; organizationists (*tanzimiyyin*) 25, 96, 101, 196, 219, 231; public/hidden faces of 9, 11, 16, 189–90; rebuilding an undefined organization 23–8, 268–9; reformers (*islahiyyin*) 42, 43, 96, 100, 225; two Gama'at al-Ikhwan al-Muslimin 276; *see also the entries below related to* MB; Guidance Bureau; the *tanzim*

MB, ban of 5, 145; 1948 ban 1; 1954 ban 27, 268; 2013 ban 1, 189, 263; 'illegal but tolerated' 5, 16, 19; *al-mahzura* 4–5; MB, declared as 'terrorist organization' 1, 48; MB's illegal status 5–6, 14, 26, 27, 37, 271, 282; repression of MB by the state 2, 5, 25, 95, 96, 99, 143, 189, 240, 242, 283; resistance to legalization after lifting the ban 268, 271; stigma 155, 185; strategies to get around the ban 170

MB and Egyptian society 7–12, 97–8, 137, 282; debate on 7–9; institutional embedding 270; social embedding 10, 22, 35, 40, 45, 155, 275, 282; the *tanzim* 97

MB electoral campaigns 38, *39*, 41, 72, 95, 109, 151, 155, 174; 2013 parliamentary elections 273; collective mediation 79–80; door-to-door canvassing 82; electoral leaflets 16, 83; electoral mobilization 40, 51, 54, 86, 93; external networks: the *'izba* politics 87–92; 'Ali Fath

medical caravan organized by 169

Misr al-Qadima (Cairo) 7

Misr al-Qawiyya (Strong Egypt Party) 215

Mitchell, Richard 9, 283

Mitchell, Timothy 6, 51

Mohamed Mahmoud Street clashes (2012) 239

monarchy (Egyptian monarchy) 26, 36

morality: Islam/religious morality 139, 142, 175–7, 183; *sawtak amana* (civic morality) 80–2, *81*, 88, 91, 92

Morsi, Mohamed 25, 236; 2012 presidential elections 2, 263, 271, 274; calls for resignation 266; comparing MB's internal problems to Morsi's presidency failures 279; coup d'état by al-Sisi 2; criticism of 237, 238, 275; failure of Morsi's presidency 280, 281; fall of 1, 9, 242, 263; head of the parliamentary bloc of MB 101; *al-kharuf* (the sheep) 275; popular disappointment under 8; as president of FJP 269; violent and authoritarian practices of 263

*mosalsal* 3–4

MP (Member of Parliament): legislative work 265, 267; NDP MPs 31, 134, 139; nuwwab/MPs as 'state agents' 29; politicization of MP's role 32; role of 28, 29, 30–1, 274; state apparatus and 30–1; *see also* MB MPs; Parliament

*mu'ayyidin see* supporters

Mubarak, Gamal 38

Mubarak, Hosni 1, 245; crony capitalism 55; electoral engineering 31; Islam 93; MB under 4, 5, 21, 36, 189, 273, 282; 'moderate Islamism' 24; neoliberalism 29

al-Muhammadi 'Abd al-Maqsud, Sheikh 60, 66, 247; autonomy as MP 103, 110, 136; charity 145; electoral campaign 72–3, 75, 80, 87; electoral leaflet 73, 74, *81*; ethical conduct 181; 'everyday state' and local legitimacy 117–21, *121*, 123, 136; face-to-face meeting with residents

125, 126–30, 131–3; GS 73–4, 108, 151, 181; Islamic Alliance 73–4, 109; Labor Party 75, 108, 109; local court of justice in the MP's office 131–3; LPC 74, 108–109, 117, 118, 181; MP offices 103–10; multiple identities 130–1, 133; parliamentary interventions 116; politics of goodness *141*, 181–2; public work 72–6; Qur'an 73, 80, 93; religion and politics 72–3, 80; rootedness 75; symbolic economy of disinterestedness 76, 92, 130; *see also* Helwan

*muhibbin/muhibb see* sympathizers

Mukhtar, 'Isam 65, 144; disguise of his Brotherhood identity 77–8, 134, 136; electoral campaign 83, 86, 89–91, 154–5, 210; electoral leaflet *84*; 'everyday state' and parliamentary pressure 115–16, *117*, 232; few resources owned by 113, 116, 136; GS 77; MP office/staff 110–13, 136; politics of goodness *140*; public work 77–8, 163–4, 232, 255–6; symbolic economy of disinterestedness 77, 78–9; the *tanzim* and 79

Mungi, Mohamed 60, 66

Mustafa (dissident MB blogger) 83, 86, 87–8, 111, 208–10, 214–16; 6 April 2008 Facebook call for general strike 213, 219; 2011 Revolution 214, 221; 2011–12 parliamentary elections 221–2; al-'Adl (Justice) Party 221; defection from MB 214, 221; ElBaradei, Mohamed 221; 'I Am with Them' *(Ana ma'ahum)* 215, 219; ideological dissatisfaction 215; MB party's program draft 216–17; moral career 214, 216–22; *ukhuwwa* 218, 220; 'Waves in a Sea of Change' *(Amwag bahr al-taghyir/Amwag)* 215, 217, 219; *see also* MB internal dissent and defection

Nabil, Hagg 88, 89–90, 91, 154

al-Nahda Square 263

Nasr al-Din, Isma'il 60, 61, 157–8; *ibn*

*al-balad* 61
Nasser, Gamal Abdel 29, 30; MB under 1, 22, 283
Nasserism 73, 264, 266
Nazif, Ahmed 96
NDP (National Democratic Party) 7, 264, 283; 2011 dissolution 1, 265, 267; businessmen/business leaders 54, 55, 184; clientelism 8; corruption 251; election brokers and 90, 91; election campaigners 85, 92; election candidates 51, 55–6, 58, 63, 65–6, 90, 91, 92; electoral system 32, *34–5*; ethical conduct, NDP/MB comparison 165–7, 176–8, 184, 251, 283; independent candidates and 32, 55, 115; MPs 31, 134, 139; NDP/MB networks interrelationship 92, 283; patronage 8; religion and 93; social services provided by 10, 163, 169, 184; state apparatus 66
neoliberalism 29, 119, 245, 275
New Wafd Party 36, 37, 43
newspapers: *Abna' Helwan* 169; *al-Dustur* 59; *Helwan al-youm* 61; *Sawt Helwan* 59; *al-Sha'b* 65; *al-Usbu'* 59; *see also* media
NGOs (non-governmental organizations) 117, 153, 281–2; charitable NGOs 24; state control of 47
'non-Brothers' 11, 148, 182, 212, 228
Nuh, Mukhtar 65
Nuqrashi Pasha, Mahmoud Fahmy 1

Palestinian cause 83, 186, 201, 240
Parliament (Egypt) 29; 1979 dissolution 30; 2011 dissolution 267; 2012 dissolution 267; 2012 Parliament 267; FJP members in 1, 12; parliamentary politics 28; politics of *khayr* 275; state bourgeoisie 29, 30; subordinated to the executive 31; *see also* MB MPs; MP
party system 31–2; party-based electoral system 32; Political Parties Commission 31–2
patronage 53, 61, 267, 268; MB 70, 72,

130; NDP 8; patron–client relationship 14, 130; *see also* clientelism
People's Assembly *see* Parliament
polarization 7, 20, 264, 273
political legitimacy 266, 275
politicization 8, 142, 255; of elections 38–40; *mazlumin* and virtuous neighbors 255–63; MB, politicization and ethical conduct 142, 255; MB, politicization of social services 9, 10, 15, 37, 70, 72, 142, 272–3; MPs' role, politicization of 32
politics: formality/informality tensions in institutional political sphere 21; institutionalized informality 21, 28; Islam in 22; municipal authorities, absence of 30; non-professionalism of political actors 22, 42; non-specialization of 21–2, 28, 29–31, 37, 40; political liberalization 22, 24, 28; 'politics from below' 6, 251; *see also* MB and politics
politics of goodness 10; collapse of 20, 276, 283; definition 139; depolitization/non-politicized practices 10; Mubarak era 245; NDP MPs 139; post-Mubarak era 276; *see also* MB MPs' politics of goodness; social services
the poor: MB and 8, 9, 53, 140, 160–1; NDP and 53
Prophet Mohamed 156, 199, 211
protests/demonstrations: 2003 210; 2004–2005 96; 2008 259; 2013, 30 June demonstrations 2, 266; media and 96; strikes 58, 213, 219, 259; 'thugification' of protesters 262–3; workers 57–8
public space 271; appropriation by the state 123; MB 259; MB MPs and 136, 146, 169–70; women in 262–3
public work (*al-'amal al-'amm*): 'Ali Fath al-Bab, 69–70, 72, 174; MB electoral candidates 46–51, *47*, 68; al-Muhammadi, Sheikh 72–6; Mukhtar, 'Isam 77–8, 163–4, 232, 255–6; NDP MPs 139; *see also* MB MPs' politics of

goodness; MB social services

al-Qassas, Mohamed 240
Qur'an 4, 86, 140, 175; Bakri, Mustafa 93;
    'If you support God, He will support
    you' 243; MB and 176–7, 183, 201,
    207, 208–209, 212; al-Muhammadi,
    Sheikh 73, 80, 93
Qutb, Sayyid 25, 196, 201, 202, 242
Qutbism 196–7

Rab'a (NGO in exile) 277–80
Rab'a al-'Adawiyya Square, Cairo 244,
    263, 276, 281
Rabi', 'Amr Hashim 115
Radi, Mohsen 264–6
Rafiq (dissident MB blogger) 214, 215–16,
    222–6, 231, 233; 2007 arrest and
    incarceration 224; 2010 election cam-
    paign 222–3, 225; 2011 Revolution
    215, 225; defection from MB 214,
    225, 226, 238; ideological dissatisfac-
    tion 215; 'paradoxical loyalty' 215,
    223; tortured love of *ukhuwwa* 222–6;
    'tube' and SIM card 226–9; *see also*
    MB internal dissent and defection
Ramadan 3, 158; food distribution during
    102, 112–13, 141
redistribution 29, 53–4, 88, 275
religion 181; religious determinism 242–3,
    244; *see also* Islam
research methodology 41, 263–4; ethno-
    graphic approach 8, 10, 11, 13–16;
    evidential paradigm 13–14; fieldwork
    12–13, 17–19, 264; interviews 13,
    191; investigating 'open secrecy'
    12–19; local offices of MB MPs
    12–13, 16; 'open secrecy' hypothesis
    15; role of the researcher 16–19;
    sociological case studies 191–2;
    sources 13
Rida, Rashid 179
Rock-Singer, Aaron 230
rumors 185, 195, 226, 247, 266

Sabbahi, Hamdin 266
Sabiq, Sayyid, Sheikh 201, 202; *Fiqh*

*al-Sunna* 180
al-Sadat, Anwar: assassination of 24,
    32, 36, 96; economic liberalization
    23, 29; electoral engineering 31;
    Islamic charities 23; Islamism 23;
    liberalized autocracy 22;
    MB under 1, 22–4
Salafism 8, 179, 198–9, 202, 207, 222, 267;
    Salafization of MB 197
Salah (al-Muhammadi's successor as can-
    didate, Helwan) 104, 109, 200, 201,
    203, 251, 256–8, 273
al-Sallab, Mustafa 63, 64–5, 88, 116, 163–
    4, 166–7, 178
SCAF (Supreme Council of the Armed
    Forces) 279
Schwartz, Olivier 8, 53–4, 161
Secret Apparatus (*al-tanzim al-sirri*) 25,
    26, 48
sectarianism 189, 190, 197, 242–3, 244;
    *see also* MB recruitment, cultivation,
    promotion
Shafiq, Ahmed 266
*shakluh kwayyes* 198, 199–200, 204, 211,
    226, 227, 236; MB internal discipline
    through 234; MB promotion and
    232–3; *see also* MB recruitment, culti-
    vation, promotion
shari'a 36, 37
al-Shater, Khayrat 25, 95, 220, 238, 271
*shura* (collective consultation) 209, 217–18,
    232, 235, 236; loss of trust in 239,
    240, 242
Singerman, Diane 82–3
al-Sisi, Abdel Fattah, General 2, 272, 274,
    283
social embedding: electoral politics and
    28–35; MB 10, 22, 35, 40, 45, 155,
    275, 282
social services (*khidma*, pl. *khadamat*) 10,
    12, 283; 2011 Revolution and break-
    down of local politics 267; electoral
    politics and social embedding 28–35;
    Islamic charities 23; MPs' role in 28,
    29, 30; state and political institutions
    29, 31; *see also* MB social services;
    politics of goodness; welfare

industrial workers by subdistrict 67; demographic disparities between subdistricts 67; electoral campaign 86; electoral constituencies of 66; employees in the public sector by subdistrict, all occupations 69; Labor Party 114; MB candidates in 39, 65–6; MB MP staff, guest *na'ib* and self-managing offices 113–14; professionals in technical and scientific occupations by subdistrict 69; services and sales workers by subdistrict 68; stable relationship networks 56, 57; technicians and clerks by subdistrict 68; women activists 113; *see also* 'Ali Fath al-Bab,

trade unions 50, see also ETUF

*ukhuwwa* (sense of brotherhood) 196, 214, 218; as double-edged sword 214, 220; MB internal dissent and defection 236, 240, 241, 242; moral superiority and exclusion 227; 'oration of the Brothers' ritual *(du'a' al-ikhwan)* 218; Rafiq, tortured love of *ukhuwwa* 222–6

*ulama* (clerics) 23, 50, 180, 202

universities: 'Islamic groups' (gama'at islamiyya) 23; MB and 2, 3, 23–4; student unions 23, 43, 46, 210, 240; students' dismissal from universities 4

Veyne, Paul 244

vote: clientelism 53; electoral bribes 55; election brokers *(samasir)* 55, 63, 88, 90, 91; exchange of votes for money 55; making vote 33, 51, 63, 65; voting cards 33, 82, 90; *see also* electoral system/politics; voters

voters 251, 253–5, 270, 274–5; 2012 MB's incoherent communication strategy and 271; canvassing voters 82–3, 86, 109, 172, 256, 257–8; electoral roll 56, 60, 82; producing voters 80–4; *sawtak amana* 80–2, *81*, 88, 92; workers 57, 63, 70; *see also* electoral system/politics; vote

Wahhabism 197

Wasat Party 27

*wasta* (connections) 125, 128, 130, 167; merit vs *wasta* 130

Weber, Max 164–5

welfare 184; declining state welfare provision 29; depoliticization of welfare provision 8, 10; electoral politics and 19; relocation of welfare into goodness 139, 275

Wickham, Carrie R. 7

Wissam and Farid 233–9, 243, 269; 2006–11 occasional disagreement not turning into opposition 240; 2011–13 widespread disagreement and multiple opposition 241–2; 2014–present: exile, fragmentation, opposition 234, 236, 240, 242, 276–80, 281; *see also* MB internal dissent and defection

women: 2005 elections 86; *da'iyya* 158, 159; defusing police repression by turning to women activists 262; dress code 159, 198–9, 260; as election candidates 78; electoral system and 86, 79; ethical conduct 186; in MB 113, 159–64, 185–6; in MB's election campaigns 79, 85–6; MB MPs' politics of goodness and 159–64, 175–7, 186; mobilization of female MB supporters 86; Muslim Sisters 86, 215, 260, 262, 282; 'politics of respectability' 262–3; in public space 262–3; 'thugification' of protesters 262–3; women's electoral rally, Alexandria 259–62

al-Za'farani, Ibrahim 241

*zakat* committees 70, 77, 79, 93, 102, 104, 145, 146, 147–8